Books by Lois McMaster Bujold

PALADIN OF SOULS

LOIS McMASTER BUJOLD

HarperTorch
An Imprint of HarperCollinsPublishers

◆

HARPERTORCH
An Imprint of HarperCollins*Publishers*
10 East 53rd Street
New York, New York 10022-5299

Copyright © 2003 by Lois McMaster Bujold
Excerpt from *The Hallowed Hunt* copyright © 2005 by Lois McMaster Bujold
ISBN 0-380-81861-2

First HarperTorch paperback printing: May 2005
First Eos hardcover printing: October 2003

HarperCollins®, HarperTorch™, and ◆ ™ are trademarks of HarperCollins Publishers Inc.

Maps by Lois McMaster Bujold and Carol Collins

Printed in the United States of America

Visit HarperTorch on the World Wide Web at www.harpercollins.com

10 9 8 7 6 5 4 3 2 1

For Sylvia Kelso,
syntax wrangler and
Ista partisan first class

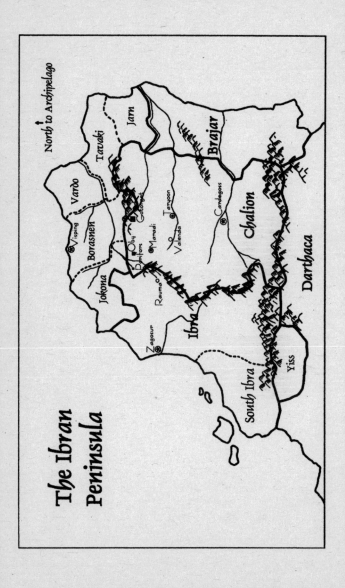

The Ibran Peninsula

North to Archipelago

Tavaki

Jarn

Vardo

Brajar

Visping

Borasnen

Oby

Cardegoss

Jokona

Maradi

Tenoon

Chalion

Valenda

Reumaot

Darthaca

Zagosur

Ibra

Yiss

South Ibra

Ista's Pilgrimage route

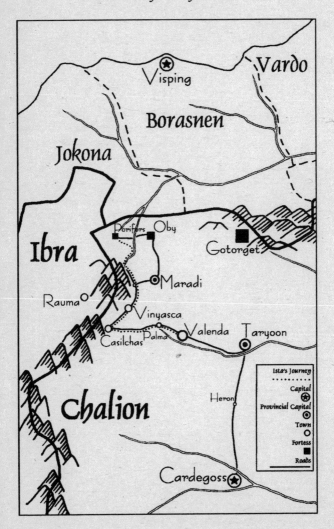

PALADIN OF SOULS

I

Ista leaned forward between the crenellations atop the gate tower, the stone gritty beneath her pale hands, and watched in numb exhaustion as the final mourning party cleared the castle gate below. Their horses' hooves scraped on the old cobblestones, and their good-byes echoed in the portal's vaulting. Her earnest brother, the provincar of Baocia, and his family and retinue were last of the many to leave, two full weeks after the divines had completed the funeral rites and ceremonies of the interment.

Dy Baocia was still talking soberly to the castle warder, Ser dy Ferrej, who walked at his stirrup, grave face upturned, listening to the stream, no doubt, of final instructions. Faithful dy Ferrej, who had served the late Dowager Provincara for all the last two decades of her long residence here in Valenda. The keys of the castle and keep glinted from the belt at his stout waist. Her mother's keys, which Ista had collected and held, then turned over to her older brother along with all the other papers and inventories and instructions that a great lady's death entailed. And that he had handed back for permanent safekeeping not to his sister, but to good, old, honest dy Ferrej. Keys to lock out all danger . . . and, if necessary, Ista in.

It's only habit, you know. I'm not mad anymore, really.

It wasn't as though she wanted her mother's keys, nor her mother's life that went with them. She scarcely knew what she wanted. She knew what she feared—to be locked up in some dark, narrow place by people who loved her. An enemy might drop his guard, weary of his task, turn his back; love would never falter. Her fingers rubbed restlessly on the stone.

Dy Baocia's cavalcade filed off down the hill through the town and was soon lost from her view among the crowded red-tiled roofs. Dy Ferrej, turning back, walked wearily in through the gate and out of sight.

The chill spring wind lifted a strand of Ista's dun hair and blew it across her face, catching on her lip; she grimaced and tucked it back into the careful braiding wreathing her head. Its tightness pinched her scalp.

The weather had warmed these last two weeks, too late to ease an old woman bound to her bed by injury and illness. If her mother had not been so old, the broken bones would have healed more swiftly, and the inflammation of the lungs might not have anchored itself so deeply in her chest. If she had not been so fragile, perhaps the fall from the horse would not have broken her bones in the first place. If she had not been so fiercely willful, perhaps she would not have been on that horse at all at her age . . . Ista looked down to find her fingers bleeding, and hid them hastily in her skirt.

In the funeral ceremonies, the gods had signed that the old lady's soul had been taken up by the Mother of Summer, as was expected and proper. Even the gods would not dare violate her views on protocol. Ista imagined the old Provincara ordering heaven, and smiled a little grimly.

And so I am alone at last.

Ista considered the empty spaces of that solitude, its fearful cost. Husband, father, son, and mother had all filed down to the grave ahead of her in their turn. Her daughter was claimed by the royacy of Chalion in as tight an embrace as any grave, and as little likely to return from her high place, five gods willing, as the others from their low ones. *Surely I am done.* The duties that had defined her, all accomplished. Once, she had been her parents' daughter. Then great, unlucky Ias's wife. Her children's mother. At the last, her mother's keeper. *Well, I am none of these things now.*

Who am I, when I am not surrounded by the walls of my life? When they have all fallen into dust and rubble?

Well, she was still Lord dy Lutez's murderer. The last of that little, secret company left alive, now. *That* she had made of herself, and that she remained.

She leaned between the crenellations again, the stone abrading the lavender sleeves of her court mourning dress, catching at its silk threads. Her eye followed the road in the morning light, starting from the stones below and flowing downhill, through the town, past the river . . . and where? All roads were one road, they said. A great net across the land, parting and rejoining. All roads ran two ways. They said. *I want a road that does not come back.*

A frightened gasp behind her jerked her head around. One of her lady attendants stood on the battlement with her hand to her lips, eyes wide, breathing heavily from her climb. She smiled with false cheer. "My lady. I've been seeking you everywhere. Do . . . do come away from that edge, now . . ."

Ista's lips curled in irony. "Content you. I do not yearn to meet the gods face-to-face this day." *Or on any other. Never again.* "The gods and I are not on speaking terms."

She suffered the woman to take her arm and stroll with her as if casually along the battlement toward the inner stairs, careful, Ista noted, to take the outside place, between Ista and the drop. *Content you, woman. I do not desire the stones.*

I desire the road.

The realization startled, almost shocked her. It was a new thought. *A new thought, me?* All her old thoughts seemed as thin and ragged as a piece of knitting made and ripped out and made and ripped out again until all the threads were frayed, growing ever more worn, but never larger. But how could *she* gain the road? Roads were made for young men, not middle-aged women. The poor orphan boy packed his sack and started off down the road to seek his heart's hope . . . a thousand tales began that way. She was not poor, she was not a boy, and her heart was surely as stripped of all hope as life and death could render it. *I am an orphan now, though. Is that not enough to qualify me?*

They turned the corner of the battlement, making toward the round tower containing the narrow, winding staircase that gave onto the inner garden. Ista cast one last glance out across the scraggly shrubs and stunted trees that crept up to the curtain wall of the castle. Up the path from the shallow ravine, a servant towed a donkey loaded with firewood, heading for the postern gate.

In her late mother's flower garden, Ista slowed, resisting her attendant's urgent hand upon her arm, and mulishly took to a bench in the still-bare rose arbor. "I am weary," she announced. "I would rest here for a time. You may fetch me tea."

She could watch her lady attendant turning over the risks in her mind, regarding her high charge untrustingly. Ista frowned coldly. The woman dropped a curtsey. "Yes, my lady. I'll tell one of the maids. And I'll be *right back.*"

I expect you will. Ista waited only till the woman had rounded the corner of the keep before she sprang to her feet and ran for the postern gate.

The guard was just letting the servant and his donkey through. Ista, head high, sailed out past them without turning round. Pretending not to hear the guard's uncertain, "My lady . . .?" she walked briskly down the steepening path. Her trailing skirts and billowing black velvet vest-cloak snagged on weeds and brambles as she passed, like clutching hands trying to hold her back. Once out of sight among the first trees, her steps quickened to something close to a run. She had used to run down this path to the river, when she was a girl. Before she was anybody's anything.

She was no girl now, she had to concede. She was winded and trembling by the time the river's gleam shone through the vegetation. She turned and strode along the bank. The path still held its remembered course to the old footbridge, across the water, and up again to one of the main roads winding around the hill to—or from—the town of Valenda.

The road was muddy and pocked with hoofprints; perhaps her brother's party had just passed on its way to his provincial seat of Taryoon. He had spent much of the past two weeks attempting to persuade her to accompany him there, promising her rooms and attendants in his palace, under his benign and protective eye, as though she had not rooms and attendants and prying eyes enough here. She turned in the opposite direction.

Court mourning and silk slippers were no garb for a country road. Her skirts swished around her legs as though she were trying to wade through high water. The mud sucked at her light shoes. The sun, climbing the sky, heated her velvet-clad back, and she broke into an unladylike sweat. She walked on, feeling increasingly uncomfortable and foolish. This was madness. This was just the sort of thing that got women locked up in towers with lack-witted attendants, and hadn't she had enough of that for one lifetime? She hadn't a change of clothes, a plan, any money, not so much as a copper vaida. She touched the jewels around her neck. *There's money.* Yes, too much value—what country-town moneylender could match for them? They were not a resource; they were merely a target, bait for bandits.

The rumble of a cart drew her eyes upward from picking her way along the puddles. A farmer drove a stout cob, hauling a load of ripe manure for spreading on his fields. He turned his head to stare dumfounded at the apparition of her on his road. She returned him a regal nod—after all, what other kind could she offer? She nearly laughed out loud, but choked back the unseemly noise and walked on. Not looking back. Not daring to.

She walked for over an hour before her tiring legs, dragging the weight of her dress, stumbled at last to a halt. She was close to weeping from the frustration of it all. *This isn't working. I don't know how to do this. I never had a chance to learn, and now I am too old.*

Horses again, galloping, and a shout. It flashed across her mind that among the other things she had failed to provision herself with was a weapon, even so much as a belt knife, to defend herself from assault. She pictured herself matched against a swordsman, any swordsman, with any weapon she could possibly pick up and swing, and snorted. It made a short scene, hardly likely to be worth the bother.

She glanced back over her shoulder and sighed. Ser dy Ferrej and a groom pounded down the road in her wake, the mud splashing from their horses' hooves. She was not, she thought, quite fool enough or mad enough to wish for bandits instead. Maybe that was the trouble; maybe she just wasn't crazed *enough*. True derangement stopped at no boundaries. Mad enough to wish for what she was not mad enough to grasp—now there was a singularly useless lunacy.

Guilt twinged in her heart at the sight of dy Ferrej's red, terrified, perspiring face as he drew up by her side. "Royina!" he cried. "My lady, what are you doing out here?" He almost tumbled from his saddle, to grasp her hands and stare into her face.

"I grew weary of the sorrows of the castle. I decided to take a walk in the spring sunshine to solace myself."

"My lady, you have come over five miles! This road is quite unfit for you—"

Yes, and I am quite unfit for it.

"No attendants, no guards—five gods, consider your station and your safety! Consider my gray hairs! You have stood them on end with this start."

"I do apologize to your gray hairs," said Ista, with a little real contrition. "They do not deserve the toil of me, nor does the remainder of you either, good dy Ferrej. I just . . . wanted to take a walk."

"Tell me next time, and I will arrange—"

"By myself."

"You are the dowager royina of all Chalion," stated dy Ferrej firmly. "You are Royina Iselle's own *mother*, for the five gods' sake. You cannot go skipping off down the road like a country wench."

Ista sighed at the thought of being a skipping country wench, and not tragic Ista anymore. Though she did not doubt country wenches had their tragedies, too, and much less poetic sympathy for them than did royinas. But there was nothing to be gained by arguing with him in the middle of the road. He made the groom give up his horse, and she acquiesced to being loaded aboard it. The skirts of this dress were not split for riding, and they bunched uncomfortably around her legs as she felt for the stirrups. Ista frowned again as the groom took the reins from her and made to lead her mount.

Dy Ferrej leaned across his saddle bow to grasp her hand, in consolation for the tears standing in her eyes. "I know," he murmured kindly. "Your lady mother's death is a great loss for us all."

I finished weeping for her weeks ago, dy Ferrej. She had sworn once to neither weep nor pray ever again, but she had forsworn herself on both oaths in those last dreadful days in the sickroom. After that, neither weeping nor praying had seemed to have any point. She decided not to trouble the castle warder's mind with the explanation that she wept now for herself, and not in sorrow but in a sort of rage. Let him take her as a little unhinged by bereavement; bereavement passed.

Dy Ferrej, quite as tired out as she by the past weeks of grief and guests, did not trouble her with further conversation, and the groom did not dare. She sat her plodding horse and let the road roll up again beneath her like a carpet being put away, denied its use. What was her use now? She chewed her lip and stared between her horse's bobbing ears.

After a time, its ears flickered. She followed its snorting

glance to see another cavalcade approaching down a connecting road, some dozen or two riders on horses and mules. Dy Ferrej rose in his stirrups and squinted, but then eased back in his saddle at the sight of the four outriders clad in the blue tunics and gray cloaks of soldier-brothers of the Daughter's Order, whose mandate encompassed the safe conveyance of pilgrims on the road. As the party rode closer, it could be seen that its members included both men and women, all decked out in the colors of their chosen gods, or as close as their wardrobes could manage, and that they wore colored ribbons on their sleeves in token of their holy destinations.

The two parties reached the joining of the roads simultaneously, and dy Ferrej exchanged reassuring nods with the soldier-brothers, stolid conscientious fellows like himself. The pilgrims stared in speculation at Ista in her fine somber clothes. A stout, red-faced older woman—*she's not any older than I am, surely*—offered Ista a cheery smile. After an uncertain moment, Ista's lips curved up in response, and she returned her nod. Dy Ferrej had placed his horse between the pilgrims and Ista, but his shielding purpose was defeated when the stout woman reined her horse back and kneed it into a trot to come up around him.

"The gods give you a good day, lady," the woman puffed. Her fat piebald horse was overburdened with stuffed saddlebags and yet more bags tied to them with twine and bouncing as precariously as its rider. It dropped back to a walk, and she caught her breath and straightened her straw hat. She wore Mother's greens in somewhat mismatched dark hues proper to a widow, but the braided ribbons circling her sleeve marched down in a full rank of five: blue wound with white, green with yellow, red with orange, black with gray, and white twined with cream.

After a moment's hesitation, Ista nodded again. "And you."

"We are pilgrims from around Baocia," the woman announced invitingly. "Traveling to the shrine of the miraculous death of Chancellor dy Jironal, in Taryoon. Well, except for the good Ser dy Brauda over there." She nodded toward an older man in subdued browns wearing a red-and-orange favor marking allegiance to the Son of Autumn. A more brightly togged young man rode by his side, who leaned forward to frown quellingly around him at the green-clad woman. "He's taking his boy, over there—isn't he a pretty lad, now, eh?"

The boy recoiled and stared straight ahead, growing flushed as if to harmonize with the ribbons on his sleeve; his father was not successful in suppressing a smile.

"—up to Cardegoss to be invested in the Son's Order, like his papa before him, to be sure. The ceremony is to be performed by the holy general, the Royse-Consort Bergon himself! I'd so like to see *him*. They say he's a handsome fellow. That Ibran seashore he comes from is supposed to be good for growing fine young men. I shall have to find some reason to pray in Cardegoss myself, and give my old eyes that treat."

"Indeed," said Ista neutrally at this anticipatory, but on the whole accurate, description of her son-in-law.

"I am Caria of Palma. I was wife of a saddler there, most lately. Widow, now. And you, good lady? Is this surly fellow your husband, then?"

The castle warder, listening with obvious disapproval to such familiarity, made to pull his horse back and fend off the tiresome woman, but Ista held up her hand. "Peace, dy Ferrej." He raised his brows, but shrugged and held his tongue.

Ista continued to the pilgrim, "I am a widow of . . . Valenda."

"Ah, indeed? Why, and so am I," the woman returned brightly. "My first man was of there. Though I've buried three husbands altogether." She announced this as though it were an achievement. "Oh, not all together, of course. One at a time." She cocked her head in curiosity at Ista's high mourning colors. "Did you just bury yours, then, lady? Pity. No wonder you look so sad and pale. Well, dear, it's a hard time, especially with the first, you know. At the beginning you want to die—I know I did—but that's just fear talking. Things will come about again, don't you worry."

Ista smiled briefly and shook her head in faint disagreement, but was not moved to correct the woman's misapprehension. Dy Ferrej was clearly itching to depress the creature's forwardness by announcing Ista's rank and station, and by implication his own, and perhaps driving her off, but Ista realized with a little wonder that she found Caria amusing. The widow's burble did not displease her, and she didn't want her to stop.

There was, apparently, no danger of that. Caria of Palma pointed out her fellow pilgrims, favoring Ista with a rambling account of their stations, origins, and holy goals; and if they rode sufficiently far out of earshot, with opinions of their manners and morals thrown in gratis. Besides the amused veteran dedicat of the Son of Autumn and his blushing boy, the party included four men from a weavers' fraternity who went to pray to the Father of Winter for a favorable outcome of a lawsuit; a man wearing the ribbons of the Mother of Summer, who prayed for the safety of a daughter nearing childbirth; and a woman whose sleeve sported the blue and white of the Daughter of Spring, who prayed for a husband for *her* daughter. A thin woman in finely cut green robes of an acolyte of the Mother's Order, with a maid and two servants of her own, turned out to be neither midwife nor physician, but a comptroller. A wine merchant rode to give thanks and redeem his pledge to the Father for his safe return with his caravan, almost lost the previous winter in the snowy mountain passes to Ibra.

The pilgrims within hearing, who had evidently been riding with Caria for some days now, rolled their eyes variously as she talked on, and on. An exception was an obese young man in the white garb, grimed from the road, of a divine of the Bastard. He rode along quietly with a book open atop the curve of his belly, his muddy white mule's reins slack, and glanced up only when he came to turn a page, blinking nearsightedly and smiling muzzily.

The Widow Caria peered at the sun, which had topped the sky. "I can hardly wait to get to Valenda. There is a famous inn where we are to eat that specializes in the most delicious roast suckling pigs." She smacked her lips in anticipation.

"There is such an inn in Valenda, yes," said Ista. She had never eaten there, she realized, not in all her years of residence.

The Mother's comptroller, who had been one of the widow's more pained involuntary listeners, pursed her mouth in disapproval. "I shall take no meat," she announced. "I made a vow that no gross flesh would cross my lips upon this journey."

Caria leaned over and muttered to Ista, "If she'd made a vow to swallow her pride, instead of her salads, it would have been more to the point for a pilgrimage, I'm thinking." She sat up again, grinning; the Mother's comptroller sniffed and pretended not to have heard.

The merchant with the Father's gray-and-black ribbons on his sleeve remarked as if to the air, "I'm sure the gods have no use for pointless chatter. We should be using our time better—discussing high-minded things to prepare our minds for prayer, not our bellies for dinner."

Caria leered at him, "Aye, or lower parts for better things still? And you ride with the Father's favor on your sleeve, too! For shame."

The merchant stiffened. "That is *not* the aspect of the god to which I intend—or need—to pray, I assure you, madam!"

The divine of the Bastard glanced up from his book and murmured peaceably, "The gods rule all parts of us, from top to toe. There is a god for everyone, and every part."

"*Your* god has notably low tastes," observed the merchant, still stung.

"None who open their hearts to any one of the Holy Family shall be excluded. Not even the priggish." The divine bowed over his belly at the merchant.

Caria gave a cheerful crack of laughter; the merchant snorted indignation, but desisted. The divine returned to his book.

Caria whispered to Ista, "I like that fat fellow, I do. Doesn't say much, but when he speaks, it's to the point. Bookish men usually have no patience with me, and I surely don't understand *them*. But that one does have lovely manners. Though I do think a man should get him a wife, and children, and do the work that pays for them, and not go haring off after the gods. Now, I have to admit, my dear second husband didn't—work, that is—but then, he drank. Drank himself to death eventually, to the relief of all who knew him, five gods rest his spirit." She signed herself, touching forehead, lip, navel, groin, and heart, spreading her hand wide over her plump breast. She pursed her lips, raised her chin and her voice, and called curiously, "But now I think on it, you've never told us what you go to pray for, Learned."

The divine placed his finger on his page and glanced up. "No, I don't think I have," he said vaguely.

The merchant said, "All you called folk pray to meet your god, don't you?"

"I have often prayed for the goddess to touch *my* heart," said the Mother's comptroller. "It is my highest spiritual goal to see Her face-to-face. Indeed, I often think I have felt Her, from time to time."

Anyone who desires to see the gods face-to-face is a great fool, thought Ista. Although that was not an impediment, in her experience.

"You don't have to pray to do that," said the divine. "You just have to die. It's not hard." He rubbed his second chin. "In fact, it's unavoidable."

"To be god-touched in *life*," corrected the comptroller coolly. "*That* is the great blessing we all long for."

No, it's not. If you saw the Mother's face right now, woman, you would drop weeping in the mud of this road and not get up for days. Ista became aware that the divine was squinting at her in arrested curiosity.

Was *he* one of the god-touched? Ista possessed some practice at spotting them. The reverse also held true, unfortunately. Or perhaps that calflike stare was just shortsightedness. Discomforted, she frowned back at him.

He blinked apologetically and said to her, "In fact, I travel on business for my order. A dedicat in my charge came by chance across a little stray demon possessed by a ferret. I take it to Taryoon for the archdivine to return to the god with proper ceremony."

He twisted around to his capacious saddlebags and rummaged therein, trading the book for a small wicker cage. A lithe gray shape turned within it.

"Ah-ha! So that's what you've been hiding in there!" Caria rode closer, wrinkling her nose. "It looks like any other ferret to me." The creature stood up against the side of the cage and twitched its whiskers at her.

The fat divine turned in his saddle and held up the cage to Ista's view. The animal, circling, froze in her frown; for just a moment, its beady eyes glittered back with something other than animal intelligence. Ista regarded it dispassionately. The ferret lowered its head and backed away until it could retreat no farther. The divine gave Ista a curious sidelong look.

"Are you sure the poor thing isn't just sick?" said Caria doubtfully.

"What do you think, lady?" the divine asked Ista.

You know very well it has a real demon. Why do you ask me? "Why—I think the good archdivine will certainly know what it is and what to do with it."

The divine smiled faintly at this guarded reply. "Indeed, it is not much of a demon." He tucked the cage away again. "I wouldn't name it more than a mere elemental, small and unformed. It hasn't been long in the world, I'd guess, and so is little likely to tempt men to sorcery."

It did not tempt Ista, certainly, but she understood his need to be discreet. Acquiring a demon made one a sorcerer much as acquiring a horse made one a rider, but whether skilled or poor was a more open question. Like a horse, a demon could run away with its master. Unlike a horse, there was no dismounting. To a soul's peril; hence the Temple's concern.

Caria made to speak again, but the path to the castle split off at that point, and dy Ferrej reined his horse aside. The widow of Palma converted whatever she'd been about to say to a cheery farewell wave, and dy Ferrej escorted Ista firmly off the road.

He glanced back over his shoulder as they started down the bank into the trees. "Vulgar woman. I'll wager she has not a pious thought in her head! She uses her pilgrimage only to shield her holiday-making from the disapproval of her relatives and get herself a cheap armed escort on the road."

"I believe you are entirely right, dy Ferrej." Ista glanced back over her shoulder at the party of pilgrims advancing down the main road. The Widow Caria was now coaxing the divine of the Bastard to sing hymns with her, though the one she was suggesting more resembled a drinking song.

"She had not one man of her own family to support her," dy Ferrej continued indignantly. "I suppose she can't help the lack of a husband, but you'd think she could scare up a brother or son or at least a nephew. I'm sorry you had to be exposed to that, Royina."

A not entirely harmonious but thoroughly good-natured duet rose behind them, fading with distance.

"I'm not," said Ista. A slow smile curved her lips. *I'm not.*

2

Ista sat in her mother's rose arbor, twisting a fine handkerchief in her fingers. Her lady attendant sat near her, poking at a piece of embroidery with a needle as narrow as, though rather sharper than, her mind. Ista had paced the garden round and round in the cool morning air till the woman, her voice rising, had begged her to stop. She paused now in her sewing to stare at Ista's hands, and Ista, irritably, set the tortured scrap of linen aside. Beneath her skirts, safely hidden, one silk-slippered foot took up a nervous—no, furious—drumming.

A gardener bustled about, watering the flowers in the tubs placed around all the doorways for the Daughter's Season, just as he had done for years under the direction of the old Provincara. Ista wondered how long it would be before those drilled habits died away—or would they continue forever, as if the old lady's meticulous ghost still oversaw each task? But no, her soul had truly been taken up, and out of the world of men; there were no new ghosts in the castle, or Ista would have felt them. All the sundered spirits left here were ancient and tired and fading, a mere chill in the walls at night.

She breathed out through pursed lips, flexing both curtained feet. She had waited several days to spring to her castle warder the proposal that she go on pilgrimage this season, in hopes that he would have forgotten the Widow Caria. A pilgrimage in humility, with only a small company; few attendants, simple gear, no royal train a hundred riders long, as he seemed instantly to think would be the minimum required. Dy Ferrej had thrown up a dozen annoyingly practical objections, and wondered at her sudden piety. He'd dismissed Ista's hint that she sought penance for her sins, being under the impression that she could have committed none to speak of under his good guard. Which was, she had to admit, certainly the case for such gross sins of the flesh as he imagined; dy Ferrej was not a theologically subtle man. As Ista's arguments had grown more intense, dy Ferrej had grown more stolid and cautious, till Ista had to bite back a frantic urge to scream at the man. The more fiercely she pleaded, the worse she made her case sound in his ears, she was sure. A galling paradox.

A page trotted across the garden, favoring Ista with a most peculiar bow in passing, a sort of bending in midbounce. He disappeared into the keep. A few minutes later dy Ferrej appeared with the page at his heels, and trod gravely back across the garden. The castle keys, mark of his wardship, jingled at his belt.

"Where away, dy Ferrej?" Ista called idly. She forced her feet to stillness.

He paused and gave her a bow, suitable to her rank and his dignity and girth, and made the page do his over correctly as well. "I am told some riders from Cardegoss have arrived, Royina." He hesitated briefly. "Your argument that I, by my oath to you and yours, owed you obedience as well as protection has been much on my mind."

Ah-ha, so that one had struck home. *Good.* Ista smiled slightly.

He smiled slightly back, the openly relieved expression on his features edged with triumph. "As my pleas did not seem to move you, I wrote to court to ask those to whom you *will* listen to add their voices, and their more august authority, to my own. Old dy Ferrej indeed has no right to thwart you, save for whatever forbearance he may be owed—no, that you may bestow upon him in charity—for his years of service—"

Ista's lips thinned at his words. *I cry a foul.*

"But Royina Iselle and Royse Bergon are your liege lords now, as well as having concern for your safety as their mother, and I believe Chancellor dy Cazaril is a man whose opinion you do somewhat regard. If I'm not mistaken, some calming advice arrives with these messengers." He nodded in satisfaction and moved off.

Ista clenched her teeth. She declined to call down curses on Iselle, Bergon, or Cazaril. Or, in truth, on *Old dy Ferrej*, as he was pleased to style himself—a disputant's ploy, he was scarcely more than a decade older than Ista. But the tension in her body seemed almost to constrict her breathing. She half believed that in their urgency to guard her from old madness, her earnest protectors would drive her mad anew.

The clack of horses' hooves, voices, and the calls of grooms floated around the curve of the keep. Abruptly, Ista rose and paced after dy Ferrej. Her lady attendant disentangled herself from her embroidery, scrambled to her feet, and pattered after her, making little protesting noises through sheer habit, Ista decided.

In the cobbled entry court, two riders in the garb of the Daughter's Order were dismounting under dy Ferrej's benevolent and welcoming eye. They were certainly not local men from the temple at Valenda—nothing about their clothing or gear was mismatched, crude, or rustic. From their polished boots up through neat blue trousers and tunics, clean embroidered white wool vest cloaks, and the gray hooded cloaks of their order, their clothing shouted of Cardegoss tailoring. Weapons and their housings were clean and meticulously cared for, the brightwork polished and the leather oil-rubbed—but not new. One officer-dedicat was a little above middle height, light and wiry. The shorter fellow was deeply muscled, and the heavy broadsword that hung from his baldric was clearly no courtier's toy.

As dy Ferrej finished speaking a welcome and directing the servants, Ista stepped up beside him. She narrowed her eyes. "Gentlemen. Do I not know you?"

Smiling, they handed off their reins to the cluster of castle grooms and swept her courtly bows. "Royina," the taller murmured. "A pleasure to see you again." Not giving her a chance to be discomfited with shaky memory, he added, "Ferda dy Gura; my brother Foix."

"Ah, yes. You are those young men who rode with Chancellor dy Cazaril on his great Ibran mission, three years ago. I met you at Bergon's investiture. The chancellor and Royse Bergon praised you highly."

"Kind of 'em," murmured the stout one, Foix.

"Honored to serve you, lady." The elder dy Gura came to a species of attention before her, and recited, "Chancellor dy Cazaril presents us to you with his compliments, to escort you upon your journey, Royina. He begs you will regard us as your right hand. Hands." Ferda faltered and extemporized, "Or right and left hand, as the case may be."

His brother raised an impertinent eyebrow at him, and murmured, "But which is which?"

Dy Ferrej's satisfied look gave way to a startled one. "The chancellor *approves* this, this . . . venture?"

Ista wondered what less flattering word he had just swallowed.

Ferda and Foix looked at each other. Foix shrugged and turned to dig in his saddlebag. "M'lord dy Cazaril gave me this note to give into your hand, lady." With a cheerful flourish, he presented a paper folded with both a large red chancellery seal and dy Cazaril's personal stamp, a crow perched on the letters CAZ pressed in blue wax.

Ista took it with thanks, and considerable mystification. Dy Ferrej craned his neck as she broke it open on the spot, scattering wax on the cobbles. She turned a little away from him to read it.

It was brief, and written in a fine chancellery script, addressing her with all her full formal titles; the heading was longer than the body of the letter. It read: *I give you these two good brothers, Ferda and Foix dy Gura, to attend you as captains and companions upon your road, wherever it may take you. I trust they may serve you as well as they have served me. Five gods speed you on your journey. Your most humble and obedient,* and a semicircle with trailing scrawl, dy Cazaril's signature.

In the same vile handwriting—dy Cazaril's fingers had more strength than delicacy, Ista recalled—was written a postscript: *Iselle and Bergon send a purse, in memory of the jewels pawned for another jaunt, that bought a country. I have entrusted it to Foix. Do not be alarmed by his humor, he is much less simple than he looks.*

Slowly, Ista's lips curled up. "I think that is very clear."

She handed off the letter to the hovering dy Ferrej. His face fell as his eyes sped down the lines. His lips made an O, but were too well trained, perhaps, to complete the expletive. Ista credited the old Provincara for that.

Dy Ferrej looked up at the brothers. "But—the royina cannot take to the roads with only two outriders, no matter how excellent."

"Certainly not, sir." Ferda gave him a little bow. "We brought our full troop. I left them down in town to batten upon the temple's larder, except for the two men I dispatched to another task. They should return tomorrow, to complete our numbers."

"Other task?" said dy Ferrej.

"Marshal dy Palliar seized our going this way to add a chore. He sent up a fine Roknari stallion that we captured in the Gotorget campaign last fall, to cover the mares at our order's breeding farm at Palma." Ferda's face grew animated. "Oh, I wish you'd had a chance to see him, Royina! He bounds from the earth and trots on air—the most glorious silver coat—silk merchants would swoon in envy. Hooves that ring like cymbals when they strike the ground, tail like a banner flying, mane like a maiden's hair, a marvel of nature—"

His brother cleared his throat.

"Er," concluded Ferda, "a very fine horse, withal."

"I suppose," dy Ferrej said, staring into the middle distance with the chancellor's note still in his hand, "we could write to your brother dy Baocia in Taryoon for a detachment of his provincial cavalry, in addition. And ladies of his household, to wait upon you in full panoply. Your good sister-in-law, perhaps—or some of your nieces may be old enough . . . ladies of his court, and your own attendants, of course, and all the necessary maids and grooms. And we must send down to the temple for a suitable spiritual conductor. No, better—we should write to Cardegoss and ask Archdivine Mendenal to recommend a divine of high scholarship."

"That would take another ten days," said Ista in alarm. *At least.* Her thrill at dy Ferrej's forced reversal sank in dismay. If he had his way, so far from escaping, she would be constrained to crawl over the countryside trailed by a veritable army. "I wish no such delay. The weather and the roads are much improved now," she threw in a little desperately. "I would prefer to take advantage of the clear skies."

"Well, well, we can discuss that," he said, glancing up at the fair blue day as if allowing her the point, safely minor. "I'll speak with your ladies and write to your brother." His mouth turned down in thought. "Iselle and Bergon plainly mean some message by that purse. Perhaps, Royina, they intend for you to pray for a grandson on your pilgrimage? That would indeed be a great blessing to the royacy of Chalion, and a very befitting purpose for your prayers." The idea clearly held more charm for him than it did for her, as he'd been enormously pleased recently by the birth of his own first grandson. But since it was the first positive remark he'd yet made about her . . . venture, she forbore to wrest it from him.

The dy Gura brothers and their horses were led off to the hospitality of the castle and its stables, respectively, and dy Ferrej hurried about his self-imposed tasks. Ista's woman promptly began gabbling about all the problems of selecting clothing for such an arduous journey, for all the world as if Ista ·proposed an expedition across the mountains to Darthaca or beyond, instead of a pious amble around Baocia. Ista considered pleading a headache to make her stop her chatter, concluded it would ill serve her purposes, and set her teeth to endure.

❧

The woman was still prattling and worrying by late afternoon. Trailed by three maids, she dodged about Ista's rooms in the old keep, sorting and re-sorting piles of gowns, robes, cloaks, and shoes, trading off the need for colors appropriate for Ista's high mourning with preparation for every likely or unlikely contingency. Ista sat in a window seat overlooking the entry court, letting the endless words flow over her like a drip from a gutter spout. Her headache was now quite real, she decided.

A clatter and bustle at the castle gate announced, unusually, another visitor. Ista sat up and peered through the casement. A tall bay horse clopped in through the archway; its rider wore the castle-and-leopard tabard of the chancellery of Chalion over more faded clothing. The rider swung down, bouncing on—oh, *her* toes; the courier was a fresh-faced young woman with her hair in a black braid down her back. She pulled a bundle from behind her saddle and unrolled it with a snap to reveal a skirt. With decidedly perfunctory modesty, she hitched up her tunic and wrapped the garment around her trousers at her slim waist, shaking out the hem around her booted ankles with a cheerful swing of her hips.

De Ferrej appeared below; the girl unsealed her chancellery pouch and held it upside down to drop out a single letter. Dy Ferrej read the direction and tore it open then and there, by which Ista deduced it was a personal missive from his beloved daughter Lady Betriz, attendant upon the Royina Iselle at court. Perhaps it contained news of his grand-

son, for his face softened. Was it time yet for first teeth? If
so, Ista would hear of the infant's achievement in due
course. She had to smile a little.

The girl stretched, restored her pouch, checked her
horse's legs and hooves, and turned the animal over to the
castle groom with some string of instructions. Ista became
conscious of her own lady-in-waiting peering over her
shoulder.

Ista said impulsively, "I would speak to that courier girl.
Fetch her to me."

"My lady, she had only the one letter."

"Well, then, I'll have to hear the news of court from her
lips."

Her woman snorted. "Such a rude girl is not likely to be
in the confidence of the court ladies at Cardegoss."

"Nonetheless, fetch her."

It might have been the sharp tone of voice; in any case,
the woman moved off.

At length, a firm tread and an aroma of horses and leather
announced the girl's arrival in Ista's sitting room, even before her woman's dubious, "My lady, here is the courier as
you asked." Ista swung round in the casement seat and
stared up, waving her woman out; she departed with a dis-
approving frown.

The girl stared back with slightly daunted curiosity. She
managed an awkward bob, halfway between a bow and a
curtsey. "Royina. How may I serve you?"

Ista scarcely knew. "What's your name, girl?"

"Liss, my lady." After a moment of rather empty silence
she offered, "Short for Annaliss."

"Where do you come from?"

"Today? I picked up my dispatch case at the station in—"

"No—altogether."

"Oh. Um. My father had a little estate near the town of
Teneret, in the province of Labra. He raised horses for the
Brother's Order, and sheep for the wool market. Still does,
as far as I know."

A man of substance; she was not escaping some dire poverty, then. "How did you become a courier?"

"I had not thought about it, till one day my sister and I came to town to deliver some horses to the temple, and I saw a girl gallop in riding courier for the Daughter's Order." She smiled as if in some happy memory. "I was on fire from that moment."

Perhaps it was the confidence of her calling, or of her youth and strength; the girl, while very polite, was by no means tongue-tied in the royina's presence, Ista noted with relief. "Aren't you afraid, out there alone on the roads?"

She tossed her head, making her braid swing. "I outride all danger. So far, anyway."

Ista could believe it. The girl was taller than Ista, but still shorter and slighter than the average man, even the wiry fellows favored for couriers. She would sit her horse lightly. "Or . . . or uncomfortable? You must ride in heat, cold, all weather . . ."

"I don't melt in the rain. And the riding keeps me warm in the snow. If I have to, I can sleep wrapped in my cloak on the ground under a tree. Or up it, if the place seems chancy. It's true the courier station bunks are warmer and less bumpy." Her eyes crinkled with humor. "Slightly."

Ista sighed in faint awe of such boundless energy. "How long have you been riding for the chancellery?"

"Three years, now. Since I was fifteen."

What had Ista been doing at age fifteen? Training to be a great lord's wife, she supposed. When Roya Ias's eye had fallen on her, at about the age this girl was now, the schooling had seemed to succeed beyond her family's wildest dreams—till the dream had melted into the long nightmare of Ias's great curse. Now broken, thank the gods and Lord dy Cazaril; now broken these three years gone. The choking fog of it had lifted from her mind that day. The dullness of her life, the stalemate of her soul since then was just long habit.

"How came your family to let you leave home so young?"

The girl's flickering amusement warmed her face like the sun through green leaves. "I believe I forgot to ask, come to think on it."

"And the dispatcher allowed you to sign on without your father's word?"

"I believe he forgot to ask, too, being in great need of riders just then. It's amazing how the rules change in a pinch. But with four other daughters to dower, I didn't expect my father and brothers to run down the road to drag me back."

"You went that very day?" asked Ista, startled.

The white grin widened—she had healthy teeth, too, Ista noted. "Of course. I figured if I had to go home and spin one more skein of yarn, I'd scream and fall down in a fit. Besides, my mother never liked my yarn anyway. She said it was too lumpy."

Ista could sympathize with *that* statement. A reluctant answering smile lifted her lips. "My daughter is a great rider."

"So all Chalion has heard, my lady." Liss's eyes brightened. "From Valenda to Taryoon in one night, and dodging enemy troops the while—*I've* never had such an adventure. Nor won such a prize at the end of it."

"Let us hope the wings of war will not brush Valenda so close again. Where do you go next?"

Liss shrugged. "Who knows? I'll ride back to my station to await the next pouch my dispatcher hands to me, and go where it takes me. Swiftly if Ser dy Ferrej writes some reply, or slowly to spare my horse if he does not."

"He will not write tonight . . . ." Ista scarcely wanted to let her go, but the girl looked disheveled and dirty from the road. Surely she would wish to wash and take refreshment. "Attend on me again, Liss of Labra. The castle takes dinner in an hour or so. Wait upon me there and dine at my table."

The girl's dark brows rose in brief surprise. She bow-curtseyed again. "At your command, Royina."

The old Provincara's high table was set exactly as it had been a thousand—ten thousand—times before, on days when no festival brought relief from the monotony. Granted it was comfortable, in the small dining chamber of the newest building within the castle walls, with fireplace and glazed windows. The same small company, too: Lady dy Hueltar, who was Ista's mother's aging relative and longtime companion; Ista; her principal lady attendants; solemn dy Ferrej. By tacit agreement, the old Provincara's chair still stood empty. Ista had not moved to claim the central seat, and perhaps in some misplaced notion of her grief, none had urged her to.

Dy Ferrej arrived, escorting Ferda and Foix, both looking very courtly. And young. The courier girl entered in their wake and made polite bows. She had faced Royina Ista bravely enough alone, but the atmosphere of staid age here was enough to melt the sinews of strong soldiers. She took her seat stiffly and sat as if trying to make herself smaller, though she eyed the two brothers with interest. The aroma of horses was much fainter now, although Lady dy Hueltar wrinkled her nose. But one more place setting—not the old Provincara's—still stood empty across from Ista.

"Do we expect a guest?" Ista inquired of dy Ferrej. One of the elderly people's elderly friends, perhaps; Ista dared not hope for anything more exotic.

Dy Ferrej cleared his throat and nodded at old Lady dy Hueltar.

Her seamed face smiled. "I asked the Temple of Valenda to send us a suitable divine to be your spiritual conductor upon your pilgrimage, Royina. If we are not to send to Cardegoss for a court-trained scholar, I thought we might request Learned Tovia, of the Mother's Order. She may be a lesser theologian, but she is a most excellent physician, and knows you of old. Such a relief to have someone familiar, should we be taken with any female complaints upon the road, or . . . or if your old troubles should flare up. And none could possibly be more proper to your sex and status."

A relief to whom? Divine Tovia had been a bosom friend to the old Provincara and to Lady dy Hueltar; Ista could quite imagine the trio enjoying a gentle jaunt in the spring sunshine together. Five gods, had Lady dy Hueltar assumed *she* would be going along also? Ista suppressed an unworthy desire to scream, just like Liss in fear of being cocooned in her endless skeins of wool.

"I knew you would be pleased," Lady dy Hueltar murmured on. "I thought you might wish to begin discussing your holy itinerary with her over dinner." She frowned. "It's not like her to be late."

Her frown vanished, as a servant entered and said, "The divine is here, my lady."

"Oh, good. Show her in at once."

The servant opened his mouth as if to speak, but then bowed and retreated.

The door swung wide again. A puffing figure of totally unexpected familiarity entered, and stopped, stranded upon a wall of stares. It was the fat young divine of the Bastard that Ista had met upon the road those two weeks or so ago. His white robes were only somewhat cleaner now, being free of loose detritus, but mottled with permanent faint stains about the hem and front.

His beginning smile grew uncertain. "Good evening, gentle ladies and my lords. I was told to attend here upon a certain Lady dy Hueltar. Something about a divine being wanted for a pilgrimage . . . ?"

Lady dy Hueltar recovered her voice. "I am she. But I had understood the temple was sending the Mother's physician, Divine Tovia. Who are you?"

That had almost come out *Who* are *you?* Ista felt, but for Lady dy Hueltar's grip on good address.

"Oh . . ." He bobbed a bow. "Learned Chivar dy Cabon, at your service."

He claimed a name of some rank, at least. He eyed Ista and Ser dy Ferrej; the recognition, Ista thought, ran two ways, as did the surprise.

"Where *is* Learned Tovia?" asked Lady dy Hueltar blankly.

"I believe she has ridden out upon a medical call of some special difficulty, at some distance from Valenda." His smile grew less certain still.

"Welcome, Learned dy Cabon," said Ista pointedly.

Dy Ferrej woke to his duties. "Indeed. I'm the castle warder, dy Ferrej; this is the Dowager Royina Ista . . ."

Dy Cabon's eyes narrowed, and he stared sharply at Ista. "*Are* you, now . . ." he breathed.

Dy Ferrej, ignoring or not hearing this, introduced the dy Gura brothers and the other ladies in order of rank, and lastly, and a bit reluctantly, "Liss, a chancellery courier."

Dy Cabon bowed to all with indiscriminate good cheer.

"This is all wrong—there must be some mistake, Learned dy Cabon," Lady dy Hueltar went on, with a beseeching sideways glance at Ista. "It is the dowager royina *herself* who proposes to undertake a pilgrimage this season, in petition of the gods for a grandson. You are not—this is not— we do not know—is a divine of the Bastard's Order, and a man at that, *quite* the most appropriate, um, person, um . . ." She trailed off in mute appeal for someone, anyone, to extract her from this quagmire.

Somewhere inside, Ista was beginning to smile.

She said smoothly, "Mistake or no, I feel certain that our dinner is ready to be served. Will you please grace our table this evening with your scholarship, Learned, and lead us in the meal's invocation to the gods?"

He brightened vastly. "I should be most honored, Royina."

Smiling and blinking, he seated himself in the chair Ista indicated and looked hopeful as the servant passed among them with the basin of lavender-scented water for washing hands. He blessed the impending meal in unexceptionable terms and a good voice; whatever he was, he was no country rustic. He tucked into the courses presented with an enthusiasm that would have warmed the Provincara's cook's heart, could he have witnessed it, discouraged as he was by his long thrall to elderly, indifferent appetites. Foix kept pace with him with no apparent effort.

"Are you of those Cabons related to the present Holy General dy Yarrin of the Daughter's Order?" Lady dy Hueltar inquired politely.

"I believe I am some sort of third or fourth cousin to him, lady," the divine replied after swallowing his bite. "My father was Ser Odlin dy Cabon."

Both dy Gura brothers stirred with interest.

"Oh," said Ista in surprise. "I believe I met him, years ago, at court in Cardegoss." *Our Fat Cabon*, as he was jovially dubbed by the roya; but he'd died as bravely as any thinner gentleman of the roya's service at the disastrous battle of Dalus. She added after a moment, "You have the look of him."

The divine ducked his head in apparent pleasure. "I am not sorry for it."

Some impulse of mischief prompted Ista to ask, because it was certain no one else present would, "And are you also a son of Lady dy Cabon?"

The divine's eye glinted in response over a forkful of roast. "Alas, no. But my father took some joy in me nonetheless, and settled a dower upon me at the Temple when I came of the age for schooling. For which I—eventually— came to thank him very much. My calling did not come upon me as a lightning bolt, to be sure, but slowly, as a tree grows." Dy Cabon's round face and divine's robes made him look older than he was, Ista decided. He could not be above thirty, perhaps much less.

For the first time in a long while, the conversation turned not on various people's illnesses, aches, pains, and digestive failures, but widened to the whole of Chalion-Ibra. The dy Gura brothers had considerable witness to report of last year's successful campaign by the Marshal dy Palliar to retake the mountain fortress of Gotorget, commanding the border of the hostile Roknari princedoms to the north, and young Royse-Consort Bergon's seasoning attendance there upon the field of battle.

Ferda said, "Foix here took a bad knock from a Roknari war hammer during the final assault on the fortress, and was much abed this winter—a mess of broken ribs, with inflammation of the lungs to follow. Chancellor dy Cazaril took him up as a clerk while his bones finished knitting. Our cousin dy Palliar thought a little light riding would help him regain his condition."

A faint blush colored Foix's broad face, and he ducked his head. Liss's gaze at him sharpened a trifle, though whether imagining him with sword or with pen in hand Ista could not tell.

Lady dy Hueltar did not fail to register her usual criticism of Royina Iselle for riding to the north to be near her husband and these stirring events, even though—or perhaps that was, because—she had been brought safely to bed of a girl thereafter.

"I do not think," said Ista dryly, "that Iselle staying slugabed in Cardegoss would have resulted in a boy, however."

Lady dy Hueltar mumbled something; Ista was reminded of her own mother's sharp critique when she had borne Iselle to Ias, those long years ago. As if anything she might have done would have made it come out any differently. As if, when it had come out differently in her second confinement, it was any better . . . her brow wrinkled in old pain. She looked up to intersect dy Cabon's sharp glance.

The divine swiftly turned the subject to lighter matters. Dy Ferrej had the pleasure of trotting out an old tale or two for a new audience, which Ista could not begrudge him. Dy Cabon told a warm joke, albeit milder than many Ista had heard over the roya's table; the courier girl laughed aloud, caught a frown from Lady dy Hueltar, and held a hand over her mouth.

"Please don't stop," said Ista to her. "No one has laughed like that in this household for weeks. Months." *Years.*

What might her pilgrimage be like if, instead of dragging

a lot of tired guardians out on a road that suited their old bones so ill, she could travel with people who *laughed*? Young people, not brought low by old sin and loss? People who *bounced*? People to whom, dare she think it, she was an elder to be respected and not a failed child to be corrected? *At your command, Royina*, not, *Now, Lady Ista, you know you can't . . .*

She said abruptly, "Learned dy Cabon, I thank the Temple for taking thought for me, and I shall be pleased to have your spiritual guidance upon my journey."

"You honor me, Royina." Dy Cabon, sitting, bowed as deeply as he could over his belly. "When do we leave?"

"Tomorrow," said Ista.

A chorus of objection rose around the table: lists of persons and support not assembled, ladies-in-waiting, their maids, their grooms, of clothing, gear, of transport animals, of dy Baocia's small army not yet arrived.

She almost added weakly, *Or as soon as all can be arranged*, but then stiffened her resolve. Her eye fell on Liss, chewing and listening with detached fascination.

"You are all correct," Ista raised her voice to override the babble, which died in relief. She went on, "I do not have youth, or energy, or courage, or knowledge of how to make my way upon the road. So I shall commandeer some. I shall take the courier, Liss, to be my lady-in-waiting and my groom in one. And none more. That shall save three dozen mules right there."

Liss nearly spat out the bite she was chewing.

"But she's only a courier!" gasped Lady dy Hueltar.

"I assure you Chancellor dy Cazaril will not begrudge her to me. Couriers hold themselves ready to ride wherever they are ordered. What say you, Liss?"

Liss, eyes wide, finished gulping, and managed, "I think I'd make a better groom than waiting lady, Royina, but I will try my best for you."

"Good. None could ask more."

"You are the dowager royina!" dy Ferrej almost wailed. "You cannot go out on the roads with so little ceremony!"

"I plan a pilgrimage in humility, dy Ferrej, not a march in pride. Still . . . suppose I were not a royina? Suppose I were some simple widow of good family. What servants, what reasonable precautions would I take then?"

"Travel incognito?" Learned dy Cabon caught the idea instantly, while the rest were still gobbling in misdirected resistance. "That would certainly remove many distractions from your spiritual study, Royina. I suppose . . . such a woman would simply ask the Temple to provide her with escort in the usual way, and they would fill the request from the riders available."

"Fine. That has been done for me already. Ferda, can your men ride tomorrow?"

The cacophony of protest was overridden by dy Gura's simple, "Certainly. As you command, Royina."

The shocked silence that followed was decidedly baffled. And even, possibly, a little thoughtful, if that was not too much to hope.

Ista sat back, a smile turning her lips.

"I must take thought for a name," she said at length. "Neither dy Chalion nor dy Baocia will do, unsimple as they are." Dy Hueltar? Ista shuddered. *No.* She ran down a mental list of other minor relatives of the provincars of Baocia. "Dy Ajelo would do." The Ajelo family had scarcely crossed her view, and never once provided a lady-in-waiting to assist in Ista's . . . keeping. She bore them no ill will. "I shall still be Ista, I think. It's not so uncommon a name as to be remarked."

The divine cleared his throat. "We need to confer a little tonight, then. I do not know what route you desire of me. A pilgrimage should have both a spiritual plan and, in necessary support of it, a material one."

And hers had neither. And if she did not assert one, one would surely be foisted upon her. She said cautiously, "How have you led the pious before, Learned?"

"Well, that depends much upon the purposes of the pious."

"I have some maps in my saddlebags that might supply some inspiration. I'll fetch them, if you like," Ferda offered.

"Yes," said the divine gratefully. "That would be most helpful."

Ferda hurried out of the chamber. Outside, the day drew toward sunset; and the servants moved quietly about the room, lighting the wall sconces. Foix leaned his elbows comfortably on the table, smiled amiably at Liss, and found room for another slice of honey-nut cake while they waited for his brother's return.

Ferda strode back into the dining chamber in a very few minutes, his hands full of folded papers. "Here . . . no, here is Baocia, and the provinces to the west as far as Ibra." He spread a stained and travel-worn paper out on the table between the divine and Ista. Dy Ferrej peered anxiously over dy Cabon's shoulder.

The divine frowned at the map for a few minutes, then cleared his throat and looked across at Ista. "We are taught that the route of a pilgrimage should serve its spiritual goal. Which may be simple or manifold, but which will partake of at least one of five aims: service, supplication, gratitude, divination, and atonement."

Atonement. Apology to the gods. *Dy Lutez*, she could not help thinking. The chill memory of that dark hour still clouded her heart, on this bright evening. Yet who owed Whom the apology for that disaster? *We were all in it together, the gods and dy Lutez and Ias and I.* And if abasing herself on the altar of the gods was the cure for that old wound, she had eaten dirt enough already for a dozen dy Lutezes. Yet the scar still bled, in the deep dark, if pressed.

"I once saw a man pray for mules," Foix remarked agreeably.

Dy Cabon blinked. After a moment he asked, "Did he get any?"

"Yes, excellent ones."

"The gods' ways are . . . mysterious, sometimes," murmured dy Cabon, apparently digesting this. "Ahem. Yours—

Royina—is a pilgrimage of supplication, for a grandson as I understand it. Is it not?" He paused invitingly.

It is not. But dy Ferrej and Lady dy Hueltar both made noises of assent, and Ista let it pass.

Dy Cabon ran his finger over the intricately drawn chart, thick with place names, seamed with little rivers, and decorated with rather more trees than actually stood on Baocia's high plains. He pointed out this or that shrine devoted to the Mother or the Father within striking distance of Valenda, describing the merits of each. Ista forced herself to look at the map.

To the far south, beyond the map's margins, lay Cardegoss, and the great castle and fortress of the Zangre of evil memory. *No.* To the east lay Taryoon. *No.* West and north, then. She trailed her finger across the map toward the spine of the Bastard's Teeth, the high range that marked the long north–south border of Ibra, so recently united with Chalion in her daughter's marriage bed. North along the mountains' edge, some easy road. "This way."

Dy Cabon's brow wrinkled as he squinted at the map. "I'm not just sure what . . ."

"About a day's ride west of Palma is a town where the Daughter's Order has a modest hostel, rather pleasant," remarked Ferda. "We've stayed there before."

Dy Cabon licked his lips. "Hm. I know of an inn near Palma that we might reach before nightfall, if we do not tarry on the road. It has a most excellent table. Oh, and a sacred well, very old. A minor holy place, but as Sera Ista dy Ajelo desires a pilgrimage in humility, perhaps a small start will serve her best. And the great shrines tend to be crowded, this time of year."

"Then by all means, Learned, let us avoid the crowds and seek humility, and pray at this well. Or table, as the case may be." Ista's lips twitched.

"I see no need to weigh out prayer by the grain, as though it were dubious coin," replied dy Cabon cheerily, encouraged by her fleeting smile. "Let us do both, and return abundance for abundance." The divine's thick fingers made calipers of themselves and stepped from Valenda to Palma to the spot Ferda had tapped. He hesitated, then his hand turned once more. "A day's ride from there, if we arise early enough, is Casilchas. Sleepy little place, but my order has a school there. Some of my old teachers are still there. And it has a fine library, considering the small size of the place, for many teaching divines who have died have left it their books. I grant a seminary of the Bastard is not exactly . . . exactly *apropos* to the purpose of this pilgrimage, but I confess I should like to consult the library."

Ista wondered, a little dryly, if the school also had a particularly fine cook. She rested her chin upon her hand and studied the fat young man across from her. Whatever *had* possessed the Temple of Valenda to send him up to her, anyway? His half-aristocratic ancestry? Hardly. Yet experienced pilgrimage conductors usually had their charges' spiritual battle plans all drawn out in advance. There were doubtless books of devotional instruction on the topic. Perhaps that was what dy Cabon wanted from the library, a manual that would tell him how to go on. Perhaps he had slept through a few too many of those holy lectures, in Casilchas.

"Good," said Ista. "The Daughter's hospitality for the next two nights, the Bastard's thereafter." That would put her at least three full days' ride from Valenda. A good start.

Dy Cabon looked extremely relieved. "Excellent, Royina."

Foix was mulling over the maps; he'd pulled out one of all Chalion, necessarily less detailed than the one dy Cabon studied. His finger traced the route from Cardegoss north to Gotorget. The fortress guarded the end of a chain of rough, if not especially high, mountains that ran partway along the border between Chalion and the Roknari princedom of Borasnen. Foix's brows knotted. Ista wondered what memories of pain the name of that fortress evoked in him.

"You'll want to avoid that region, I think," said dy Ferrej, watching Foix's hand pause at Gotorget.

"Indeed, my lord. I believe we should steer clear of all north-central Chalion. It is still very unsettled from last year's campaign, and Royina Iselle and Royse Bergon are already starting to assemble forces there for the fall."

Dy Ferrej's brows climbed with interest. "Do they think to strike for Visping already?"

Foix shrugged, letting his finger slide up to the north coast and the port city named. "I'm not sure if Visping *can* be taken in a single campaign, but it were good if it could. Cut the Five Princedoms in two, gain a seaport for Chalion that the Ibran fleet might find refuge in . . ."

Dy Cabon leaned over the table, his belly pressing its edge, and peered. "The princedom of Jokona, to the west, would be next after Borasnen, then. Or would we strike toward Brajar? Or both at once?"

"Two fronts would be foolish, and Brajar is an uncertain ally. Jokona's new prince is young and untried. First pinch Jokona between Chalion and Ibra—pinch it off. Then turn to the northeast." Foix's eyes narrowed, and his pleasant mouth firmed, contemplating this strategy.

"Will you join the campaign in the fall, Foix?" Ista asked politely.

He nodded. "Where the Marshal dy Palliar goes, the dy Gura brothers will surely follow. As a master of horse, Ferda will likely be pressed into assembling cavalry mounts by midsummer. And, lest I miss him and start to pine, he'll find some hot, dirty job for me. Never any lack of those."

Ferda snickered. Foix's returning grin at his brother seemed entirely without resentment.

Ista thought Foix's analysis sound, and had no doubt how he'd come by it. Marshal dy Palliar and Royse Bergon and Royina Iselle were none of them fools, and Chancellor dy Cazaril had a deep wit indeed, and not much love for the Roknari coastal lords who had once sold him to slavery on the galleys. Visping was a prize worth playing for.

"We shall steer west, and away from the excitement, then," she said. Dy Ferrej nodded approval.

"Very good, Royina," said dy Cabon. His sigh was only a little wistful, as he refolded Ferda's maps and handed them back. Did he fear his father's martial fate, or envy it? There was no telling.

The party broke off shortly thereafter. The planning and complicated itinerary-listing and complaints from Ista's women went on and on. They would never stop arguing, Ista decided; but she could. She would. *You can't solve problems by running away from them*, it was said, and like the good child she had once been, she had believed this. But it wasn't true. Some problems could *only* be solved by running away from them. When her lamenting ladies at last blew out the candles and left her to her rest, her smile crept back.

3

ISTA SPENT THE EARLY MORNING SORTING THROUGH HER
wardrobe with Liss, searching for clothing fit for the road
and not merely a royina. Much that was old lingered in Ista's
cupboards and chests, but little that was plain. Any ornate or
delicate gown that made Liss wrinkle her nose in doubt went
instantly into the discard pile. Ista did manage to assemble a
riding costume of leggings, split skirt, tunic, and vest-cloak
that showed not a scrap of Mother's green. Finally, they
ruthlessly raided the wardrobes of Ista's ladies and maids, to
the latters' scandal. This resulted at the last in a neat pile of
garments—practical, plain, washable, and, above all, *few*.

Liss was clearly happier to be sent off to the stables to select the most suitable riding horse and baggage mule. *One*
baggage mule. By midday Ista's feverish single-mindedness
resulted in both women dressed for the road, the horses saddled, and the mule packed. The dy Gura brothers found them
standing in the cobbled courtyard when they rode through
the castle gate heading ten mounted men in the garb of the
Daughter's Order, dy Cabon following on his white mule.

The grooms held the royina's horse and ushered her to the
mounting block. Liss leapt up lightly on her tall bay with no

such assistance. In the spring of her life Ista had ridden much; hunted all day and danced till the moon went down, at the roya's glittering court when she'd first come there. She, too, had been too long abed in this castle of age and grievous memory. A little light duty to regain condition was just what was wanted.

Learned dy Cabon clambered from his mule long enough to stand up on the mounting block and intone a mercifully brief prayer and blessing upon the enterprise. Ista bowed her head, but did not mouth the responses. *I want nothing of the gods. I've had their gifts before.*

Fourteen people and eighteen animals just to get her on the road. What about those pilgrims who somehow managed this with no more than a staff and a sack?

Lady dy Hueltar and all of Ista's ladies and maids trooped down to the courtyard, not to wish her farewell, it transpired, but to weep pointedly at her in one last, decidedly counter-productive, bid to make her change her mind. In the teeth of all evidence to the contrary, Lady dy Hueltar wailed, "Oh, she's not *serious*—stop her, for the Mother's sake, dy Ferrej!" Gritting her teeth, Ista let their cries bounce off her back like arrows glancing from chain mail. Dy Cabon's white mule led out the archway and down the road at a gentle amble, but even so the voices fell behind at last. The soft spring wind stirred Ista's hair. She did not look back.

❧

They reached the Inn at Palma by sunset, barely. It had been a very long time, Ista reflected as she was helped down from her horse, since she had spent a whole day in the saddle, hunting or traveling. Liss, plainly bored with the pilgrimage's placid pace, jumped down off her animal as though she'd spent the afternoon lounging on a couch. Foix had apparently worked through whatever stiffness lingered from his injuries earlier in the brothers' journey. Even dy Cabon didn't waddle as though he hurt. When the divine offered her his arm, Ista took it gratefully.

Dy Cabon had sent one of the men riding ahead to bespeak beds and a meal for the party, fortunately as it turned out, for the inn was small. Another party, of tinkers, was being turned away as they arrived. The place had once been a narrow fortified farmhouse, now made more sprawling with an added wing. The dy Gura brothers and the divine were given one chamber to share, Ista and Liss another, and the rest of the guardsmen were assigned pallets in the stable loft, although the mild night made this no discomfort.

The innkeeper and his wife had set up two tables near the sacred spring, in a little grove behind the building, and hung lanterns lavishly in the trees. The thick moss and ferns, the bluebells and the bloodroots with their starry white blooms, the interlaced boughs, and the gentle gurgle of the water running over the smooth stones made a more lovely dining chamber, Ista thought, than she had sat in for many a year. They all washed their hands in springwater brought in a copper basin and blessed by the divine, and needing no other perfume. The innkeeper's wife was famous for her larder-keeping. A pair of servants kept busy lugging out heavy trays and jugs: good bread and cheese, roast ducks, mutton, sausages, dried fruit, new herbs and spring greens, eggs, dark olives and olive oil from the north, apple nut tarts, new ale and cider—simple fare, but very wholesome. Dy Cabon made flattering inroads upon these offerings, and even Ista's appetite, numbed for months, bestirred itself. When she finally undressed and lay down beside Liss in the clean little bed in the chamber under the eaves, she fell asleep so quickly she barely remembered it next morning.

Rising again, as the early light fell through the half-open casement window, proved briefly awkward. Through sheer ingrained habit, Ista stood still for a time and waited to be dressed, like a doll, till she realized her new maidservant would require instruction. At that point it became easier to sort out and draw on her garments herself, though she did ask for help with some of the fastenings. They snagged for a moment upon the problem of Ista's hair.

"I don't know how to dress ladies' hair," Liss confessed when Ista handed her the brush and sat on a low bench. She stared doubtfully at Ista's thick dun mane, hanging to her waist. Ista had, perhaps ill-advisedly, picked out her former attendant's careful, tight, elaborate braiding before bed. The hair's own curl had reasserted itself during the night, and it was now beginning to snarl, and perhaps growl and snap.

"You do your own, presumably. What do you do with it?"

"Well, I put it in a braid."

"What else?"

"I put it in two braids."

Ista thought a moment. "Do you do the horses?"

"Oh, yes, my lady. Snail braids, and dressed with ribbons, and fringe knots with beads for the Mother's Day, and for the Son's Day the fountain knots along the crest, with feathers worked in, and—"

"For today, put it in one braid."

Liss breathed relief. "Yes, my lady." Her hands were quick and clever; much quicker than Ista's former attendants. The results, well, they suited modest Sera dy Ajelo becomingly enough.

The whole party met in the grove for dawn prayers, for this the first full day of Ista's pilgrimage. Dawn by courtesy, anyway—the sun had been up for some hours before the inn's guests. The innkeeper, his wife, and all their children and the servants were also turned out for the ceremony, as the visit of a divine of notable scholarship was evidently a rare event. Besides which, Ista thought more cynically, there was the possibility that were he flatteringly enough received, the divine might recommend other pilgrims to this decidedly minor holy attraction.

As this wellspring was sacred to the Daughter, dy Cabon stood on the bank of the rivulet in the sun-dappled shade and commenced with a short springtime prayer from a small book of occasional devotions he carried in his saddlebag. Exactly why this well was sacred to the Lady of Spring was a little unclear. Ista found the innkeeper's assertion that it was the true secret location of the miracle of the virgin and the water jar a trifle unconvincing, as she knew of at least three other sites in Chalion alone that claimed that legend. But the beauty of the place was surely excuse enough for its holy reputation.

Dy Cabon, his stained robes seeming almost white in this pure light, pocketed his book and cleared his throat for the morning lesson. Since the tables behind them stood set and waiting for breakfast to be served when prayers were done, Ista was confident that the sermon would be succinct.

"As this is the beginning of a spiritual journey, I shall go back to the tale of beginnings we all learned in our childhoods." The divine closed his eyes briefly, as if marshaling memory. "Here is the story as Ordol writes it in his *Letters to the Young Royse dy Brajar.*"

His eyes opened again, and his voice took up a storyteller's rhythm. "The world was first and the world was flame, fluid and fearsome. As the flame cooled, matter formed and gained vast strength and endurance, a great globe with fire at its heart. From the fire at the heart of the world slowly grew the World-Soul.

"But the eye cannot see itself, not even the Eye of the World-Soul. So the World-Soul split in two, that it might so perceive itself; and so the Father and the Mother came into being. And with that sweet perception, for the first time, love became possible in the heart of the World-Soul. Love was the first of the fruits that the realm of the spirit gifted back to the realm of matter that was its fountain and foundation. But not the last, for song was next, then speech." Dy Cabon, speaking, grinned briefly and drew another long breath.

"And the Father and the Mother between them began to order the world, that existence might not be instantly consumed again by fire and chaos and roiling destruction. In their first love for each other they bore the Daughter and the

Son, and divided the seasons of the world among them, each with its special and particular beauty, each to its own lordship and stewardship. And in the harmony and security of this new composition, the matter of the world grew in boldness and complexity. And from its strivings to create beauty, plants and animals and men arose, for love had come into the fiery heart of the world, and matter sought to return gifts of spirit to the realm of spirit, as lovers exchange tokens."

Satisfaction flickered across dy Cabon's suety features, and he swayed a trifle with his cadences as he became absorbed by his tale. Ista suspected they were getting to his favorite part.

"But the fire at the heart of the world also held forces of destruction that could not be denied. And from this chaos rose the demons, who broke out and invaded the world and preyed upon the fragile new souls growing there as a mountain wolf preys upon the lambs of the valleys. It was the Season of Great Sorcerers. The order of the world was disrupted, and winter and spring and summer and fall upended one into another. Drought and flood, ice and fires threatened the lives of men, and of all the marvelous plants and artful creatures that matter, infected by love, had offered on the altar of the World-Soul.

"Then one day a powerful demon lord, wise and wicked by the consumption of many souls of men, came upon a man living alone in a tiny hermitage in a wood. Like a cat who thinks to toy with her prey, he accepted the beggar's hospitality and waited his chance to leap from the worn-out body he presently possessed to the fresh new one. For the man, though clad in rags, was beautiful: his glance was like a sword thrust and his breath, perfume.

"But the demon lord was confounded when he accepted a little earthen bowl of wine, and drank it in one gulp, and prepared to pounce; for the saint had divided his own soul, and poured it out into the wine, and given it to the demon of his own free will. And so for the first time, a demon gained a soul, and all the beautiful and bitter gifts of a soul.

"The demon lord fell to the floor of the woodland cell and howled with all the astonished woe of a child being born, for he was born in that moment, into the world of both matter and spirit. And taking the hermit's body that was his free gift, and not stolen nor begrudged, he fled through the woods in terror back to his terrible sorcerer's palace, and hid.

"For many months he cowered there, trapped in the horror of his self, but slowly the great-souled saint began to teach him the beauties of virtue. The saint was a devotee of the Mother, and called down Her grace to heal the demon of his sin, for with the gift of free will had come the possibility of sin, and the burning shame of it, which tormented the demon as nothing had ever done before. And between the lash of his sin and the lessons of the saint, the demon's soul began to grow in probity and power. As a great sorcerer-paladin, with the Mother's favor fluttering upon his mailed sleeve, he began to move in the world of matter, and fight the baleful soulless demons on the gods' behalf in the places where They could not reach.

"The great-souled demon became the Mother's champion and captain, and She loved him without limit for his soul's incandescent splendor. And so began the great battle to clear the world of demons run rampant and restore the order of the seasons.

"The other demons feared him, and attempted to combine against him, but could not, for such cooperation was beyond their nature; still their onslaught was terrible, and the great-souled demon, beloved of the Mother, was slain on the final battlefield.

"And so was born the last god, the Bastard, love child of the goddess and the great-souled demon. Some say He was born on the eve of the last battle, fruit of a union upon Her great couch, some say the grieving Mother gathered up the great-souled demon's shattered dear remains from the stricken field and mixed them with Her blood, and so made the Bastard by Her great art. However so, their Son, of all the gods, was given agency over both spirit and matter, for He in-

herited as servants the demons that His father's great sacrifice
had conquered and enslaved and so swept out of the world.

"What *is* certainly a lie," dy Cabon continued in a suddenly more prosaic, not to mention irate, tone of voice, "is
the Quadrene heresy that the great-souled demon took the
Mother by force and so engendered the Bastard upon Her
against Her great will. A scurrilous and senseless and blasphemous lie . . ." Ista wasn't sure if he was still paraphras-
ing Ordol, or if that was his own gloss. He cleared his throat
and finished more formally, "Here ends the tale and tally of
the advent of the *five* gods."

Ista had heard various versions of the tally of the gods
what seemed several hundred times since childhood, but she
had to admit, dy Cabon's delivery of the old story had the
eloquence and sincerity to make it seem almost new again.
Granted, most versions did not give the complex story of the
Bastard more space than the rest of the Holy Family put together, but people had to be allowed their favorites. Despite
herself, she was moved.

Dy Cabon returned to ritual and called down the fivefold
benison, asking of each god the proper gifts, leading the re-
spondents in praise in return. Of the Daughter, growth and
learning and love; of the Mother, children, health, and healing; of the Son, good comradeship, hunting, and harvest; of
the Father, children, justice, and an easy death in its due time.

"And the Bastard grant us . . ."—dy Cabon's voice, fallen
into the soothing singsong of ceremony, stumbled for the
first time, slowing—"in our direst need, the smallest gifts:
the nail of the horseshoe, the pin of the axle, the feather at
the pivot point, the pebble at the mountain's peak, the kiss in
despair, the one right word. In darkness, understanding." He
blinked, looking startled.

Ista's chin snapped up; for an instant, her spine seemed to
freeze. *No. No. There is nothing here, nothing here, nothing
here. Nothing, do you hear me?* She forced her breath out
slowly.

It was not the usual wording. Most prayers asked to be

spared the fifth god's attention, the master of all disasters
out of season as He was. The divine hastily signed himself,
touching forehead, lip, navel, groin, and heart, hand spread
wide upon his chest above his broad paunch, and signed
again in the air to call down blessing upon all assembled
there. The company, released, stirred and stretched, some
breaking into low-voiced talk, some strolling away to their
day's tasks. Dy Cabon came toward Ista, rubbing his hands
and smiling anxiously.

"Thank you, Learned," Ista said, "for that good beginning."

He bowed in relief at her approval. "My very great pleasure, my lady." He brightened still further as the inn's servants hurried to bring out what promised to be a very hearty
breakfast. Ista, a little shamed by the excellence of his effort
to have purloined the divine with false pretenses of a sham
pilgrimage, was heartened by the reflection that dy Cabon
was clearly enjoying his work.

❧

The country west of Palma was flat and barren, with only a
few trees clustering in the watercourses that broke up the
long dull vistas. Grazing, not crop farming, was the main
work of the thinly scattered old fortified farmsteads along
the seldom-used road. Boys and dogs tended sheep and cattle, all dozing together in the distant patches of shade. The
warming afternoon seemed to hold a long silence that invited sleep, not traveling, but given their late start, Ista's
party pushed on through the soft and somnolent air.

When the road widened for a time, Ista found herself riding with dy Cabon's fine sturdy mule on one side and Liss's
rangy bay on the other. As an antidote to dy Cabon's infec-
tious yawns, Ista inquired of him, "Tell me, Learned, whatever happened to that little demon you were carrying when
first we met?"

Liss, who'd been riding along with her feet out of the stirrups and her reins slack, turned her head to listen.

"Oh, all went well. I gave it up to the archdivine of Taryoon, and we oversaw its disposition. It is safely out of the world now. I was actually returning to my home from there when I spent the night in Valenda, and, well." A jerk of his head at the string of riders trailing them indicated his unexpected new duty with the royina.

"A demon? You had a demon?" said Liss in a tone of wonder.

"Not *I*," corrected the divine fastidiously. "It was trapped in a ferret. Fortunately, not a difficult animal to control. Compared to a wolf or a bull." He grimaced. "Or a man, seeking to plunder the demon's powers."

Her face screwed up. "How do you send a demon out of the world?"

Dy Cabon sighed. "Give it to someone who's going."

She frowned at her horse's ears for a moment, then gave up the riddle. "What?"

"If the demon is not grown too strong, the simplest way to return it to the gods is to give it into the keeping of a soul who is going to the gods. Who is dying," he added to her blank look.

"Oh," she said. Another pause. "So . . . you slew the ferret?"

"It is, alas, not quite so easy as that. A free demon whose mount is dying simply jumps to another. You see, an elemental escaped into the world of matter cannot exist without a being of matter to lend it intelligence and strength, for by its nature it cannot create such order for itself. It can only steal. In the beginning it is mindless, formless, as innocently destructive as a wild animal, at least until it learns more complicated sins from men. It is constrained in turn by the power of the creature or person upon whom it battens. A dislodged demon will always seek to leap to the strongest soul in its vicinity, creature to larger creature, animal to man, man to greater man, for it becomes what it . . . eats, in a sense." Dy Cabon drew breath and seemed to look into some well of memory. "But when a divine of long experience is finally dying in his or her order's house, the demon can be forced to jump to them. If the demon is weak enough, and the divine strong of heart and mind even in the last extremity, well, the matter solves itself." He cleared his throat. "Persons great-souled and grown detached from the world, and longing for their god. For a demon can tempt a weaker person to sorcery with promises to extend life."

"Rare strength," said Ista after a moment. Had he just come from such an extraordinary deathbed scene? It seemed so. She did not wonder at his air of daunted humility.

Dy Cabon gave a wry shrug of acknowledgment. "Yes. I don't know if I will ever . . . Fortunately, stray demons are rare. Except that . . ."

"Except what?" Liss prodded, when no more of this rarified theological discourse seemed to be forthcoming.

Dy Cabon's lips twisted. "The archdivine was most disturbed. Mine was the third such fugitive that has been captured this year in Baocia alone."

"How many do you usually catch?" asked Liss.

"Not one a year in all of Chalion, or so it has been for many years. The last great outbreak was in Roya Fonsa's day."

Ias's father; Iselle's grandfather, dead these fifty years.

Ista considered dy Cabon's words. "What if the demon is not weak enough?"

Dy Cabon said, "Ah. Indeed." He was silent for a moment, staring at his mule's limp ears, hanging out to either side of its head like oars. "That is why my order gives much thought and effort to removing them when they are still small."

The road narrowed then, curving down to a small stone bridge over a greenish stream, and dy Cabon gave Ista a polite salute and pushed his mule ahead.

4

THE NEXT DAY'S RIDING BEGAN EARLY AND RAN LONG,
but slowly the barrens of Baocia fell away behind them. The
country grew more rolling, better watered, and better
wooded, running up toward the mountains just visible on the
western horizon. It was still a bony land at heart.

The town wall of Casilchas hugged a rocky outcrop
above a stream running clear and chill with spring runoff
from the distant heights. Gray and ochre stone, rough or
dressed, formed both walls and buildings, here and there en-
livened with plaster dyed pink or pale green, or with painted
wooden doors or shutters, rich red or blue or green in the angled light of the late-spring afternoon. *One might drink this
light like wine and grow intoxicated on color*, Ista thought,
as their horses clopped down the narrow streets.

The town's temple fronted a small plaza paved with irregular slabs of granite fitted together like a puzzle. Opposite it, in what had the look of some local aristocrat's old
mansion bequeathed to the order, Ista's party found the Bastard's seminary.

A smaller hatch in the ironbound slab-planked double
doors opened at dy Cabon's pounding, and the porter came

out. He met the divine's first greetings with discouraging
headshaking. Dy Cabon disappeared inside for a few minutes. Then both doors swung wide, and grooms and dedicats
scurried to assist the party with horses and baggage. Ista's
horse was led within. Three stories of ornate wooden-bal-
conies rose above a cobbled courtyard. A white-gowned
acolyte hurried up with a mounting block. A senior divine
bowed and offered humble welcome. It was Sera dy Ajelo's
name he spoke, but Ista had no illusions; it was Ista dy
Chalion to whom he scraped. Dy Cabon might have been
less discreet than she wished, but there was no doubt it won
them better rooms, eager servants, and the best care for their
tired mounts.

Wash water was brought almost on their heels to the
room where Ista and Liss were guided. No rooms at the seminary were large, Ista suspected, but theirs had space for a
bed, a truckle bed, and a table and chairs, with a balcony
overlooking the town wall and the stream behind this main
building. Meals for both women were brought soon thereafter on trays, with hastily arranged pots of blue and white
flowers for the season as well.

After supper Ista took her handmaiden, with Ferda and
Foix for escort, and strolled around the town in the fading
light. The two officer-dedicats made a handsome pair, in
their blue tunics and gray cloaks, swords carried with cir-
cumspection, not swagger; and not a few Casilchas maidens'—and matrons'—heads turned as they passed. Liss's
stride and height nearly matched that of the dy Gura brothers, a display of youth and health to make silks and jewels
look like tawdry toys. Ista felt herself as splendidly attended
as ever she had been at the roya's court.

The temple was of the standard plan, if of small scale:
four domed lobes, one for each member of the Holy Family,
around an open court where the holy fire burned on its central hearth, with the Bastard's Tower freestanding behind
His Mother's court. The walls were built of the native gray
stone, though the roof arches were finely carved wood, with

a small riot of brightly painted demons, saints, holy animals, and plants appropriate to each god cavorting along the beams. For lack of any better entertainment, they all attended the evening services there. Ista was weary of the gods, but she had to admit, the singing was a pleasure; the seminary contributed a white-robed and enthusiastic choir. The pious effect was only slightly spoiled by the choir leader peeking periodically at Ista for her reaction. Ista sighed inwardly and made sure to smile and nod, to assuage the woman's anxiety.

Three days of riding had tired both people and animals; tomorrow both would rest here. A little elusive ease seemed to have crept in to Ista's spirit—whether its source was sunlight, exercise, cheerful young company, or distance from Valenda, she hardly knew, but she was grateful for it. She slid her body under the feather quilt, finding the narrow bed more luxurious than many more ornate but less comfortable ones in royal castles, and fell asleep before Liss stopped rolling over in her truckle.

Ista dreamed, and knew she was dreaming.

She crossed a paved castle courtyard in a late-spring or early-summer noon. A stone-arched walk ran around the court's edge, the fine alabaster pillars carved with a tracery of vines and flowers in the Roknari style. The sun shone down high and hot; the shadows were black accent marks at her feet. She climbed—no, floated—up the stone stairs at the end, leading up over the arched walk to a wooden gallery, and along it. At the far end, a room: she passed softly into it without opening the carved door, which seemed to part and close around her skin like water.

The room was dim and cool, but a grid of light fell through the shutters onto the woven rugs, making the muted colors briefly blaze. In the room, a bed; on the bed, a form. Ista drifted closer, like a ghost.

The form was a man, asleep or dead, but very pale and still. His long, lean body was dressed in an undyed linen robe, folded across his chest and bound at the waist with a linen belt. On his left breast, a patch of dark red blood seeped through the cloth.

Despite the wiry length of his frame, the bones of his face were almost delicate: brow wide, jaw fine, chin somewhat pointed. His skin was unmarred by scar or blemish, but faint lines pressed across the forehead, framed the lips, fanned from the eyes. His dark, straight hair was brushed back from his forehead, the hairline high, receding; it flowed down over the pillow to his shoulders like a river of night, rippling with tiny gleams of moonlight from the silver threads. His brows were arched, winging; nose straight; lips parted.

Ista's ghostly hands unbound the belt, folded back the linen robe. The hair trailing down his chest was sparse, until it thickened at his crotch. The bird that nested there was fine and fair, and Ista smiled. But the wound beneath his left breast gaped like a small, dark mouth. As she watched, blood began to well from it.

She pressed her hands over the dark slit to staunch the flow, but the red liquid oozed up between her white fingers, a sudden flood, washing across his chest, spreading in a scarlet tide across the sheets. His eyes flew open, he saw her, and he gasped.

Ista woke, shot up, pressed her knuckles to her mouth to stifle her cry. She expected to taste blood, hot and sticky, and was almost shocked not to. Her body was drenched in sweat. Her heart was hammering, and she was panting as though she had been running.

The room was dark and cool, but moonlight filtered through the shutter slats. On her truckle, Liss muttered and turned over.

It had been one of *those* dreams. The real ones. There was no mistaking them.

Ista clutched her hair, opened her mouth in a rictus, screamed silently. Breathed, "*Curse You.* Whichever one of

You this is. Curse You, one and five. Get out of my head. Get out of my head!"

Liss made a little cat sound and mumbled sleepily, "Lady? You all right?" She sat up on her elbow, blinking.

Ista swallowed for control and cleared her tight throat. "Just an odd dream. Go back to sleep, Liss."

Liss grunted agreeably and rolled back over.

Ista lay back, clutching her feather coverlet to her despite her sweat-dampened body.

Was it starting again?

No. No. I won't have it. She gasped and gulped, and barely kept from breaking into sobs. In a few minutes, her breathing steadied.

Who had that man been? It was no one she had ever seen in her life, she was certain. She would know him instantly if she ever saw him again, though; the fine shape of his face felt burned into her mind like a brand. And . . . and the rest of him. Was he enemy? Friend? Warning? Chalionese, Ibran, Roknari? Highborn or low? What did the sinister red tide of blood mean? No good thing, of that she was quite certain.

Whatever You want from me, I can't do it. I've proved that before. Go away. Go away.

She lay trembling for a long time; the moonlight had turned to gray predawn mist before she fell asleep again.

❧

Ista was awakened not by Liss slipping out, but by Liss slipping back in. She was embarrassed to discover her handmaiden had let her sleep through morning prayers, rudeness both as a pilgrim, however false, and as a real guest.

"You looked so tired," Liss excused herself when Ista chided her. "You did not seem to sleep well last night."

Indeed. Ista had to admit, she was glad for the extra rest. A breakfast was brought to her on a tray by a bowing acolyte, also not usual for a pilgrim so laggard as to miss the morning's start.

After dressing and having her hair done up in a slightly more elaborate braid than usual—not looking too much like a horse, she hoped—she walked with Liss about the old mansion. They fetched up in the now-sunny court. Sitting on a bench by the wall, they watched the denizens of the school hurry past on their tasks, students and teachers and servants. *Another* thing Ista liked about Liss, she decided, was that the girl didn't chatter. She conversed pleasantly enough when spoken to; the remainder of the time she fell without resentment into a restful silence.

Ista felt a cool breath on her neck from the wall she leaned against: one of this place's ghosts. It wove around her like a cat seeking a lap, and she almost raised her hand to shoo it away, but then the impression faded. Some sad spirit, not taken up by the gods, or refusing them, or lost somehow. New ghosts kept the form they'd had in life, for a while, often violent, harsh, outraged, but in time they all came to this faded, shapeless, slow oblivion. For such an old building, the ghosts here seemed few and tranquil. Fortresses—like the Zangre—were usually the worst. Ista was resigned to her lingering sensitivity, as long as no such wasted souls took form before her inner eye. *Seeing* such a spirit would mean some god breathed too near, that her second sight was leaking back—and all that went with it.

Ista considered the courtyard in her dream. It was no place she'd ever been before, of that she was sure. She was equally convinced it was a real place. To avoid it . . . to certainly avoid it, all she had to do was crawl back to the castle at Valenda and stay there till her body rotted around her.

No. I will not go back.

The thought made her restless, and she rose and prowled the school, Liss dutifully at her heels. Many acolytes or divines, passing her on the balcony walks or in the corridors, bowed and smiled, by which she concluded dy Cabon's indiscretion had now been widely shared. Pretending to be Sera dy Ajelo was well enough; having half a hundred total strangers assiduously pretend along with her felt oddly irritating.

They looked into a succession of small rooms crammed with books, packed in shelves and piled on tables: dy Cabon's desired library. To Ista's surprise, Foix dy Gura was curled up in a window seat with his nose in a volume. He looked up, blinked, rose, and made a little courtesy. "Lady. Liss."

"I did not know you read theology, Foix."

"Oh, I read anything. But it's not all theology. There are hundreds of other things, some very odd. They never throw anything away here. There's a whole locked room where they keep the books on sorcery and demons, and, um, the lewd books. Chained."

Ista raised her brows. "That they may not be opened?"

Foix's grin flashed. "That they may not be carried off, I think." He held out the book in his hand. "There are more verse romances like this. I could find you one."

Liss, staring around in wonder at what might have been more books in one place than she'd ever seen in her life, looked hopeful. Ista shook her head. "Later, perhaps."

Dy Cabon poked his head through the door and said, "Ah. Lady. Good. I've been seeking you." He heaved his bulk within. Ista hadn't seen him since they'd arrived, she realized, not even at the evening services. He looked fatigued, gray and puffy under the eyes. Had he been up late in some forced study? "I request—beg—some private audience with you, if I may."

Liss looked up from where she'd been peering over Foix's shoulder. "Should I leave you, Royina?"

"No. The correct thing for a lady-in-waiting to do, should her mistress wish private speech with some gentleman not of her immediate family, is to place herself out of earshot, but within sight or call."

"Ah." Liss nodded understanding. Ista would never have to repeat the instruction. Liss might be untutored, but five gods, what a joy it was to finally have an attendant with all her wits about her.

"I could read to her, in this chamber or the next," Foix immediately volunteered.

"Um . . ." Dy Cabon gestured to a table and chairs visible through an archway in the next room. Ista nodded and passed in before him. Foix and Liss settled back into the cozy window seat.

More discussion of their holy itinerary was due, she suspected, and tedious letters to be written thereafter apprising dy Ferrej of their planned route. Dy Cabon held her chair, then edged around the table to seat himself. She could hear Foix's voice begin to murmur in the next chamber, too softly to make out the words from here, but in the cadences of some strong, striding narrative stanzas.

The divine tented his hands on the table before him, stared at them for a moment, then looked her in the face. In a level tone he asked, "Lady, why are you *really* on this pilgrimage?"

Ista's brows rose at this utterly blunt beginning. She decided to return straight speech for straight speech; it was rare enough in a royina's hearing and ought to be encouraged. "To escape my keepers. And myself."

"You have not and had not, then, any real intention to pray for a grandson?"

Ista grimaced. "Not for all the gods in Chalion would I insult Iselle or my new granddaughter Isara so. I still remember how I was chided and shamed for bearing a daughter to Ias, these nineteen years ago. The selfsame brilliant girl who is now the brightest hope the royacy of Chalion has had in four generations!" She controlled her fierce tone, which clearly had taken dy Cabon aback. "Should a grandson come, in due time, I shall of course be very pleased. But I will not beg the gods for any favor."

He took this in, nodded slowly. "Yes. I had come to suspect something of a sort."

"It is, I grant, a trifle impious to use a pilgrimage so, and abuse the good guards the Daughter's Order lends me. Though I'm quite sure I'm not the first to make holiday at the gods' expense. My purse shall more than compensate the Temple."

"That does not concern me." Dy Cabon waved away these pecuniary considerations. "Lady. I have read. I have talked to my superiors. I have taken thought. I have—well, never mind that now." He drew a breath. "Are you aware, Royina—do you realize—I have found reason to think, you see, that you may be extraordinarily spiritually gifted." His gaze upon her face was deeply searching.

Found reason where? What garbled, secret tales had the man heard? Ista sat back; did not, quite, recoil. "I am afraid that is not so."

"I believe you underestimate yourself. Seriously underestimate yourself. This sort of thing is, I admit, rare in a woman of your rank, but I have come to realize you are a very unusual woman. But I believe that, with prayer, guidance, meditation, and instruction, you might reach a pitch of spiritual sensitivity, of fulfilled calling, that, well, that most of us who wear our god's colors only dream about and long for. These are not gifts to be lightly cast aside."

Not lightly, indeed. With great violence. How in five gods' names had he come by this sudden delusion? Dy Cabon's eager face, she realized, was afire with the look of a man seized by a grand idea. Was he picturing himself as her proud spiritual mentor? He would not be turned from his conviction that he was called to aid her to some life of holy service by any vague excuses on her part. He would not be stopped by anything less than the whole truth. Her stomach sank. *No.*

Yes. It was not, after all, as though she had not made full confession before, to another god-gripped man. Perhaps these things grew easier with practice.

"You are mistaken. Understand, Learned. I have walked down that road already, to its bitterest end. Once, I was a saint."

It was his turn to recoil, in astonishment. He gulped. "*You* were a vessel of the gods?" His face bunched up with consternation. "That explains . . . something. No, it doesn't." He grasped his hair, briefly, but let it go unravaged. "Royina, I do *not* understand. How came you to be god-touched? When was this miracle?"

"Long, long ago." She sighed. "Formerly, this story was a state secret. A state crime. I suppose it is no longer. Whether it will in time become rumor or legend or dead and buried, I know not. In any case, it is not to be shared, not even with your superiors. Or, if you seem to have cause to do so, take your instruction first from the Chancellor dy Cazaril. He knows all the truth of it."

"They say he is very wise," said dy Cabon, wide-eyed now.

"For once, they say right." She paused, marshaling her thoughts, her memories, her words. "How old were you when Roya Ias's great courtier, Lord Arvol dy Lutez, was executed for treason?"

Dy Lutez. Ias's boyhood companion, brother in arms, greatest servant throughout his darkly troubled thirty-five-year reign. Powerful, intelligent, brave, rich, handsome, courteous . . . there seemed no end to the gifts that the gods—and the roya—had piled upon the glorious Lord dy Lutez. Ista had been eighteen when she'd married Ias. Ias and his right arm dy Lutez had reached their fifties. Dy Lutez had arranged the marriage, the aging roya's second, for already there were worries about Ias's sole surviving son and heir, Orico.

"Why, I was a young child." He hesitated, cleared his throat. "Though I heard it talked about, later in my life. The rumor was . . ." He stopped abruptly.

"The rumor you heard was that dy Lutez had seduced me and died for it at my royal husband's hands, yes?" she supplied coolly.

"Um, yes, lady. Was it—it wasn't—"

"No. It was not true."

He breathed covert relief.

Her lips twisted. "It was not me he loved in that way, but Ias. Dy Lutez should have been a lay dedicat of *your* order, I think, instead of holy general of the Son's."

In addition to bastards, the occasional artist, and other jetsam of the world, the Bastard's Order was the refuge of those to whom it was not given to conform to the fruitful relations between men and women overseen by the great Four, but to seek their own sex. At this distance in time, space, and sin it was almost amusing to watch dy Cabon's face as he unraveled her polite description.

"That must have been . . . rather difficult for you, as a young bride."

"Then, yes," she admitted. "Now . . ." She held out her hand and opened it, as if letting sand pass through her fingers. "It is beside the point. Far more difficult was my discovery that since the calamitous death of Ias's father, Roya Fonsa, a great and strange curse had been laid upon the royal house of Chalion. And that I had brought my children into it, unknowing. Not told, not warned."

Dy Cabon's lips made an O.

"I had prophetic dreams. Nightmares. For a time, I thought I was going mad." For a time, Ias and dy Lutez had left her in that terror, alone, uncomforted. It had seemed then, and still seemed now, a greater betrayal than any trivial sweaty graspings under the sheets could ever be. "I prayed and prayed to the gods. And my prayers were answered, dy Cabon. I spoke to the Mother face-to-face, as close as I am to you now." She shivered still in memory of that overwhelming incandescence.

"A great blessing," he breathed in awe.

She shook her head. "A great woe. Upon the instruction of the gods, as given to me, we—dy Lutez, and Ias, and I—planned a perilous ritual to break the curse, to send it back to the gods from whom it had once been spilled. But we—*I*, in my anxiety and fear, made a mistake, a great and willful mistake, and dy Lutez died in the midst of it as a direct result. Sorcery, miracle, call it what you will, the ritual failed, the gods withdrew from me . . . Ias in his panic put the treason rumor about, to account for the death. That bright star of his court, his best beloved, murdered, buried—then defamed, which was all but to be murdered again, for dy Lutez had loved his high honor better than his life."

Dy Cabon's brow wrinkled. "But . . . was not this posthumous slander of Lord dy Lutez by your husband equally a slander of you, lady?"

Ista faltered at this unconsidered view. "Ias knew the truth. What other opinion mattered? That the world should think me, falsely, an adulteress, seemed far less hideous than that it should know me truly a murderess. But Ias died of grief thereafter, deserting me, leaving me to wail in the ashes of the disaster, mind-fogged and accursed still."

"How old were you?" asked dy Cabon.

"Nineteen when it began. Twenty-two when it ended." She frowned. When had that begun to seem so . . .

"You were very young for so great a burden," he offered, voicing almost her own thought.

Her lips thinned in denial. "Officers like Ferda and Foix are sent to fight and die at no greater age. I was older then than Iselle is now, who bears the whole of the royacy of Chalion upon her slim shoulders, not just the woman's half."

"But not alone. She has great courtiers, and Royse-Consort Bergon."

"Ias had dy Lutez."

"Whom did *you* have, lady?"

Ista fell silent. She could not remember. Had she truly been so alone? She shook her head, drew breath. "Another generation brought another man, humbler and greater than dy Lutez, of deeper mind, more equal to the task. The curse was broken, but not by me. Yet not before my son Teidez died of it as well—of the curse, of my failure to lift it when he was a child, of betrayal by and of those who should have protected and guided him. Three years ago, by the labor and sacrifice of others, I was released from my long bondage. Into the silence of my life in Valenda. Unbearable silence. I am not *old*—"

Dy Cabon waved his plump hands in protest. "Indeed, no, my lady! You are quite lovely still!"

She made a sharp gesture, cutting off his misconstrual. "My mother was forty when I was born, her last child. I am forty now, in this ill-made spring of her death. One-half my life lies behind me, and half of *that* stolen from me by Fonsa's great curse. One-half lies before. Shall it hold only a long, slow decay?"

"Surely not, lady!"

She shrugged. "I have made this confession twice now. Perhaps some third occasion will release me."

"The gods . . . the gods may forgive much, to a truly penitent heart."

Her smile grew bitter as desert brine. "The gods may forgive Ista all day long. But if Ista does not forgive Ista, the gods may go hang themselves."

His "Oh" was very small. But, earnest faithful creature, he had to try again. "But to turn away so—dare I say it, Royina—you betray your gifts!"

She leaned forward, lowered her voice to a husky growl. "No, Learned. You daren't."

He sat back and was very quiet for several moments after that. At length, his face screwed up again. "Then what of your pilgrimage, Royina?"

She grimaced, waved a hand. "Pick a route to the best-laid tables, if you wish. Let us go anywhere, so long as it does not return to Valenda." *So long as it does not return to Ista dy Chalion.*

"You must go home eventually."

"I would throw myself off a precipice first, except that I would land in the arms of the gods, Whom I do not wish to see again. That escape is blocked. I must go on living. And living. And living . . ." She cut off her rising tones. "The world is ashes and the gods are a horror. Tell me, Learned, what other place is there for me to go?"

He shook his head, eyes very wide. Now she'd terrorized him, and she was sorry for it. She patted his hand contritely. "In truth, these few days of travel have brought me more ease than the past three years of idling. My flight from Valenda may have begun as a spasm, as a drowning man strikes upward to the air, but I do believe I start to breathe, Learned. This pilgrimage may be a medicine despite me."

"I . . . I . . . Five gods grant it may be so, lady." He signed himself. She could tell by the way his hand hesitated at each holy point that it was not, this time, a gesture of mere ritual.

She was almost tempted to tell him about her dream. But no, it would just excite him all over again. The poor young man had surely had enough for one day. His jowls were quite pale.

"I will take, um, more thought," he assured her, and scraped his chair back from the table. His bow to her, as he rose, was not that of conductor to charge, nor of courtier to patron. He gave her the deep obeisance of piety to a living saint.

Her hand shot out, grabbed his hand halfway through its gesture of boundless respect. "*No*. Not now. Not then. Not ever again."

He swallowed, shakily converted his farewell to a nervous bob, and fled.

5

THEY LINGERED TWO MORE DAYS IN CASILCHAS, WAITING
out a slow spring rain, wrapped in a hospitality that Ista
found increasingly uncomfortable. She was invited to meals
in the seminary's refectory not of scholarly austerity, but
near banquets in her near honor, with senior divines and
local notables of the town discreetly jostling for a place at
her table. They still addressed her as Sera dy Ajelo, but she
was forced to trade the new ease of her incognito for her old
constrained court manners, learned in too stern a school, it
seemed, ever to be forgotten. She was gracious; she was attentive to her hosts; she complimented and smiled and gritted her teeth and sent Foix to inform the elusive dy Cabon
that he must finish his inquiries, whatever they were, immediately. It was time to travel on.

The days that followed were much better, a pleasant ram-
ble through the blooming countryside from one minor shrine
to another, nearly the escape Ista had hoped for from her pilgrimage. Moving steadily northwest, they passed out of
Baocia into the neighboring province of Tolnoxo. Long
hours in the saddle were interspersed with invigorating
tramps about places of historical or theological interest—

wells, ruins, groves, shrines, famous graves, commanding heights, formerly embattled fords. The young men of the party searched the military sites for arrowheads, sword shards, and bones, and argued over whether the blotches upon them were, or were not, heroic bloodstains. Dy Cabon had acquired another book for his saddlebag's library, of the history and legends of the region, from which he read improving paragraphs as opportunities presented. Despite the odd succession of humble inns and holy hostels, quite unlike anything she had ever experienced as a royina or even as the youngest daughter of a provincar, Ista slept better than she had in her own bed for . . . as long as she could remember. The disturbing dream did not return, to her secret relief.

Dy Cabon's first few morning sermons after Casilchas showed the results of his hasty researches, being plainly cribbed from some volume of model lessons. But the next few days brought more daring and original material, heroic tales of Chalionese and Ibran saints and god-touched martyrs in the service of their chosen deities. The divine made contorted connections between each day's tale and the sites they were to view, but Ista was not deceived. His stories of the famous miracles that men and women had performed as vessels of the gods' powers made Ferda's and Foix's and even Liss's eyes shine with a spirit of emulation, but Ista found the divine's message, on all its several levels, entirely resistible. He watched her anxiously for her responses; she thanked him coolly. He bowed and bit back disappointment, but also, fortunately, the temptation to reopen the subject more directly.

A break in dy Cabon's oblique campaign occurred as they wound through the foothills of the western ranges and arrived at the town of Vinyasca, just in time for the mid-spring festival. This feast day fell at the apogee of the season, exactly midway between the Daughter's Day and the Mother's. In Vinyasca, it was also tied to the renewal of the trade caravans over the snowy passes from Ibra, bringing new wine and oil, dried fruit and fish, and a hundred other delicacies of that milder land, as well as exotic fare from even farther shores.

A fairground had been set up outside the town walls, between the rocky river and a pine grove. Mouthwatering smoke rose up from roasting pits behind tents displaying handicrafts and produce of the area's maidens, who competed for honors in the goddess's name. Liss shrugged at the tent of embroidery, sewing, and wool work; dy Cabon and Foix returned disappointed from a reconnoiter of the tent of foodstuffs to report that it did not offer morsels to any but the judges.

Food might be the focus, but youthful energy could not be denied. For all that it was a young women's festival, young men vied for their gazes in a dozen contests of skill and daring. Ista's guard, kindling at the challenges, begged for their commander's indulgence and dispersed to try their luck, although Ferda meticulously apportioned pairs in turn to be at her call at all times. Ferda's sternness eroded abruptly when he discovered the horse races. Having no one else's leave to beg, he sought Ista's, and she hid a smile and sent him off to ready his mount.

"My courier horse," said Liss in a voice of longing, "could make all these country nags look like the plow horses they undoubtedly are."

"I'm afraid the women's race was earlier," said Ista. She'd seen the winner led past, horse and girl festooned with blue-and-white garlands, surrounded by cheerful relatives.

"*That* was for the *young* maidens," said Liss, her voice tinged with scorn. "There are some older women getting ready for the longer one—I saw them."

"Are you sure they were not just grooms, or relatives, or owners?"

"No, for they were tying colors on their sleeves. And they had the look of riders."

As Liss did, indeed. She was doing her best to keep her face dignified, but she was rising on her toes.

"Well," said Ista, amused, "if Foix at least will undertake not to abandon me—"

Foix, smiling, favored her with a loyal bow.

"Oh, thank you, my lady!" cried Liss, and was gone as

though racing afoot, back to the inn's stable where they had stowed their mounts.

Ista strolled about the makeshift grounds on Foix's arm, taking care to observe any contests in which her own men competed. A contest to gallop with a javelin picking off small rings set up on posts was won by one of her guard; a match that involved leaping from a horse to grapple a young steer to the ground was won by the steer. All brought back their prizes for their officer Foix to hold, and therefore Ista to notice; she felt half courtly, half maternal, and commiserated the dusty, limping steer-wrestler with as many words as she spared to congratulate the luckier contestants.

She had accepted her guard troop at first as an unavoidable encumbrance, and ignored them. But over the days of her journey she had learned names, faces, life stories—most very short. They had begun to look less like blank-faced soldiers, responsible for her, and more like overgrown children. She did not care for this oppressive shift in her perceptions. She did not want to be responsible for them. *I had no luck with sons.* Yet loyalty must run two ways, or else become betrayal in the egg.

As the contenders assembled for the horse race, Foix found Ista a spot on the slope overlooking the road, above most of the rest of the eager crowd. In a gallant's gesture he spread his vest-cloak, carried over his arm in the warmth of the bright afternoon, on the ground for Ista to settle upon. They had a fine view of the start and finish point, which was a large stump by the roadside. The course ran down the valley road for about two miles, circled a stand of oak trees crowning a mound, and returned by the same route.

Some twenty or so horses and their riders milled about in the wide space on the road. Ferda dy Gura, on his shining black beast, was shortening his stirrups and studying the others when Liss trotted up on her leggy bay. He turned to stare at her in surprise, but no delight. He apparently said something sharp, for Liss's face fell. She looked up in a moment and returned a rather bitten-out remark. Ferda leaned toward her and said something else, longer. She jerked her horse away, flushing; the angry color faded in a moment, to be replaced by a thoughtful frown, then a tight smile.

"Now, what was that all about?" Ista wondered aloud.

Foix, sitting at her feet, smirked. "I believe my brother was seeking to display his prowess to Liss, not to compete with hers. I fear he did not handle his surprise well." He settled back on one elbow with an air of enjoyable interest that did not seem entirely due to the colorful excitement of the upcoming race.

"So why aren't you down there?" she asked him. "Do your ribs still trouble you?"

"No, lady. But I'm no great rider." His eyes narrowed with amusement. "I'll choose my ground, when I do, with more wit." He was not, Ista suspected, referring to contests in a rural festival.

Under the direction of a pair of shouting organizers, the riders arranged themselves in an uneven, jostling line across the road. Vinyasca's town divine, a blue-and-white sash wrapped around his waist, stood on the stump and intoned a short blessing to dedicate the race to the goddess, then held up a blue kerchief. His hand dropped. With yells from both riders and onlookers, the horses plunged off.

At first, the horses clashed for position in a heart-stopping melee—one rider fell—but by the time the leaders were partway to the turning point, the line was spreading out. Liss's bay and Ferda's black both ran near the front of the pack. Ista squinted anxiously into the distance, lips parted, breath coming faster. When the racers appeared again around the mound of oaks, the two shared a clear and widening lead. Ista's party all broke into cheers.

Halfway back along the road from the trees, Liss threw a glance over her shoulder at Ferda and his laboring black, then leaned forward low over her horse's neck. The rangy bay seemed to rise and float over the ground, and the gap between them widened rapidly.

Even Ista found herself cheering then: "Yes! Go! Ha!"

Liss was two dozen horse lengths ahead as she neared the stump. But then, suddenly, she sat bolt upright. Her horse's stride abruptly shortened; in a few more yards the bay was nearly bouncing in place. Ferda's foam-flecked black flashed past, and Liss eased her reins and let her mount canter demurely after him. Her animal looked as though it was ready to run another race just like this one, and Ista was reminded that a typical courier leg was fifteen or so miles. The cries of the onlookers took on a decidedly bewildered tone. The rest of the field pelted past the finish point, and the crowd swirled down onto the road.

Foix, one arm wrapped around his knees as he rocked, held his hand over his mouth and choked back sputtering noises.

Ferda was standing in his stirrups, astonished and red with exertion and fury. He was nevertheless fêted as the winner by the dubious locals, who shot many looks over their shoulders at Liss. Liss put her nose in the air and walked her horse past him toward the town and the waiting stables. Ferda looked as though he wanted to fling his blue-and-white garland on the ground in front of her in a rage, but couldn't so insult the goddess or his hosts.

"If this is a courtship," said Ista to Foix, "might you not advise your brother on his, ah, method?"

"Not for all the world," said Foix, who had gained control of his breathing again. Little squeaks still leaked out now and then. "Nor would he thank me if I did. Now, mind you, my lady, I would throw myself between my brother and a Roknari crossbow quarrel without hesitation. In fact, I have. But there must be limits to fraternal self-sacrifice, I think."

Ista smiled dryly. "Is that the way of it? I see."

Foix shrugged. "Well, who knows? Time must tell."

"Indeed." It reminded Ista quite of old court politics, in miniature. She must advise Liss against creating untoward dissension in her little troop, whether by accident or design. Foix . . . she wasn't sure Foix needed anyone's advice.

Foix scrambled to his feet, eyes alight. "I must go congratulate my brother on his victory. It's not a moment to be missed." He turned to help her up from the ground with a panache that would not have been out of place in Cardegoss.

Later in the afternoon, when Liss had returned to Ista's side, Foix found a wood-chopping contest. He tackled this humble but vigorous exercise with his shirt off, before the ladies' eyes. He bore no serious scars on his muscular torso, though his flesh was slightly mottled still, Ista noted. She suspected his broadsword swing would be as handsome as his work with an ax. But he was either not quite as recovered from his injuries as he'd claimed, or interestingly subtle, for he came in a cheerful second. He clapped the winner on the shoulder, bought the man a congratulatory flagon of ale, and departed whistling.

❧

Ista had no opportunity to speak alone with her handmaiden till mid-evening. They withdrew after supper to the balcony of her inn room, a choice chamber overlooking the town square. In the paved space below, a feast had given way to music and dancing, illuminated by hundreds of beautiful pierced metal lanterns scattered around the square and hung from the trees in front of the temple, shedding a lacy light. It was not excessively rowdy yet, for the young women were well chaperoned by their families. Later in the evening, when the maidens had all gone in, Ista expected more serious drinking to commence.

Ista settled in a chair brought out for her; Liss leaned on the wooden rail and watched the dancers wistfully.

"So," said Ista after a time, "what had you and Ferda to say to each other that so inflamed you both, before your race?"

"Oh." Liss grimaced, turning half around. "Stupid things. He said it was unfair for me to enter because my courier horse was too fine and fit for this country competition. As though *his* horse was not the finest Cardegoss could yield! And then he said it was not a proper contest for a woman—

with half a dozen other women there! A race in the name of the goddess! The men in it only rode on their women's behalf—he entered in *your* honor."

"A trifle inconsistent, I grant you," murmured Ista.

"He was odious. Well! I showed him."

"Mm, but you also showed him half right. Your horse did clearly overmatch the humble beasts of Vinyasca."

"So did his. If I should not have entered for that reason, neither should he."

Ista smiled in silence, and Liss, after a moment, turned once more to watch the dancers. In the country dances here, men and women danced sometimes apart, in hand-clasped circles, and sometimes together, in complicated patterns sung out above the music by a caller. Most were rather vigorous, with a swirling of skirts and petticoats and rhythmic foot stamping.

Ista tried to decide if this flurry between her two principal attendants was a problem, or its opposite. In truth, she did not even know if her handmaiden, so hastily snatched up into her service, *was* a maiden. The riding girls of the courier cadre presumably took care not to become pregnant, lest they lose their livelihood, but that did not necessarily mean they were sexually abstinent, or innocent, or ignorant. Quite the reverse, since innocence based in ignorance was unfit to protect itself.

In Ias's court, Ista could not help having learned some things about how men and women—or other combinations of participants—could pleasure each other without risking the consequences of children. Ista didn't know how many of these secrets the riding girls passed around in their dormitories, nor how much they were taught by the women who supervised them, themselves former couriers looking out for their charges. In any case, as a farm girl involved in breeding animals, Liss was doubtless better informed of the basics than Ista had been at a like age. But emotions were as like to wreak havoc in a tightly confined court as physicalities.

Ista was also unsure if either dy Gura brother intended

honorable courtship, or merely seduction. The social gap between landless minor aristocrat and landed yeoman's child might tend to the latter, but it was not impossibly wide for the former. Especially given a dowry, though that seemed a dubious hope in Liss's case.

But a very little time in Liss's insouciant company had certainly brought both brothers to attention, and no wonder. The girl was beautiful and bright, the young men were healthy and vigorous . . . in all, Ista saw good reason not to rush to repair the breach, lest she replace one problem with a much less tractable one.

Still, she probed: "So what do you think of the dy Guras?"

"Ferda was all right at first, but lately he's grown priggish."

"He feels his responsibilities keenly, I think."

Liss shrugged. "Foix, well, Foix is all right, I suppose."

Would Foix be crushed to hear this tepid judgment? Perhaps not. Ista ventured a hint. "I trust no men of my guard have made offensive advances to you. In order to testify to her lady's honor, a handmaiden must herself be above reproach."

"No, they all seem to take their oaths to the goddess most seriously." She sniffed. "Or else Ferda selected them for like-minded priggishness." A merry smile brought a dimple to the side of her mouth. "The good divine, now, he wasted no time. *He* propositioned me that first night in Palma."

Ista blinked in surprise. "Ah," she said cautiously. "One must remember that not everyone in the Bastard's Order is of that, um, preference." She considered how to phrase her next question. "You need not endure affront, regardless of any man's rank or calling. In fact, as my dependent, you should not. It is quite proper to complain to me if there is such a problem."

Liss tossed her head. "I suppose I ought to have been insulted, but he managed to be quite charming about it, really. He took his rejection in good part and went off to try the chambermaid."

"I received no complaints!"

Liss snickered. "I don't think she had any. When they came out of her room later, she was giggling. It made me wonder what I'd missed."

Ista tried to set a good stern example by not laughing, and failed. "Oh, dear."

Liss grinned back and returned to gazing enviously at the dancers. After a time, Ista couldn't bear it anymore, and gave her leave to join the party. Liss looked delighted with the unexpected treat, and startled Ista a trifle by popping directly over the balcony to hang one-handed and drop onto the pavement. She scampered off.

It felt odd to be alone. Ista drew a few slightly rude, if not unamiable, calls from passing men in the street, which she didn't know how to handle and therefore ignored. The men trod off more rudely and less amiably. Liss had exchanged such banter earlier, with easy cheer, and sent their drunken admirers on their way chuckling. *This is not my world.* Yet she had ruled it once, supposedly, from a clouded distance in Cardegoss.

Ferda dy Gura emerged onto the neighboring balcony, found Ista by herself, glared a would-be serenader into slinking away, and chided her, albeit in the politest terms, for dispensing with her attendant. He vanished again, only to exit the inn below—by the doorway—and plunge into the crowd to retrieve Liss. When they came in sight again, they both had their fists clenched. Whatever hot exchange they were having, however, they muffled before they came back within Ista's hearing.

Ista led the way to bed. The festival continued noisily for some hours, but did not keep her awake.

❧

Deep in the night, she opened her dreaming eyes to find herself in the mysterious castle courtyard again. This time the scene was dark—this very night? What seemed the same waning moon that was passing over Vinyasca gave a sickly, inadequate light. But the shadows were not impenetrable, for a strange glow hung in the air, like a rope made of white fire. It ran across the court and up the stairs, disappearing through the same heavy door at the end of the gallery. Ista's dream-self scarcely dared to touch it, though it drew her eyes. She followed it again, up the stairs, along the boards. Through the door.

The bedchamber was darker than the courtyard, shutters closed, moonless, but illuminated still; the rope of fire seemed to be rising up from the heart of the man stretched on the bed. The pale flames flickered all along his body as though he burned, coiling from his chest, flowing away . . . and then Ista wondered if she was looking at a rope, or a conduit. And where that conduit emptied out. She glanced back along the floating line of light and was moved to grasp it, let it tow her along to its destination as a cable might pull a drowning woman from the water.

Her dream-hand reached, gripped; the line broke, shattering under her fingers, spattering away in bright ripples.

The man on the bed woke, panted, started half-up. Saw her. Stretched out a burning hand.

"You!" he gasped. "Lady! Help me, in the god's name—"

Which god? Ista could not help thinking, in a sort of tilted hysteria. She dared not grasp that terrifying fiery hand, for all that it reached for her. "*Who are you?*"

His wide eyes devoured the sight of her. "She speaks!" His voice cracked. "My lady, I pray, don't go—"

Her eyes snapped open in the dimness of the little inn chamber in Vinyasca.

Nearly the only sound was Liss's slow, regular breathing on her pallet across the room. The festival dance had evidently ended, the last drunken revelers departed for home, or at least passed out in doorways along the route.

Silently, Ista swung her feet out of bed and padded to the locked shutters to the balcony. She eased up the latch and slipped out. The only lights were a pair of wall lanterns, burning low, flanking the closed doors of the temple across the plaza. She gazed up into the night sky at the waning moon. She knew it for the same moon as in her vision. The place, the man, were as real as she, wherever they were. So did the strange man dream this night of Ista, as Ista dreamed of him? What did his dark straining eyes see that made him reach out so desperately, and was he as bewildered by her as she was by him?

His voice had been rich in timbre, though scraped thin with pain or fear or exhaustion. But he had spoken in the Ibran tongue shared by Ibra and Chalion and Brajar, not in Roknari or Darthacan—albeit with a north Chalionese accent tinged by Roknari cadences.

I cannot help you. Whoever you are, I cannot help. Pray to your god, if you want rescue. Though I do not recommend it.

She fled the moonlight, locked the shutter, huddled back into her bed as soundlessly as she could, careful not to wake Liss. She pulled her feather pillow over her head. It blocked all vision except the very one she did not want to see, burning in her mind's eye. When she woke again on the morrow, all the events of the previous day would seem a more faded dream than this. She clenched her hands in her sheets and waited for the light.

❧

As Liss was braiding Ista's hair, soon after dawn the next morning, there came a knock on their chamber door, and Foix dy Gura's voice: "My lady? Liss?"

Liss went to the door and opened it onto the gallery that ran around the inn's interior well court. Foix, fully dressed for the road, gave her a nod, adding a little bow to Ista, who came up behind Liss's shoulder.

"Good morning, my lady. Learned dy Cabon sends his abject apologies, but he cannot lead prayers this morning. He is fallen very ill."

"Oh, no," said Ista. "Is it serious? Should we send someone to the temple to ask for a physician?" Vinyasca was much smaller than Valenda; was the Mother's Order here large enough to support a physician of good learning?

Foix rubbed his lips, which kept trying to quirk up in a smile. "Ah, I think not quite yet, my lady. It may just be something he ate yesterday. Or, er . . . wine-sickness."

"He was not drunk when I last saw him," said Ista doubtfully.

"Mm, that was earlier. Later, he went off with a party from the local temple, and, well, they brought him back quite late. Not that one can diagnose with certainty through a closed door, but his groans and noises sounded quite like wine-sickness to me. Horribly familiar, brought back memories. Mercifully blurred memories, but still."

Liss smothered a laugh.

Ista gave her a quelling frown, and said, "Very well. Tell your men to stand down and leave their horses to their hay. We shall attend the morning service at the temple instead, and decide whether to take to the road again . . . later. There is no hurry, after all."

"Very good, my lady." Foix gave her a nod and a little salute, and turned away.

Early services filled an hour, although it seemed to Ista that they were curtailed, and not well attended; the local divine was rather pale and wan himself. Afterward, she and Liss and Foix idled about the quiet town. The festival tents were being taken down and folded away. They walked along the river over the racecourse, and Foix encouraged Liss to give a blow-by-blow account of her ride, details of horses and riders that Ista had scarcely registered. Liss explained that her remarkable burst of speed, late in the race, was partly illusory; it had merely been that the other horses were starting to flag at that stage. Ista was pleased to note that her five-mile walk did not exhaust her as it had that day when she'd fled the castle in Valenda, and she didn't think it was wholly due to wearing more suitable clothing and shoes.

Learned dy Cabon emerged from his room around noon, his face the color of dough. Ista took one look at him, canceled the day's travel plans, and sent him back to bed. He crept away mumbling pitifully grateful thanks. She was relieved to see he was not feverish. Foix's diagnosis of wine-sickness seemed sound, confirmed when the divine slunk out again, shamefaced, in the evening and took a supper of toast and tea, turning down with loathing an offer of watered wine.

❧

By the next morning dy Cabon seemed fully recovered, although his sunrise sermon again reverted to a model from his book. Ista's party took to the road while the air was yet cool, fording the rocky river and climbing the hill road out of Vinyasca, heading north.

The country they rode through, on the dry side of the mountains, was sparsely wooded: stands of pine and ever-green oak with scrub between, gray rocks poking up through the yellow weeds. The soil was far too poor for much farming, except in patches and terrace gardens grubbed out and hand-tended, and the thinly populated area around Vinyasca soon gave way to utter wilderness. The road led up and down, one little valley looking much like the next. Sometimes old bridges or culverts, not in the best repair, crossed the streams tumbling down from the distant heights on their leftward side, but more often their horses and mules had to pick their way across boulder-studded fords. They stopped in the early afternoon to picnic by such a stream; the water was this land's one rich gift, clear and pure and cold.

The evening's goal was a reputed holy site tucked high in the hills, the village birthplace of a saintly woman healer, devotee of the Mother, whose miracles had all taken place far from here. Or else, Ista reflected as she rode along, they would have been far more obscure. The scampering golden rock gophers that popped up and chittered inhospitably as they passed would not have written them down and passed them around to attract foreign travelers in after-generations. After the visit, their route would descend to the easier roads in the Chalionese plains. And swing south again toward Baocia and home?

She did not want to go back. Yet how long could she go on like this, trailing these young men around the countryside on random roads? They would be wanted soon for harsher services, as the lords of Chalion prepared for the autumn campaign in the north. *Well, then, let us all dodge our duties a little longer.* The weather was mild, the season was right; the warm afternoon breathed a scent of mountain thyme and sage. The smell of blood and sweat and iron would overtake them all soon enough.

The track widened, curving around a wooded slope and then descending. Ferda and dy Cabon rode ahead, followed by one of the young guards and Foix. Liss rode close behind Ista, and the rest trailed after.

Ista felt it first as a wave of emotion: hot, confused menace; pain and desperation; a terrible shortness of breath. A moment later, her horse planted all four feet and came to an abrupt, trembling halt. Its head came up sharply, and it snorted.

From the shadows of the trees, the bear charged. Its head was lowered, its great shoulder crest stood up, its bronze fur rippled like water in the slanting afternoon light. It moved incredibly fast for such a bulky, low-slung creature, and its snarl split the air like a saw.

Every horse and mule in the party tried to wheel and bolt. The young guard ahead of Ista, Pejar, swung left as his panicked mount shied right, and they parted company. Ista didn't see him hit the ground, for her own horse reared then, squealing. Too late, she tried to shorten her reins, grab mane. Her saddle pommel hit her hard in the stomach, her saddle jerked away from under her, and then the ground came up in a whirl, knocking her wind half out. Dizzied, she rolled to her feet, missing her lunge for a flapping rein.

Horses were galloping away in all directions, their furious riders sawing at their reins in an effort to regain control. Pejar's horse, its saddle empty, was far down the track already, Ista's horse bucking and kicking in its wake. The young man, flat on the ground, was staring up in terror as the drooling bear loomed over him. Was the animal mad, to so attack? Ordinarily these mountain bears were elusive, shy; and this was no mother defending cubs, but a large male.

It's not a bear. Or—not only a bear. Gasping, fascinated, Ista staggered nearer. Despite the initial impression of terrifying energy, it wasn't a well bear, either. Its fur, now that she saw it more closely, was mangy, falling out in patches, and despite its large frame, its flesh was thin. Its legs trembled. It stared up at Ista as if as fascinated by her as she was by it.

It seemed to her as though its essential bear-ness was almost eaten away, from the inside out. The eyes that stared back at her had a red intelligence that owed nothing to any animal mind. *It has caught a demon. And the demon has nearly devoured it.*

And now the rider seeks another mount.

"How *dare* you," Ista grated. Not even a humble bear deserved *this. You don't belong here, demon. Go back to your accursed master.* Their gazes locked; she stepped closer; the bear stepped back from the white-faced boy. Another step. Another. The bear-demon lowered its head almost to the ground, its eyes wide and white-ringed, snuffling, backing away in fear.

"Royina, I come!" With a grunting cry, Foix appeared from the corner of Ista's vision, vest-cloak billowing, swinging his broadsword in a mighty arc. His lips were drawn back, strong teeth clenched with the effort of his strike.

"No, Foix!" Ista screamed, too late.

The heavy blade took the bear's head in one blow, and went on to bury itself in the soil beneath. Blood burst briefly from the creature's neck, and the head rolled away over the ground. One front paw spasmed; the big furry body dropped in a heap.

Ista seemed to see the demon with every sense but her eyes, a palpable force, a blood-tinged fire, a smell like hot metal. It roared toward her, then, suddenly, scrambled back in a sort of bestial terror. It hesitated a desperate moment between Foix and the boy on the ground. Then it flowed into Foix.

Foix's eyes widened. "What?" he said, in a weirdly conversational tone. Then his eyes rolled back, and he collapsed.

6

LISS WAS THE FIRST TO GET CONTROL OF HER MOUNT AND gallop back; she swung down off her bay, breathless with confusion and alarm. The groaning Pejar pushed himself up to a sitting position and boggled at the beheaded bear. His brow wrinkled in bewilderment at the sight of Foix lying on the ground beside the carcass, which still leaked hot blood. "Sir . . . ?"

The fall from her horse had shaken Ista's stomach, but it was the concussion from the demon's passage that reverberated in her bones. Her mind felt unnaturally distanced from her body. She pulled off her vest-cloak, folded it, and knelt to try to drag Foix's heavy body around and pillow his head.

Liss said, "Lady, wait—was he stunned when his horse threw him? There may be broken bones . . ."

"Did his horse throw him? I didn't see." That would explain why he had been first to reach the bear, certainly. "No, he was not hurt then. He slew the beast." *More's the pity.*

"He slid right over the crupper onto his, um. Backside. I suppose there were no bones to break there." Liss wrapped one rein around her arm to hold her snorting, backing horse, and knelt to help, poking her head up for an impressed glance at the evidence of carcass, sword, and distant head. "Five gods, what a blow." She stared down at Foix. His face was the color of porridge. "What's the *matter* with him?"

Ferda rode up next, took one look, and vaulted from his horse not even bothering to keep a rein. "Foix! Royina, what has happened?" He knelt to run his hands over his brother's body, searching for the injury, obviously expecting to see bloody damage from some massive clawed swipe. His brows knotted as he found none. He started to try to turn Foix over. Dy Cabon labored up, minus his mule, gasping for breath.

Ista grasped Ferda's arm. "No, your brother was not struck."

"He chopped off the bear's head. Then he just . . . fell over," confirmed Pejar.

"Was the beast mad, to attack like that?" panted dy Cabon. He bent over his belly to brace his hands on his knees and stare around as well.

"Not mad," said Ista in a flat voice. "Demon-ridden."

Dy Cabon's eyes widened, searching her face. "Are you sure, Royina?"

"Entirely sure. I . . . felt it." *It felt me.*

Ferda rocked back on his heels, looking dumfounded.

"Where did it . . ." Dy Cabon's voice trailed off as he surveyed the shaken guard, Ista upright and in apparent possession of her wits. Foix lying as though bludgeoned. "It didn't go into *him*, did it?"

"Yes." Ista moistened her lips. "It was backing off. I tried to stop him, but all he saw was a mad bear, I think, seeming to menace me."

Dy Cabon's lips repeated the word, *Seeming?* His gaze upon her sharpened.

Dy Cabon's manifest belief finally convinced the stunned Ferda. His face nearly crumpled in tears. "Learned, *what will happen to Foix?*"

"That depends"—dy Cabon swallowed—"much on the nature of the demon in question."

"It was bearish," reported Ista, still in that same flat voice.

"It may have consumed other creatures before the bear, but it could not have ingested the nature or intelligence of a man yet. It had no speech." *But now it possesses a very banquet of words and wits.* How quickly would it start its feast?

"*That* will change," muttered dy Cabon, echoing Ista's own thought. He took a deep breath. "Nothing will happen instantly," he asserted more loudly. Ista did not quite like the too-hearty tone of that. "Foix can resist. If he chooses. An inexperienced demon needs time to grow, to learn."

To dig in, Ista's thought supplied. To tap a soul's strength, to prepare for siege. Did it follow that an experienced demon, fat with many souls of men, could conquer in a breath?

"Still, we should give it as little time as possible to . . . as little time as possible. A temple at one of the provincial seats will have the means, the scholars to deal with this. We must take him at once to the archdivine of Taryoon—no. That would take a week." He stared out over the hills toward the distant plains. "The provincial temple at Maradi is closer. Ferda, where are your maps? We must find the speediest route."

The other guardsmen were riding up, having captured the loose horses and mules. One towed Ferda's mount. Ferda rose to search his saddlebags, but turned back quickly as Foix stirred and groaned.

Foix's eyes opened. He stared up at the sky and the ring of faces hovering anxiously over him, and his brows drew down in a wince. "*Oh,*" he muttered.

Ferda knelt by his head, his hands opening and closing helplessly. "How do you feel?" he ventured at last.

Foix blinked. "I feel very strange." He made a clumsy gesture with one hand—it looked like a paw, swiping—and tried to roll over and stand up. He ended up on all fours instead. It took him two more tries to gain his feet. Dy Cabon held one arm and Ferda the other as he blinked again and moved his jaw back and forth a few times. He reached his hand toward his mouth, missed, and tried again. His fingers probed as if reassuring himself he felt a jaw and not a muzzle. "What happened?"

For a long moment, no one dared to answer. He looked around at their horror-stricken stares with increasing dismay.

Dy Cabon finally said, "We think you have contracted a demon. It was riding the bear when it attacked."

"The bear was dying," said Ista. Even in her own ears, her voice sounded oddly detached. "I tried to warn you."

"It's not true, is it?" Ferda asked. Begged. "This cannot be."

Foix's face went still, inward; his eyes were fixed, unseeing for half a dozen breaths. "Oh," he said again. "Yes. It is . . . is that what . . ."

"What?" Dy Cabon tried to make his voice gentle, but it came out edged with anxiety.

"There is something . . . in my head. Frightened. All in a knot. As though trying to hide in a cave."

"Hm."

It was becoming apparent that Foix was not about to turn into a bear, demon, or anything else much but a bewildered young man just yet. The seniors of the party, supporting Foix, all went a short distance away and sat on the ground to consult the maps. A couple of the guardsmen discussed the carcass in low voices and decided its diseased skin was not worth the peeling, though they collected the teeth and claws for souvenirs, then hauled it away off the road.

Ferda sorted out his map of the region and smoothed it over a wide, flat stone. His finger traced a line. "I believe our most efficient route to Maradi is to stay on this very track for another thirty miles or so, to this village. Then turn and descend almost due east."

Dy Cabon glanced up toward the sun, already fallen behind the wall of mountains to their west, though the sky still glowed deep blue. "We'll not make it there before this night falls."

Ista dared to touch the map with one white finger. "If we continue only a little, we'll come to that crossroad up to the old saint's village that we intended to visit. We've already bespoken food and fodder and beds there. And we could start again early." And there would be strong walls between them and any more bears. Although not between them and the demon—a reflection she resolved to keep to herself.

Ferda frowned. "Six extra miles each way. More, if we mistake the track again." Just such a deceptive fork in the road had cost them an hour, earlier in the day. "Half a day's travel lost. We carry enough food and fodder for one night— we can restock where we turn east." He hesitated, and said more cautiously, "That is, if you are willing to endure the discomforts of a night in camp, Royina. The weather looks to continue fair, at least."

Ista fell silent. She misliked the scheme, but misliked still more the hint that she would put her comfort above her loyal officer's clear need. Split the party, send the speediest riders on ahead with Foix? She misliked that idea as well. "I . . . have no preference."

"How do you feel about riding?" Ferda asked his brother.

Foix was sitting with his brow furrowed and an inward look, like a man with a stomachache. "Huh? Oh. No worse than usual. My rump hurts, but that has nothing to do with . . . with the other thing." He was quiet a moment longer, then added, "Except indirectly."

Ferda said in a voice of military decision, "Let us push on as far and fast as we can tonight, then."

A murmur of agreement ran around the little council squatting by the stone. Ista pressed her lips closed.

They put Foix back up on his nervous horse—it took two men to hold the beast, and it sidled and snorted at first, but then settled as they set out again. Dy Cabon and Ferda rode close to Foix on either side. Protectively. Too late.

Ista stared at their backs as they continued down the road, such as it was. Her sense of the demon's presence, briefly so searing, was muted again. Was it occluded by matter, or perhaps deliberately hiding itself within its new fleshly lair? Or was it her deficiency? She had suppressed her sensitivity for so long, extending it again was like stretching a withered muscle. It hurt.

Lord dy Cazaril claimed that the world of the spirit and

the world of matter existed side by side, like two sides of a coin, or a wall; the gods were not far away in some other space, but in this very one, continuously, just around some strange corner of perception. A presence as pervasive and invisible as sunlight on skin, as though one stood naked and blindfolded in an unimaginable noon.

Demons as well, though they were more like thieves putting a hand through a window. What occupied Foix's space, now? If both brothers came up behind her, would she know which was which without looking?

She closed her eyes, to test her perceptions. The creak of her saddle, the plodding of the other mounts, the faint crack as a hoof struck a stone; the smell of her horse, of her sweat, of the cool breath of pines . . . nothing more, now.

And then she wondered what the demon saw when it looked at Ista.

They made camp by another clear stream when there was barely enough light left to find firewood. The men gathered plenty; Ista suspected she was not the only one worried about wildlife. They also built her and Liss a little bower, of sorts, with logs and branches, floored with a hay of hastily cut yellow grasses. It did not look especially bear-proof to her.

Foix rejected being treated as an invalid and insisted on gathering wood as well. Ista watched him discreetly, and so, she noticed, did dy Cabon. Foix heaved over one good-sized log only to find it rotten, crawling with grubs. He stared down at his find with a very odd look on his face.

"Learned," he said quietly.

"Yes, Foix?"

"Will I turn into a bear? Or into a madman who thinks he's a bear?"

"No. Neither," said dy Cabon firmly. Though whether truly, Ista suspected even he did not know. "That will wear off."

Dy Cabon spoke to reassure, but did not seem to partake of the comfort himself. Because if the demon became less bearlike, it could only be because it was growing more Foix-like?

"Good," sighed Foix. His face screwed up. "Because those look *delicious*." He kicked the log back over again with rather more force than was necessary and went to look for a drier deadfall.

Dy Cabon lingered by Ista. "Lady . . ."

Five gods, his plaintive tone of voice was just like Foix's, a moment ago. She barely turned her soothing *Yes, dy Cabon?* into a sharper, "What?" lest he take her for mocking him.

"About your dreams. The god-touched ones you had, so long ago."

Not long ago enough. "What about them?"

"Well . . . how do you know when dreams are real? How do you tell good prophecy from, say, bad fish?"

"There is nothing good about prophecy. All I can tell you is, they are unmistakable. As if more real than memory, not less." Her voice went harsh in sudden suspicion. "Why do you ask?"

He tapped his fingers nervously against the side of one broad hip. "I thought you might instruct me."

"What, the conductor conducted?" She tried to turn this off lightly, though her stomach chilled. "The Temple would disapprove."

"I think not so, lady. What apprentice would not seek advice from a master, if he could? If he found himself with a commission far beyond his skills?"

Her eyes narrowed. Five gods—and never had the oath seemed more apropos—what dreams had come to him? Did a lean man lie in a sleep like death, on a bed in a dark chamber . . . she would not even hint of that secret vision. "What dreams have you been having?"

"I dreamed of you."

"Well, so. People do dream of those they know."

"Yes, but this was before. Once, before I ever saw you that first day out riding on the road near Valenda."

"Perhaps . . . were you ever in Cardegoss as a child, or elsewhere, when Ias and I made a progress? Your father, or someone, might have put you on his shoulder to see the roya's procession."

He shook his head. "Was Ser dy Ferrej with you then? Did you wear lilac and black, ride a horse led by a groom down a country road? Were you forty, sad and pale? I think not, Royina." He looked away briefly. "The ferret's demon knew you, too. What did it see that I did not?"

"I have no idea. Did you ask it before you dispatched it?"

He grimaced and shook his head. "I did not know enough to ask. Then. The next dreams came later, more strongly."

"What dreams, Learned?" It was almost a whisper.

"I dreamed of that dinner in the castle in Valenda. Of us, out on the road, with almost this company. Sometimes Liss and Ferda and Foix were there, sometimes others." He looked down, looked up, confessed: "The temple in Valenda never sent me to be your conductor. They only sent me up to convey Learned Tovia's apologies, and to say that she would call on you as soon as she returned. I stole your pilgrimage, Royina. I thought the god was telling me to."

She opened her mouth, to do no more than breathe out. She made her voice very neutral, letting her hands grasp the sapling she leaned against, behind her back, to still their trembling. "Say on."

"I prayed. I drew us to Casilchas so that I might consult my superiors. You . . . spoke to me. The dreams ceased. My superiors suggested I bestir myself to really be your spiritual conductor, since I had gone so far already, and lady, I have tried."

She opened a hand to assuage his concern, though she was not sure he could see it in the failing light. So, his peculiar convictions about her spiritual gifts, back in Casilchas, had come from a more direct source than old gossip. Through the sparse trees, the firelight was starting up from two pits dug in the sandy stream bank, in cheery defiance of the gathering night. The fires looked . . . small, at the feet of these great hills. The Bastard's Teeth, the range was called, for in the high passes they bit travelers.

"But then the dreams started up again, a few nights past. New ones. Or a new one, three times. A road, much like this. Country much like this." His white sleeve waved in the shadows. "I am overtaken by a column of men, Roknari soldiers, Quadrene heretics. They pull me from my mule. They—" He stopped abruptly.

"Not all prophetic dreams come true. Or come true as first seen," said Ista cautiously. His distress was very real, it seemed to her, and very deep.

"No, they could not be." He grew almost eager. "For they slew me in a different cruel way each night." His voice slowed in doubt. "They always started with the thumbs, though."

And she and Liss had laughed at his wine-sickness . . . drowning dreams, was he? That didn't work. She'd tried it herself, long ago in Ias's court. "You should have told me this! Much earlier!"

"There cannot be Roknari here, now. They would have to cross two provinces to reach this place. The whole country would be aroused." His voice seemed to be trying to push back the darkness with reason. "That dream must belong to some other, later future."

You cannot push back the darkness with reason. You have to use fire. Where had that thought come from? "Or no future. Some dreams are but warnings. Heed them, and their menace empties out."

His voice went very small, in the darkness. "I fear I have failed the gods, and this is to be my punishment."

"No," said Ista coldly. "The gods are more ruthless than that. If they use you up in their works, they have no more interest in you than a painter in a crusted and broken brush, to be cast aside and replaced." She hesitated. "If they still lash and drive you, you may be sure it means they still want something from you. Something they haven't got yet."

"Oh," he said, no louder.

She gripped the tree. She wanted to pace. Could they get off this road? It was farther back to Vinyasca, now, than it was to go forward. Could they strike down this streambed to the plains? She imagined waterfalls, thorn tangles, sudden rock faces over which it was impossible either to ride or lead their mounts. They would think her mad to insist upon such a wild course. She shivered.

"You are right about the Roknari, though," she said. "Single spies, or small groups in disguise, might penetrate this far south unseen. But nothing strong enough to overcome our well-armed company, in any case. Even Foix is not out of the muster."

"True," he allowed.

Ista bit her lip, looking around to be quite sure the young man had gone out of earshot back to the camp. "What about Foix, Learned? For a moment, I saw—it was as if I saw the bear's spirit. It was more riddled and decayed than its body, writhing in an agony of putrefaction. Will Foix . . . ?"

"His danger is real, but not imminent." Dy Cabon's voice firmed on this surer ground, and his white-clad bulk straightened. "What he has gained by accident, some sinful or shortsighted or desperate men actually seek by design. To capture a demon, and feed it slowly on themselves in exchange for its aid—so men turn sorcerers. For a time. Quite a long time, some of them, if they are clever or careful."

"Who ends up in charge, then?"

He cleared his throat. "Almost always the demon. Eventually. But with this young elemental, Foix would be master at first, if he made the attempt. I do not mean to discuss this with him, or plant the suggestion, and I beg you will be careful, too, Royina. The more . . . intertwined they become, the harder they will be to separate."

He added lowly, "But where are they *coming* from? What rip in hell is leaking them back into the world in such sudden numbers? My order is called to be guardians upon that march, as surely as troops of the Son's or the Daughter's Orders ride out in the sun armed with swords and shields against more material evil. The fifth god's servants walk singly in the darkness, armed with our wits." He heaved a disconsolate sigh. "I could wish for a better weapon, just now."

"Sleep will sharpen all our wits, we must hope," said Ista. "Perhaps the morning will bring some better counsel."

"I pray it may be so, Royina."

He walked her back through the brush to her bower. Ista forbore to wish him pleasant dreams. Or any dreams at all.

❧

The anxious Ferda roused everyone at dawn except his brother. Only when breakfast was ready to be served did he squat beside that bedroll and carefully touch the heavy sleeping form upon the shoulder. Liss, passing by Ista lugging a saddle, paused and watched this worried tenderness, and her lips pinched with distress.

They wasted little time eating, breaking camp, and taking again to the stony, winding track. The irregular hills discouraged speed, but Ferda led at a steady pace that ate the miles nonetheless. The morning and the road slowly fell behind them.

The company was largely silent, pushing along lost in who-knew-what sober reflections. Ista could not decide which development she liked least, Foix's acquisition or dy Cabon's dreams. Foix's bear-demon might be mischance, if chance it was. Dy Cabon's dreams were plain warnings, perhaps deceptive to heed, but perilous to ignore.

The concatenation of the uncanny beginning to swirl about Ista set her neck hairs standing and her teeth on edge. She felt a disturbing sense of having stepped into a pattern not yet perceived. *Yes. We turn for home at Maradi.*

Her silent decision brought no relief; the tension remained, like a cable strained to snapping. Like the breathless pressure that had shot her out the postern gate and down the road in court mourning and silk slippers, that morning in Valenda. *I must move. I cannot be still.*

Where? Why?

The hill country here was even drier than farther south, though the streams still ran full from the spring melt, above. The gnarled pines grew smaller and more scattered, and long bony washes almost devoid of vegetation became more frequent. When they topped a rise, dy Cabon glanced back over their track. He pulled his mule up abruptly. "What's that?"

Ista twisted in her saddle. Just coming over the distant crest of the descending ridge behind them was a rider—no, riders.

Foix called, "Ferda? You have the better eyes."

Ferda wheeled his horse and squinted in the bright light; the sun was growing hotter, climbing toward noon. "Men on horses." His expression grew grim. "Armed—I see chain mail—spears. Their armor is in the Roknari style . . . Bastard's dem—five gods! Those are the tabards of the prince-dom of Jokona. I can see the white birds on the green even from here."

They still looked like green blurs to Ista, though she squinted, too. She said uneasily, "What are they doing here, in this peaceful land? Are they merchant's guards, leading a caravan? Emissaries?"

Ferda stood in his stirrups, craned his neck. "Soldiers. All soldiers." He glanced around at his little company and touched his sword hilt. "Well, so are we."

"Ah . . . Ferda?" said Foix after a moment. "They're still coming."

Ista could see his lips move as he kept count. Rank on rank, riding two or three abreast, the interlopers poured over the lip of the hill. Ista's own count had passed thirty when dy Cabon, whose face had gone the color of lard, signed himself and looked across at her. He had to cough before he could form words. They seemed to catch on his dry lips. "Royina? I do not think we want to meet these men."

"I am certain of it, Learned." Her heart was starting to pound.

The column's leaders had seen them, too. Men pointed and yelled.

Ferda dropped his arm and shouted back over his company, "Ride on!"

He led the way down the track at a brisk canter. The baggage mules resisted being towed at this speed, and slowed the men who had them in charge. Dy Cabon's more willing mule did better at first, but it grunted with each stride at the jouncing weight it bore. So did dy Cabon. When they reached the top of the next rise, half a mile on, they could see that the Jokonan column had dispatched a squad of a double dozen riders out ahead, galloping with the clear intent of overtaking Ista's party.

Now it was a race, and they were not fitted for it. The baggage mules might be abandoned, but what of the divine's beast? Its nostrils were round and red, its white hair was already starting to lather at its neck and shoulder and between its hind legs, and despite dy Cabon's kicks and shouts it kept breaking from a canter into a bone-jarring fast trot. It shook dy Cabon like a pudding; his face went from scarlet to pale green and back again. He looked close to vomiting from the exertion and terror.

If this was the raiding column it appeared—and how in five gods' names had it appeared from the *south* of them, so unheralded?—Ista might cry ransom for herself and the Daughter's men. But a divine of the fifth god would be treated as heretic and defiled—they would indeed start by cutting off dy Cabon's thumbs. And then his tongue, and then his genitals. After that, depending on their time and ingenuity, whatever ghastly death the Quadrene soldiers could devise, or urge each other on to—hanging, impalement, something even worse. Three nights he'd dreamed of this, dy Cabon had said, each different. Ista wondered what death could possibly be more grotesque than impalement.

The country offered poor cover. The trees were small,

and even if any overhung the road, she wasn't sure they could boost the wheezing divine up one. His white robes, dirty as they were, would shine like a beacon through the leaves. They'd show up for half a mile through the scrub, as would his mule. But then they topped another rise, temporarily out of sight of their pursuers, and at the bottom of this wash . . .

She lashed her horse forward beside Ferda's, and shouted, "The divine—he must not be taken!"

He looked back over his company and signed agreement. "Exchange horses?" he cried doubtfully.

"Not good enough," she shouted back. She pointed ahead. "Hide him in the culvert!"

She slowed her horse, letting the others pass her, till dy Cabon's mule labored up. Foix and Liss reined back with her.

"Dy Cabon!" she cried. "Did you ever dream about being pulled out of a culvert?"

"No, lady!" he quavered back between jounces.

"Hide you in that one, then, till they all pass over you." Foix—Foix was in hideous danger if taken, too, if the Quadrenes should learn of his demon affliction. They might well take him for a sorcerer and burn him alive. "Did you dream of Foix with you?"

"No!"

"Foix! Can you stay with him—help him? Keep both your heads down and don't come out, no matter what!"

Foix glanced down the track at the cover she pointed to and seemed to understand the plan at once. "Aye, Royina!"

They scraped to a halt over the culvert. The streamlet here did not fill it full, though it would be a cramped, wet, uncomfortable crouch, especially for dy Cabon's quivering bulk. Foix swung down, threw his reins to Pejar, and caught the gasping divine as he half fell from his animal. "Wrap this around you, hide those white robes." Foix tossed his gray cloak around dy Cabon, hustling him off the road. Another guard began grimly towing dy Cabon's mule; relieved of its great burden, it broke again into a canter. A canter wasn't going to be enough, Ista thought.

"Look after each other!" she cried in desperation. The pair was already scrambling into the low mouth of the culvert, and she could not tell if they heard her or not.

They started forward once again. There was another here who must not be taken by the rough soldiery, she thought. "Liss!" she called. The girl rode nearer. Ista's horse was dark with sweat, blowing; Liss's tall bay still cantered easily.

"Ride ahead—"

"Royina, I won't leave you—"

"Fool girl, listen! Ride ahead and carry warning to anyone you pass, Jokonan raiders are coming. Raise the countryside! Get help and send it back!"

Understanding dawned in her face. "Aye, Royina!"

"Ride like the wind! Don't look back!"

Liss, face set, saluted her and bent over her horse's neck. Its stride lengthened. The three or four galloping miles they'd covered so far were clearly but a warm-up for it. In moments, the bay outpaced every horse in the party and started to draw ahead.

Yes, fly, girl. You don't even have to outride the Jokonans, as long as you can outride us . . .

As they topped the next rise, where the road swung out around a bulge in the hill, Ista looked back. There was no sign whatever of the divine or Foix. The first Jokonan riders were galloping across the culvert without pausing or looking down, intent on their quarry ahead. The tightness in Ista's chest eased a little, even as she gasped for breath.

At last, her whirling brain began to take thought for herself. If captured, should she maintain her incognito? What worth would a minor female cousin of the rich provincar of Baocia seem to them? Would Sera dy Ajelo's status be enough to buy safety for her men as well as her? But the dowager royina of Chalion, Royina Iselle's own mother, was far too exciting a prize to let fall into the grubby hands of a pack of Jokonan soldier-bandits. She glanced around at her grimly intent outriders. *I don't want these loyal young men to die for me. I don't want any man to die for me, ever again.*

Ferda galloped up beside her horse, pointed back. "Royina, we must cut loose the mules!"

She nodded understanding, gulped for breath. Her legs ached from gripping the heaving sides of her mount. "Dy Cabon's saddlebags—they must be got rid of—hidden—all his books and papers will reveal him, they might go back and search! And mine as well, I have letters in my own name—"

His lips drew back in a grimace of understanding; he stood in his stirrups and fell behind. She turned in her saddle and scrabbled at the rawhide ties holding her bags behind her cantle. Happily, Liss had tied them intelligently; the strong knots came loose at Ista's pull.

Ferda again galloped up beside her; now he had the divine's heavy pair of bags over his pommel. She glanced back. The loosed baggage mules and dy Cabon's white beast were falling behind, stumbling to a halt, wandering gratefully from the road.

They were approaching a bridge over a strong freshet. Ferda held out his arm in demand, and she swung her bags over to him. He reared his horse atop the bridge and violently heaved first one set of bags, then the other, over the crumbling stone balustrade to the downstream side. The bags floated away, bumping on the rocks, sinking slowly out of sight. Ista briefly regretted the divine's books, and their purses of money—but not their damning correspondence and other signs of identity.

This prudence cost them still more of the implacably closing space between them and the Jokonan leaders. Ista put her weight in her stirrups and concentrated on urging her flagging horse up the next rise. Perhaps turning aside to capture the baggage mules would slow their pursuers. *Some of them.* The enemy had plenty of men to spare, it seemed. She had glimpsed the beginnings of their column; she had yet to glimpse its end.

What they were seemed plain enough. Both sides had

played these evil games of raid and reprisal across the borders here for generations, the boundaries that the Chalionese Quintarians were slowly pushing back to the north. In the disputed regions, men grew up expecting to raid for a living as though it were some job of work. Sometimes the game was played by elaborate rules of etiquette, with businesslike arrangements for ransoms mixed with bizarre contests of honor. Sometimes there were no rules, and it was no game, and honor dissolved in sweaty, screaming, bloody horrors.

How desperate were their pursuers? They seemed to have dropped from the very sky. They were a province and a half away from the borders of Jokona, hustling down an obscure hill road. Fresh troops, circling to attack some target, or worn ones, running for home? If they wore the prince's tabards, they at least were not a spontaneous gang of semi-bandit younger sons and ruffians out for what they could grab, but men of greater discipline bent on some larger mission. Presumably.

Atop the next rise, her horse stumbling, Ista again gained a long view of the road ahead. Liss's rangy bay was well out in the distance, still galloping.

Ista's heart caught. Plunging down the scrubby hillside toward Liss pelted another dozen Jokonan riders. A scouting screen of cavalry, sent before the main force, clearly. Ista's eye tried to guess angles, distances, speeds. The Jokonans descended as if to pluck Liss from the road as a hawk snatches a squirrel from a tree branch. Liss had not seen them yet, could not possibly hear Ista if she screamed out a warning. Ferda rose in his stirrups, a look of helpless horror on his face; he whipped his mount, but could beat no more speed out of the strained animal.

Closer, closer the raiders drew—Liss looked aside at last, saw them. Surely even *her* great-hearted horse must be reaching the limits of its endurance . . . She flashed past the leaders. A crossbow glinted, a quarrel sped through the air. Ferda yelled in anguish, but the shot, loosed at too great a range and from the back of a heaving horse, went wide.

The patrol reached the road. Their officer gesticulated. A pair of riders split off and rode in pursuit of Liss. The rest wheeled around and bunched to a halt across the road. Waiting.

Ferda cursed, looked back, looked forward, teeth gritting; he threw back his cloak and touched his sword hilt. He cast a worried look aside at Ista, obviously trying to think how to screen her if his dwindling company attempted to burst through the new blockade. Ista followed his glance back. More and more riders were pouring over the ridge behind them, seemingly without end.

Once blood was drawn, events would spin rapidly out of control. Death would cry for death.

"Ferda!" Ista screamed. It came out a croak. "There is no way. We must halt, surrender on terms!"

"No, Royina!" His face bunched in agony. "By my oath and honor, no! We will die to defend you!"

"You will better defend me alive with your wits and self-control, Ferda!" Except they'd left the best wits and self-control in the party back along the road in a culvert. She drew a long breath, pinned a moral fear vaster than her physical terror by its neck to the ground, pushed the words past her lips. "By my command! We must halt!"

Ferda clenched his jaw, but really, it was hardly a decision anymore. The main body of Jokonans was almost on their heels, squeezing them up against the line across the road. Ista could see half a dozen crossbows raised among the waiting riders, from steadier platforms this time.

Ferda flung up his hand. "We halt!" The spent horses of his company stumbled to a ragged stop. Men threw back cloaks, reached for weapons. "Do not draw!" Ferda roared.

Some cried aloud in dismay and protest. Some were red-faced with tears of frustration and hot strain. But they obeyed. They knew how the game was played, too, as well as Ista. And knew as well as she how it was violated.

The Jokonans, swords out and spears and bows at the ready, crowded up on both sides of them and slowly closed in.

7

ISTA STOOD IN HER STIRRUPS, WRAPPED HER DRY TONGUE around her rusty Roknari. ~I cry ransom~. And in Ibran: "I am the Sera dy Ajelo, and the provincar of Baocia is my patron! I pledge his ransom upon myself and upon all these men of mine! All of them!" And repeated in Roknari, to be sure: ~Ransoms for all!~

An officer rode forward from his men. He was marked by a better grade of chain mail, fine decorations in pressed gold leaf on the leather of bridle, saddle, and scabbard, and a green silk baldric worked in gold-and-white thread with the flying pelicans of Jokona. His typical crinkled Roknari bronze-blond hair was done up in crisscrossing rows of braids ending in a queue. His eyes summed the Chalionese numbers; perhaps took in the garb and badges of the Daughter's Order with a slight tinge of respect? Ista, who had silently repudiated her prayers in her mind during all the weeks of her pilgrimage, though she'd moved her lips by rote in the responses, prayed now in her hammering heart: *Lady, in this Your season of strength, cast a cloak of protection over these Your loyal servants.*

In passable Ibran, the officer cried, "Throw down your weapons!"

One last, anguished hesitation; then Ferda shrugged back his vest-cloak and pulled his baldric off over his head. His scabbard and sword struck the dirt with a clank. His belt knife succeeded them. The men of his company followed suit with equal reluctance. Half a dozen crossbows and the pair of spears were lowered more carefully on the growing heap. Their lathered, blowing horses stood quiescent as Ferda and his men were made to dismount and sit on the ground a little way off, surrounded by Jokonans with drawn swords and cocked bows.

A soldier seized the bridle of Ista's horse and made motions to her to get down. Her legs almost gave way as her boots hit the ground; her knees felt like custard. She jerked back from his raised hand, though she realized almost at once that he'd only meant to grab her elbow to keep her from falling. The officer approached and gave her a demisalute, possibly meant to be reassuring.

"Chalionese noblewoman." It was half a question; her plain dress did not quite support her claimed status. His eyes searched for, and did not find, jewelry, rings, brooches. "What are you doing here?"

"*I* have every right to be here." Ista lifted her chin. "You have interrupted my pilgrimage."

"Quintarian devil-worshipper." He spat, ritually, but to the side. "What do you pray for, eh, woman?"

Ista raised one brow. "Peace." She added, "And you will address me as *Sera*."

He snorted, but seemed convinced, or at least grew less curious. Half a dozen men were starting to poke in the saddlebags; with a spate of Roknari too fast for Ista to follow, he strode among them and shoved them back.

She saw why as the rest of the column draggled up, and a couple of men carrying the green pouches of royal clerks rode hastily forward, followed by what were obviously the senior officers. Now the bags were all pulled off and looted in a much more systematic fashion, with a running inventory. The clerks were there to make sure that the prince of

Jokona's one-fifth share was properly counted. One of them walked about, stylus busy upon his tablet, noting the horses and their gear. No question but that this was an official expedition of some kind, and not some spontaneous banditry.

The officer reported to his seniors; Ista heard the word *Baocia* twice. One of the men rummaging through the saddlebags straightened up with a glad cry; Ista thought he might have found a purse, but instead he waved Ferda's maps. He rushed over to his officers, crying in Roknari, ~Look, my lords, look! Charts of Chalion! Now we are not lost!~

Ista blinked. Then she began to look around more carefully.

The mounts of the men who'd overtaken them were every bit as lathered and exhausted as their own, and Ista, remembering Liss's remarks about horses flagging late in the race, wondered if her party might not have outridden them after all, but for being trapped by the advance patrol. The men looked hot, worn, filthy, stubbled. Their fine Roknari pattern-braids were in disarray, as if they had not been redone for days or even weeks. The men riding up late looked worse. Many were bandaged or bruised or scabbed, and most of them led extra horses with empty saddles, sometimes three or four in a string. Not booty, for most of the animals were decked in Roknari-style gear. Some might be remounts. Not all. The baggage train that limped up behind them all was strangely scant.

If the baggage train marked the end of their company, and there was no sign of Foix or dy Cabon among the prisoners . . . Ista permitted herself a shiver of hope. Even if the clerks counting horses counted men as well, and noted the two empty saddles, by the time they circled back to search, Foix would surely have moved the divine and himself to better cover. If Foix was as quietly sly on his feet as he was with his tongue—if the bear-demon had not put his mind in too much disarray—if the Jokonans had not simply slain them and left their bodies by the roadside . . .

One thing was certain. These Jokonans were not men

moving to some secret attack. They were fleeing a defeat, by every sign, or some dreadfully costly victory. Running north for home. She was glad for Chalion, but increasingly anxious for herself and Ferda and his men. Tense, exhausted, strained men on the ragged edge of their endurance made worrisome captors.

The officer came back and directed her to sit by the roadside in the mottled shadow of a small, bent tree, some odd northern species with wide palmate leaves. Foix's bags yielded a purse of gold that cheered the prince's clerks, and the officers eyed her with a shade more respect, or at least, calculation. They pulled apart the baggage from the captured mules, as well. Ista turned her face away and declined to notice the soldiers raucously playing about with her clothing. The officer inquired more closely into her relationship with the provincar of Baocia, and Ista trotted out Sera dy Ajelo's imaginary family tree. He seemed anxious to ascertain that the wealthy provincar would actually deliver a ransom for her.

"Oh, yes," said Ista distantly. "He will come in person, I expect." *With ten thousand swordsmen at his back, five thousand archers, and the Marshal dy Palliar's cavalry as well.* It occurred to her that if she did not want men to die for her, she'd gone about it in exactly the wrong way. But no. There might yet be chances to escape, or be traded out at a tiny fraction of her real worth, if her incognito held. Liss . . . had Liss made it away? No soldiers had yet returned along the track dragging her resisting behind them, nor as a limp corpse tossed over a saddle.

The officers argued over the maps, while the men and animals rested in what shade could be found, and the flies buzzed around them. The Ibran-speaking officer brought her water in a rather noisome skin bag, and she hesitated, licked dusty cracked lips, and drank. It was fairly fresh, at least. She indicated he should take it to Ferda and his troop, and he did. At length, she was put back up on her own horse, with her hands lashed to the pommel, the horse in turn roped with several others following the baggage train. Ferda's men were towed in a like line, but farther forward, surrounded by more armed soldiers. The advance scouts were redeployed, and the column started north once more.

Ista stared around at her fellow prisoners, tied to horses as she was. They were oddly few in number, some dozen debilitated men and women, and no children at all. Another older woman rode near her, jerked along in another string of tired horses. Her clothes, though filthy, were finely made and elaborately decorated—clearly no common woman, but someone whose family might offer a rich ransom. Ista leaned toward her. "Where do these soldiers come from? Besides Jokona."

"Some Roknari hell, I think," said the woman.

"No, *that* would be their destination," murmured Ista back.

A sour smile lifted one corner of the woman's mouth; good, she was not shocked stupid, then. Or at least, not anymore. "I do pray so, hourly. They took me in the town of Rauma, in Ibra."

"Ibra!" Ista glanced leftward at the mountain range rising in the distance. They must have scrambled out of Ibra over some little-used pass, and dropped down into Chalion to cut north for home. And the pursuit must have been fiery, to drive them to such a desperate ploy. "No wonder they seemed to have fallen from the sky."

"Where in Chalion are we?"

"The province of Tolnoxo. These raiders still have over a hundred miles to go to safety, across the rest of Tolnoxo and all of Caribastos, before they reach the border of Jokona. If they can." She hesitated. "I have hopes that they have lost their secrecy. I think some of my party escaped."

The woman's eyes flared hot, briefly. "Good." She added after a little, "They fell upon Rauma at dawn, by surprise. It was well planned—they must have swung wide around some dozen better-prepared towns closer to the border. I had brought my daughters into town to make offerings at the

Daughter's altar, for my eldest was—pray the goddess, still is—to be married. The Jokonans were more interested in booty than rapine and destruction, at first. They left the rest of the temple alone, though they held all they'd caught there at sword's point. But then they delayed their withdrawal to pull down the Bastard's Tower, and to torment the poor divine who had it in her charge." The woman grimaced. "They caught her still in her white robes; there was no chance to hide her. They slew her husband, when he tried to defend her."

For a woman devoted to the fifth god, the Quadrenes would also start with the thumbs and tongue. Then rape, most likely, prolonged and vicious.

"They burned her in her god's tower, in the end." The woman sighed. "It seemed almost a mercy by then. But their blasphemy cost them all they'd gained, for the march of Rauma's troops came upon them while they were still in the town. The Son give him strength for his sword arm! He had no mercy upon them, for the divine had been his half sister. He had got her the benefice, I suppose, to keep her in comfort."

Ista hissed sympathy through her teeth.

"My daughters escaped in the chaos . . . I think. Perhaps the Mother heard my prayers, for in my terror I did offer myself in exchange for them. But I was thrown upon a horse and carried off by these raiders who broke and retreated, for they could guess by my clothes and jewels I would profit them."

She bore no jewels now, naturally.

"Their greed bought me some consideration, although they used my maid . . . hideously. I think she is still alive, though. They abandoned all their lesser prisoners in the wilderness, because they were slowing them on the climb. If they all stayed together, and did not panic, they may have helped each other to rescue by now. I hope . . . I hope they carried the wounded."

Ista nodded understanding. She wondered what Prince Sordso of Jokona could possibly be about, permitting—no, dispatching—this raid. It seemed more a probe than the first wave of an invasion. Perhaps it had been intended merely to stir up North Ibra, tie down the old roya's troops in a broad defense, and so prevent them from being sent in support of Chalion in the autumn campaign against Visping? If so, the strategy had been a little too swiftly successful. Although these men might have been an intentional sacrifice without even knowing it . . .

The not-too-badly wounded also rode with the baggage train. The severely wounded, Ista supposed, had been left along the route to the dubious mercy of the column's recent victims. One man caught Ista's eye. He was an older officer, very senior judging by his clothing and gear. He bore no bandage or visible wound, but he rode along tied to his saddle like a prisoner, slack-faced and moaning, his braids tumbled down. His mumbled words were not intelligible even in Roknari, Ista judged. Had he suffered a blow to the head, perhaps? His drooling disturbed her, and his noises set her teeth on edge; she was secretly relieved when the baggage train shuffled its order and he was led farther from her.

A few miles up the road they came upon the men who'd been sent in pursuit of Liss, both riding one stumbling horse, leading the second one lamed. They were greeted with inventive Roknari cursing and cuffs from their furious commander; both ruined horses were turned loose and replaced with two of the many spares. Ista concealed a grim smile. More consulting of Ferda's maps followed, and more scouts were dispatched. The column lumbered on.

An hour later they came to the hamlet where Ista's party had planned to turn east and take the road to Maradi. It was wholly abandoned, not a person to be found, nor any animal but a few stray chickens, cats, and rabbits. *Liss made it this far, it seems,* Ista thought with satisfaction. The Jokonans ransacked it quickly, taking what food and fodder they could find, argued about setting it afire, made more debate over the maps, and finally hastened north on the dwindling continuation of their road. Prudence and discipline still held, if tenuously, for they left the hamlet standing behind them, with no rising column of black smoke, visible for miles, to mark their passing. The sun fell behind the mountains.

Dusk was thickening when the column turned off the easier but dangerously open road and began scrambling up what would in any other season have been a dry wash. A stream gurgled down the middle of it now. After a couple of miles, they turned to the north again, making their way through brush to an area denser with trees and cover. Ista wondered how futile an attempt at concealment it would prove—they'd left enough hoof marks, broken vegetation, and dung in their wake that even she could have tracked them.

The Jokonans made camp in a shaded dell, lighting only a few fires, and those just long enough to sear their stolen chickens. But they had to give their horses time to eat their looted fodder and grain, and regain strength. The half-dozen women prisoners were put together, given bedrolls no worse than the Jokonans themselves used—probably the same. Their food was also no worse than what their captors ate. In any case, it did not seem to be grilled cat. Ista wondered if she was sleeping in a dead man's bedding, and what dreams it would bring her.

Something useful would be a nice change. It wasn't quite a prayer. But no prophetic dreams, and few of the usual kind, came to her as she tossed, dozing badly and waking with a start at odd noises, or when one of the other women started sobbing in her blankets, inadequately muffled.

One of the injured Jokonans died in the night, apparently from a fever brought on by his wounds. His burial in the dawn was hasty and lacking in ceremony, but the Brother in His mercy took up his soul nonetheless, Ista thought; or at least, she felt no distraught ghost as she passed the sad shallow scraping in the soil. Her son Teidez had died of an infected wound. She watched for a moment when no Jokonan eyes were on her, and covertly made the Quadrene sign of blessing toward the gravesite, for whatever comfort it might bring to a dead boy lost in a foreign land.

The column did not return to the road, but pushed on north through the hilly wilderness. Necessarily, they went more slowly, and she could feel her captors growing more tense with every passing hour.

The mountains to their left dwindled; at some point toward evening, they crossed the unmarked boundary into the province of Caribastos. The wilderness grew patchy, forcing detours that swung wide and secretly around walled towns and villages. Streams grew fewer. The Jokonans stopped early to camp by such a brook, and to rest their horses. As a Chalionese border province with the Five Princedoms, Caribastos was better armed, its fortresses in better repair, and its people more alert for the endemic warfare. The Jokonan column would likely try to cross it under the cover of darkness. Three more marches, Ista estimated.

The valuable captive women were again set aside under the trees, brought food, left alone. Until the Ibran-speaking officer, flanked by two of his seniors, approached them in the level light of sunset. He had some papers in his hand, and an intent, disturbed expression on his face. He stopped before Ista, sitting on a log with her back to a tree. She kept silence, making him speak first.

"Greetings, *Sera*." He gave the title an odd emphasis in his mouth. Without another word, he handed her the papers.

It was a letter, half-finished, rumpled from a sojourn in a saddlebag. The handwriting was Foix's, strong and square. Ista's heart sank even before she read the salutation. It was addressed to Chancellor dy Cazaril, in Cardegoss. After a respectful and unmistakable listing of the great courtier's offices and ranks, it began:

"My Dearest Lord:
   "I continue my report as I may. We have left Casilchas behind and come at length to Vinyasca: there is to be a festival here tomorrow. I was glad to be shut of Casilchas. Learned dy Cabon has no notion of proper secrecy or even discretion. By the time he was

done blundering about, half the town knew full well that Sera dy Alejo was the dowager royina, and came to court her, which I think did not please her much.

"Upon further observation, I am coming to agree with you; Royina Ista is not mad in any usual sense, though there are times when she makes me feel very strange and foolish, as though she sees or senses or knows things I do not. She still spends long periods in silence, somewhere far off in her sad thoughts. I do not know why I ever thought women chattered. It would be some relief if she would talk more. As for whether her pilgrimage is the result of some god-driven impulse, as you feared after your long prayers in Cardegoss, I still cannot tell. But then, I rode beside towering miracles with you for weeks and never knew, so that shows nothing.

"The Daughter's festival should be a welcome diversion from my worries. I will continue this tomorrow."

The next day's date followed, and the neat writing recommenced.

"The festival went well"—there followed two paragraphs of droll description. *"Dy Cabon has gone off to get very drunk. He says it is to blot out bad dreams, though I think it is more likely to induce them. Ferda is not best pleased with him, but the divine has had closer to do with Royina Ista than any of us, so perhaps he needs it. At first I thought him a fat nervous idiot, as I wrote you before, but now I begin to wonder if the idiot may not be me.*

"I will write more on this head at our next stop, which is to be some dire hamlet in the hills where some saint came from. I'd be from there, too, if I had the choice. I should be able to dispatch this letter securely from the Daughter's house in Maradi, if we turn that way. I will try to suggest it. I do not think we

should venture any farther north, and I have run out of things to read."

The letter broke off there, with half a page left to fill. Foix had evidently been too shaken to add a report on the bear before the Jokonans had overtaken them next day.

Ista looked up. One Jokonan, dark-haired and younger, was watching her with a delighted, avaricious smile. The older, shorter one, who wore a green baldric more heavily encrusted with gold and who she thought was the expedition's commander, or at any rate surviving senior officer, frowned more thoughtfully. She read wider strategic considerations in his eyes, far more disturbing than mere greed. The Ibran-speaking officer looked apprehensive.

She made one more effort to clutch her torn incognito to her, futile as it seemed. She held out the paper in an indifferent hand. "What is this to me?"

Her translator took it back. "Indeed. Royina." He favored her with a bow in the Roknari court style, right hand sweeping down before him, thumb tucked in the palm: one part irony, one part wariness.

The commander said in Roknari, ~So, this is Royina Iselle's infamous mad mother, truly?~

~It seems so, my lord.~

~The largesse of the gods has fallen upon us,~ said the dark-haired one in a voice that vibrated with excitement. He made the Quadrene four-point sign of blessing, touching forehead, navel, groin, and heart, his thumb carefully folded inward. ~In one lucky blow, all of our pains are repaid and our fortunes are made.~

~I thought they kept her locked up in a castle. How is it they were so careless as to let her out to wander about on the roads like this?~ said the commander.

~Her guard could not have anticipated us here. *We* did not anticipate us here,~ the dark-haired one said.

The commander frowned at the letter, though it was plain he could not read more than one word in three of it without the help of his officer. ~This spy of their chancellor babbles too carelessly of the gods. It is impious.~

And it worries you. Good, Ista thought. It was hard to think of Foix as a spy. Although her estimate of his subtlety and wits rose another notch, for he'd not let fall the least hint of his mandate to report upon her. It made perfect sense in retrospect, of course. If he had been writing to anyone in the world but Lord dy Cazaril, it would have offended Ista deeply, but all of Chalion was in the chancellor's charge— and her own debt to the man was as boundless as the sea.

The commander cleared his throat, and continued to Ista in heavily accented Ibran, "You think you are god-touched, mad queen?"

Ista, sitting very still, allowed her lips to curve up just a trifle, enigmatic. "If you were god-touched, you would not have to ask. You would know the answer."

He jerked back, eyes narrowing. "Blasphemous Quintarian."

She gave him her best impassive stare. "Inquire of your god. I promise you shall meet Him soon. His mark is on your brow, and His arms are open to receive you."

The dark-haired one made a noise of inquiry; the Ibran-speaking officer translated her cool remark, an arrow shot at random from Ista's point of view. Although it hardly needed communion with the gods to make that prophecy, given the Jokonan raiders' precarious situation. The commander's lips thinned still more, but he made no further attempt to cross words with her. He at least seemed to grasp how much more perilous his retreat had grown due to her presence here as a prisoner. Liss's escape had been a greater disaster than he'd first guessed.

The women were moved up beside the commander's campsite, and two extra guards were assigned to watch them—to watch Ista, she had no doubt. This put paid to any dream of slipping away into the woods in darkness, in some moment of confusion or inattention.

The evening continued unsettled. A Jokonan soldier was dragged in and whipped for some infraction—attempted desertion, most likely. The senior officers sat close together and debated—sometimes breaking into angry oaths, too loud, then quickly muffled—about whether to hold the column together for mutual defense or break up into small groups and finish the flight to Jokona in better secrecy.

It wouldn't be long before some no longer waited for orders to break and run. Ista had spent part of the long ride, earlier, distracting her mind by counting the Jokonan numbers—the sum had come to some ninety-two men. It would be interesting to count again when the light returned tomorrow. The fewer their company, the less defense staying together would become. How long before the column was forced into splitting by default?

The Jokonan commander had every reason, internal and external, to push on as quickly as possible, and Ista was not surprised when she was wakened at midnight and lashed to a horse again. This time, however, she was moved up from the baggage train and put in hand of the Ibran-speaking officer himself. Two other riders flanked them closely. The column moved off in the darkness, stumbling and cursing.

She had at first expected provincial troops from Tolnoxo to come pelting up behind them on their too-visible trail, but they had certainly crossed out of that district many miles back. With every passing hour, the odds shifted: not attack from behind, but ambush from the front, grew likelier now. It made a certain tactical sense—let the Jokonans expend their energy transporting themselves to a battlefield picked by their enemies.

And yet . . . was it possible that Liss had still maintained Ista's incognito, only telling the authorities that a minor noblewoman on pilgrimage had been snapped up by these unwelcome transients? Ista could picture the provincar of Tolnoxo holding back just long enough to let the fleeing Jokonans become the problem of the provincar of Caribastos. Dy Cabon and Foix would not have permitted any such laggard approach, though—had they made it to safety? Were they still lost in the hills? Overcome or diverted by Foix's demon elemental, grown abruptly stronger in power, wit, and will as it feasted on that sharp mind?

Led on by who knew what reports from their scouts, the Jokonans left the thin woods and took to a dark road, putting several miles behind them at a fast trot. It was close to dawn when they turned in to a half-filled riverbed, the horses' hooves crunching loudly through the gravel and sand. If men had to speak, they rode close and leaned toward each other. Ista licked dry lips, stretching her aching back as much as she could with her hands tied in front of her. She had been left a length of cord between her lashed-together wrists and the saddle ring to which the rope was knotted, and if she lifted her hands and bent, she could just scratch her nose. It had been too long since she'd been permitted to drink, or eat, or piss, and the insides of her knees were rubbed raw.

And what if the column evaded ambush altogether, slipping over the border to Jokona after all? No question but that she would be handed over to Prince Sordso, taken to his palace, put up in comfort, nay, luxury, with attendants . . . many watchful attendants. Had she escaped one castle only to end up prisoner in another—and worse, made into a political lever against the few people she loved . . . ?

Blackness gave way to grayness, shadows to shapes to forms tinged with color, as the starry sky paled in the predawn. A low mist hung on the water and curled up over the flat banks, and the horses stirred it like milk as they passed. A little cliff, carved out by the riverlet, rose on their left, the reddish colors of its layers just beginning to glow.

A rock plunked into the dark water that slid along at the cliff's feet. Her flanking guard snapped his head around at the sudden noise.

A *thwack*—a crossbow bolt bloomed in his chest. He barely cried out as he fell into the gravel. A moment later, she felt the shock of his death like a lightning strike across her senses, dizzying her. Her horse was jerked abruptly into a trot, into a canter. All around her, men began to cry out, yell orders, curse. Answering shouts, and more arrows, rained down from above.

Five gods, let the attack be swift. Ferda and his men were in the greatest immediate peril, as the Jokonans might be inspired to slay their most dangerous prisoners at once before turning on the new enemy. Another death, and another, slashed across her inner senses like white fire even as her outer senses were thrown into a whirl of motion. She jerked her sore wrists back and forth in frustration against her bindings, but the knots had been tied tight and had failed to work loose even through the long night ride. Kicking her feet free of the stirrups and heaving off to one side in some mad effort to dismount would break her wrists before it broke their lashings; then she would merely be dragged.

A thundering of hooves, shouts, and screams rose from the front of the column; some bellowing cavalry charge down the river valley met the Jokonan van in a shock and clash of metal. Horses squealed and grunted and fell. More shouts came from the rear. The officer towing her yanked his reins up so sharply his horse reared. He stared around in panic.

The commander galloped toward him out of the melee, sword out, shouting in Roknari, motioning some others to follow. They swept up Ista and her captor and broke to the side, scrambling over the low bank there. The leading swordsmen cut their way through some crossbowmen in unfamiliar gray tabards who were running toward the fight. The half-dozen Jokonans and Ista burst past more riders and galloped wildly into the scrublands bordering the river's trees.

Ista's head was pounding, her vision blurred, alternately darkened and whited out with the stunning impacts of the deaths, so many souls in one place and moment violently uprooted from their bodies. She dared not pass out and fall—at this speed, her hands might well be torn off. All she could think was how unfair it had been to that poor soldier who'd been whipped last night, when his very commanders didn't hesitate to desert *him* . . .

She could see nothing but her horse's neck stretched before her, its ears laid back, and the hard ground whipping by below. Her foolish frightened horse didn't even have to be pulled, but raced the animal beside it until it threatened to become the leader, and her captor the follower. Their course bent away to the right in a wide curve. They slowed at last as they passed into a more rugged area, low hillocks clad in scattered woods at last hiding them from the view of any pursuit. Was there any pursuit?

The commander finally took time to sheathe his sword. He had not blooded it, Ista noted. He led the way into the wilderness, dodging and turning among the rocks and trees. Ista suspected he had no thought of choosing a route beyond confusing trackers, and would shortly be confused himself, again. Well, he could probably find north, and with so few followers to hide, perhaps that was all he needed to know. The woodlands thickened. They climbed a rise, descended a ravine. Ista tried to estimate how many miles they'd come from the point of attack. Five or six, at least.

She considered her own danger, as the horses picked their way slowly among the stones of the rivulet, and she caught her breath again. It was scarcely worse than before. She did not fear rape, or malicious torture, though she would doubt-less share whatever hardships the Jokonans did in their hasty flight. These officers had lost everything—their men, their equipment, their booty, their honor, even their way. But if only they could present Ista to him, the prince of Jokona would forgive their every disaster. She was their hope of re-demption. They would not let her go for money or threat, nor surrender her for life itself. So death by design did not await her at their hands, no; but death by misadventure or over-wrought bad judgment, oh, yes, very possible. It hardly seemed an improvement.

They wound down the ravine for over a mile. It deepened and the sides grew steeper, wooded and overhung, but in the distance she could see a hazy paleness. They rounded a turn to discover the ravine opening suddenly out onto a flat, bright little river.

Framed by the sides, blocking the outlet, stood a lone horseman. Ista's breath caught in a chill, or was that a thrill? The horse's charcoal-gray sides were heaving and wet, its nostrils round and red, but it pawed the ground and shifted nervously, its muscles bunching in readiness. The man did not seem out of breath at all.

His dark reddish hair was unbraided, cut short in the Chalionese style, and curled around his ears in tangled strands. A short-trimmed beard covered his jaw. He wore chain mail, heavy leather vambraces, a gray tabard worked with gold over all. The tabard was splashed with blood. His eyes flicked as he counted up the odds: narrowed, glittered.

He swung his sword wide in salute. The hand that tightened on the hilt was filthy and blood-crusted. For just a moment, the most thoroughly fey smile Ista had ever seen on a man's face glinted more brightly than the steel.

He clapped his heels to his horse's sides and charged forward.

8

IN THE FACE OF THIS THUNDERING CONVICTION, THE EX-hausted Jokonans hesitated a moment too long. The attack-ing horseman passed between the first two before they had their own swords half drawn, and left them both reeling from bloody slashes even as he bore down on the man tow-ing Ista. The man cried out and dodged, scrabbling for his weapon; with a deep hiss and hum, the horseman's heavy blade parted the taut lead line. Ista's freed horse shied back.

The gray horse reared beside her. The blade swung up, was somehow transferred to a left hand no less capable than the right, flashed around edge upward, and snaked between Ista's hands and the saddle to which they were tied. She scarcely had time to clench her fingers back out of the way before the razor-honed blade yanked up again, parting her bindings, and whipped past her face. The horseman shot her a grin over his shoulder as sharp-edged as his blade, yelled, and spurred his steed onward.

With a fierce gasp of satisfaction, Ista untangled her wrists from the hated cords and began to lean forward and grab for her reins. Her captor in turn wheeled his horse around, barging into hers and nearly unseating her, and beat her to the snatch. He dragged the reins over her horse's head. "Get away, get away!" she shrieked, beating at his clutching arm. With his own reins and his sword held awkwardly in his off hand, he was unbalanced, leaning far out; in a moment of terrified inspiration, she suddenly grabbed his sleeve instead, braced in her stirrups, and yanked as hard as she could. The startled Jokonan officer toppled out of his saddle and down to smack onto the stones of the rivulet.

She hoped her horse stepped on him as it danced aside, but she couldn't be sure. The smooth wet stones were coated with green algae, slippery underfoot; her mount heaved and jerked as it stumbled. Her reins now trailed, in danger of being trampled under her horse's front hooves. She leaned past her pommel, grabbed, missed, grabbed, caught them, let the dirty leather slide through her dirty fingers, and came upright and in control of her own movement for the first time in days. Swords were clanging and scraping. She looked around wildly.

One of the trailing soldiers was trying to beat their attacker back toward the others, while the second rider maneuvered for position to strike at the swordless side. The commander urged his horse closer to the melee, but his left hand, clumsily clutching his sword, was clapped over his right arm. Blood welled between his fingers and ran down his sleeve, making his reins slippery in his grasp. Another Jokonan soldier, who had been riding on the far side of the forward trio and so escaped the first onslaught, had managed to get his crossbow unshipped from his saddle ties and was frantically winding it while his horse sidled and snorted. A quarrel was clutched in his teeth. He spat the lethal bolt into his hand, slapped it into position, and began to raise his bow for aim. The target was moving, but the range was very short.

Ista bore no weapon . . . she aimed her horse, beating its sides with her spurless heels, and drove it into an unwilling trot across the rivulet. It bounded over the water and landed in a canter of sorts; she yanked its head around and forced it to carom into the crossbowman's steed. He cursed as the string twanged and his shot flew wide. He swung the heavy crossbow backhanded at her head, but missed as she ducked away.

The commander screamed in Roknari over his shoulder at the crossbowman, ~Take the woman! Get her to Prince Sordso!~ The gray horseman, leaving both rear guardsmen unhorsed and bleeding, pounded forward, guiding his horse with his knees, rising in his stirrups, readying a powerful two-handed swing. The luckless commander's last order was cut off abruptly, together with his head. Ista had a flashing view of falling body, spurting blood, shying horse, the glaring fire of an anguished soul ripped from its anchorage, and the dizzied thought, *Now do you believe my prophecies?*

And, even more dizzied: *Do I?*

Gleaming sword and gray horse both swung around without pause to charge the crossbowman, now frenziedly winding again. The sword passed from right to left hand once more, and its point dropped like a lance. The momentum of horse and swordsman was monstrous, and perfectly aligned; the sword's point smashed into the bowman's chest and pierced his chain mail, unseating him and carrying him over his horse's rump to pin his corpse to a tree behind him. His buffeted horse fell and scrambled up, flanks heaving as it plunged off. For a moment, the heavy sword was ripped from its deadly master's hand, but he spun his horse around immediately, lunged for the hilt, and yanked it free again. The dead Jokonan slumped to the ground, his blood watering the tree's roots.

Ista nearly fainted at the white whirl of screaming, distraught souls swirling around her. She clutched her pommel and forced herself to stay upright, open eyes denying the second sight. The worst gore now spread before her eyes was less terrifying than these unwanted visions. How many had died . . . ? The commander, the crossbowman . . . neither of the two rear guardsmen were going to stir again, either. One horse and rider were gone, their exit marked by a trail of blood. At the ravine's mouth, the translator-officer, his sword abandoned in the green-and-red muck, was scrambling up on a loose horse. He jerked it around and galloped downstream without looking back.

Not even breathing heavily, blood dripping from his sword's lowered tip, the gray horseman frowned after him for a moment, then turned and looked in concern at Ista. He nudged his horse toward hers.

"My lady, are you all right?"

"I'm . . . uninjured," she gasped back. The ghostly visions were fading like the lingering dazzlement in eyes that had stared too directly at the sun.

"Good." His grin flashed again, exhilarated—battle-drunk? His wits were clearly unimpaired by fear, but also by anything resembling good sense. Sensible men didn't charge six desperate enemy soldiers by themselves.

"We saw you carried off," he continued. "We split up to quarter the woods for you; I thought you must come out this way." His face turned as he checked the ravine's rim for any sign of further threatening motion; his eyes narrowed in satisfaction at finding none. He wiped his sword clean upon his befouled tabard, raised it in a brief salute to her, and sheathed it with a satisfied click. "May I know what lady I have the honor and pleasure of addressing?"

"I . . ." Ista hesitated. "I am the Sera dy Ajelo, cousin to the provincar of Baocia."

"Hm." His brows drew down. "I'm Porifors." He glanced toward the ravine's bright mouth. "I must find my men."

Ista flexed her hands. She hardly dared touch her darkly lacerated wrists, crusted, bleeding, and abraded. "And I mine, but I have been tied to this fool of a horse since midnight last night. Without rest or food or water, which first seemed cruel but now seems kind. If you would cap your morning's heroism, do me the kindness of guarding this animal and my modesty while I find a bush." She glanced doubtfully up the ravine. "Or a rock, or whatever. Although I doubt my horse has any more desire to go another step than I do."

"Ah," he said, in a tone of amused enlightenment. "But of course, Sera."

He swung lightly off his warhorse and reached for her reins. His smile faded at the sight of her wrists. She dismounted like a sack of grain falling; strong hands caught her. They left smudged red prints upon her tunic. He held her upright a moment to be sure she had control of her feet.

His smile vanished altogether as he looked her up and down. "There is a deal of blood on your skirts."

She followed his glance. The folds of her split skirt were mottled with patches of blood, dried and fresh, at the knees. That last gallop had flayed her raw skin to shreds. "Saddle sores. Trivial hurts, for all that they are mine."

His brows rose. "What do you call severe, then?"

She staggered away past the beheaded commander. "That."

His head tilted, conceding the point.

She tottered beyond the bodies and up the ravine a short way to find some rocks *with* bushes. She returned to find him kneeling by the streamlet. He smiled and offered her something on a leaf; she squinted, and recognized it after a bewildered moment as a slice of strong tallow soap.

"*Oh*," she breathed. It was all she could do not to burst into tears. She fell to her knees and washed her hands beneath a chill freshet that spurted over the rocks, then, more carefully, her hurt wrists. She drank then from her cupped hands, handful after dripping handful.

He laid a small linen-wrapped packet on a flat stone and opened it to reveal a pile of clean rags cut for bandages. From his saddlebag, presumably; the Jokonans had used up all such preparations of their own. "Sera, I fear that I must ask* you to ride some distance farther. Better you should clean and pad your knees first, eh?"

"Oh. Yes. My thanks, sir." She sat on a rock, removed her boots for the first time in recent memory, and carefully rolled up one skirt leg, peeling it away from the crusted sores where it had stuck and dried. He hovered, cleaned hands opening to help, but closed them again as she stoically carried on. The soap next, painful but relieving. And revealing. The deep scarlet abrasions oozed yellow fluid.

"Those will be a week, healing," he remarked.

"Probably."

As a horse soldier, he had no doubt treated saddle sores before, and diagnosed with authority. He watched a moment more as if to be sure she was going to be all right, stretched his fingers and rubbed his face, then rose and went to turn over the bodies.

His examination was methodical, and not for looting, for he barely glanced at the rings or pins or purses the corpses yielded. Any papers he happened upon, however, he examined and folded carefully away in his tunic. This Porifors—or dy Porifors; he had not said if it was first name or last—was an officer, no question, and one with a steady head: some military vassal of the provincar of Caribastos, or trained up like such a battle lord. Foix's letter, it appeared, had either been left with the deserted column or gone with one of the escapees.

"Can you tell me, Sera, what were the other prisoners in the Jokonan train?"

"Few, the gods be thanked. Six women from Ibra, and seven men, that the Jokonans judged valuable enough to drag over the mountains with them. And twelve, no, eleven guardsmen of the Daughter's Order, who had undertaken to convey my pilgrimage, captured by the Jokonan column these . . . two days back." Only two days? "I have good hope that one of my guardsmen and some others from my party escaped back in Tolnoxo, when we were first overtaken."

"You were the only lady of Chalion among those taken?" His brow wrinkled further.

She nodded shortly, and tried to think of something useful to say to this intent officer. "These raiders rode under the seal of Prince Sordso, for they had tally officers accounting the prince's fifth. They came up through Ibra, and pillaged the town of Rauma there, then escaped over the passes when the march of Rauma followed hotly. The one you beheaded over there"—she nodded toward the sad corpse—"was the senior, though I do not believe he was the original commander. As of yesterday, their numbers were about ninety-two, though some may have deserted in the night before they ran afoul of your ambush."

"Tolnoxo . . ." He dusted his hands, rose from the last corpse, and strolled over to examine her progress. She was just tying strips around the pad on her second knee. His meticulous courtesy somehow made her more, not less, conscious of the fact that she was alone with a strange man. "No wonder. You are now less than thirty miles from the border of Jokona. That column covered nearly a hundred miles, these past two days."

"They were pushing. They were afraid." She glanced around the scene. Iridescent green flies were beginning to gather, an ugly buzzing in the damp shade. "Not afraid enough to stay home in the first place, unfortunately."

His lips twisted in a sour smile. "Perhaps next time their fear will have improved." He scratched his beard. It was not the reddish dark of his hair, but lighter, shot with gray. "Your first battle, Sera?"

"Of this sort, yes." She tied off the last strip and yanked the knot tight.

"Thank you for jostling the fellow with the crossbow. A timely blow, that."

He'd noticed? Five gods. She'd thought him fully occupied. "You are most welcome."

"You keep your wits about you, I see."

"I know." She glanced up at his surprised snort. She said unsteadily, "If you are too kind to me, I shall start to weep, and then we shall be undone."

He looked a little taken aback, but then nodded. "Cruel lady, to forbid me to be kind! So it shall be. We must ride now, to a safer place to lie up. Swiftly and with care, for I think yours were not the only stragglers and survivors. I hope we may meet with some of my own, first." He frowned around. "I'll send them back to collect these, and their horses."

She glanced at the silent scene. The bodies lay sprawled; none of the weary horses had wandered far. The shrieking visions had faded altogether—she did not say, *thank the gods*—but the ravine still seemed to reverberate with woe. She couldn't wait to escape it.

He helped her to her feet; she nodded gratefully. With every minute of rest, her body seemed to be seizing up. Much more, and she wouldn't be able to walk *or* ride.

Or mount. His attempt to give her a leg up failed when she gasped with pain; then he simply took her about the waist and lifted her. She wasn't a tall woman, but neither was she the willow-whip she'd been at eighteen. Unfair—the man had to be as old as she was, but his strength was clearly unimpaired by whatever years had grayed his beard. Of course, patrolling these marches, he would be in constant training. He swung up on his own tall horse with easy grace. Ista thought the beautiful dark-dappled animal must be of the same breed as Liss's leggy bay, lean-muscled and bred to speed and endurance.

He led the way to the riverbed and turned upstream. She could see his own horse's prints in the gravel and sand, coming down, but, reassuringly, no others. After a few minutes' ride, the prints turned to—or rather, from—the thin woods lining the river. The two of them continued on beside the flowing water. Her tired horse's steps were short and stiff; only the presence of the other horse, she thought, kept it moving. *Just like me.*

She studied her rescuer in this better light. Like his horse and sword, the rest of his gear was of the finest quality, but forbore gaudy jeweled studs or metallic inlay. Not a poor officer, then, but serious about his business. To survive twenty years on this frontier, as his beard and the weathering of his face suggested he must have, a man had to be paying close attention to what he was doing.

That face drew her eyes. Not a boy's face, fresh and full-blooded like Ferda's or Foix's, nor an aging man's face, sagging like dy Ferrej's, but a face in the full strength of its maturity. Perfectly balanced on the apogee of its life. Pale, though, for all his obvious vigor. Perhaps the past winter in Caribastos had been unusually dreary.

A stunning first impression was not the same thing as love at first sight. But surely it was an invitation to consider the matter.

What of her and love, after all? At eighteen, she had been lifted up by Lord dy Lutez into the bright, easy, poisoned triumph of her high marriage to Roya Ias. It had spiraled down into the long, dark fog of her widowhood and the curse, blighting mind and heart both. The entire center of her life was a blackened waste, its long years not to be recovered nor replaced. She'd had neither the life nor the learning from it that other women her age could be assumed to possess.

For all the relentless idealism surrounding virginity, fidelity, and celibacy—for women—Ista had known plenty of ladies of rank in Ias's court who had taken lovers, openly or in secret. She had only the vaguest idea how they'd gone about it. Such carryings-on hadn't happened in the Dowager Provincara's minor court in Valenda, of course; the old lady had held neither tolerance for the nonsense nor, indeed, kept any such nonsensical young persons about her, with the sole exception of her embarrassing mad daughter Ista. In Ista's two trips to Cardegoss since the destruction of the curse, in the old Provincara's train for Iselle's coronation and to visit little Isara last autumn, she had fairly waded through courtiers, to be sure. But it had seemed to her that she'd read not desire, but merely avarice in their eyes. They'd wanted the royina's favors, not Ista's love. Not that Ista felt love. Ista felt nothing, on the whole, she decided.

The past three days of numb terror excepted, perhaps. Yet even that fear had seemed to lie on the other side of some sheet of glass, in her mind.

Still—she glanced sideways—he was a striking man. For an hour yet, she might still be modest Ista dy Ajelo, who could dream of love with a handsome officer. When the ride was done, the dream would be over.

"You are very silent, lady."

Ista cleared her throat. "My wits were wandering. I am stupid with fatigue, I expect." They had not reached safety yet, but when they did, she imagined she would fall like a tree. "You must have been up all night as well, preparing that most splendid reception."

He smiled at that, but said only, "I have little need of sleep, these days. I'll take some rest at noon."

His eyes, returning her study, disturbed her with their concentration. He looked as though she presented some deep quandary or puzzle to him. She looked away, discomfited, and so was first to spot the object floating down the stream.

"A body." She nodded toward it. "Is this the same river my Jokonan column was riding down, then?"

"Yes, it curves around here . . ." He forced his horse out into the rippling water, belly deep, leaned over, and grabbed the corpse by the arm to drag it sloshing up on the sand. It was not clad in Daughter's blue, Ista saw with relief. Just another ill-fated young soldier, who would grow no older now.

The officer grimaced down at it. "Lead scout, it appears. I'm tempted to leave him to ride the river as courier down to Jokona. But there will doubtless be others, more voluble, to carry the news. There always are. He can be collected with the rest." He abandoned the sodden thing and clucked his horse onward. "Their column had to turn this way, to avoid both the stronghold of Oby and the screen of Castle Porifors. Which was originally designed to look south, not north, after all. Better they should have split up and crept past us in twos and threes; they'd have lost some that way, but not all. They were too tempted by the shortest route."

"And the surest, if they knew the river went to Jokona. They seemed to have trouble with their directions. I don't think this line of retreat was in their original plan."

His eye glinted with satisfaction. "My b . . . best advisor

always said it must be so, in such a case. He was right as usual. We camped upon this river last night, therefore, and took our ease while the Jokonans delivered themselves to us. Well, except for our scouts, who wore out a few horses keeping contact."

"Is it much farther to your camp? I think this poor horse is almost done." Her animal seemed to stumble every five steps. "It is my own, and I don't wish to lame it worse."

"Yes, we could almost have tracked these Jokonans just by the ruined horses they abandoned in their wake." He shook his head in soldierly censure. His own elegant mount, for all its hard use that morning, appeared superbly cared for. A slight smile flitted across his face. "Let us by all means relieve your horse."

He shifted his horse up to her side, dropped his reins on its withers, reached across, plucked her from her saddle, and balanced her sideways upon his lap; Ista choked back an undignified yelp of protest. He did not follow up this startling move with any attempt to steal a kiss or other shameless familiarity, but merely reached around her to take up his reins with one hand and catch up her horse's reins to tow it along with the other. Leaving her to wind her arms around *him* for security. Gingerly, she did so.

His cool strength was almost shocking, in this proximity. He did not reek of dried sweat, as she had expected—she had no doubt she stank worse herself, just now. The congealing blood, stiffening in dark patches on his gray tabard, had little odor as yet, for all that a chill of death seemed to hang about him. She rested in the curve of his arm away from the dampest stains, intensely conscious of the weight of her thighs across his. She had not relaxed in the circle of a man's arms for . . . for as long as she could remember, and she did not do so now. Limp exhaustion was not the same thing as relaxation.

He dropped his face to the top of her head; it seemed to her that he inhaled the scent of her hair. She trembled slightly.

He murmured in a voice of concern, "Now, I'm only being kind to your horse, mind you."

Ista snorted softly, and felt his body's tension slacken a trifle at the reassurance of her half laugh. It was wonderful to imagine letting go one's guard, if only for a moment. To pretend that safety was something another could give as a gift. It could only be for a few more moments; he would certainly not have blocked his sword arm with her in this way if they weren't nearly within sight of his camp. But presumably, as long as she pretended, so would he. So she clung, and let herself be rocked along, her eyelids drooping.

Hoofbeats on gravel, a shout; she knew it was friends before she even looked up, for no new tautness flowed into his easy embrace. *Your dream is done. Time to wake up.* She sighed.

"My lord!" cried a horseman. One of a trio in gray tabards, she saw through her eyelashes, trotting down the river's side in the sunny midmorning. The mail-clad soldiers broke into a canter and pulled up around them in a laughing mob. "You have her!" the speaker continued. "I might have known."

Her rescuer's voice was amused, and possibly a trifle smug. "I should think you might."

She considered the heroic picture they presented atop the dappled warhorse, and what a fine show it made for this lord's men. It would be gossiped about tonight in his troop, no doubt. And so a commander maintained his mystique—she did not begrudge him the calculation, if calculation it was. If, as a man, he had also obtained some bonus of pleasure from this courtly cuddle of her exhausted self, well, she could not begrudge that either.

The men vented a spate of brief reports: of prisoners taken, of the area secured, of wounded treated or transported to the nearest town in carts, of bodies counted.

"We're not done rounding up all who fled, then," said their commander. "Though I begin to doubt the accuracy of our alarms from my Lord dy Tolnoxo. We seem to have only ninety Jokonans to account for, not two hundred as he claimed. You'll find five more dead ones downstream. One that I pulled from the stream about three miles down, I think must have fallen when we first struck their van. Four more near the mouth of a ravine a mile or so farther, where I caught up with them attempting to make off with this lady. Take some men and collect them and their horses and gear, and put them with the rest, to be listed." He tossed the reins of Ista's horse to one of the men. "See carefully to this beast—it belongs to the Sera, here. Bring its gear to my tent. I'll be found there for a little. Have any who were involved in delivering the captives from the baggage train report to me at once. I'll ride to inspect the wounded and prisoners in the afternoon."

Ista roused herself to ask the soldier, "There were some men of the Daughter's Order, taken prisoner by the Jokonans—are they safe?"

"Yes, I saw several such."

"How many?" she asked urgently.

"I don't know exactly, my lady—there are some in the camp." He jerked his head upstream.

"You shall be reunited with them in a moment, and have all their accounts of the morning's business," her rescuer soothed her. He exchanged salutes with his men, and they all departed in their several new directions.

"Whose are these excellent soldiers?" asked Ista.

"Mine, happily," he replied. "Ah, my apologies; I failed to introduce myself fully in all my haste. Arhys dy Lutez, March of Porifors, at your service, Sera. Castle Porifors guards all the sharp point of Chalion between Jokona and Ibra, and its men are the honed edge of that blade. Five gods be thanked, a somewhat easier task now that Ibra is made all peaceful in the Royina Iselle's arms."

She froze in his gentle grip. "Dy Lutez?" she repeated, aghast. "Are you any relation to . . . ?"

He stiffened in turn; his cheerful amiability cooled. But his suddenly studied voice remained light. "The great chancellor and traitor, Arvol dy Lutez? My father."

He was not either of dy Lutez's two principal heirs, sons

of the chancellor's first marriage who had trailed after him at court in Ista's time. The famous courtier's three acknowledged bastards had all been girls, disposed to high and lucrative marriages long ago. Dy Lutez had been twice a widower by the time Ista had first met him, his second wife already a decade dead. This Arhys must be a son of that second wife, then. The one whom dy Lutez, in the prime of his manhood, had abandoned at her country estates so that he might go haring off after Ias, at court or in the field, unimpeded. A northern heiress, yes, Ista recalled that much.

His voice went a little harsh. "Does it startle you that a traitor's son serves Chalion well?"

"Not at all." She turned her eyes up to trace the bones of his face, so close to her view. Arhys must take something in his fine chin and straight nose from his mother, but the appalling energy of the man was all dy Lutez. "He was a great man. You have . . . something of the look of him."

His brows shot up; he turned his head around to look at her in an entirely new way, a muffled, eager urgency. She had not realized how masked he was, until it slipped. "Truly? You once met him? To look at?"

"What, had not you?"

"Not to remember. My mother had a painting, but it was bad." He frowned. "I was almost old enough to be brought to court at Cardegoss, when he . . . died. I *was* old enough. But . . . perhaps it was better so." The eagerness cloaked itself, settled back to its secret lair. His brief smile was faintly embarrassed. A mature man of forty, pretending not to care for the grief of a young man of twenty. Ista took back her belief in her own numbness, for this inadvertent flash of self-revelation wrenched like a knife in her stomach.

They rounded a bend in the river to discover its inward curve lapping a meadow edged with woods. The grass was trampled and littered with the detritus of a camp half-struck, dead campfires and scattered gear. At distant horse lines strung between trees, a few men saddled up mounts or tied baggage to mules. Men packed, men sat, a few men slept on blankets or on the bare ground. Some officers' tents sheltered beneath a grove on the meadow's far side.

A dozen men rushed dy Lutez as soon as he came in view, cheering, shouting greetings and questions, pelting him with news and demanding orders. A familiar figure in blue ran stiffly in their wake.

"Ah! Ah! She is spared!" Ferda dy Gura cried joyously. "*We* are spared!"

He looked as though he had been dragged backward through thorn scrub for about a mile, dirty, exhausted, and pale with fatigue, but hale: no bandages, no blood, limping no worse than his own saddle soreness and a few bruises might account for. Ista's heart melted with relief.

"Royina!" he cried. "Thank the gods, one and five! Praise the Daughter of Spring! I was sure the Jokonans had snatched you away at the last! I've all who can still ride out with the march of Porifors's men, searching for you—"

"Our company, Ferda—were any hurt?" Ista struggled upright, a hand upon the march's arm, as Ferda pushed his way up to the dappled horse's shoulder.

He ran a hand through his sweat-stiff hair. "One was hit in the thigh by a quarrel from the march's men, bad luck, one had his leg broken when his horse fell on him. I set two to tend them, while we wait for the physicians to get free of the worse hurt fellows. The rest are as well as might be. Me, too, now that my heart isn't being plowed through the dirt in terror for you."

Arhys dy Lutez had grown still as stone, beneath her. "Royina?" he echoed. "*This* is Dowager Royina Ista?"

Ferda looked up, grinning. "Aye, sir? If you are her rescuer, I shall kiss your hands and feet! We were in agony when we counted the women captives and found her gone."

The march stared at Ista as though she had transmuted into some startling creature of myth before his eyes. *Perhaps I have.* Which of the several versions of the death of his father at Roya Ias's hands had he heard? Which lie did he believe true?

"My apologies, March," said Ista, with a crispness she did not feel. "The Sera dy Ajelo was my chosen incognito, for humility's sake on my pilgrimage, but for safety's sake thereafter." Not that it had worked. "But now I am delivered by your bravery, I can dare to be Ista dy Chalion once more."

"Well," he said after a moment. "Dy Tolnoxo wasn't wrong about everything after all. What a surprise."

She glanced up through her lashes. The mask was back, now, tied tight. The march let her down very carefully into Ferda's upreaching arms.

9

ISTA CLUNG TO FERDA'S ELBOW AS HE ESCORTED HER across the trampled greensward and poured out an excited account of the dawn's battle as witnessed from somewhat farther forward in the column. She did not follow one sentence in three, though she gathered he was greatly enamored of Arhys dy Lutez's warcraft. The meadow wavered before her gaze. Her head seemed poorly attached, and not always the same size. Her *eyes* throbbed, and as for her legs . . .

"Ferda," she interrupted gently.

"Yes, Royina?"

"I want . . . a piece of bread and a bedroll."

"This rough camp is no place for your repose—"

"Any bread. Any bedroll."

"There may be some women I can find for your attendants, but they are not what you are used to—"

"Your bedroll would do."

"Royina, I—"

"If you do not give me a bedroll at once, I am going to sit down on the ground right here and start to cry. Now."

This threat, delivered in a dead-level tone, seemed to get through at last; at least, he stopped worrying about all the things he thought she ought to have, that weren't here, and provided what she asked for, which was. He led her to the officers' tents by the trees, picked one apparently at random, poked his head inside, and ushered her within. It was stuffy and warm, and smelled of mildew, strange men, leather, horses, and oil for blades and mail. There was a bedroll. She lay down on it, boots, bloody skirts, and all.

Ferda returned in a few minutes with a piece of brown bread. She held up one hand and gave a vague wave; he pressed the morsel into it. She gnawed it sleepily. When the tent's owner returned . . . someone else could deal with him. Foix could have convinced him that this blatant theft was an honor to be devoutly treasured, she had no doubt. Ferda might do almost as well. She was worried about Foix and dy Cabon. Were they still afoot in the wilderness? Liss had clearly escaped and reached Maradi, but what had she done after that? Had they found each other yet? And . . . and . . .

❧

She pulled open gluey eyes and stared upward. Points of light leaked through the tent fabric's rough weave, winking as a faint breeze moved the leaves overhead. Her body felt beaten, and her head ached. A half-chewed morsel of bread lay where it had fallen from her hand. Afternoon? By the evidence of the light and her bladder, no later.

An apprehensive female voice whispered, "Lady? Are you awake?"

She groaned and rolled over to find that Ferda, or someone, had found attendants for her after all. Two rough-looking camp followers and a clean woman in the Mother's green of a medical acolyte awaited her wakening. The acolyte, it transpired, had been conscripted from the nearest town by one of the march's couriers. They shortly proved to have more practical skills among them than the whole troop of highborn ladies back in Valenda who had formerly plagued Ista with their services.

Fully half of her own clothes had been retrieved from the Roknari spoils, presumably by Ferda or one of his men, and set in a pile on the opposite bedroll. Abundant wash water, tooth-sticks and astringent herb paste, medications and new bandages, a thorough brushing and replaiting of her feral hair, nearly clean garments—when Ista limped from the tent into the early-evening light on the acolyte's arm, she felt, if not royal, at least womanly again.

The camp was quiet, though not deserted; small groups of men came and went on mysterious postbattle errands. No one, it appeared, wished to load her aboard another horse at once, which saved her a fit of hysterics for which she had no stamina. She could only be grateful. Some cleaned-up, if exhausted-looking, men of her guard now had their own campfire in the grove, and had borrowed camp followers. She was invited to a seat upon an upturned log, hastily chopped into the form of a chair and thoughtfully padded with folded blankets. Upon this makeshift throne she idly watched a dinner being prepared for her company. She dispatched the acolyte to offer her medical services to any of her men who might still have unattended hurts; the woman returned hearteningly soon. At length, Ferda appeared. He, too, seemed to have snatched some sleep, to Ista's relief, although clearly not enough.

As aromatic smoke rose from the fire, Arhys dy Lutez rode in accompanied by a dozen officers and guards. He approached her and offered a bow that would not have been out of place in a noble's palace in Cardegoss. He inquired politely after her treatment, accepting her assurances of its excellence rather doubtfully.

"In Cardegoss, in the summer, the court ladies frequently made picnics in the forest, and pretended to rustic delights," she told him. "It was quite fashionable to dine upon a tapestry spread under a grove much like this, in weather equally fine." Minus the wounded men and strewn battle gear, granted.

He smiled. "I hope we may soon do better by you. I have

a few matters to attend to here, and reports to dispatch to my lord the provincar of Caribastos. But by tomorrow morning our road should be safe and clear of Jokonan stragglers. It is my desire and honor to welcome you to the hospitality of Castle Porifors, until your hurts and weariness are healed and your men restored, and then to lend you escort where you will."

Her lips pursed, considering this. She felt the solicitous weight of his stare upon her. "Is Porifors the closest haven?"

"It is the strongest hold. There are villages and towns that lie closer, but their walls are lesser, and they are, frankly, but humble places. A half a day's ride more for you, no worse, and that in easy stages, I promise. And"—a smile flickered across his lips, a flash of charm and warmth—"I confess, it is my home; I should be pleased and proud to show it to you."

Ista ignored her heart, melting like wax in a candle flame. Yet taking up his society must lead to further speech with him, which must lead to . . . what? Ferda, she noticed, was watching her with fervent hope. The young officer-dedicat breathed an open sigh of satisfaction when she said, "Thank you, my lord. We shall be pleased for the rest and refuge." She added after a moment, "Perhaps the lost members of our company may find us there, if we tarry a time. When you write to dy Caribastos, would you ask him to pass the word that we seek them anxiously, and to speed them there if—when—they are found?"

"Certainly, Royina."

Ferda whispered to her, "And if you are lodged in a secure fortress, then I can seek them, too."

"Perhaps," she murmured back. "Let us reach it, first."

At Ferda's earnest invitation, the march lingered by their fire, as the sun went down and the camp followers, thrown on their mettle by Ista's royal presence, produced a surprisingly complex meal. Ista had not known that one could bake bread, redolent with herbs, garlic, and onions, in a pan over an open fire. Arhys refused the food, saying he had already eaten, but accepted a mug of watered wine, or rather, water tinted with a splash of wine.

He excused himself early. Ista could see the glow from the candles in his tent as he scribbled at whatever campaign desk his servants carried along on such forays, receiving rolls of the dead and wounded and captured, dispatching orders and reports and letters to be carried away in the dark by swift riders. She saw one of the captured Jokonan tally officers marched in for a long interview. When she retired to her purloined tent again, now cleared of its owner's gear and strewn with scented herbs, Arhys's working lights still shone through his tent walls, like a lantern in the long night.

✦

Their departure was delayed in the morning by matters of Arhys's troop and delegations from the town where he had sent the Jokonan prisoners, which she could see annoyed him, but at last the tents were folded. A fresh horse of the march's company was presented to her, a pretty white gelding, clad in her own saddle and trappings. She had noted the young soldier who brought it to her riding it about the meadow earlier, presumably to take its edge off and be certain it was suitable for a lady to ride. A tired, aging lady. She would have preferred a staircase to board it, but made do with the soldier's nervous leg up.

"I hope he will do for you, Royina," said the young man, ducking his head. "I picked him out myself. We miss our master of horse, since he has fallen ill—my lord tries to do two men's tasks. But all will be easier when we return to Porifors."

"I'm sure it will."

It was a much-expanded company that clambered out of the river valley and across the dry countryside. Forty horsemen in the gray tabards of Porifors rode ahead, mail-clad and armed, before Ista and Ferda's reduced troop. A long train of baggage mules and servants followed after, then another twenty men for rear guard. They struck a track, then turned north upon a greater road. Scouts came and went, ahead and along the fringes, to exchange brief but apparently reassuring reports with Arhys's alert officers.

They settled down to a steady plod through the warm morning. At length, Arhys won free of the plucking demands of his command long enough to drop back and ride by her side.

He saluted her with good cheer, now that he had his little army headed in the preferred direction. "Royina. I trust you slept well, and that this last ride is bearable?"

"Yes, I'll do. Though I believe I would mutiny at a trot."

He chuckled. "None shall ask it of you, then. We'll rest a space at noon, and come to Porifors in time for a rather better dinner than I could offer you last night."

"Then we shall dine very well indeed. I look forward to it." The courtesies fell automatically from her lips. But by the tension in his smile, he wanted more than an exchange of pleasantries.

"I feel I must apologize for not recognizing you yesterday," he continued. "The courier from Tolnoxo who brought warning of the column told us a wild tale that you were among the taken, but all his reports were very garbled. Yet when I saw the Jokonan officers hustling a woman away, I thought they might be true after all. Then your alias confused me anew."

"You owe me no apology. I was overcautious, as it proved."

"Not at all. I . . . never thought to meet you. In the flesh."

"I must say, I am quite glad you did. Or I should have woken up someplace unpleasant in Jokona this morning."

He smiled briefly and glanced across at Ferda, riding on Ista's other side as a contented audience to all this noble speech. Curiosity wrestled with dread in Ista's stomach, and won. She took the hint and waved Ferda out of earshot. "My good dedicat, leave us a little." With a disappointed look, he tightened his reins and dropped behind. She and Arhys were left riding together side by side, pearl-white horse and charcoal-gray, an elegant picture and as nice a balance between private and proper as could likely be obtained. She felt a pang of loneliness for Liss, and wondered where the girl was now. Carrying on competently, no doubt.

Arhys regarded her through slightly lidded eyes, as though he contemplated enigmas. "I should have known at once. I've felt a gravity in your presence from the moment I first saw you. And yet you did not look like what I thought bright Ista should have been."

If this was the start of some suave dalliance, she was too tired to deal with it. If it was something else . . . she was *much* too tired. She finally managed, "How did you imagine me?"

He waved vaguely. "Taller. Eyes more blue. Hair more pale—honeyed gold, the court poets said."

"Court poets are paid to lie like fools, but yes, it was lighter in my youth. The eyes are the same. They see more clearly now, perhaps."

"I did not picture eyes the color of winter rain, nor hair the shade of winter fields. I wondered if your long grief brought you to this sad season."

"No, I was always a dull dab of a thing," she tossed off. He did not laugh. It would have helped. "I grant you, age has improved nothing but my wits." *And even they are suspect.*

"Royina—if you can bear to—can you tell me something of my father?"

Alas, I didn't think this interest was all for my rain-colored, weeping eyes. "What is there to say that all men do not know? Arvol dy Lutez was good at all things to which he turned his hand. Sword, horse, music, verse, war, government . . . If his brilliance had any flaw, it was in his very versatility, which stole away the sustained effort that would . . ." She cut off her words, but the thought flowed on. Dy Lutez's many great starts, she realized at this distance, had not been matched by nearly as many great finishes. Fragrant in the flower, green and cankered in the fruit . . . *Yes. I should have realized it then, even then. Or, if my girl's judgment was too weak, where was that of the gods, who have no such excuse?* "He was the delight of every eye that fell upon him." *Except mine.*

Arhys stared down at his horse's withers. "Not dull," he said after a moment. "I have seen more beautiful women, but you anchor my eye . . . I cannot explain it."

A suave courtier, she decided, would never commit the blunder of admitting the existence of women more lovely than his current auditor, and would have gone on to explain himself at poetic length. Mere dalliance might be dismissed with a smile. Arhys's remarks were considerably more worrisome, taken in earnest.

He continued, "I begin to understand why my father would risk his life for your love."

Ista, with regret, forbore to scream. "Lord Arhys. Stop."

He glanced across at her, startled, then realized she did not mean halt his horse. "Royina?"

"I see the romantic rumors penetrated all the way to Caribastos. But there is no lapse in his exquisite taste to explain away, for Arvol dy Lutez was never my lover."

Taken thoroughly aback, he digested her words for a moment. At last he offered cautiously, "I suppose . . . you've no reason, now, to tell other than the truth."

"I never told other than the truth. The clapping iron tongues of rumor and slander were not mine. I was silent, mostly." And any less at fault, therefore? Hardly.

His forehead wrinkled as he worked this through. "Did Roya Ias not believe your protestations of innocence?"

Ista rubbed her brow. "I see we must back up a little. What have you imagined to be the truth of those fatal events, all these years?"

He frowned uneasily. "I believed . . . I concluded . . . my father was tortured to confess his fault in loving you. And when, to protect you or his honor, he would not speak, the inquisitors went too far in their duress, and he died in accident there in the Zangre's dungeons. The charges of peculation and secret dealings with the roya of Brajar were got up to cloak Ias's guilt, afterward. A truth tacitly admitted by Ias when the dy Lutez legacy was not attaindered, as real traitors' estates are, but let to flow to his heirs."

"You are shrewd," she remarked. And about three-quarters correct. He lacked only the secret core of the events. "Dy Lutez was very nearly as brave as that, indeed. It is as good a tale as any, and better than most."

His gaze flicked to her. "I have offended you, lady. My abject pardon."

She sought better control of her tone. She desperately wanted him to know that she had not been his father's lover. And why? What did it matter, at this late hour? His beliefs about dy Lutez, the father who, as far as she could tell, had ignored him utterly, were noble and romantic, and why should she take that heart's lone legacy from him now?

She studied his tall, easy power from the corner of her eye. Well, *that* question answered itself, didn't it?

It was pointless to replace his bright lie with some other lie. But to explain the truth, in all its dark complexity—and complicity—could hardly advance any secret romantic dream of hers.

Perhaps, when she knew him better, she might dare to tell all. *What, that his father was drowned by my word? How well will I have to know him for that?*

She took a long breath. "Your father was not a traitor, in bed or out of it. He was as courageous and noble a man as ever served Chalion. It took a task beyond all human fortitude to break him." Failure, at the sticking point. Failure wasn't treason, even if the rubble it left in its wake was every bit as dire.

"Lady, you bewilder me."

Her nerve broke. *Even as dy Lutez's did, aye?* "It is a state secret, and Ias died before ever releasing me from my sworn silence. I promised I would never tell a living soul. I can say no more, except to assure you that you need bear your father's name with no shame."

"Oh," he echoed, his brows drawing down. "A state secret. Oh."

And the poor man *accepted* that, dear gods. She wanted to shriek. *Gods, why have you brought me here? Have I not been punished enough? Does this amuse you?*

She spoke with a lightness she did not feel. "But enough of the dead past. Tell me of the breathing now. Tell me more about yourself." A conversational gambit that should serve for the rest of their ride; she would not have to bestir herself for more than an occasional noise of interest, if he was like most courtiers she had known.

He shrugged. "There's not that much to tell. I was born in this province, and have lived here all my life. I have ridden in its defense since boyhood. My mother died when we— when I was about twelve. I was raised by her faithful—by other relatives, and brought up to a soldier's trade by need. Porifors actually came to me through my mother, confirmed to me by the provincar when I grew old enough to hold it. My father's great possessions went mostly to his elder family, though a few estates here in Caribastos came to me by the sheer logic of it—I believe there was some trading among the executors, but it was all over my head at the time." He fell silent.

Finished, apparently. His father, brilliant raconteur as he had been, could have held a table enthralled for an evening with no more encouragement than that.

He stared around, squinting into the sharp-edged northern light, and added one codicil. "I love this land. I would know every mile of it in the dark."

She followed his eye around the horizon. The mountains had dwindled away altogether, into a wide, rolling country, open to the bright sky. It was warm enough for olive groves, shining silver-green largesse scattered here and there across the long slopes. A few walled villages sat like light-gilded toys at the edges of sight. In this peaceful day, yokes of oxen plowed far valleys. A tall wheel groaned in a watercourse, its voice softened by distance, lifting moisture to irrigate the garden plots and rows of vines embroidered upon the lower and more fertile ground. Along the heights, the gray bones of the world poked through the thinner soil, soaking in the sun like old men on a plaza bench.

I think you left some hard turns out of your tale, too. But that last remark had the weight and density of a truth too large to be denied. How like a man, to change from mask to mask like a player, concealing all intention, yet leave his heart out on the table, carelessly, unregarded, for all to behold.

A scout rode up and greeted his commander with a deferential salute. Arhys rode aside for a moment to confer with him, then blinked up at the sun and frowned. "Royina, I must attend to a few things. I look forward to further pleasure in your company." With a grave nod he excused himself from Ista's side.

Ferda returned, smiling in reasonably well-suppressed curiosity. In a few minutes, some of the baggage mules and servants were sent trotting on ahead, escorted by half a dozen armed outriders. In a few more miles, the road curved into a long shallow valley, green and silver with trees and vines. A walled village sheltered there by the little watercourse. In the olive grove near the stream, the servants were setting up a couple of tents, starting a fire, and assembling food.

Lord Arhys, Ista, Ferda's company, and about a dozen guardsmen turned aside into the grove. The rest of the baggage train and soldiers rode on without looking back.

Ista smiled gratefully as Ferda helped her down from her white horse. The young soldier reappeared to whisk it away to be watered and cared for, and another invited Ista, on Ferda's arm, to the shade of an ancient olive tree while her luncheon was prepared. They had made her a seat with saddles, rugs, and folded blankets soft enough to ease even her tired limbs. With his own hands Lord Arhys brought her a mug of watered wine, then quaffed down another, again more water than wine.

He wiped his mouth and handed off the mug to a hovering servant. "Royina, I must take a little rest. My people should supply all your wants. The other tent is for you, should you wish to retire."

"Oh. Thank you. This pleasant shade will do for now, though." They were both modest officers' tents, quick to pitch and fold; his larger command tent had evidently been sent on with the baggage train.

He bowed and trod away, to duck into his tent and disappear. Small wonder he seized the quiet hour if, as Ista suspected, he'd been up all night for two nights running. His servant followed him in, then reemerged a few minutes later to sit down cross-legged before the closed flap.

The acolyte, her temporary handmaiden, inquired into her needs, which were few, and disposed herself beside Ista in the shade. Ista encouraged her to idle conversation, learning much of local village life by the way. The camp followers brought her food, watched anxiously as she ate it, and looked relieved and elated when she smiled and thanked them.

This village was too small to support a temple, but learning that a shrine to the Daughter Herself stood in the village square by its fountain, Ferda and his remaining men went off after eating to give thanks there for their late deliverance. Ista bid them go with her goodwill, feeling no need to find some special place to seek the gods; they seemed to press on her in all places, at all times, equally. Someplace they were guaranteed to *not* be, now that might be worth a pilgrimage. She half dozed in the quiet, bleached afternoon. The acolyte curled up on the blankets by her side in frank sleep. Her snore was quite ladylike, more like a loudly purring cat.

Ista readjusted a blanket and leaned against the bark of the tree. The gnarled bole must be five hundred years old. Had this village stood here that long? It seemed so. Chalionese, Ibran, a number of Roknari principalities, Chalionese again . . . its masters had passed over it like tides across a strand, and yet still it remained, and carried on. For the first time in days Ista could feel her body start to really relax, in the safety of this calm hour, in the continuity of centuries. She allowed her eyes to close, just for a little.

Her thoughts grew formless, drifting on the edge of dreams. Something about running about the castle of Valenda, or possibly the Zangre, and arguing about clothes that did not fit. Flying birds. A chamber in a castle, candlelit.

Arhys's face, crumpled in dismay. His mouth opened in an O of shock, his hands reaching out in horror as he stumbled forward. He uttered a hoarse noise, between a grunt and a cry, rising to a wail of woe.

Ista shot awake, her breath drawing in, the cry still seeming to ring in her ears. She sat up and stared around, her heart beating rapidly. The acolyte slept on. Some men sat in the shade across the grove near the horse lines, playing at a game of cards. Others slept. No one else seemed to have heard the shocking sound; no heads turned toward Arhys's tent. The servant was gone from his place before its entrance.

It was a dream . . . wasn't it? And yet it had too much density, too much clarity; it stood out from the mind-waverings that had preceded it like a stone in a stream. She forced herself to lean back again, but her ease did not return. Tight bands seemed to circle her chest, constricting her breath.

Very quietly, she put out a hand and rose to her feet. No one was watching her just now. She slipped across the few yards of sunlight between her tree and the next, and back into the shade. She paused at the tent door. If he was asleep, what excuse would she give for waking him? If awake and, say, dressing, what reason for barging in upon his privacy?

I must know.

Ista lifted the tent flap and stepped inside, her eyes adjusting to the shadows. The tent's pale fabric, thin enough that she could see the narrow shadows of the olive leaves moving on the roof, glowed with the light outside, which glinted also through half a hundred pinholes.

"Lord Arhys? Lord Arhys, I . . ." Her whisper died.

Arhys's tunic and boots were folded on a blanket on the right. He lay faceup on a low camp cot on her left, covered only with a light linen sheet, his head near the door. A thin braid of gray-and-black cloth was bound about his upper arm, next to the skin, marking some private prayer to the Father of Winter.

His lids were closed, gray. He was unmoving, flesh pale and translucent as wax. Leaking through the linen over his left breast, a splotch of bright red burned.

Ista's breath stopped, choking her scream. She dropped to her knees beside the cot. *Five gods, he is assassinated!* But how? No one had entered this tent since the servant had come out. Had the servant fatally betrayed his master? Was he some Roknari spy? Her trembling hand flicked back the sheet.

The wound beneath his left breast gaped like a small, dark mouth. Blood oozed slowly from it. A dagger thrust, perhaps, angled up into the heart. *Does he yet live?* She pressed her hand to that mouth and felt its sticky kiss upon her palm, desperate for some thump or flutter to show his heart yet beat. She couldn't tell. Dare she lay her ear to his chest?

A hideous flash of memory burned through her mind's eye, of her long, lean dream-man, and the red tide of blood welling up between her fingers in a flood. She snatched her hand away.

I have seen this wound before. She could feel her own pulse racing, beating in her neck and face, drumming in her ears. Her head felt stuffed with cotton batting.

It was the right wound, she would swear to it, exact in every detail. But it was on the wrong man.

Gods, gods, gods, what is this terror?

Even as she watched, his lips parted. His bare chest rose in a long inhalation. Starting from the edges, the wound slowly pressed closed, the dark slit paling, tightening. Smoothing. In a moment, it was only a faint pink scar ringed by a drying dapple of maroon. He exhaled in a light moan, stirring.

Ista scrambled to her feet, her right hand clenching around its stickiness. With a breathless stride, she slipped through the tent flap and stood blinking in the afternoon. Her face felt bloodless. The shaded grove seemed to spin before her eyes. She walked quickly around to the back of the tent, sheltering between it and the great, thick olive bole, out of view for a moment while she caught her breath. She heard the cot creak, movement on the other side of those opaque fabric walls, a sigh. She opened her right palm and stared down at the carmine smear across it.

I do not understand.

In another minute or two, she felt she could walk again without stumbling, breathe without screaming, and hold her face still and closed. She made her way back to her seat and plunked down. The acolyte stirred and sat up. "Royina? Oh, is it time to ride on already?"

"I think so," said Ista. Her voice, she was pleased to note, came out without tremor or upward slide. "Lord Arhys arises . . . I see."

He pushed the flap aside and stepped out; he had to bend his head to do so. He had his boots on again. He straightened, his fingers fastening the last frog of his tunic. His unstained, unpierced tunic. He stretched, and scratched his beard, and smiled around, the very picture of a man arising from a refreshing post-luncheon nap. Except that he had eaten nothing . . .

His servant scurried back, to help him pull tabard and sword baldric over his head. The little man supplied a light gray linen vest-cloak as well, elaborately embroidered with gold thread on the margins, and adjusted the hang to a pleasantly lordly swing about Arhys's calves. A lazy-voiced order or two sent his people to work making their cavalcade ready for the road once more.

The acolyte rose to gather her things and pack them away. Ferda passed by, heading for the horse lines. Ista softly called him to her side.

She stared away. In a deliberately uninflected voice, she

said to him, "Ferda. Look into my right palm and tell me what you see."

He bent over her hand, straightened. "Blood! My lady, did you take an injury? I'll fetch the acolyte—"

"Thank you, I am unhurt. I merely wished to know . . . if you saw what I saw. That's all. Carry on, please." She wiped her hand upon the blankets and extended her other arm for him to help her to her feet. She added after a moment, "Do not speak of this."

His lips pursed in puzzlement, but he saluted and continued on his way.

The second portion of the ride was much shorter than Ista had expected, a mere five miles or so up over the next ridge and into a somewhat wider watercourse. The road switched back and forth a few times, angling down the steep slope, then ran beside the little river. Arhys moved up and down along the column, but fetched up toward the end by her side and Ferda's. "Look, there." He pointed ahead, an expansive wave. "Castle Porifors."

Another walled village, much larger than the last, nestled by the stream at the foot of a tall rocky outcrop. Along the outcrop's crown, commanding a long view of the valley, an irregular array of rectangular walls loomed, broken only sparingly by round towers. The blank walls, pierced by arrow slits and capped by crenellations, were of fine-cut stone, palest gold in the liquid light. Elaborate twining carvings, running in bands of contrasting bright white stone around the walls, marked it as the best Roknari masonry work of a few generations back, when Porifors had been built to guard Jokona from Chalion and Ibra.

Arhys's upturned face held a strange expression for a moment, drinking in the sight, at once eager and tense, longing and reluctant. And for the briefest, lid-squeezed flash, weary beyond measure. But he then turned to Ista with a more open smile. "Come, Royina! We're almost there."

More of the baggage train split off at the village, and most of the soldiers. Arhys led his remaining troop and Ferda's past those lesser walls and up a narrower road, single file, winding across the slope. Green bushes clung dizzily to the rocks with roots like grasping fingers. The horses' haunches bunched and flexed, pushing them up the last breathless incline. Cries of greeting rang down from above, echoing off the boulders. Had they been attackers, arrows and stones would have fallen on their heads just as readily.

The cavalcade circled the walls and approached a drawbridge lowered over a sharp natural cleft in the rocks, its downward plunge adding another twenty or so free feet to the wall's height. Arhys, now at the head of his troop, waved and gave a great whoop, then cantered his horse through the archway with a clatter like a drumroll.

Ista followed at a saner pace, to find herself in what seemed a sudden other world, a garden gone amok. The rectangular entry court was lined with big pots of blooming flowers and succulent shrubs. One open wall was covered with an array of more pots, secured in wrought-iron rings driven into the walls, exploding with color—purple, white, red, blue, searing pink—dripping with green vines trailing down over the pale severe stone. A second wall boasted an espaliered apricot tree, grown immense across it, twining with an equally ancient almond, both in bloom. At the far end of the court, an arcade of harmonious stone pillars held up a balcony. A delicately carved staircase descended like a white alabaster waterfall into the court.

A tall young woman, her face glowing with joy, fairly flew down the stairs. Black hair was braided up from her temples, framing her rose-tinted ivory features, but was freed to ripple like flowing silk over her shoulders. Light linens graced her slim body, and a pale green silk robe with wide gilt-edged sleeves fluttered about her, billowing like a sail as she descended. Arhys jumped from his dappled horse and flung his reins to a groom barely in time to open his arms to the impact of her frantic, fragrant embrace. "My lord, my lord! Five gods be praised, you are come back safe!"

The young soldier had appeared at Ista's horse's head and

stood ready to help her dismount, but his head turned to mark this play with open, if tolerantly amused, envy in his eyes.

"What an incredibly lovely young woman," Ista said. "I did not realize Lord Arhys had a daughter."

He managed to look back around to her, and hurried to hold her stirrup. "Oh, my lord's daughter does not live here, Royina . . ."

She came about from her dismount, upright on her feet, as Arhys strode up to her, the young woman clinging to his arm.

"Royina Ista," said Arhys, breathless with pride and a long kiss. "May I have the pleasure and honor of presenting to you my wife, Cattilara dy Lutez, Marchess of Porifors."

The black-haired young woman dipped in a curtsey of surpassing gracefulness. "Dowager Royina. My household is honored beyond all deserving by your presence here. I hope I may do everything possible to make your sojourn with my lord and myself a memorable delight."

"Five gods give you a good day, Lady of Porifors," Ista choked. "I'm sure you shall."

10

FLANKED BY TWO SMILING LADIES-IN-WAITING, THE YOUNG marchess led Ista through a cool, dim archway under the balcony and into an inner court. Ferda and Ista's medical acolyte followed less certainly, until gestured forward by Lord Arhys. The courtyard was graced by a small marble pool in the shape of a star, its water bright, and more pots of succulents and flowers. Lady Cattilara darted up the stairway to the second-floor gallery and paused to wait, staring in concern as the acolyte helped Ista labor upward on her sore legs. Ferda hurried to lend his arm. Ista grimaced in mingled gratitude and annoyance.

Their footsteps echoed on the boards toward a corner where a short tower loomed, until Lord Arhys stopped abruptly. "Catti, no! Not these chambers, surely!"

Lady Cattilara paused outside the carved double doors her woman had been about to open, and smiled back at Arhys in uncertainty. "My lord? They are the best rooms of the house—we cannot offer the dowager royina less!"

Arhys strode to her side, lowered his voice, and said through his teeth, "Have some sense!"

"But they are swept and garnished for her—"

"No, Catti!"

She stared up at him in dismay. "I—I'm sorry, my lord. I'll . . . I'll think of something. Else."

"Five gods, please you do," he snapped back, exasperation leaking into face and voice. With an effort, he recovered an expression of bland welcome.

Lady Cattilara turned, smiling stiffly. "Royina Ista. Won't you . . . come to my rooms to rest and refresh yourself before dinner? Just this way . . ."

She eased back past them, and they all reversed direction toward a similar set of doors on the opposite end of the gallery. Ista found herself, briefly, next to Arhys.

"What is the problem with the chambers?" she asked.

"The roof leaks," he growled after a moment.

Ista cast a look at the bright blue, cloudless sky. "Oh."

The men were excluded at these new doors.

"Shall I bring your things here, then, Royina?" asked Ferda.

Ista glanced apprehensively at Arhys.

"Yes, for now," he answered, apparently finding this other, if temporary, lodging more acceptable. "Come, dy Gura, I'll show you and your men to your quarters. You will wish to see to your horses, of course."

"Yes, my lord. Thank you." Ferda gave Ista a parting salute and followed Arhys back down the stairs.

Ista entered the chamber past the lady-in-waiting, who had paused to hold the door open for her. The woman smiled and bobbed a curtsey.

Ista felt an immediate sense of ease from having come at last to what were obviously a woman's private quarters. A softened light filtered through elaborate lattices at the narrow windows on the far wall. Wall hangings, and vases of cut flowers, brightened the austere whitewashed angles. A door, closed, gave interior access to some adjoining chamber, and Ista wondered if it was Arhys's. The walls were crowded with chests, variously carved, inlaid, or ironbound; Cattilara's women whisked away piles of clothing and other evidences of disorder, and set a feather-stuffed cushion on one such trunk for Ista to rest upon. Ista glanced through the lattices, which gave a view onto the roof of another inner court, and settled her aching body down gingerly.

"What a pleasant room," Ista remarked, to allay Lady Cattilara's obvious awkwardness at having her refuge so suddenly invaded.

Cattilara smiled in gratitude. "My household is anxious to honor you at our table, but I thought perhaps you would wish to wash and rest, first."

"Yes, indeed," said Ista fervently.

The acolyte ducked a curtsey at the castle's chatelaine, and said firmly, "And it please you, lady, the royina should have her dressings changed as well."

Cattilara blinked. "You are injured? My lord did not say, in his letter . . ."

"Some minor scrapes. But yes, wash and rest, before all." Ista had no intention of neglecting her hurts. Her son Teidez had died, it was said, of an unattended injury upon his leg scarcely worse than a scratch, which had taken a febrile infection. Ista suspected complicating factors beyond the natural; prayers the boy had certainly had poured upon him, but they had gone unanswered.

Lady Cattilara cast off her moment of discomfort in a flurry of activity, ordering her ladies and her maids to these practicalities. Tea and dried fruit and bread were offered, basins and a hip bath trundled in, and water carried up; the acolyte and Cattilara's women tended not only Ista's body but washed her hair as well. By the time these welcome ablutions were concluded, and Ista rewrapped in borrowed robes, her hostess was quite cheerful again.

Under her direction, the ladies carried in armloads of garments for Ista's inspection, and Cattilara opened her jewel cases.

"My lord said you had lost all your belongings to the Jokonans," Cattilara said breathlessly. "I beg you to accept whatever of mine may please you."

"As my journey was intended as a pilgrimage, I actually carried but little, and so it was but little loss," said Ista. "The gods spared me my men; all else may be repaired."

"It sounded a terrible ordeal," said Cattilara. She had gasped in consternation when the acolyte had uncovered the admittedly ugly lesions on Ista's knees.

"The Jokonans had it worse, in the end, thanks to your lord and his men."

Cattilara glowed with pleasure at this oblique commendation of the march. "Is he not fine? I fell madly in love with him from the first moment I saw him, riding into the gates of Oby with my father one autumn day. My father is the march of Oby—the greatest fortress in Caribastos, bar the provincar's own seat."

Ista's lips quirked. "I grant you, Lord Arhys on horseback makes a most striking first impression."

Cattilara burbled on, "He looked so splendid, but so sad. His first wife had died in childbed, oh, years before, when his little daughter Liviana was born, and it was said he did not look at other women after her. I was but fourteen. My father said I was too young, and it was only a girl's infatuation, but I proved him wrong. Three years did I campaign with my father for my lord's favor, and I won such a prize!"

Indeed. "Have you been wedded long?"

"Almost four years, now." She smiled in pride.

"Children?"

Her face fell, and the volume of her voice. "Not yet."

"Well," said Ista, in an effort to bridge this unexpected chasm of secret woe that flashed so plainly in the girl's face, "you are indeed young . . . let us see these garments."

Ista's heart sank, contemplating Cattilara's offerings. The marchess's tastes ran to bright, airy, fluttering confections that doubtless flattered her tall slenderness exceedingly well. Ista suspected they would make her own short body look like a dwarf dragging a curtain. Her mouth sought less blunt excuses. "I am still in mourning for the recent death of my lady mother, alas. And my pilgrimage, though most rudely interrupted by those Jokonan raiders, is far from concluded. Perhaps something in the colors proper to my grief . . . ?"

The elder of Cattilara's ladies glanced at Ista and at the bright silks, and seemed to correctly interpret this. Much rummaging in chests and some trips to other storage places produced at length some dresses and robes of sterner cut and much-less-trailing hemlines, in suitable black and lilac. Ista smiled and shook her head at the jewel case. Cattilara contemplated the choices therein, and suddenly curtseyed and excused herself.

Ista heard her steps outside on the gallery turn in again almost at once; then through the wall, a reverberation of voices, Cattilara's and a man's. Lord Arhys had returned, evidently. His timbre and cadences were distinctive. The light steps dashed back, then slowed to a lady's dignity. Cattilara entered, her lips curled up with satisfaction, and held out her hand.

In it lay a rich silver mourning brooch set with amethysts and pearls.

"My lord has not very many pieces inherited from his great father," she said shyly, "but this is one of them. He'd be honored if you would choose to have it, for those past times' sake."

Ista, surprised by the sight, vented a huff of a laugh. "Indeed. I know the piece. Lord dy Lutez used to wear it in his hat, upon occasion." Roya Ias had given it to him—one of the least of his many gifts, which had run to half his royacy before it all had come crashing down.

Cattilara gazed at her with eyes shining, Ista would swear, in a muted romantic glow. The marchess, presumably, shared her husband's heroic theories about his father's fall. Ista was still not sure if Arhys had believed her denial of a sexual involvement with a man whose reputation as a lover had been scarcely less famous than his reputation as a soldier, or if he'd merely acceded to her story for courtesy's sake. Did he imagine her still in mourning for dy Lutez? For

Ias? For lost love of whatever object? The brooch was an ambiguous message, if message it was.

Arhys's flesh beneath her hand, as she had touched that misplaced wound, had been stiff and cool as wax. And yet he had risen, walked and rode, talked, kissed his wife, laughed or growled as grumpily as any breathing husband might. Ista might have convinced herself by now that she'd had a hallucination, or a dream, but for Ferda's witness to the material reality of the blood on her palm.

Ista wrapped her hand around the mystery of his intentions, and said, "Thank you, and thank your lord for me."

Cattilara looked immensely pleased with herself.

Ista was laid down upon Lady Cattilara's bed with her still-damp hair spread out on a linen towel, under the guard of the acolyte on a stool across the chamber. Cattilara swept her ladies out before her and left her honored guest to rest until the evening meal was served. Probably, Ista thought, to dash off and oversee its preparation. In the quiet of the dim chamber, exhaustion and the immense relief of clean skin and clothing lent Ista a sensation—illusion?—of having come to sanctuary at last. Her headache could just be a touch of fever from her sores and her nightmare ride . . . despite the lingering hum of tension on the edge of her nerves, her eyelids drooped.

At a cool breath on her cheek, they opened again in irritation. No surprise that this castle had ghosts—all old fortresses did—nor that they emerged to investigate a visitor . . . She rolled onto her side. A faint white blob floated in her vision. As she stared, dismayed and frowning, two more slipped out of the walls and collected with it, as if drawn to her warmth. Ancient spirits, these, formless and decayed to near oblivion. Merciful oblivion. Her lips drew back in a fierce frown. "Be gone, sundered," she whispered. "I can do nothing for you." A swipe of her hand scattered the shapes like fog, and they dispersed from her inner sight. No mirror would reflect these visions, no companion share them.

"Royina?" the acolyte's voice came in a dozy murmur.

"Nothing," said Ista. "I dream."

No dream, that, but her inner vision grown clear again. Undesired, unwelcomed, resented. And yet . . . she was come to a very murky place, in this bright afternoon. Perhaps she was going to need such clarity.

The gods give no gifts without hooks embedded.

Remembering her vivid, disturbing dream from earlier, Ista hardly dared allow herself to drop off again. She half dozed for the turning of a glass, until Cattilara and her ladies came to collect her again.

The senior lady-in-waiting dressed Ista's hair in what was obviously an accustomed style, braided back from her face and falling loose behind. On Cattilara, the fall made fascinating ripples; Ista suspected her own dun mop, snarling at her nape, had more the effect of a mat of scouring weed. But a lavender linen shift, with a black silk overrobe pinned together beneath her breasts by the mourning brooch, made a suitably dignified display. Display, she was fairly certain, would be her next task.

Summer's heat came early to this northern province. The tables had been set up in the court, and the meal timed for when the westering sun dropped below the roofline, the advancing shadow sparing the diners the light's hammering. The head table, at the court's far end, faced the star fountain, and two other longer ones ran perpendicular to it.

Ista found herself set at Lord Arhys's right hand, with Lady Cattilara on her other side. If Arhys had been stunning in mail and leather, splashed with blood, he was devastating in a courtier's garb of gray touched with gold, and splashed with verbena. He smiled warmly. Ista's heart turned over; she gathered the shreds of her reserve and returned cooler greetings, then forced herself to look away from him.

Ferda was given an honored place beyond the marchess. An elderly gentleman in the robes of a Temple divine was seated one space over from Lord Arhys's left hand. One of Arhys's senior officers began to approach them, but halted at the two fingers Lord Arhys held up above the empty seat, nodded understanding, and went to take a place at one of the lesser tables.

Lady Cattilara, watching this, leaned behind Ista to murmur to her husband, "My lord. With these honored guests, surely tonight we should use the place."

Arhys's eyes darkened. "Tonight least of all, then." His brows bent at her in a scowl; one finger touched his lips. In warning?

Cattilara settled back, her mouth taut. She twitched it back into a smile for Ista's sake, and addressed a polite triviality to Ferda. Ista was pleased to see the remainder of Ferda's company, refreshed and washed and lent clean clothes, scattered along the other tables. Arhys's officers and Cattilara's women and a few habitués in Temple dress made up the rest. Important citizens from the town at the castle's feet would doubtless be paraded before Ista at ensuing meals.

The elderly divine shuffled to his feet and quavered the prayers: of thanksgiving for the previous day's victory and marvelous rescue of the royina, of supplication for the healing of the wounded, of blessing upon the meal about to be served. He continued with some special if slightly vague reference to the steadfastness of Ferda and his men, in this the Daughter's Season, which Ista could see gratified the officer-dedicat. "And as ever, we especially beg the Mother, with Her Season impending, for the recovery of our Lord dy Arbanos." He made a gesture of blessing over the empty chair at Lord Arhys's left hand, and Arhys nodded, sighing under his breath. A nearly wordless murmur of assent ran round the officers at the other tables, and, Ista saw, some bleak frowns.

As the servants began to pass among them with pitchers of wine and water and the first platters of food, Ista asked, "Who is Lord dy Arbanos?"

Cattilara eyed Arhys warily, but he merely replied, "Illvin dy Arbanos, my master of horse. He has been . . . unwell, these two months. I save his seat, as you see." His last remark had almost a mulish air. He added after a long moment, "Illvin is also my half brother."

Ista sipped at her goblet of watered wine, drawing family trees in her head. Another dy Lutez bastard, unacknowledged? But the great courtier had made a point of claiming all his scattered progeny, with regular prayers and offerings to the Bastard's Tower for their protection. Perhaps this one had been got upon some woman already married, then folded silently into her family by the acquiescence of her cuckolded husband . . . ? The name suggested it. Silently, yet not secretly, if this dy Arbanos had claimed a place of the march and had his claim honored.

"It was a great tragedy," Cattilara began.

"Too great to darken this evening's celebration with," growled Arhys. No gentle hint, that.

Cattilara fell silent; then, with obvious effort, evolved some inconsequential chatter about her own family in Oby, remarks upon father and brothers and their clashes with the Roknari stragglers along their border during last fall's campaigns. Lord Arhys, Ista noted, took little upon his plate, and that little merely pushed about with his fork.

"You do not eat, Lord Arhys," Ista ventured at last.

He followed her glance to his plate with a rather pained smile. "I am troubled with a touch of tertiary fever. I find starving it to be the most effective treatment, for me. It will pass soon."

A group of musicians who had seated themselves in the gallery struck up a lively air, and Arhys, though not Cattilara, took it for pretext enough to let the limping conversation pause. Shortly after, he excused himself and went to consult with one of his officers. Ista eyed the empty seat beyond him, its place fully set. Someone had laid a cut white rose across the plate, in offering or prayer.

"Lord dy Arbanos appears to be much missed, in your company," said Ista to Cattilara.

She glanced across the courtyard to locate her husband, leaning over another table in conversation and safely out of earshot. "Greatly missed. Truly, we despair of his recovery, but Arhys will not hear . . . it is very sad."

"Is he a much older man than the march?"

"No, he's my lord's younger brother. By two years, nearly. The two have been inseparable most of their lives— the castle warder raised them together after the death of their mother, my father says, and made no distinction between them. Illvin has been master of horse here for Arhys for as long as I can remember."

Their mother? Ista's mind ratcheted backward over the hypothesized family tree. "This Illvin . . . is not a son of the late Chancellor dy Lutez, then?"

"Oh, no, not at all," said Cattilara earnestly. "It was a great romance, though, I've always thought, in its day. It is said—" She glanced around, blushed a little, and lowered her voice, leaning in toward Ista. "The Lady of Porifors, Arhys's mother—it is said, when Lord dy Lutez left her to attend court, she fell in love with her castle warder, Ser dy Arbanos, and he with her. Dy Lutez hardly ever returned to Porifors, and the date for Lord Illvin's birth . . . well, it just didn't work. It was a very open secret, I gather, but Ser dy Arbanos did not acknowledge Illvin until after their mother died, poor lady."

And another reason for dy Lutez's long neglect of his northern bride emerged . . . but which was cause and which effect? Ista's hand touched the brooch at her breast. What a quandary this Illvin must have posed for dy Lutez's vanity and possessiveness. Had it been a gracious and forgiving gesture, to yield him legally to his real father, or a mere relief to slide the bastard boy off the crowded roll of dy Lutez's heirs?

"What illness befell him?"

"Not exactly an illness. A very unexpected . . . tragedy, or cruel accident. Made worse by all the guesses and uncertainly. It was a great grief to my lord, and shock to all of Porifors . . . oh, but he returns to us." Lord Arhys had straightened and was heading back to his high place. The officer to whom he had been speaking rose, gave him an acknowledging half salute, and made his way out of the courtyard. Cattilara lowered her voice still further. "It disturbs my lord deeply to speak of it. I will tell you all the tale of it privately, later, hm?"

"Thank you," said Ista, not knowing quite how to respond to all this mysterious evasion. She knew what she wanted to ask next. *Is Lord Illvin a long, lean man, with hair like a stream of frosted night?* Dy Arbanos the younger might, after all, be short, or round as a barrel, or bald, or with hair of flaming red. She could ask, Cattilara would say so, and the knot in Ista's stomach could then relax.

The plates were cleared. Some soldiers, under the direction of the officer Arhys had dispatched, brought in an array of boxes, chests, bags, and assorted armloads of weapons and armor, to lay in heaps before the high table. The spoils of yesterday morning's battle, Ista realized. Lord Arhys and Lady Cattilara went together to lift a small chest to Ista's place and open it before her.

Ista's head nearly jerked back at the reek of mortality and woe that rose from the mess of gauds piled within. It was not, she realized at once, a stink she sensed with her nose. It seemed she was to be the first inheritor of the Jokonan disaster. A select mound of rings and pins and bracelets of finer workmanship or obvious femininity gleamed in the fading light. How much of it had been lately stolen from Rauma? How much intended for Jokonan girls who would not see their suitors again? She took a breath, fixed a befitting smile of gratitude upon her face, and mustered a few appropriate words, commending Arhys and his men on their courage and swift response to the raiders' incursion, raising her voice to carry her compliments to the far tables.

An especially fine sword was then presented to Ferda, to his obvious pleasure. Cattilara bestowed a few pieces upon her ladies, Arhys distributed the bulk to his officers, with personal words or jokes, and the residue was disposed to the divine for prayers in the town temple. A young dedicat, apparently the elderly divine's personal prop, took charge of it with thanks and blessings.

Ista let her finger glide over the contents of her box. It made her skin crawl. She did not want this mortal legacy. Well, there was a solution for that. She started to pick out one ring for her brave handmaiden, formed of tiny galloping gold horses—where *was* Liss by now? But after a hesitant moment, her hand drifted to a curved dagger with a jeweled hilt. It had a certain elegant practicality that seemed more in the riding girl's style. With a sigh, recalling that all her money was at the bottom of a river in Tolnoxo, she withdrew a few trinkets for vails as well. She laid both ring and dagger aside, and pushed the box down toward Ferda.

"Ferda. Pick out the best piece for your absent brother. And the four next best for our wounded and the men who were left with them. Something appropriate for dy Cabon, too. Each man of your company may then take what he likes. The rest, please see that it comes to the Daughter's Order, with my thanks."

"Certainly, Royina!" Ferda smiled, but then his smile faded. He leaned closer across the marchess's empty seat. "I wanted to ask you. Now that you are indeed delivered to a place of safety, and look to be secure here under the march's protection for a time, may I have your leave to go and search for Foix, and Liss and the divine?"

I do not know what this strange place is, but I do not name it safety. She could not say so aloud. Almost, she wanted to order him to ready his men for her departure tomorrow. *Tonight.* Impractical, impossible. Impolite. The Daughter's men were nearly as exhausted as she was. Half their horses were still back on the road with Porifors's grooms, being brought along in slow stages.

"You are as much in need of rest as any of us," she temporized.

"I will rest better when I know what has happened to them."

She had to allow the truth of that, but the thought of being trapped here without her own escort sent a shiver of unease along her nerves. She frowned in uncertainty as Lady Catti-lara fluttered back to her place.

Lord Arhys also returned, to lower himself into his chair with a covertly weary sigh. Ista asked after his letters of inquiry on her missing people's behalf. He listened in what seemed to Ista especially grave sympathy to Ferda's concern for his brother, but opined that it was too early for a reply. By tacit agreement, no one mentioned the complication of the bear-demon.

"We know that Liss, at least, found her way to the provincar of Tolnoxo," argued Ista. "Others might have given warning of the raiders, but only she knew that I was among the taken. And if she made it to safety, she will surely have had the sense to ask for searchers for your brother and the good divine."

"That's . . . true." Ferda's lips wrinkled, tugged between reassurance and worry. "If they listened to her. If they gave her shelter . . ."

"The chancellery's courier stations will have given her refuge even if dy Tolnoxo did not, though if he did not reward her courage with a proper hospitality—*and* her pleas with all aid—he will certainly hear from me about it. And from Chancellor dy Cazaril, too, I warrant. By Lord Arhys's letters, the world will shortly know where we have fetched up. If our strays find their way to Porifors while you are running about hunting for them, Ferda, you will miss them all the same. In any case, you surely cannot intend to hare off in the dark, tonight. Let us see what counsel—or messages—tomorrow morning brings."

Ferda had to agree to the sense of that.

A cool twilight was falling in the court. The musicians concluded their offering, but no dancing or masque was presented. The men made sure that the last of the wine did not go to waste, and final prayers and blessings were offered. The divine doddered away on his dedicat's arm, trailed by his rustic temple's people. Arhys's officers made slightly

awed courtesies to the dowager royina, seeming honored to
be permitted to kneel and kiss her legendary hands. But
from the way they strode off afterward, faces already intent
upon anticipated tasks, Ista was reminded that this was a
working fortress.

Cattilara made to put a helpful hand under her elbow as
she rose.

"*Now* I can take you to your rooms, Royina," she said,
smiling. She glanced briefly at Arhys. "They are not so
large, but . . . the roof is in better repair."

The food and the wine, Ista had to admit, had combined
to destroy any ambition of hers for further movement
tonight. "Thank you, Lady Cattilara. That would be good."

Arhys formally kissed her hands good night. Ista was uncertain if his lips were cool or warm, confused by the disturbing tingle their imprints left on her knuckles. In any
case, they did not burn with fever, though when he raised his
clear gray eyes to hers, *she* flushed.

Trailed by the usual gaggle of women, the marchess took
her arm and strolled with her through another archway beneath the gallery and down a short arcade. They turned again
and went under another looming line of buildings to emerge
in a small, square courtyard. The evening was still luminous,
but overhead, the first star shone in the high blue vault.

*A stone-arched walk ran around the court's edge, the fine
alabaster pillars carved with a tracery of vines and flowers
in the Roknari style . . .*

Neither hot noon nor chill half-moon midnight, but still
the same court as in Ista's dreams, every detail identical,
unmistakable, engraved on her memory as if with chisel and
awl. Ista felt faint. She could not decide if she felt surprised.

"I think I should like to sit down," she said in a thin voice.
"Now."

Cattilara glanced, startled, at the trembling of Ista's hand
on her arm. Obediently, she guided Ista to a bench, one of
several around the courtyard's margin, and sat down with
her. The time-polished marble beneath Ista's fingers was

still warm from the heat of the day, though the air was cooling, growing soft. She gripped the stone edge briefly, then forced herself to sit straight and take a deep breath. This place seemed an older part of the fortress. It lacked the ubiquitous pots of flowers; only the legacy of the Roknari stonecutters kept it from being severe.

"Royina, are you all right?" asked Cattilara diffidently.

Ista considered various lies, or truths for that matter—*My legs hurt. I have the headache.* She settled on, "I will be, if I rest a moment." She considered the marchess's anxious profile. "You were going to tell me what struck down Lord Illvin." With difficulty, Ista kept her eyes from turning toward *that* door, in the far corner to the left of the stairs to the gallery.

Cattilara hesitated, frowning deeply. "It is not so much what, as who, we think."

Ista's brows climbed. "Some evil attack?"

"That, to be sure. It was all very complicated." She glanced up at her waiting women and waved them away. "Leave us, please you." She watched them settle out of earshot on a bench at the court's far end, then lowered her voice confidentially. "About three months ago, the spring embassy came from Jokona, to arrange the trade of prisoners, set ransoms, obtain letters of safe passage for their merchants, all the things such envoys do. But *this* time, with a most unexpected offering in their train—a widowed sister of Prince Sordso of Jokona. An elder sister, married twice before, I gather, to some dreadful rich old Jokonan lords, who did what old lords do. I don't know if she refused to be sacrificed so again, or if she'd lost her value in that market with her age—she was almost thirty. Though really, she was still fairly attractive. Princess Umerue. It soon became clear that her entourage sought a marriage alliance with my lord's brother, if he proved to please her."

"Interesting," said Ista neutrally.

"My lord thought it a good sign, that it might be a way to secure Jokona's acquiescence in the coming campaign against Visping. If Illvin were willing. And it was soon evident that Illvin—well, I'd never seen his head turned round like that by any woman, for all he pretended otherwise. His tongue was always quicker to bitter jest than to honeyed compliments."

If Illvin was only a little younger than Arhys . . . "Had not Lord Illvin—Ser dy Arbanos?—been married before?"

"Ser dy Arbanos now, yes—he inherited his father's title almost ten years ago, I think, though there was not much else to go with it. But no. Two times he was almost betrothed, I think, but the negotiations fell through. His father had devoted him to the Bastard's Order for a period in his youth, for his education, though he said he did not develop a calling. But as time ran on, people made assumptions. I could see that always annoyed him."

Ista recalled making similar assumptions about dy Cabon, and grimaced wryly. Still, even if this Princess Umerue had grown seriously shopworn, a union with a minor Quintarian lord, and a bastard to boot, was a curiously reduced ambition for such a highborn Quadrene. Her maternal grandfather was the Golden General himself, if Ista recalled the old marriage alliances of the Five Princedoms aright. "Did she plan to convert, if the courtship proved successful?"

"In truth, I am not sure. Illvin was so taken by her, he might well have gone the other way himself. They made a remarkable couple. Dark and golden—she had this classic Roknari skin, the color of fresh honey, and hair that nearly matched it. It was very . . . well, it was all very plain which way things were going. But there was one who was not happy."

Cattilara drew a deep breath, her eyes shadowed. "There was a Jokonan courtier in the princess's train who was consumed with jealousy and resentment. He'd wanted her for himself, I suppose, and could not see why she was being bartered to an enemy instead. Lord Pechma's rank and wealth were scarcely more than poor Illvin's, though of

course he had not Illvin's military reputation. One night . . .
one night, she sent away her attendants, and Illvin . . . visited her." Cattilara swallowed. "We think Pechma must have
seen, and followed. Next morning, Illvin was nowhere to be
found, until her women entered her chambers and discovered the most dreadful scene. They came and woke my lord
and me—Arhys would not let me enter the chambers, but it
was said"—her voice dropped still lower—"Lord Illvin was
found naked, all tangled in her sheets, senseless, bleeding.
The princess had fallen dead near the window, as though she
had been struggling to escape or call for help, with a poisoned Roknari dagger lodged in her breast. And Lord
Pechma, and his horse and gear, and all the purse of the
Jokonan party that had been entrusted to him, were gone
from Porifors."

"Oh," said Ista.

Cattilara swallowed, and knuckled her eyes. "My lord's
men and the princess's servants rode out together, looking
for the murderer, but he was long fled. The entourage became a cortege, and took Umerue's body back to Jokona. Illvin . . . never awoke. We are not sure if it was from some vile
Roknari poison on the dagger that pierced him, or if he fell
and hit his head, or if he was struck some other dire blow.
But we are terribly afraid his mind is gone. I think that horror grieves Arhys more than even Illvin's death would have,
for he always set great store by his brother's wits."

"And . . . how was this received in Jokona?"

"Not well, for all that they brought their evil with them.
The border has been very tense, since. Which did you some
good, after all, for all my lord's men were in readiness to
ride out when the provincar of Tolnoxo's courier galloped
in."

"No wonder Lord Arhys is on edge. Appalling events indeed." *Leaking roofs, indeed.* Ista could only be grateful to
Arhys's short temper, not to be lodged tonight in Princess
Umerue's death chamber. She considered Cattilara's horrific
account. Lurid and agonizing, yes. But there was nothing

uncanny about it. No gods, no visions, no blazing white fires that yet did not burn. No mortal red wounds that opened and closed like a man buttoning his tunic.

I would look upon this Lord Illvin, she wanted to say. *Can you take me in to view him?* And what excuse would she give for her morbid curiosity, this dubious desire to enter a man's sickroom? In any case, she did not want to gawk at the high laid low. What she really wanted was to mount a horse—no—a cart, and be carried far from here.

It had grown dark enough to drain the color from her sight; Cattilara's face was a fine pale blur. "It has been a very long day. I grow weary." Ista climbed to her feet. Cattilara sprang to assist her up the stairs. Ista gritted her teeth, let her left hand lie lightly on the young woman's arm, and pushed her way up with her right hand on the railing. Cattilara's ladies, still conversing among themselves, straggled after them.

As they reached the top, the door at the far end swung open. Ista's head snapped around. A runty, bowlegged man with a short grizzled beard emerged, carrying a mess of dirty linens and a bucket with a closed lid. Seeing the women, he set his burdens down outside the door and hastened forward.

"Lady Catti," he said in a gravelly voice, ducking his head. "He needs more goat's milk. With more honey in't."

"Not now, Goram." With an irritated wrinkling of her nose, Cattilara waved him off. "I'll come soon."

He ducked his head again, but his eyes gleamed from under his thick brows as he peered across at Ista. Curious or incurious, she could hardly tell in these shadows, but she felt his stare like a hand on her back as she turned right to follow Cattilara into the suite of rooms waiting for her on the gallery's other end.

His footsteps clumped away. She glanced back in time to see the door on the far end open and close once more, an orange line of candlelight flaring, narrowing, and blinking out.

II

CATTILARA'S LADIES WRAPPED ISTA IN A GRACEFUL, GAUZY
nightdress, and tucked her into a bed covered in the finest
embroidered linens. Ista had them leave the candle in its
glass vase burning on her table. The women tiptoed out and
shut the door to the outermost of the two chambers, where
the acolyte and a maid would sleep tonight, within the royina's call. Ista sat up on a generous bank of pillows, contemplating the wavering light and the darkness it drove
back. Contemplating her options.

It was possible to resist sleep for days on end, till the
room swayed and strange, formless hallucinations spurted
across one's vision like sparks spitting from a fire. She'd
tried that, once, when the gods had first troubled her dreams,
when she'd feared she was going mad and Ias had let her go
on thinking so. It had ended badly. It was possible to drown
one's wits, and dreams, in drink. For a little while. She'd
tried that, too, and it had worked even less well, in the long
run. There was no refuge from the gods to be had in madness, either; quite the reverse.

She brooded about what might be lying, on a bed not dis-
similar to this if less delicately perfumed, in that room on

the other end of the gallery. Actually, she rather thought she knew quite precisely how the bed, and the rugs, and the room—and its occupant—appeared. She didn't even need to look. *I never saw Goram the groom before, though.* Although she supposed his existence was implied.

So, You dragged me here, whichever of You harries me. But you cannot force me through that door. Nor can you open it yourselves. You cannot lift so much as a leaf; bending iron or my will is a task equally beyond your capacities. They were at a stand, she and the gods. She could defy them all day long.

But not all night long. Eventually, I must sleep, and we all know it.

She sighed, leaned over, and blew out her candle. The hot wax smell lingered in her nose, and the dazzle of its light left a colored smear in her eyes as she rolled over and thumped her pillow into shape beneath her shoulder. *You cannot open that door. And You cannot make me do it, either, send what dreams You will.*

Do Your second-worst. Your worst, you have done to me already.

🙥

Her sleep at first was formless, dreamless, blank. Then she swam for a little in ordinary dreams, their anxious absurdities melting one into another. Then she stepped into a room, and all was changed; the room was solid, square, its angles unyielding as any real place, though not any place she'd yet been. Not Lord Illvin's chamber. Not her own. It was bright afternoon outside, by the light falling through the tracery of the shutters. She knew it for a room in Castle Porifors by its style, then she realized she *had* glimpsed it once before, in a flash of candlelight. Lord Arhys had cried out . . .

All was serene and empty now. The chamber was clean and swept. And unpeopled, but for herself—no, wait. A door opened.

A familiar figure was briefly backlit by the hazy light falling into the flower-decked court beyond. It filled the door from side to side, heaved its hips through, let the door swing shut. Briefly, her heart lifted in joy and relief to see Learned dy Cabon safe and well.

Except . . . it was not dy Cabon. Or not dy Cabon only.

He was fatter, brighter, whiter. Faintly androgynous. Did that flesh swell as if to contain the uncontainable? His garments were spotless—by that alone, Ista might have known the difference—and luminous as the moon. Above the creases of his smile, cheerfully echoed by the curves of his chins, the god's eyes glinted at her. Wider than skies, deeper than sea chasms, their complexity bent inward endlessly, each layer a lamination of other layers, repeated into infinity, or the infinitesimal. Eyes that might simultaneously contemplate each person and living thing in the world, inside and out, with equal and unhurried attention.

My Lord Bastard. Ista did not speak His name aloud, lest He mistake it for a prayer. Instead, she said lightly, "Aren't I a little overmatched?"

He bowed over his immense belly. "Small, yet strong. I, as you know, cannot lift a leaf. Nor bend iron. Nor your will. My Ista."

"I am not yours."

"I speak in hope and anticipation, as a suitor may." His smile bunched his fat face tighter.

"Or with the trickery of a rat."

"Rats," he observed, sighing, "are low, shy, straightforward creatures. Very limited. For trickery, one wants a man. Or a woman. Trickery, treachery . . . truth, triumph . . . traps for bears . . ."

She twitched at this possible reference to Foix. "You want something. The gods' tongues can grow quite honeyed, when they want something. When I wanted something—when I prayed on my face, arms outflung, in tears and abject terror—for *years*—where were You then? Where were the gods the night Teidez died?"

"The Son of Autumn dispatched many men in answer to your prayers, sweet Ista. They turned aside upon their roads, and did not arrive. For He could not bend their wills, nor their steps. And so they scattered to the winds as leaves do."

His lips curved up, in a smile more deathly serious than any scowl Ista had ever seen. "Now another prays, in despair as dark as yours. One as dear to me as Teidez was to my Brother of Autumn. And I have sent—you. Will you turn aside? As Teidez's deliverance did? At the last, with so few steps left to travel?"

Silence fell between them.

Ista's throat was clogged with rage. And more complicated things, a boiling mixture even she could not separate and name. A stew of anguish, she supposed. She snarled through her teeth, "Lord Bastard, you *bastard.*"

He merely grinned, maddeningly. "When the man arises who can make you laugh, solemn Ista, angry Ista, iron Ista, then will your heart be healed. You have not prayed for this: it's a guerdon even the gods cannot give you. We are limited to such simples as redemption from your sins."

"The last time I tried to follow the gods' holy addled inadequate instructions, I was betrayed into murder," she raged. "But for You, I wouldn't *need* redemption. I don't want to be part of You. If I thought I could pray for oblivion, I would; to be smudged, blotted out, erased, like the sundered ghosts, who die to death indeed, and so escape the world's woe. What can the gods give *me?*"

His brows twitched up in an expression of remarkably disingenuous goodwill. "Why, work, sweet Ista!"

He stepped closer; beneath his feet, the boards creaked and groaned, dangerously. She almost retreated just for the fearful vision of the pair of them crashing through the floor into the chamber beneath. He held his hands lightly above, but not quite touching, her shoulders. She noticed, with extreme annoyance, that she was nude. He leaned forward over his belly, its equator bumping hers, and murmured, "My mark is on your brow."

His lips brushed her forehead. The spot burned like a brand.

He has given me back the gift of second sight. Direct, unguided perception of the world of spirit, *His* realm. She remembered how the print of the Mother's lips had seared her skin, just like this, in that long-ago waking vision that had led to such disastrous consequences. *You may press Your gift on me, but I need not open it. I refuse it, and defy You!*

His eyes glinted with a brighter spark. He let his fat hands drift down over her bare back, and hugged her in tighter to his girth, and bent again, and kissed her on the mouth with an utterly smug lascivious relish. Her body flushed with an embarrassing arousal, which only infuriated her more.

The dark infinities abruptly vanished from those eyes, so close to hers that they crossed. A merely human gaze grew wide, then appalled. Learned dy Cabon choked, recovered his tongue, and leapt backward like a startled steer.

"Royina!" he yelped. "Forgive me! I, I, I . . ." His gaze darted around the chamber, flicked to her, grew wider still, and sought the ceiling, the floor, or the far walls. "I don't quite know where I am . . ."

He was not, now, her dream, she was quite certain of it. She was his. And he would remember it vividly when he awoke, too. Wherever he was.

"Your god," snapped Ista, "has a *vile* sense of humor."

"What?" he asked blankly. "He was here? And I *missed* Him?" His round face grew distraught.

If these were real dreams, each the other's . . . "Where are you now?" asked Ista urgently. "Is Foix with you?"

"What?"

Ista's eyes sprang open.

She was lying on her back in the dark bedchamber, tangled in her fine linen sheets and Cattilara's translucent nightclothes. Quite alone. She spat a foul word.

It was drawing toward midnight, she guessed; the fortress had fallen silent. In the distance, filtering through her window lattices, the faint sawing of insects grated. A night bird warbled a low, liquid note. A little dull moonlight seeped in, rendering the room not quite pitch-black.

She wondered whose prayers could have drawn her here. All sorts of persons prayed to the Bastard as the god of last resort, not just those of dubious parentage. It could be any-one in Porifors. Except, she supposed, a man who'd never woken from an exsanguinated collapse. *If ever I find who has done this to me, I'll make them wish they'd never so much as recited a rhyme at bedtime . . .*

A cautious creak and scuff of steps sounded on the stairs to the gallery.

Ista fought her way clear of the sheets, swung her bare feet onto the boards, and padded silently to the window that gave onto the court. She unbarred the wooden inner shutter and swung it back; fortunately, it did not squeak. She pressed her face to the ornate iron lace of the outer grating and peered into the court. The waning moon had not yet dropped below the roofline. Its sickly light angled onto the gallery.

Ista's dark-adapted eyes could make out clearly the tall, graceful form of Lady Cattilara, in a pale robe, unattended, gliding along the balcony. She paused at the door at the far end, gently swung it open, and slipped within.

Am I to follow? Sneak and spy, listen at windows, peer in like a thief? Well, I will not!

No matter how benighted curious You make me, curse You . . .

By no force could the gods compel her to follow Lady Cattilara to her afflicted brother-in-law's bedchamber. Ista closed the shutter, turned, marched back to her bed. Bur-rowed under the covers.

Lay awake, listening.

After a few furious minutes, she rose again. She silently lifted a stool to the window and sat, leaning her head against the iron lattice, watching. Faint candlelight leaked through the gratings opposite. At length, it went out. A little time more, and the door half opened again, just wide enough for a slim woman to twist through. Cattilara retraced her steps, descended the stairs. She did not appear to be carrying anything.

So, she oversaw the sick man's care. Not beneath a chatelaine's duties, for a man so highborn, an officer so essential, a relative so close and, apparently, esteemed by her husband. Perhaps Lord Illvin was due some midnight medication, some hopeful treatment that the physicians had ordered. There were a dozen possible mundane, harmless explanations.

Well, a handful.

One or two, at least.

Ista hissed through her teeth and returned to her bed. It was a long, galling time before she slept again.

❦

For a woman who had still been flitting around the castle secretly at midnight, Lady Cattilara appeared at Ista's chambers much too soon after dawn, bursting with cheerful hospitality and the plan of dragging Ista to the temple in the village for morning prayers of thanksgiving. With an effort, Ista suppressed the twinging tension the young marchess's presence induced in her. When Ista arrived in the flower-decked entry court to discover Pejar holding a horse for her, it was too late to beg off. Muscles still sore, feeling altogether decrepit, in anything but a thankful mood, she let herself be loaded aboard. Pejar led her mount at a decorous pace. Lady Cattilara walked ahead in the procession, head high, arms swinging freely, and had breath to spare to sing a hymn with her ladies as they descended the treacherous twisting path.

The village of Porifors, tightly crowded behind its gates, was clearly a town-in-waiting for either more walls, or a reign of peace in which walls might be dispensed with. Its temple likewise was small and old, the altars of the four gods hardly more than arched niches off the central court, the Bastard's Tower one of those temporary outbuildings that had lasted beyond all expectation, or desire. Nevertheless, after the services the old divine was eager to show the dowager royina all of his temple's little treasures. Ferda signed Pejar to attend Ista and excused himself, claiming he would not be gone long. Ista's lips twitched at his timing.

The treasures proved not so little after all, as the temple was recipient of largesse from many of Lord Arhys's more successful raids and forays. Lord Illvin's name, too, came up often in the divine's enthusiastic inventory. Indeed, yes, the crime that had laid him low was a terrible, terrible event. Alas, that the rural temple physicians here could do naught for him, though there was still hope that wiser men imported from one of the greater cities in Ibra or Chalion might yet work wonders, when the agents Lord Arhys had dispatched finally succeeded in getting one here. The divine had run through his most interesting, or lurid, tales of provenance and had progressed to a detailed account of the building plans for a new temple, pending peace and the march and marchess's patronage, before Ferda returned.

His face was grave. He paused to kneel briefly in the niche of the Lady of Spring, his eyes closing and his lips moving, before coming to Ista's side.

"Excuse me, Learned," Ista ruthlessly overrode the divine's monologue. "I must speak to my good officer-dedicat."

They returned to the Lady's niche. "What, then?" asked Ista quietly.

His voice was equally quiet. "The morning courier from Lord dy Caribastos has ridden in. No news of Foix or dy Cabon, or of Liss. I therefore ask your leave to take two of my men and search for them." He glanced across in judicious admiration at Lady Cattilara, who had taken over the task of listening politely to the divine. "You are clearly in the best of hands, here. It will only take a few days to ride up to Maradi and back—Lord Arhys undertakes to lend us some good, fresh horses. I'd expect to return before you are ready to travel again."

"I . . . mislike this. I do not care to dispense with your support, should some emergency arise."

"If Lord Arhys's troops cannot protect you, my handful could do no more," said Ferda. He grimaced. "As we have proved, I fear. Royina, under ordinary circumstances I would defer to you without hesitation." His voice grew lower still. "But then there is the matter of the bear."

"Dy Cabon is better fit to deal with those complications than either of us."

"If he lives," said Ferda heavily.

"I am sure he does." Ista decided she didn't want to explain how she knew. Worse, she could not likewise vouch for Foix.

"I know my brother. He can be forceful and persuasive. And tricky, if the first does not serve. If . . . his will is not quite his own, and yet is informed by all his wits . . . I'm not sure dy Cabon could handle him. *I* can. I have ways." His face was lightened, temporarily, by a brief fraternal grin.

"Mm," said Ista. Persuasion, it seemed, ran in the family.

"And then there is Liss," he said more vaguely.

What there was about Liss, he did not expand upon, and Ista mercifully forbore to prod him. "I do dearly wish she were back by my side, that is so." She added after a moment, "And dy Cabon." Perhaps especially dy Cabon. Whatever the god was about, the bewildered young divine figured in it as well.

"Then may I have your leave, Royina? Dedicat Pejar can serve all your needs in this minor court, I am sure. And he is eager enough to do so."

Ista let the little flash of Cardegoss arrogance pass without comment. Were Porifors an ordinary rural court, Ferda would doubtless be correct. "Do you mean to go now?"

He ducked his head. "At once, please you. If there is any problem, the sooner I arrive, the better." He added to her frowning silence, "And if there isn't, then the sooner I may return."

She sucked on her lower lip in doubt. "And there is, as

178   Lois McMaster Bujold

you say, the matter of the bear." *Traps for bears*, the god had said. *His* accursed pet, escaped. No point in praying to the god for protection, either; if he could directly control his wild demons fled into the realm of matter, he presumably would, and not let his divine weakness depend upon human weakness.

"Very well," she sighed. "Go on, then. But return quickly."

He offered a strained smile. "Who knows? I may meet them coming down the road from Tolnoxo and be back before nightfall." He knelt and kissed her hand, gratefully. By the time she drew a second breath, the flapping of his vest-cloak had already vanished out the temple's doors.

Luncheon, Ista discovered to her dismay, was to be a fête in the dowager royina's honor in the village square, complete down to a choir of village children offering a selection of songs, hymns, and earnest and not especially rhythmic local dances. Lord Arhys was not present; the young marchess did the honors for the castle, in a warm style obviously much approved by the proud and anxious parents. More than once, Ista caught her looking at the littlest ones with open longing in her eyes. When the urchins had stamped through their last erratic caper, and Ista had had her hands kissed by all and sundry, she was loaded back aboard her horse and permitted to escape. Surreptitiously, she wiped upon the animal's mane the slimy offering left on her fingers by the waif with the cold. She was by this time almost glad to see that horse. Almost.

❧

Dismounted again back in the floral entry court, Ista was just trying to decide whether she was annoyed or glad for Lady Cattilara's delicately worded suggestion that perhaps a lady of the royina's age would care for an afternoon nap, when a whoop at the gate cried against its closing.

"Hallo, Castle Porifors! Courier from Castle Oby!"

Ista spun on her heel at the familiar, boisterous voice.

Riding through the gate on a fat and lathered yellow nag was Liss. She wore her castle-and-leopard tabard, and held up a leather pouch in the official style, its wax seals bouncing on their strings. Her shirt, beneath the tabard, was as wet with sweat as the horse, and her face flushed with sunburn. Her mouth went round as she gazed about at the pots of color and greenery.

"Liss!" Ista cried in delight.

"Ha, Royina! So you *are* here after all!" Liss kicked loose her stirrups, swung her off leg up over her horse's neck, and jumped down. Grinning, she knelt courtier-fashion at Ista's feet; Ista raised her by her hands. It was all she could do not to hug her.

"How came you here, on this horse—did Ferda find you?"

"Well, I came here on this horse, of course, great slug that it is. Ferda? Is Ferda safe? Hallo, Pejar!"

The sergeant-dedicat at Ista's elbow grinned back broadly. "The Daughter be thanked, you made it!"

"If the tales I heard were true, you all were in worse case than I ever was!"

Ista said anxiously, "Ferda left here not three hours ago—you must have passed him on the road to Tolnoxo, surely?"

Liss's brow wrinkled. "I came in by the road from Oby, though."

"Oh. But how came you to be at—oh, come, come, sit with me and tell me everything! How I have missed your currying and grooming!"

"Yes, dearest Royina, but I must first hand off my letters, since I am a courier again for today, and see to this beast. It isn't mine, five gods be thanked. It belongs to the courier station midway between here and Oby. I should be grateful for a bucket of water, though."

Ista motioned to Pejar, and he nodded and dashed off.

Cattilara and her ladies drifted up. The marchess smiled in inviting puzzlement at the courier girl, and at Ista. "Royina . . . ?"

"This is my most loyal and brave royal handmaiden, Annaliss of Labra. Liss, make a curtsey to Lady Cattilara dy Lutez, Marchess of Porifors, and likewise these . . ." Ista went down the ranks of Cattilara's ladies, who goggled at the courier girl. Liss complied with a series of friendly little dips at the string of introductions.

Pejar dashed up with a sloshing bucket. Liss grabbed it in passing and plunged her whole head in. She came up for air with a sigh of relief, and her soaked black braid swung droplets in an arc that nearly spattered Cattilara's recoiling ladies. "Ah! That's better. Five gods, but Caribastos is a hot country in this season." She allowed the bucket to continue to the horse, giving its side a hearty pat.

Pejar said eagerly, as the horse shoved at him getting its nose in the water, "We were sure you must have warned that crossroads village, but where you went after that, we could not guess."

"My good courier mount was done in by the time I reached there, but my tabard and chancellery baton persuaded them to lend me another. They had no soldiers fit to fight the Jokonans, so I left them to save themselves and rode east as fast as I could whip the poor blowing plow horse. Did the villagers escape harm?"

"They were all fled by the time we got there, close to sunset," said Pejar.

"Ah, good. Well, right after that same sunset I reached a courier station on the main road to Maradi, and once I'd convinced them I wasn't raving, they got the hunt up. Or so I thought. I slept there, and rode in to Maradi the next morning at a saner pace only to find the provincar of Tolnoxo just then leading his cavalry out the gates in pursuit. As fast as the Jokonans were moving, I greatly feared he was already too late."

"It did prove so," agreed Ista. "But a courier reached Castle Porifors in time for Lord Arhys to set an ambush along the line of the Jokonan retreat."

"Yes, that must have been one of the fellows who rode directly from my courier station, five gods rain blessings on their wits. One of them said he was native to this region. I'd hoped he might know what he was about."

"Did you hear anything of Foix and Learned dy Cabon?" asked Ista urgently. "We never saw them again after we hid them in that culvert."

Liss shook her head, frowning. "I told of them at the courier station, and I warned Lord dy Tolnoxo's lieutenants, when we passed, to be on watch for them both. I was not sure then if they'd been taken by the Jokonans, as you were, or if they had got away, or would follow the road forward or back or strike into the scrub, or what. So I went to the temple at Maradi, and found a senior divine of Learned dy Cabon's order, and told her of all our troubles, and that our divine was likely out on the road and much in need of help. And she undertook to send some dedicats to seek them."

"*That* was well thought of," Ista said, her voice warm with approval.

Liss smiled gratefully. "It seemed little enough. I waited a day at the chancellery's office in Maradi, but no word came back from Lord dy Tolnoxo's column. So I bethought me of a faster route south and volunteered to ride courier to Oby. I reckoned, since it was the greater fortress, you would most likely be rescued by its soldiers and brought there. Then I flew—I don't think any courier has ridden that road faster than I did, that day." She shoved a strand of wet hair out of her sunburned face, raking it back with her fingers. "All were still in suspense when I arrived at the fortress that night. But my labors were repaid next morning, when the letter came there from the march of Porifors that you were all safely rescued. Oby's lord and men had gone out on patrol for the Jokonans, too, but they came riding back that afternoon."

"My father is the march of Oby," observed Cattilara, an eager tinge leaking into her voice. "Did you see him?"

Liss made her unique half bow, half curtsey again. "He is in good health, my lady. I begged the boon from him of riding courier to Porifors, so I might most speedily rejoin the royina." She held up her pouch. "He saw me off at dawn this morning. I received this from his own hands. There may be something in here for you—ah." Her eye brightened at the approach of Porifors's castle warder, an aging, landless lordling who reminded Ista much of Ser dy Ferrej, except for being stringy instead of stout. The groom Goram followed in his wake. The warder took the pouch in charge, to Liss's obvious relief, and hastened away with it, after directing the groom to assist with the courier's horse.

"You must be exhausted," said Lady Cattilara, whose eyes had widened more than once during Liss's account. "Such a frightening ordeal!"

"Oh, but I love my task," said Liss cheerfully, slapping her dirty tabard. "People give me fast horses and get out of my *way*."

Ista's lips twitched up at this. Reason enough for joy, indeed.

But at least it appeared that she hadn't let Ferda go off on a fool's errand, for all that he had missed Liss on the road. And that she could hope that by the time he reached Maradi, he would find his bear-ridden brother and his conductor safely in the temple's charge there.

Liss, attempting to follow her horse as Goram led it away, made little excusing bows in all directions.

Ista said smoothly, "When my handmaiden has seen to her mount, she will be in need of a bath, as I was. And, I pray you, a loan of clothing as well. Her things were stolen by the Jokonans along with mine." Actually, Liss's extremely scant wardrobe had mostly been in her saddlebags. But Ista judged that Cattilara's ladies' noses were in the air at more than the reek of horses and sweat from the lowborn, high-riding girl.

"And fodder, pray you, dear Royina!" Liss called over her shoulder.

"It shall be worthy of your great ride, the fame of which shall reach Cardegoss itself in my next letter," Ista promised.

"So it is quick, it may be anything you please!"

Liss was a long time in the stables, but at last she presented herself at Ista's new quarters. Cattilara's ladies, local petty lords' daughters who had nearly fallen over themselves for the honor of serving the dowager royina, were clearly less taken with the chore of serving Liss. But a bath Liss had, under Ista's firm eye, in between snatching bites from the tray of bread, olives, cheese, and dried fruit, and sloshing down cup after cup of lukewarm herb tea. Her rank riding clothes were sent off with the servants to be properly washed.

Cattilara's castoffs suited Liss's height and age much better than they did Ista's, even if they were a trifle too generously cut in the chest for the riding girl. Liss laughed in delight and awe, waving about one trailing, delicate sleeve, and Ista smiled at her pleasure with the unfamiliar richness.

One person's delight in Liss was unalloyed; the medical acolyte finally had someone to assume the care of Ista's hurts so that she might return to her neglected temple and family. Liss hadn't finished drying before the acolyte finished her tutelage, turned over a supply of bandages and ointments, gathered her things, received a suitable vail from Ista for her pains, and scampered off for home.

Dinner that afternoon was presented in a smaller chamber off the courtyard of the star fountain, and proved to be an almost entirely female gathering, under Lady Cattilara's dominion. No chair was left ritually empty.

"Does Lord Arhys not dine tonight?" Ista asked as she was seated at the marchess's right hand. *Or ever?* "I should think his tertiary fever would worry you."

"Not nearly as much as his military duties," Lady Cattilara confided with a sigh. "He has taken some men on a patrol toward the northern border. My heart will be in my mouth till he returns. I am in agony inside with terror for him when he rides out, though of course I smile, and do not let him guess. If anything ever happened to him, I believe I would go mad. Oh." She covered her gaffe with a sip of wine and held her cup up to Ista in salute. "But *you* understand, I'm sure. I wish I could keep him by my side forever."

"Is not his superior military craft a part of his"—*admittedly appalling*—"attractiveness? Hobble him, and you risk killing the very thing you admire in the attempt to preserve it."

"Oh, no," said Lady Cattilara seriously. Denying, but not answering, the objection, Ista noted. "I do make him write to me every day, when he is gone. If he forgot, I should be quite cross with him"—her lips turned up, and her eyes sparkled with laughter—"for a whole hour at least! But he doesn't forget. Anyway, he's supposed to be back by nightfall. I'll watch for him on the road from the north tower, and when I see his horse, my heart will stop choking me and start beating a thousand times a minute instead." Her face softened in anticipation.

Ista bit hard into a large mouthful of bread.

The food, in any case, was excellent. Lady Cattilara, or her castle cook, at least did not attempt to ape the excesses, or worse, what they imagined to be the excesses, of Cardegoss court feasting, but served simple, fresh fare. There did seem to be more sweets tonight, which Ista could not fault, and which Liss plainly relished, consuming an enviable portion. She was very quiet in this company, in what seemed to Ista unnecessary awe of her surroundings. Ista thought she would rather have heard Liss's tales than the local gossip that filled the time. When they had escaped the ladies and returned to the square stone court, Ista told her so, and chided her for her shyness.

"Truly," Liss admitted, "I think it's the dress. I felt a great gawk next to those highborn girls. I don't know how they manage all this fancy cloth. I'm sure I shall trip over myself and tear something."

"Then let us walk about in the colonnade, that I may stretch my scabs as the acolyte instructs, and that you may practice swishing in silks to do me honor in this court. And tell me more of your ride."

Liss shortened her steps in a most ladylike fashion, keeping to Ista's slow limp in the cool of the cloistered walkway. Ista primed her with questions about every aspect of her journey. Not that Ista needed a catalogue of every hair, fault, virtue, and quirk of every horse Liss had ridden for the past several days, but Liss's voice was such welcome music, it hardly mattered what it dwelt upon. Ista had less to report, she found, of her own ride, certainly not details of the Jokonan horseflesh, which she had mainly experienced as a penance. Nor had she desire to recall green flies gathering to feed on thickening blood.

Passing a pillar, Liss reached out to trail her fingers over the carved tracery. "It looks like stone brocade. Porifors is a far more beautiful castle than I was expecting. Is Lord Arhys dy Lutez as great a swordmaster as the marchess was bragging?"

"Yes, in fact. He slew four of the enemy who attempted to ride off with me. Two escaped." She had not forgotten them. She was almost glad, in retrospect, that the translator officer had been one of those fled. She had spoken with him, eye to eye, a few too many times for her to imagine him as a cipher, blurred into the faceless ranks of the fallen. A feminine weakness, that, perhaps, like refusing to eat any animal one had named as a pet.

"Was it true the march rode in with you upon his saddle-bow?"

"Yes," said Ista shortly.

Liss's eyes crinkled with delight. "How splendid! Too bad he's so married, eh? Is he really as handsome as his wife seems to think?"

"I can't say," Ista growled. She added in reluctant fairness, "He is, however, quite handsome."

"How fine, to have such a lord at your feet, though. I am glad you have come to such a place, after all this."

Ista changed *He wasn't exactly at my feet* to, "I do not plan to linger here."

Liss's brows rose. "The Mother's acolyte said you could not ride far yet."

"Ought not, perhaps. Not comfortably. I could at need." Ista followed Liss's admiring glance around the court, shaded in the slanting light of the late day, and tried to evolve a reason for her unease that did not involve bad dreams. A rational, sensible reason, for a woman who was not mad in the least. She rubbed at the itch on her forehead. "We are too close to Jokona, here. I do not know what treaties of mutual aid presently exist between Jokona and Borasnen, but everyone knows the port of Visping is the prize of my royal daughter's eye. What is planned to happen in the fall will be no mere border raid. And there was a terrible event here this spring that can't have helped relations with the prince of Jokona in any way." Ista did not look toward that corner room.

"You mean how Porifors's master of horse was stabbed by that Jokonan courtier? Goram told me of it while we were swabbing down that fat palomino. Odd fellow—I think he's a little simple in the head—but he knows his trade." She added, "Here, Royina, you are limping worse than my second horse. Sit, rest." She chose a shaded bench at the court's far end, the one where Cattilara's ladies had collected the previous evening, and with an air of determined heedfulness settled Ista upon it.

After a moment of silence, she gave Ista a sidelong look. "Funny old man, Goram. He wanted to know if a royina outranked a princess. Because a princess was the daughter of a prince, but you were only the daughter of a provincar. And that Roya Orico's widow Sara was a dowager royina more recent than you. I said a Chalionese provincar was worth any Roknari prince, and besides, you were the mother of the royina of all Chalion-Ibra herself, and *nobody* else is that."

Ista forced herself to smile. "Royinas do not often come in his way, I expect. Did your answers pacify him?"

Liss shrugged. "Seemed to." Her frown deepened. "Isn't it a strange thing, for a man to lie stunned like that, for months?"

It was Ista's turn to shrug. "Palsy-strokes, broken heads, broken necks . . . drownings . . . it happens that way, sometimes."

"Some recover though, don't they?"

"I think those that recover start to do so . . . sooner. Most struck down that way do not live long thereafter, unless their care is extraordinary. It's a slow, ugly death for a man. Or anyone. Better to go swiftly, at the first."

"If Goram cares for Lord Illvin half as well as he cares for his horses, perhaps that explains it."

Ista became conscious that the runty man himself had emerged from the corner chamber and hunkered down behind the balustrade, watching them. After a time he rose, came down the stairs, and crossed the court. As he neared, his steps shortened, his head drew in like a turtle's, and his hands gripped one another.

He stopped a little distance off, bent his knees, and ducked his head, first to Ista, then to Liss, then back to Ista again as if to make sure. His eyes were the color of unpolished steel. His stare, from under those bushy brows, was unblinking.

"Aye," he said at last, to a point halfway between the two women. "She's the one he was going on about, no mistake." He pursed his lips, and his gaze suddenly fixed on Liss. "Did you ask her?"

Liss smiled crookedly. "Hello, Goram. Well, I was working up to it."

He wrapped his arms around himself, rocking forward and back. "Ask her, then."

Liss cocked her head. "Why don't you? She doesn't bite."

" 'B 'n 't," he mumbled obscurely, glowering at his booted feet. "You."

Liss shrugged amused bafflement and turned to Ista. "Royina, Goram wishes you to come view his master."

Ista sat back and was silent for a long, withheld breath. "Why?" she finally asked.

Goram peered up at her, then back down at his feet. "You were the one he was going on about."

"Surely," said Ista after another moment, "no man would wish to be seen in his sickbed by strangers."

"*That's* all right," Goram pronounced. He blinked, and stared hard at her.

Liss, her eyes crinkling, cupped her hand and whispered in Ista's ear, "He was more talkative in the stalls. I think you frighten him."

Articulate smooth persuasion, Ista thought she might resist. In this odd tangle, she could hardly find an end. Urgent eyes, tongue of wood, a silent pressure of expectation . . . She could curse a god. She could not curse a groom.

She glanced around the court. Neither midnight nor noon, now; no details matched her dreams. Her dream had held neither Goram nor Liss, the time of day was all wrong . . . maybe it was safe, benign. She drew a breath.

"So, then, Liss. Let us renew my pilgrimage party and go view another ruin."

Liss helped her up, her face alert with open curiosity. Ista climbed the stairs upon her arm, slowly. Goram watched her anxiously, his lips moving, as if mentally boosting her up each step.

The women followed the groom to the end of the gallery. He opened the door, backed up, bowed again. Ista hesitated, then followed Liss inside.

12

THE ROOM WAS LIGHTER THAN SHE'D SEEN IT IN HER vision, the shutters on the far wall open now to the blue sky beyond. The effect was airy and gracious. The chamber didn't smell like a sickroom, no bunches of heavy-scented herbs hanging from the rafters failing to mask an underlying tang of feces, vomit, sweat, or despair. Just cool air, wood wax, and a faint, not unpleasing aroma of masculine occupation. Not unpleasing at all.

Ista forced her gaze to the bed, and stood rooted.

The bed was made. He rested atop the counterpane not like a man in a sickbed, but like a man who had lain down for but a moment in the middle of a busy day. Or like a corpse laid out in best garb for his funeral. Long and lean, exactly as in her dreams, but dressed very differently: not patient or sleeper, but courtier. A tan tunic embroidered with twining leaves was fastened up to his neck. Matching trousers were tucked into polished boots buckled up to his calves. A maroon vest-cloak spread beneath and beside him, and a sheathed sword lay upon the neatly arranged folds, its inlaid hilt beneath his slack left hand. A seal ring gleamed on one finger.

His hair was not merely combed back from his high forehead, but braided in neat cords up from each temple and over his crown. The dark, frosted length of it ended in a queue brought back over his right shoulder to rest upon his chest, the tail of it, beyond the maroon tie, brushed out straight. He was shaved, and that recently. A scent of lavender water tickled Ista's nostrils.

She became aware that Goram was watching her with a painful intensity, his hands flexing as they gripped each other.

All this silent beauty must be his work. What must the man on the bed have been to receive such devotion from this lackey now, when he had so plainly lost all power to punish or reward?

"Five gods," gasped Liss. "He's *dead*."

Goram sniffed. "No, he's not. He don't rot."

"But he's not breathing!"

"Does too. You can tell with the mirror, see." He sidled around the bed and picked up a tiny hand mirror from a nearby chest. With a glower at the girl from under his bristling eyebrows, he held it beneath Lord Illvin's nostrils. "See?"

Liss bent nearer across the unmoving form and cast a wary glance downward. "That's your thumbprint."

"Is not!"

"Well . . . maybe . . ." Liss straightened and backed away with a jerky gesture, as if inviting Ista to take her vacated place by the bedside and judge for herself.

Ista drew nearer under Goram's anxious eye, trying to find something to say to the grizzled fellow. "You care for him well. A tragedy, that Ser dy Arbanos should have been hewn down like this."

"Aye," he said. He swallowed and added, "So . . . go on, lady."

"I beg your pardon?"

"So . . . kiss him."

For just a moment, she pressed her teeth so hard together that her jaw twinged. But there was no suppressed merriment in Goram's seamed, strained face, no hint of japery. "I don't follow you."

He chewed on his lip. "It was a princess put him here. I thought maybe you could wake him. Being a royina and all." He added after a doubtful moment, "Dowager royina."

He was deathly serious, she saw to her dismay. She said as gently as she could, "Goram, that's a children's story. We are not children here, alas."

A slight choking noise made her glance aside. Liss's face was screwed up, but she forbore to laugh, five gods be thanked.

"You could *try*. It wouldn't hurt to *try*." He was rocking again in his unease, forward and back.

"I fear it would do no good, either."

"No harm," he repeated doggedly. "Got to try *something*."

He must have spent several hours in the meticulous preparation of the scene, of his master, for her view. What desperate hope could drive him to such bizarre lengths?

Maybe he has dreams, too. The thought clotted her breath.

The memory of the Bastard's second kiss heated her face. What if it had been not unholy jest, but another gift—one meant to be passed along? Might it be granted to her to perform a miracle of healing, as agreeably as this? *So are the saints seduced by their gods.* Her heart thumped in concealed excitement. *A life for a life, and by the grace of the Bastard, my sin is lifted.*

In a kind of fascination, she bent forward. The closely shaved skin of Illvin's jaw was stretched too thinly over the fine bones. His lips were neutral in color, a little parted upon pale, square teeth.

Neither warm nor cold, as her lips pressed upon them . . .

She breathed into that mouth. She remembered that the tongue was the organ held sacred to the Bastard, as womb for the Mother, male organs for the Father, heart for the Brother, and brain for the Daughter. Because the tongue was the source of all lies, the Quadrene heretics falsely charged. She dared secretly to trace those teeth, touch the cool tip of his tongue with hers, as the god had invaded her mouth in her dream. Her fingers spread, hovering over his heart, not quite venturing to touch, to feel for a bandage wrapped around his chest beneath that decorated tunic. His chest did not rise. His dark eyes, and she knew their color by heart already, did not open in wonder. He lay inert.

She swallowed a wail of disappointment, concealed chagrin, straightened. Found her voice, lost somewhere. "As you see. It does no good." *Foolish hope and foolish failure.*

"Eh," said Goram. His eyes were narrowed, sharp upon her. He, too, looked disappointed, but by no means crushed. "Must be something else."

Let me out of here. This is too painful.

Liss, standing watching this play, cast Ista a look of mute apology. A lecture on a handmaiden's duties in screening the importunate, the simple, and the strange from her lady's presence seemed in order, later.

"But you *are* the one he was going on about," repeated Goram in an insistent tone. Recovering his audacity, it seemed. Or perhaps the futility of her kiss had reduced his awe of her. She was, after all, merely a *dowager* royina, obviously insufficiently potent to breathe the near dead to life. "Not tall, hair curled all wild down your back, gray eyes, face all still—grave, he said you were grave." He looked her up and down and gave a short nod, as if satisfied with her graveness. "The very one."

"*Who* said—who described me so to you?" demanded Ista, exasperated.

Goram jerked his head toward the bed. "Him."

"*When?*" Ista's voice came out sharper than she'd intended; Liss jumped.

Goram's hands opened. "When he wakes up."

"*Does* he wake up? I thought—Lady Cattilara gave me to understand—he had never come out of his swoon after he was stabbed."

"Eh, Lady Catti," said Goram, and sniffed. Ista wasn't certain if he was making a comment or just clearing his nose. "But he don't *stay* awake, see. He comes up most every day for a while, around noon. We mainly try to get as much food into him as we can, while he can swallow without choking. He don't get enough. He's wasting away, you can see it. Lady Catti, she came up with a smart idea to put goat's milk down his throat with a little leather tube, and you can see that it helps, but not enough. He's too thin now. Every day, his grip is less strong."

"Is he *coherent*, when he wakes?"

Goram shrugged. "Eh."

Not an encouraging answer. But if he waked at all, why not now, for her kiss, or at any other time? Why just at the time that his brother slept his motionless sleep . . . her mind shied from the thought.

Goram added, "He does go on, sometimes. Some would say he just raves."

Liss said, "Is it uncanny, do you think? Some Roknari sorcery?"

Ista flinched at the notion. *I wasn't going to ask it. I wasn't going to suggest it. I want nothing to do with the uncanny.* "Sorcery is illegal in the princedoms, and the Archipelago." For more than just theological reasons; it was scarcely encouraged in Chalion, either. Yet given opportunity—and sufficient desperation, criminality, or hubris—a stray demon might present as much temptation to a Quadrene as to a Quintarian. More, since a Quadrene who had contracted a demon risked dangerous accusations of heretical transgression if he sought assistance from his Temple.

Goram shrugged again. "Lady Catti, she thinks it's poison from that Roknari dagger, because the wound don't heal right. I used to poison rats in the stables—never saw any that worked like this."

Liss's brows drew in, as she studied the still form. "Have you served him long?"

"Going on three years."

"As a groom?"

"Groom, sergeant, messenger, dogsbody, whatever. 'Tendant, now. The others, they're too spooked. Afraid to touch him. I'm the only one who does it really right."

She cocked her head to one side; her puzzled frown did not diminish. "Why does he wear his hair in the Roknari style? Though I must say, it suits him."

"He goes there. Went there. As the march's scout. He was good enough to pass, knows the tongue—his father's mother was Roknari, for all she learned to sign the Five, he told me once."

Footsteps sounded outside, and he looked up in trepidation. The door opened. Lady Cattilara's voice said sharply, "Goram, what are you about? I heard voices—oh. I beg your pardon, Royina."

Ista turned, crossing her arms; Lady Cattilara dipped in a curtsey, though she shot a brief scowl at the groom. She wore an apron over the fine dress she'd appeared in at dinner, and she was trailed by a maid bearing a covered pitcher. Her eyes widened a little as they passed over the courtly garb of the patient. She breathed out through her nostrils, an incensed huff.

Goram hunched, dropping his gaze, and took refuge in a sudden renewal of his unintelligible mumble.

Ista was moved by his hangdog look to try to spare him trouble. "You must excuse Goram," she said smoothly. "I asked him if I might view Lord Illvin, because . . ." Yes, why? To see if he resembled his brother? No, that was weak. *To see if he resembled my dreams?* Worse. "I perceived Lord Arhys was most troubled by his plight. I've decided to write to a certain highly experienced physician of my acquaintance in Valenda, Learned Tovia, to see if she might have any advice in the case. So I wished to be able to describe him and his symptoms very exactly. She is a stickler for precision in her diagnoses."

"That is *extremely* kind of you, Royina, to offer your own physician," said Lady Cattilara, looking touched. "My husband is grieved indeed by his brother's tragedy. If the master physicians we have sent for continue to prove unwilling to travel so far—such adepts tend to be old, we are finding—we should be most grateful for such aid." She cast a doubtful glance at the maid with the pitcher. "Do you think she would want to know how we feed him the goat's milk? I'm afraid the process is not very pretty. Sometimes he chokes it up."

The implications were clear, sinister, and repulsive. Given all the labor to which Goram had gone to present his fallen master in the most dignified possible light, Ista had no heart to watch that long body stripped of its courtly adornment and subjected to indignities, however necessary. "I expect Learned Tovia is well acquainted with all the tricks of nursing. I do not think I need to mark it."

Lady Cattilara looked relieved. With a *carry-on* gesture to the maid and Goram, she ushered Ista and Liss back out onto the gallery, and walked with them toward Ista's chambers. Twilight was gathering; the courtyard was altogether in shadow, though the highest clouds glowed peach against the deepening blue.

"Goram is a very dutiful man," Cattilara said apologetically to Ista, "but I'm afraid he's more than a trifle simple. Though he is by far the best of Lord Illvin's men who have undertaken to attend him. They are too horrified, I think. Goram had a rougher life, before, and is not squeamish. I could not begin to manage Illvin without him."

Goram's tongue was simple, but his hands were not, in Ista's judgment, for all that he seemed the exemplar of a lack-witted attendant. "He appears to have a rare loyalty to Lord Illvin."

"No great wonder. I believe he had been an officer's servant, in his younger days, and been captured by the Roknari during one of Roya Orico's ill-fated campaigns, and sold as a slave to the Quadrenes. In any case, Illvin retrieved him—on one of his trips to Jokona, I think it was. I don't know if Illvin simply bought him, or what, though it seems there was some unpleasant misadventure involved in it all. Goram has stayed by Illvin since. I suppose he's too old to go off and try to make his way elsewhere." Cattilara's gaze flicked up. "What did the poor fellow try to talk to you about?"

Liss's mouth opened; Ista's hand nipped her arm before she could reply. Ista said, "I'm afraid he's not very lucid. I had hoped he was an old retainer and could tell me about the brothers' youth, but it proved not to be the case."

Cattilara smiled in bright sympathy. "When Lord dy Lutez was still alive, and young, you mean? I'm afraid the chancellor—was he already Roya Ias's chancellor, way back then, or just a rising courtier?—didn't come much to Porifors."

"So you've explained," said Ista coolly. She allowed Cattilara to ease her and Liss into their own chambers and escape back to her nursing supervision.

Or whatever it was she did, in Illvin's service. Ista wondered if there was anything lacing that goat's milk in addition to the honey, or what strange spices might be sprinkled on that food he bolted, once a day. After which he gabbled incoherently, then slept the sun around, unable to be roused.

A seductively rational consideration, that one. Not a single dose of poison from a Roknari dagger, but an ongoing regimen, from a source much closer to home? It would account for the visible symptoms quite exactly. She was sorry she had thought of it. *Less disturbing than dreams of white fire, though.*

"Why did you pinch my arm?" Liss demanded when the door had closed.

"To stop your speech."

"Well, I figured *that*. Why?"

"The marchess was not best pleased with her groom's forwardness. I wished to save him a cuffing, or at least, sharp words."

"Oh." Liss frowned, digesting this. "I'm sorry I let him trouble you. He seemed harmless in the stables. I liked how he handled the horse. I never dreamed he would ask you for anything so foolish." She added after a moment, "You were kind not to mock him, or refuse his plea."

Kindness had nothing to do with it. "He certainly went to great pains to make it as *attractive* a proposition as possible."

The merry glint returned to Liss's eye in response to her wry tone. "*That's* so. And yet . . . it made it all seem sadder, somehow."

Ista could only nod agreement.

❧

It eased Ista's heart to have Liss's plain, practical ministrations again, readying her for bed. Liss bade her a cheerful good night and went off to sleep in the outer chamber, within call. She left the candle burning again at Ista's bidding, and Ista sat up on her pillows and meditated on the day's new revelations.

Her fingers drummed. She felt as restless as when she had used to pace round and round the battlements at Valenda Castle, till her feet blistered and the soles parted from her slippers and her attendants begged for mercy. That had been an opiate for thought, though, not its aid.

For all that it seemed a string of accidents had brought her to Porifors, the Bastard had claimed she was not here by chance. The gods were parsimonious, Lord dy Cazaril had once remarked to her, and took their chances where they found them. He had not pretended it was a positive feature, god-gnawed man that he was. Ista smiled in grim agreement.

How were prayers answered, anyway? For prayers were innumerable, but miracles were rare. The gods set others to their work, it seemed. For however vast a god might be, it had only the width of one soul at a time to reach into the world of matter: whether door, window, chink, crack, pinhole . . .

Demons, for all that they were supposedly legion, were not vast, possessing nothing like the infinite depth of *those* Eyes, but they seemed limited similarly; except that they could chew away at the edges of their living apertures, and so widen them, over time.

So who here must she reproach for praying for her advent? Or perhaps not for her, but just for help, and sending her was but a nasty jape of the Bastard's. She had absolved Lord Illvin when she'd thought him senseless, but if Goram spoke truth, he had periods of . . . if not lucidity, arousal, after all. And Goram himself had certainly made supplication of her, with the work of his hands if not words. Someone had laid that silent prayer of the white rose across Illvin's empty plate. Lady Cattilara plainly ached with the pain of her longing for a child, and her husband . . . was not what he seemed, either.

Foolish beyond hope to send a middle-aged former madwoman running down the roads of Chalion to fetch up here, and for what? Failed saint, failed sorceress, failed royina, wife, mother, daughter, failed . . . well, lover was not a role she'd ever attempted. Less even than failure, in her hierarchy of woe. At first, upon discovering Lord Arhys's relation to dy Lutez, she'd guessed this for a tribunal on the gods' parts, for her old, cold murder and sin confessed to dy Cabon back in Casilchas. Feared that she was slated to be dragged though all that stale guilt yet again: *Fetch a bucket of water for the drowning woman!*

But now . . . it seemed her self-involved expectations were mockingly thwarted. Not herself, but another, was the center of the god's attentions. Her lips puffed on a bitter laugh. And she was merely being . . . what? Tempted to meddle?

Tempted, certainly. The Bastard had plainly primed her with that salacious kiss of His. His questing tongue had sent a most cryptic message, but that part of it she had received clearly, body and mind.

What point, to wake that sleeping appetite here, now? What point ever? No dishes had been served up in tiny, backwater Valenda worth salivating over, even if the curse had not paralyzed her as much below the waist as above it. She was hardly to be faulted for failing her feminine duty to fall in love *there*. She tried to imagine dy Ferrej, or any other gentleman of the Provincara's entourage, as an object of desire, and snorted. *Just as well.* Anyway, a modest lady always kept her eyes downcast. She had been taught that rule by age eleven.

Work, the Bastard had said.

Not *dalliance*.

But what work? Healing? Enticing thought. But if so it was not, it appeared, to be effected with a simple kiss. Perhaps she'd just missed something on her first try, something obvious. Or subtle. Or profound. *Or obscene?* Though she had little heart for a second attempt. She briefly wished the god had been more explicit, then took back the wish as ill phrased.

But as disastrous as the situation already was, could even *she* make it worse? Perhaps she was here on the same principle as young physicians set to practice their experiments and new potions on the hopeless cases. So that no blame attached to their—usually inevitable—failures. *The dying, they do have at Porifors.* A little practice piece, this tightly contained domestic tragedy. Two brothers, a barren wife, one castle . . . perhaps it was not beyond her scope. Not like the future of a royacy, or the fate of the world. Not like the first time the gods had conscripted her into their service.

But why send me *in answer to a prayer, when you know perfectly well I can't do a thing without* You?

It wasn't too hard to follow the logic of *that* one to its inevitable conclusion, either.

Unless I open to You, You cannot lift a leaf. Unless You pour into me, I cannot do . . . what?

Whether a sally port was a passage or a barrier depended not on the materials of which it was made, but on its position. The free will of the door, as it were. All doors opened in both directions. She could not open the gate of herself a crack and peek out, and expect to still hold the fortress.

But I cannot see . . .

She cursed the gods methodically, in five couplets, in ferocious parody of an old childhood bedtime prayer, rolled over, and wrapped her pillow over her head. *This isn't defiance. This is shuffling.*

꩜

If any god dabbled in her dreams, Ista did not remember it when her eyes opened in the night. But regardless of the phantasms that troubled the mind, the body still had to piss. She sighed, poked her feet out of bed, and went to open the heavy wooden shutter to let in a little light. Near midnight, she guessed, by the misshapen moon's silver sheen. Well past the full, now, but the night was chill and clear. She rummaged under the bed for her chamber pot.

Finished, she eased the lid back on with a clink, frowned at how loud the noise seemed in the stillness, and pushed the pot back out of the way again. She returned to the window, intending to bar the shutters once more.

A shuffling of slippered feet sounded in the courtyard below, then scuffed quickly up the stairs. Ista held her breath, peering between the spirals of iron. Catti again, all soft, shimmering silks, flowing over her body like water as she moved in the moonlight. One would think the cursed girl would get cold.

She certainly wasn't carrying a pitcher of goat's milk this time. She wasn't even carrying a candle. Whether she clutched some smaller, more perilous vial close to her chest, or merely held her light robe closed, Ista could not tell.

She eased Lord Illvin's door open in silence and slid within.

Ista stood still at her window, staring into the dark, hands wrapped around the cold iron foliage.

All right. You win. I can't stand this any longer.

Teeth grinding, Ista sorted through her clothes presently hung on the row of wall pegs, drew down the black silk robe, and shrugged it on over her pale nightdress. She didn't wish to risk waking Liss by blundering in the dark through the outer chamber to the door. Did her window even open? She wasn't sure the iron rod holding the grating closed would move out of its stone groove at first, but it came up with a tug. The grating pushed outward. She hoisted her hips up to the sill and swung her legs out.

Her bare feet made less noise on the boards of the gallery than Catti's slippers had. As no orange glow had begun in the dark chamber opposite, Ista was unsurprised to find the inner shutters of Illvin's window open to the moonlight, too. But from Ista's vantage, easing up to the edge of the sinuous iron vines that guarded the opening, Catti was scarcely more than a dark shape moving among darker shapes, a scuff, a breath, the squeak of a floorboard softer than a mouse's cry.

The spot on Ista's forehead ached like a day-old scalding.

I can't see a benighted thing. I want to see.

Inside the room, fabric rustled.

Ista swallowed, or tried to. And prayed, Ista-fashion: or made a prayer of rage, as some claimed to do of song or the work of their hands. So long as it was from the heart, the divines promised, the gods would hear. Ista's heart boiled over.

I have denied my eyes, both inner and outer. I am not child, or virgin, or modest wife, fearing to offend. No one owns my eyes now but me. If I have not the stomach by now to look upon any sight in the world, good or evil, beautiful or vile, when shall I? It is far too late for innocence. My only hope is the much more painful consolation of wisdom. Which can grow out of knowledge alone.

Give me my true eyes. I want to see. I have to know.

Lord Bastard. Cursed be Your name.

Open my eyes.

The pain on her forehead flared, then eased.

She saw a couple of the old ghosts, first, hovering in air: not curiously, for no spirits so faded and cold could hold so coherent an emotion, but drawn as moths to a light. Catti's hand, then, impatiently swishing through the air, driving them off as one might brush away annoying insects.

She sees them, too.

Ista set aside the implications of this for later reflection as her vision began to fill with that milky fire she had seen in her dream. Illvin was the source of it, a flickering incandescence that ran the length of his body like spilled oil ignited by a brand. Catti was much darker, solider, but the details of her face, body, hands, slowly took shape and certainty. She was standing by the far side of Illvin's bed, and the rope of white fire was running out through her twisting fingers. Ista turned her head just enough to follow it, out the door, crossing the court. Without question, its liquid movement was away, not toward, the supine figure in the bed.

He was dressed again in the practical undyed linen robe, though his hair was still neatly braided. Catti reached down, plucked free the knot of the belt, and laid each half open, from shoulder to ankle. He was naked beneath except for the pale white strip of a bandage encircling his chest just below the heart, the hidden well from which that pale fire gushed and drained.

Catti's face was chill, still, nearly expressionless. She reached down to touch the bandage. The white light seemed to wind around her dark fingers like wool.

Of one thing Ista was certain: Cattilara was not the gate for any god. God light, in all its hues, was unmistakable to the inner eye. And Ista knew only one other root for such sorceries.

So where is the demon? Ista had not felt its malign presence before; what she had mainly felt in Cattilara's company was irritation. Enough to mask that deeper unease? Not entirely, it seemed in retrospect, even if Ista had misperceived her recurring clotted tension around the marchess as base envy. *Partly misperceived*, she corrected with grim honesty. Ista marshaled all the clarity of vision she could, widening her inner eye to take in all the living light that rippled in unhappy disorder around the room.

Not light: darkness, shadow. Floating under Cattilara's breastbone, a tight, dark violet knot, turned in on itself. Hiding? If so, not quite successfully, like a cat in a sack that had forgotten to pull in its tail.

But which was the possessor, which the possessed? The term *sorcerer* applied, confusingly, to both spiritual states; for all that the divines claimed they were theologically distinct, from the outside there was little practical way to tell them apart.

I can tell, it seems. But then, I'm looking from the other side. Cattilara rode this demon, not the other way around; it was her will that prevailed here, her soul that was ascendant in that lovely body. For the moment.

Cattilara ran one fingernail down Lord Illvin's torso from the hollow of his throat to his navel, and beyond. The fire seemed to intensify in its trail, divert downward as if flowing through a new channel.

She eased herself onto the bed beside him, leaned in, and began to methodically caress his body, from the shoulders downward, from the ankles upward, recentering the fountain of light over his groin. Her caresses grew more explicit. The gray eyelids never flickered, but other parts of Illvin's body began to respond to this focusing of attention. Alive he was on one level, flesh if not mind. Visibly.

Are they lovers, then? Ista's brows knotted. For all the efficient expertise, that was the most unloving touch Ista had ever seen. It sought to stimulate, not gratify, and took no satisfaction for itself. If *her* hands had the privilege of tracing that ivory skin over whipcord muscle, that darker velvet sensitivity, they would not be rough, abrupt, clawed with tension. *Her* palms would be open, drinking delight. That is . . . if she ever had the courage to touch anyone. The passion here was anger, not lust. *Lord Bastard, your blessings are being wasted in that bed.*

Catti was whispering. "Yes. That's right. Come on." The busy fingers worked. "It's not fair. Not fair. Your seed is thick, and yet my lord's has turned to water. What need have you for it? What need have you for anything?" The hands slowed again. Her eyes glittered, and her voice dropped still further. "We could ride *him*, you know. No one would ever know. Get a child all the same. It would be half Arhys's at

least. Do it now, while there's still time." Had that dark knot
beneath her breastbone fluttered?

A little silence, then her voice hissed. "*I don't want
second-best. He never liked me anyway. All his stupid jokes
I could never get. There is no man for me but Arhys. There
will never be any man for me but Arhys. Always and forever.*"

The knot seemed to cringe inward again. *Aye,* Ista
thought to it. *You are not the pregnancy she seeks, I'll warrant.*

Cattilara's hands opened: framed taut, aching flesh spinning a thread of white fire from its tip. "There. That should
hold for long enough." She eased off the bed, which creaked,
and flipped the robe almost closed again. Raised the sheet
again, very gently, and lowered it to Illvin's chest. Her hand
coursed just above the white line, not touching it, as she
slipped around the foot of the bed. Ista ducked down in a
crouch, hiding her face and hair beneath her wide black
sleeve. The creak of the door opening and closing again, the
snick of a latch. Footsteps rising on tiptoe, hurrying away.

Ista peeked over the balustrade. Catti rippled away over
the pavement below, silks fluttering behind her as she ran,
following the continuous line of light. Light that cast neither
shadow nor reflection. She, and it, vanished under the arcade.

What is this sorcery, Cattilara? Ista shook her head in bewilderment.

*I shall feed my starving eyes, then. Perhaps, when they
are full enough, they will teach me . . . something.*

And if not, I shall still have snatched a crumb.

The hinges on the door to Illvin's chamber were very
well oiled, Ista noticed. The heavy carved door moved easily. From here, she could hear faint snores from the next
chamber, beyond an inner door. Goram, or some like attendant, sleeping within call, should a miracle occur and Illvin
wake to call. Careful not to touch the floating line of light,
she eased her way around a chest and padded across the rugs
to Illvin's bedside. The opposite side from the one Catti had

taken. She delicately lifted his sheet down, opened his robe as Catti had, and studied him altogether.

Ignoring the obvious for a moment, she tried to study the swirling light, to read some pattern or message in it. The brightest was collected at his groin, temporarily, but nodes glimmered over navel, lip, and forehead as well as heart. Lip and forehead were extremely faint. She was certain he was thinner than when she had seen him in her first dream, cheeks more hollowed, ribs . . . she had not seen his ribs before, but she could surely count them now. She could mark the line of his pelvic bone, beneath his skin. Her finger traced it, paused.

He moved, barely: faint, highly recognizable twitches of lust . . . or, perhaps, the echoes of such movement, coursing back through the trembling line of light like a wave returning from some farther shore? Minutes slipped by; she could count her heartbeats. She could count his. They quickened. For the first time, his lips moved, but only to emit a low groan.

A strain, a shudder, a brighter blaring of light, then it was over. The cold fire coursed chaotically over his body, then recentered its wellspring over the dressing below his heart and pulsed on. Pumping out . . . what?

His flesh went back to looking disturbingly dead.

"So," Ista breathed. "Isn't that . . . curious."

Wisdom, or even knowledge, eluded her still. Well, some aspects of what she had just witnessed were very clear. Some . . . weren't.

Softly, she closed his robe, tied its belt. Drew the sheet up as it had been. Studied the floating line of light. She remembered her dream of it.

Dare I?

She certainly wasn't getting anywhere just staring at it. She reached forward, arched her hand around it. Paused.

Goram, I salute you.

She hitched her hip up on the bed and leaned forward. Touched her lips to Illvin's, then took a deeper caress from them. Closed her hand.

The light sputtered out.

His eyes sprang open; he inhaled her breath. She propped herself on one hand, beside his head, and gazed down into those eyes, as dark as she remembered from her first visions. His hand moved, circled up behind her head, gripped her hair.

"Oh. *That's* a better dream." Voice dusky as old honey, a soft northern Roknari-tinged accent: richer by far than she'd remembered from her own sleeping visions of him. He kissed her in return, cautiously at first, then more confidently—not so much in belief, as dizzily dispensing with belief.

She opened her hand. The light renewed itself, spiraled up from him, sped away. With a sigh of anguish, he faded again, eyelids not quite meeting. The gleam between his lashes was the more disturbing for being so motionless. Gently, she closed them for him.

She was by no means sure what she had just done, but the line of light had vanished along the whole of its length that she could see. On its terminating end, as well? And if that was the case . . . had it been another's turn to swoon? Arhys's? In Catti's arms?

Once, between ignorance, frenzied impatience, and terror, she had helped create a disaster. The night Arvol dy Lutez had died in the dungeons of the Zangre had been turbid with sorcery like this. Shot with searing visions, like this.

But set in motion by an Ista—*not* like this . . .

The terror that now throbbed dully in her head, she could do little about but endure. *In endurance, if nothing else, I am by now an expert.* Impatience she could swallow like a physician's bitter draught. Ignorance . . . she might advance upon. Like an army with banners, or just a forlorn hope, she could not say. But Ista was not ready to face another night's work like that one until she knew whether she was about to commit miracle or murder.

Swiftly, regretfully, she rose from Lord Illvin's bedside,

patted the sheet out straight, drew her black robe about her, and slipped away through the door. She ran on tiptoe along the gallery, lifted up the grating of her window, and jerked herself back through. Slid the locking rod down. Closed and barred the inner shutters. Sat back in her bed and watched the crack.

In another moment, the distant red glow from a candle wavered past, and slippered feet padded swiftly down the gallery. In a few minutes they returned the same way—slowly, pensively. In puzzlement? Whispered down the steps again.

I am ill suited to this murky task. The Bastard wasn't even her proper god. Ista had no doubt of her parentage, nor of the objects of her clumsy, stunted, hopeless desires. *Though a disaster out of season, I surely am.* But however many better godly couriers had been dispatched, she appeared to be the one who had actually arrived. *So.*

One way or another, she was determined to meet Lord Illvin awake tomorrow. What was raving incoherence to others might prove plain as god light to a madwoman.

13

THE SUN WAS BARELY OVER THE HORIZON WHEN LADY Cattilara bustled in ready to escort Ista to the morning temple services, with a ladies' archery contest and a luncheon to follow. This time, Ista had her excuses marshaled and ready.

"I'm afraid I tried to do too much, yesterday. I was feverish and ill last night. I mean to keep quietly to my chambers today and rest. Please do not think that I must be entertained every minute, Marchess."

Lady Cattilara lowered her voice to a confidential tone. "In truth, the town of Porifors has little diversion to offer. We are the frontier, here, and as harsh and simple as the task we must perform. But I have written to my father—Oby is the second town of Caribastos after the provincar's own seat. I am sure my father would be deeply honored to receive you there in a manner more befitting your rank."

"I am unfit to travel anywhere just yet, but when I am, Oby would be a most welcome halt on my return journey." Marginally less exposed than Porifors to the dangers of the border, and rather more heavily manned, Ista could not help reflecting. "That is a decision for another day."

Lady Cattilara nodded sympathetic understanding, but

looked pleased at the royina's vaguely worded acceptance. *Yes, I would imagine you would be relieved to see me shuffled off elsewhere.* Or—something would. Ista studied her.

Outwardly, she seemed the same as ever, all soft green silks and light linens over a body of yielding feminine promise. Inwardly . . .

Ista glanced at Liss, hovering solicitously to finish dressing Ista's hair and wrap her in her outer garments. A wholesome person had a soul congruent with the body, spirit occluded by the matter that generated and nourished it, and thus nearly as invisible to second sight as to the sight of the eyes. In the present god-touched magnification of her sensitivity, Ista fancied she could perceive, not intellect or emotion, but the state of the soul itself. Liss's was bright, rippling, colorful with swirling energies, and entirely centered. The maid who waited to carry off the wash water had a quieter soul, darkened with a smear of resentment, but equally congruous with the rest of her.

Cattilara's spirit was the darkest and densest, roiling with strain and secret distress. Beneath its surface another boundary lurked, darker and tighter still, like a bead of red glass dropped in a glass of red wine. The demon seemed much more tightly closed this morning than it had last night. Hiding? From what?

From me, Ista realized. The god scars upon her that were invisible to mortal eyes would surely shine like watch fires in the dusk to a demon's peculiar perceptions. But did the demon share all its observations with the mount it rode? How long, indeed, had Lady Cattilara been infested by her passenger? The dying bear had felt ragged, as if its demon were some ravenous tumor spreading tendrils into every part of it, consuming and replacing the bear's soul-stuff with itself. Whatever else Cattilara's soul was, it seemed still mostly her own.

"Did Lord Arhys return safely last night, to your heart's ease?" Ista inquired.

"Oh, yes." Cattilara's smile grew warm and secret.

"Soon your prayers to the Mother will change from supplication to thanksgiving, I'll warrant."

"Oh, I hope it may it be so!" Cattilara signed herself. "My lord has only a daughter—although Liviana is a pretty child, rising nine years old, lives with her maternal grandparents—but I know he longs for a son. If I might bear him one, he would honor me above all women!"

Above, perhaps, the memory of his first wife? Do you compete with a dead woman, girl? The blurred light of retrospective could lend a perfection hard for breathing flesh to match. Despite herself, Ista was moved to pity. "I remember this awkward period of waiting—the monthly disappointments—my mother used to write me severe letters, full of advice on my diet, as if it were *my* fault that my womb did not fill."

Cattilara's face livened with eager interest. "How unjust! Roya Ias was *quite* an old man—*much* older than Arhys." She hesitated curiously, then asked in a shyer voice, "Did you . . . do anything special? To get Iselle?"

Ista grimaced in remembered aggravation. "Every lady-in-waiting in the Zangre, whether they'd ever borne a child or not, had a dozen country remedies to press upon me."

Cattilara inquired, with unexpected wryness, "Did they offer any to Ias?"

"A fresh young bride seemed tonic enough for him." *At first.* Ias's oddly diffident early lustfulness had faded over time and with his otherwise well-concealed disappointment at a girl child's birth. Age and the curse more than accounted for the rest of his problems. Ista suspected that rather than swallowing noxious potions, he had taken to adding a private detour for stimulation by his lover before he visited her chamber. If she had continued infertile, might Lord dy Lutez have persuaded Ias to cut out the middle step and admit *him* directly to her bed? How long before the relentless expectation would have pressured Ista to compliance? Righteous indignation at such blandishment burned all the hotter when it concealed real temptation, for Arvol dy Lutez had been a striking man. That part, at least, of Cattilara's strange rage at her brother-in-law Illvin presented no block to Ista's understanding whatsoever.

Ista blinked, as a solution to the knotty problem of having Cattilara—and her demon—underfoot at Illvin's noontime awakening occurred to her. An ugly ploy, but effective. She added smoothly, "For myself, the last thing I tried before I became pregnant with Teidez was the poultice of finger-lily flowers. That remedy was the contribution of Lady dy Vara's old nurse, as I recall. Lady dy Vara swore by it. She'd had six children by then."

Cattilara's gaze grew suddenly intent. "Finger-lilies? I don't believe I know that flower. Does it grow here in the north?"

"I don't know. I thought I saw some growing near the meadow where Lord Arhys had his camp, the other day. Liss would recognize the plant, I'm sure." Behind Cattilara's shoulder, Liss's brows flew up in protest; Ista raised two fingers to command her silence. Ista went on, "The old nurse had it that they must be gathered by the supplicant herself, barefoot, at high noon when the sun is most fecund. Cut with a silver knife while praying to the Mother, the petals wrapped in a band of cheesecloth—or silk, for a lady—and worn about the waist until she next lies with her husband."

"What was the wording of the prayer?" asked Lady Cattilara.

"Nothing special, so long as it was sincere."

"This worked for you?"

"How can one be sure?" In fact, she'd never quacked herself with any of the suggestions she'd been pelted with by her well-wishers. Except for prayer. *And we all know how well that worked, in the end.* Ista mentally composed her next lure, but was cut short by her fish leaping into her net.

"Royina . . . since there is to be no ladies' fête this noon . . . might I borrow your handmaiden Liss to assist me in locating some of these wonderful blooms?"

"Certainly, Marchess." Ista smiled. "I shall rest and write letters."

"I will see you are brought luncheon," Cattilara promised, and curtseyed herself out. To go look for a silver knife and a silk scarf, Ista guessed.

"Royina," Liss hissed, when the marchess's steps had receded down the outside stairs. "I don't know anything about this flower you're talking about."

"Actually, it's a short green shoot that has little flowers dangling in a row, called Mother's bells, but it hardly matters. What I wish of you is that you get the marchess as far away from Porifors as you can persuade her to ride by noon. Let her pick any flower that isn't poisonous." Now, there was another temptation . . . Ista recalled childhood encounters with blister-ivy and stinging nettle, and smiled grimly. But whatever was going on with Cattilara was deathly serious, and no pretext for japery, no matter how the girl set Ista's teeth on edge. "Mark if she becomes suddenly anxious to return, or otherwise behaves or speaks oddly. Delay her as long as you reasonably may, however you can."

Liss frowned, her brow wrinkling. "Why?"

Ista hesitated. "When the stationmaster hands you a sealed pouch, do you peek inside?"

"No, Royina!" said Liss indignantly.

"I need you to be my courier in this."

Liss blinked. "Oh." She executed her bow-curtsey.

"The exercise will do the marchess no harm. Though . . . it would be well, also, if you are subtle in your misdirection, and take care not to offend her." That the demon dared not show itself before Ista did not guarantee that it dared not show itself at all. Ista had no idea of its powers and limits, yet.

Baffled but obliging, Liss undertook the charge. Ista ate a light breakfast in her room, opened the shutters to the morning light, and settled down with borrowed pens and paper.

First was a short, sharp note to the provincar of Tolnoxo, none too delicately conveying Ista's displeasure with his casual treatment of her courier and his failure more speedily to

produce the lost Foix and Learned dy Cabon, and a demand
of better assistance to Ferda. A more candid letter to the
archdivine of Maradi, pleading for the Temple's aid in
searching for the afflicted Foix and his companion. Liss had
found her way to Porifors speedily enough; what dire delay
could be keeping the pair of them . . . ?

Ista subdued her pent-up anxiety by penning a letter to
Chancellor dy Cazaril in Cardegoss, commending Liss and
Ferda and Foix and their company for their recent courage
and loyalty. Then a bland missive to Valenda, assuring all of
her safety, neglecting to mention any of the unpleasant details of her recent adventures. A somewhat less bland but
equally reassuring note to Iselle and Bergon, asserting that
she was safe but desiring conveyance . . . She glanced
through the iron grille toward the opposite gallery, and set
the last one aside unfinished, not so sure she desired conveyance just yet.

After a time spent thoughtfully tapping her cheek with
the feather of her quill, she reopened and added a postscript
to the letter to Lord dy Cazaril.

*My other sight has returned. There is a difficult situation
here.*

❧

At length, a page appeared to collect Liss for her noon expedition with the marchess. Sometime after that, a maid arrived with a luncheon for Ista on a tray, accompanied by a
gentlewoman of the marchess's retinue evidently detailed to
keep Ista company. Ista bade the maid set the tray on the
table and leave her, and ruthlessly dismissed the disappointed lady-in-waiting as well. As soon as their footsteps
had faded outside, Ista slipped through the outer chamber
and out the door. The sun, she noted grimly, shone down
high and hot into the stone court, making black accent marks
of the shadows. At the opposite end of the gallery, she
knocked on Lord Illvin's carved door.

It swung open. Goram's rusty voice began, "Now, did you have that fool of a cook stew the meat softer today—" then died away. "Royina." He gulped and ducked his head, but did not invite her inside.

"Good afternoon, Goram." Ista lifted her hand and pressed the door wide. He gave way helplessly, looking frightened.

The room was dim and cool, but a grid of light fell through the shutters onto the woven rugs, making the muted colors briefly blaze. Ista's eye summed the semblances with her first dream vision, but dismissed them abruptly from her attention when her second sight took in Goram.

His soul was bizarre in appearance, unlike any other that she had yet seen. It reminded her of nothing so much as a tattered cloth that had been splashed with vitriol, or eaten away by moths, until it hung together only by a few strained strings. She thought of the ragged bear. But Goram clearly was not presently demon-infested, nor was he dying. *He isn't well, though. Isn't . . . quite right.* She had to wrench her perception back to his gnarled physical surface.

"I wish to speak with your master when he wakes," she told him.

"He, um, don't always talk so's you can make out anything."

"That's all right."

The groom's head drew in upon his shoulders in the turtle hunch again. "Lady Catti, she wouldn't like it."

"Did she chide you yesterday, after I left?" *And how fiercely?*

He nodded, looking at his feet.

"Well, she's busy now. She has ridden out from the castle. You need not tell her I was here. When the servant brings Lord Illvin's tray, take it and send him away, and no one will know."

"Oh."

He seemed to digest her words a moment, then nodded and shuffled backward, allowing her entry.

Lord Illvin lay upon the bed in his linen robe, his hair un-braided and brushed back as she had first seen it in her dream. Motionless as death, but not stripped of soul-stuff; yet neither was his soul centered and congruent like Liss's, or even like tattered Goram's. It was as though it were being forcibly pulled out from his heart, to stream away in that now-familiar line of white fire. The barest tint of it remained within the confines of his actual body.

Ista took a seat on a chest by the wall to Illvin's right and studied that silent profile. "Will he wake soon?"

"Most likely."

"Carry on as you usually do, then."

Goram nodded nervously and pulled a stool and a small table up to the opposite side of the bed. He jumped up at a knock on the door. Ista leaned back out of view as he accepted a heavy tray covered with a linen towel and sent its bearer off. The manservant sounded relieved to be so dismissed. Goram settled down on his stool, his hands gripping each other, and stared at Lord Illvin. Silence settled thickly over the room.

The line of white fire gradually thinned. Drew down to the merest faint thread. Illvin's body seemed to refill, his soul-stuff deeply dense to Ista's second sight, but churning in complex agitation.

Illvin's lips parted. Abruptly, his breath drew in, then huffed out. His eyes opened to stare wildly at the ceiling. He jerked suddenly upright, his hands covering his face.

"Goram? Goram!" Panic edged his voice.

"Here, m'lord!" said Goram anxiously.

"Ah. There y'are." Illvin's speech was slurred. His shoulders slumped. His rubbed his face, dropped his hands to the coverlet, stared at his feet, the grooves deepening on his high brow. "I had that desperate dream again last night. The shining woman. Five gods, but it was vivid this time. I touched her hair . . ."

Goram looked across at Ista. Illvin's head turned to follow his glance.

His dark eyes widened. "You! *Who are you?* Do I dream still?"

"No. Not this time." She hesitated. "My name is . . . Ista. I am here for a reason, but I do not know what it is."

His lips puffed on a painful laugh. "Ah. Me, too."

Goram hastened to arrange his pillows; he fell back into them, as if this little effort had already exhausted him. Goram followed up immediately with a bite of stewed meat on a spoon, redolent with herbs and garlic. "Here's meat, m'lord. Eat, eat, quickly."

Illvin took it in, evidently before he thought to resist; he gulped it down and waved the following bite away. He turned his head toward Ista again. "You don't . . . shine in the dark, now. *Did* I dream you?"

"Yes."

"Oh." His brows knotted in bewilderment. "How do you know?" He failed to duck the insistent spoon, and was perforce silenced again.

"Lord Illvin, what do you remember about the night you were stabbed? In Princess Umerue's chambers?"

"Stabbed, me? I was not . . ." His hand felt beneath his robe for the bandage around his torso. "Curse you, Goram, why do you keep winding this benighted rag around me? I have told you . . . I have told you . . ." He clawed it away, pulled it loose, flung it down on the foot of the bed. The skin of his chest was unmarked.

Ista stood, came to the bedside, and turned the white cloth over. The dressing pad was soaked with a dull red-brown bloodstain. She angled it toward his gaze, raising her brows. He frowned fiercely and shook his head.

"I have no wound! I have no fever. I do not vomit. Why do I sleep so much? I grow so weak . . . I totter like a newborn calf . . . I cannot think . . . five gods, please not a palsy-stroke, drooling and crippled . . ." His voice sharpened in alarm. "Arhys, I saw Arhys fall at my feet. Blood—where is my brother—?"

Goram's voice went exaggeratedly soothing. "Now,

m'lord, now. The march is fine. I've told you that fifty times. I see him every day."

"Why doesn't he come to see me?" Now the slurred tongue was querulous, edging on a whine like an overtired child.

"He does. You're asleep. Don't *fret* you so." The harried Goram glowered briefly at Ista. "Here. Eat meat."

Arhys was in Umerue's chamber that night, too? Already the tale began to diverge from Cattilara's tidy version. "Did Lord Pechma stab you?" Ista asked.

Illvin blinked in confusion. He gulped down the latest bite Goram inserted, and said, "Pechma? That feckless fool? Is he still here at Porifors? What has Pechma to do with any of this?"

Ista said patiently, "Was Lord Pechma there at all?"

"Where?"

"In Princess Umerue's chamber."

"No! Why should he be? The golden bitch treated him like a slave, same as the rest. Double-dealing . . . double . . ."

Ista's voice sharpened. "Golden bitch? Umerue?"

"Mother and Daughter, but she was cruelly beautiful! Sometimes. But when she forgot to look at me, she was plain. As when I saw her before, in Jokona. But when her amber eyes were on me, *I* would have played her slave. No, not played. Been. But she turned her eyes on poor Arhys . . . all women do. . . ."

Well, yes . . .

"She saw him. She wanted him. She took him, as easily as picking up a, up a, something . . . I figured it out. I followed. She had him down on the bed. She had her mouth on his . . ."

"Meat," said Goram, and shoved in another bite.

An exotic woman, a virile man, a midnight visit, a spurned suitor . . . the roles the same, but the actors altered from Cattilara's version? Not Pechma but Illvin, the murderous intruder on some intimate scene? It hung together; it was not hard to imagine that Umerue, sent to woo Illvin for the sake of some alliance with Jokona, might for either personal *or* political reasons switch targets to his elder and more powerful brother. Cattilara was an impediment to such a design, true, but she was just the sort of bump in the road that subtle poisons were designed to smooth away.

What was harder to imagine was any such seductress getting past Cattilara to Lord Arhys in the first place. Cattilara plainly regarded Ista in the light of an elderly aunt, albeit one with a deliciously tragic romantic history, but nevertheless the marchess had made clear her claim on Arhys in every possible way before Ista's eyes. Was her fierce possessiveness just habit—or the result of a recent fright?

The new tale had a weight of likelihood. The despised bastard, half disenfranchised already, having a beautiful princess dangled before his eyes, only to have her suddenly snatched away by an elder brother who had it all *including* a beautiful wife, with no need of more; the rich, stealing from the poor . . . Reason aplenty to attempt fratricide in a jealous rage. Lesser men committed like acts everywhere, Quadrene or Quintarian, of every race and in every clime.

So: Illvin, attacking his brother and his paramour in a fit of jealousy, knifing the bitch-princess, having the weapon wrested from him and knifed in turn by the horrified Arhys, and left for dead in the sheets?

Wait. Illvin carefully stripped naked, his strangely unbloodied clothes neatly piled on a chair, the knife transferred back to Umerue's body, and *then* left for dead, Ista revised this. Her nose wrinkled in doubt.

Lord Pechma and his horse somehow got rid of, too. Concealment didn't seem Arhys's style, but—suppose he feared a war of reprisal from the prince of Jokona for the death of his beautiful—or plain—sister? Reason enough to steel himself to perform the rearrangements, to cast the blame upon the fled Jokonan courtier. Or murdered and buried Jokonan courtier, as the case might be. Arhys certainly had the strength and nerve for such an act. The misdirection would also have served to conceal Arhys's infidelity from his sleeping wife. Arhys's public prayers and concern for his fallen brother, more misdirection, or the fruit of guilt.

Another nicely tidy tale. It only failed to account for the advent of Cattilara's demon, and one mortal wound seeming to be shared between two brothers. And the fact that Cattilara seemed to know more about what was going on than Arhys did. And Ista's dreams. And the rope of fire. And the visitation of a god. And . . .

"I believe," said Lord Illvin in a thin voice, "that I am going mad."

"Well," said Ista dryly, "do you desire an experienced conductor on that road? If so, I am your woman."

He squinted at her in utter bewilderment.

From her dream in the tent, she remembered Arhys's wail of woe in a candlelit chamber. But was that an image from the past, or an image from the future?

She had no doubt that the man before her was capable of clever and subtle lies, when he had his wits about him. It was equally clear that his wits had gone away on the road as beggar boys, just now. He might babble or rave or hallucinate, but he did not lie. So . . . how many different ways might three people kill two of each other with one knife? Ista rubbed her forehead.

Goram bobbed an unhappy bow at her. "Lady. Please. He must get a chance to eat. And piss."

"No, don't let her go!" Illvin's arm shot out, fell back weakly.

She nodded at the anxious groom. "I will go out for a little. Not far. I'll come back soon," she added to the agitated Illvin. "I promise."

She let herself out onto the gallery and leaned against the wall with her arms crossed. She studied the floating line of light, reduced to a faint thread but still unbroken.

So. Illvin never saw his brother to speak with; Arhys never saw Illvin awake. Since that night, the two had never had a chance to compare their experiences, or whatever fragments they each remembered of their experiences.

Lady Cattilara, however, saw both. Spoke to both. Told whatever tales she pleased, to both.

Let us see if we can change that condition.

Ista waited a while for Goram to finish attending to his master's more intimate needs, to get him back to bed, to hastily stuff whatever foods, made soft for a sick man, down his gullet that time permitted. The rope was beginning to thicken slightly. Then noticeably. She reached out and delicately pinched thumb and forefinger around it in an O.

Lord Bastard, guide me as You will. Or, in Your case, whim.

She willed the rope to shorten, running back through her palm like spun wool. More than just sight had been included in the Bastard's gift, it seemed, for the manipulation seemed effortless. At first she mimed drawing it in hand over hand, but soon discovered she could simply bid it to flow. She kept her eye on the arcade opposite, where the passage came through from the next court.

Lord Arhys strode through onto the sun-splashed stones.

He wore light clothing suited to the hot afternoon, his gray linen vest-cloak with the gold trim swinging about his calves. He was clean, his beard new-trimmed. He yawned hugely, glanced up in concern at the corner room, saw her leaning on the balustrade, and gave her a courtier's bow.

Just wake from a nap, did you? And I know exactly how late you were up last night.

With difficulty, Ista tore her gaze from his elegant surface.

His soul was gray, strangely pale, off center, as if it lagged a little after him and left a trail of smoke.

Ah. Yes. Now I see. Ista stood up straight and moved toward the stairs, to meet him climbing up.

They came face-to-face, with her standing two steps above the tread upon which his booted feet paused. Arhys waited politely, smiling at her in puzzlement. "Royina?"

She took that strong chin in her hand, shivering at the tactile brush of his beard on her palm, leaned forward, and kissed him on the mouth.

His eyes widened, and he made a surprised muffled noise, but he did not retreat. She tasted his mouth: cool as water, and as flavorless. She drew back, sadly. *So. That didn't work either.*

His lips twisted up in a confused, enchantingly crooked grin, and he cocked his eyebrows at her as if to say, *What is this, lady?* As if women kissed him spontaneously on staircases every day, and he considered it uncivil to dodge.

"Lord Arhys," said Ista. "How long have you been dead?"

14

ARHYS'S SMILE GREW FIXED AND WARY. HE REGARDED Ista with startled concern, as if he feared the mad royina was having a relapse right in front of him, and, as her inadvertent host, he would be held responsible. "Madam—you jest . . . ?" An invitation to recant. A clear suggestion, *Please, don't do this. . . .* "My kisses are not usually so scorned!"

"I have seldom felt further from jest in my life."

He laughed uneasily. "I admit, my fevers have been a trouble to me this season, but I assure you, I am far from the grave."

"You have no fever. You don't even sweat. Your skin is the same temperature as the air. If it were not so beastly hot in this climate, more people would have noticed by now."

He continued to stare at her with the same perplexed expression.

Five gods. He really does not know. Her heart sagged.

"I think," she said carefully, "that you need to talk with your brother."

He grimaced in pain. "Would that I could. I pray for it daily. But he does not wake from his poisoned wound."

"Yes, he does. Each noon, when you have your little nap. Your only sleep of the day. Has your wife not told you this? She goes almost every day to oversee his care." *And sometimes at night, as well. Although it's not exactly* his *care that concerns her then, I expect.*

"Royina, I assure you it is not so."

"*I* just spoke with him. Come with me."

The disbelieving tilt of his mouth did not change, but when she turned and mounted the stairs again, he followed.

They entered Illvin's well-kept chamber. Goram, sitting watching his charge, saw Lord Arhys and shot to his feet, offering him his jerky, awkward bow, and a servile mutter that might have been, "M'lord."

Arhys's gaze swept down the still form in the bed. His lips thinned in disappointment. "It is all the same."

Ista said, "Lord Arhys, sit down."

"I shall stand, Royina." His frown upon her was growing less and less amused.

"Suit yourself."

The rope of white fire between the two was short and thick. Now that she knew to look for it, she could feel the demon's presence in it as well, a faint violet glow like a channel that underlay everything. It ran three ways, but only one link flowed with soul-stuff. She wrapped her hand about the bond running between the two men, squeezing it down to half its breadth. The constrained white fire backwashed into Illvin's body.

Lord Arhys's knees gave way, and he collapsed in a heap.

"Goram, help the march to a chair," Ista instructed. *Hold*, she silently commanded her invisible ligature, and it did.

She walked up by Illvin's bedside, studying the nodes of light. *Go up*, she commanded them silently, and made to push them with her hands, concentrate them at the forehead and the mouth, as Cattilara had at . . . that other theological point. The light pooled as she willed. *Stay there.* She cocked her head and studied the effect. *Yes. I think.*

Goram hurried to drag the chair, made of polished, interlaced curves of wood, out from the wall to Illvin's bedside. He hauled the startled-looking Arhys up by the shoulders and sat him in it. Arhys closed his mouth, rubbing at his face with a suddenly weak and shaking hand. Grown numb, was he? She ruthlessly stole Goram's stool and set it at the end of the bed, settling herself where she could best watch both brothers' faces.

Illvin's eyes opened; he took a breath and worked his jaw. Weakly, he began to push himself up on one elbow, until his gaze took in his brother, sitting at his right hand gaping at him.

"Arhys!" His voice rang with joy. His sudden smile transformed his face; Ista rocked back, blinking, at the engaging man so revealed. Goram bustled to shove pillows behind his back. He struggled up further, openmouthed with wonder. "Ah! Ah! You are alive! I did not believe them—they would never meet my eyes, I thought they lied to spare me—you are saved! *I* am saved. Five gods, we are *all* saved!" He collapsed back, wheezing and grinning, burst into shocking tears for five breaths, then regained control of his gasping.

Arhys stared like a stunned ox.

The slur was gone from Illvin's voice now, Ista noted with relief, though his lower limbs lay nearly paralyzed. She prayed that his wits would be likewise clarified. In a level tone that she was far from feeling, she asked, "Why did you believe your brother to be dead?"

"Ye gods, what was I to think? I *felt* that cursed knife go in—to the hilt, or I never survived a battle at some other poor bastard's expense—I could feel the push and give against my hand when it pierced the heart. I almost vomited."

Five gods, please, not fratricide. I didn't want this to be fratricide . . . She kept her voice steady despite the shaking in her belly. "How did you come to this pass? Tell me everything. Tell me from the beginning."

"*She* took him off to her chambers." He added to Arhys, "I was in a panic, because Cattilara had heard it from that meddling maidservant, and was determined to go up after you. I was sure she was unnatural by then—"

"Which she?" said Ista. "Princess Umerue?"

"Yes. The glittering golden girl. Arhys"—his grin returned, notably twisted—"if you would please stop falling over backward every time some aspiring seductress blows a kiss at you, it would be a great comfort to your relatives."

Arhys, his eyes crinkling with a delight that mirrored Illvin's, bent his head in a sheepish look. "I swear, I do nothing to encourage them."

"That, I'll grant, is perfectly true," Illvin assured Ista, as an aside. "Not that it's any consolation to the rest of us, watching the women flock past us without a glance in order to hang on him. Reminds me of a kitchen boy feeding his hens."

"It's not my doing. They throw themselves at me." He glanced at Ista, and added dryly, "On staircases, even."

"You could *duck*," suggested Illvin sweetly. "Try it sometime."

"I do, blast you. You've a highly flattering view of my ripening years if you imagine Cattilara leaves me any spare interest in dalliance, these days."

Ista wasn't quite sure how this statement squared with his actions on their first ride, but perhaps he was as charming to all rescued ladies, if only to divert them from weeping fits. With regret, Ista cut across their—obviously practiced, as well as obviously hugely relieved—banter. No doubt the god had sent her into this painful maze, baiting her with equal parts of curiosity and secret obligation, but she had no desire to linger in it. "Then why did you go to Princess Umerue's chambers? If you did."

Arhys hesitated, the levity draining from his face. He rubbed his forehead, and then his jaw and hands. "I don't quite know. It seemed like a good idea at the time."

Illvin said, "Cattilara would have it that the princess had slipped you a love potion, and you were not in control of yourself. For all my impatience with her fancies, I . . . hoped that it might be so. Because the alternative was much worse."

"What, that I'd fallen in love with Umerue?"

"No. That wasn't what I was thinking."

Ista's gaze upon him sharpened. "What were you thinking?"

Illvin's face grew introspective, grave. "Because she'd had the same effect on me. At first. Then she saw Arhys and forgot me. Dropped me to earth like a sack of bran. And . . . my wits came back to me. I finally remembered where I'd seen her before, except that it wasn't quite her—Arhys, do you recall my little trip down to Jokona about three years ago, when I went disguised as a horse dealer? The time I brought back Goram and the ground plan of Castle Hamavik."

"Yes . . ."

"I bought some stock from the lord of Hamavik. Paid too much, which made him happy and loquacious and inclined to take me for a fool. He treated me to dinner at his seaside villa, by which I might have guessed how much he'd skinned me if I hadn't known already. He showed off all his best possessions to me, including, briefly, his wife. A princess of Jokona, granddaughter of the Golden General himself, he told me, as if she were a pretty bit of blood stock he'd done a sharp trade for. Which I gather he must have, for the Regent Dowager Joen is not reputed to spend her children cheaply. Five gods, but he was a repulsive old goat. Golden she was, but she was the saddest silent mouse of a woman I'd ever seen. Drab. Fearful. *And she didn't speak more than six words of Ibran.*"

"Not the same princess, then," said Arhys. "The prince of Jokona has a pack of sisters. You mistook one for another, perhaps. Umerue's tongue was bold and witty."

"Yes. She made bilingual puns. Yet unless she has a twin sister of the same name, I'd swear her for the same woman." Illvin sighed, then his brow wrinkled. "Catti went ripping up to the princess's chambers in a fury, and I went charging after her. I was afraid of—I knew not what, but I thought, if nothing else, I might somehow warn you, and prevent a scene."

"My faithful flank man."

"*This* went beyond the bounds of duty, I thought. You were going to owe me, and I meant to collect, too. I begged Catti to at least let me go in first, but she ducked under my elbow. Our tumbling entry could not have been more ill timed. Speaking of bold tongues."

Dead men, Ista noted, couldn't blush. But they could at least look shamefaced.

"Even *I* couldn't blame Catti for going into a frenzy," Illvin continued. "But if that overdecorated dagger had been sitting at the bottom of that pile of gear instead of atop it, I might have grabbed her quicker. She went straight for the princess, screaming. Wanted to cut her face off. For understandable reasons."

"I remember that part," said Arhys slowly, as if unsure. "It comes back . . ."

"You pushed the golden slut out of the way, I seized Catti's knife hand, and between us we might have saved the moment if you hadn't tripped, lunging out of bed. Were you in such a whirl of lust that you couldn't wait to undress? If *I'd* had such an opportunity—never mind. But the best swordsman in Caribastos, hobbled by his own *trousers*—five gods, Arhys! Catti wouldn't have had the strength to drive that big blade home if she *had* been trying for you, if you hadn't toppled into us with your ankles twisted up." His indignation faded, and his excited voice slowed. "I *felt* the blade go in. I was sure we'd done you, among us all."

"It wasn't Catti's fault!" Arhys said hastily. "Oh, the look of woe upon her face—it was like being stabbed again. No wonder she . . . After that . . . after that, I don't remember."

"You fell at my feet. The fool girl yanked the blade back out of you—I shouted, *No, Catti!* Too late. Though I'm not sure if leaving it in would have staunched anything, the way you spurted. I was trying to get one hand pressed to your wound and hang on to Catti's sleeve with the other, but she twisted right out of her overrobe. Umerue was shrieking, climbing back over the bed to try to get to you—I wasn't sure why. Catti plunged the knife straight into her stomach. Umerue grabbed the hilt, then looked up and gave me the saddest look. And said *Oh*, in this lost little voice. Like . . . like her voice when first I ever saw her." His voice faded further. "She just said *Oh*. Catti's face took on a very strange air, and after that . . . *I* don't remember." He sank back on his pillows. "Why can't I . . . ?"

Ista's hands were trembling. She hid them in her skirt. "What *do* you remember next after that, Lord Illvin?" she asked.

"Waking up here. With my head buzzing. Dizzy and sick. And then waking up here again. And again. And again. And again. And—something *must* have happened to me. Was I hit from behind?"

"Cattilara said Pechma stabbed you," said Arhys. He cleared his throat. "And Umerue."

"But he wasn't there. Did he come in after us? And besides, I am not"—Illvin's hand went to his chest, beneath the sober linen, and came away smeared carmine—"ow! . . . stabbed?"

"What was Pechma like?" asked Ista, doggedly.

"He was Umerue's clerk," said Arhys. "He had a disastrous taste in clothing, and was the butt of her retinue's jokes—there's always one such feckless fellow. When Cattilara told me he had attacked Illvin, I said it was impossible. She said it had better be possible, or we'd have a war with Prince Sordso before the body was carted home. And that no one among the Jokonans would stand up for Pechma. And indeed, she proved right about that. She also said to be patient, that Illvin would recover. I was beginning to doubt, but now I see it is so!"

Ista said, "You've eaten no food for over two months, yet you didn't *wonder*?"

Illvin glanced up from his smeared hand to stare at Arhys, startled, his eyes narrowing.

"I ate. I just couldn't keep it all down." Arhys shrugged. "I seem to get enough."

"But he's going to be all right now," said Illvin slowly. "Isn't he?"

Ista hesitated. "No. He's not."

Her gaze traveled to the silent auditor of all this, half crouched by the far wall. "Goram. What did you think of Princess Umerue?"

The noise he made in his throat sounded like a dog growling. "She was bad, that one."

"How could you tell?"

His face wrinkled. "When she looked at me, I was cold afraid. I stayed out of her sight."

Ista considered his ravaged soul-stuff. *I imagine you would.*

"I would like to think that Goram helped bring me back to my senses," said Illvin ruefully, "but I'm afraid that was just the effect of Umerue's inattention."

Ista studied Goram briefly. His soul-scars were a distraction in this reckoning, she decided; they were an old injury, old and dark. If, as she was beginning to suspect, he'd once been demon-gnawed, it was well before this time. Which left . . .

"Umerue was a sorceress," Ista stated.

A brief, fierce grin flashed across Illvin's face. "I guessed it!" He hesitated. "How do you know?" And after another moment, "Who *are* you?"

I have seen her lost demon, Ista decided not to say just yet. She desperately wished dy Cabon were here now, with the theological training to unravel this tangle. Illvin was staring at her more warily of a sudden, worried—but not, she thought, disbelieving.

"They say you were seminary-trained in your youth, Lord Illvin. You can't have forgotten it all. I was told by a learned divine of the Bastard's own order that if a demon's mount dies, and the departing soul has not the strength left to drag it back to the gods, it jumps to another. The sorceress died, and the demon is in neither of you, I assure you. Who's left?"

Arhys was looking sick. For a walking corpse, this ought to have been an improvement, Ista thought, but it wasn't. "Catti has it," he whispered.

He wasn't arguing with her about this one, she noticed. Ista nodded approval, feeling absurdly like some tutor commending a pupil for getting his sums right. "Yes. Catti has it now. And *her* bidding is for it to keep you alive. Well, animate. In as far as its powers may be forced to work that way."

Arhys's mouth opened, closed. He said at last, "But . . . those things are dangerous! They consume people alive—sorcerers lose their souls to them. Catti, she must be treated—I must summon the Temple theologians, to cast it out of her—"

"Hold a moment, Arhys," said Illvin, sounding strained. "I think we need to think this through . . ."

A thumping sounded on the gallery outside: running feet. Two pairs. The door was yanked open. Cattilara, barefoot, in disarrayed riding dress, her hair wind-wild, tumbled through gasping. Liss followed, nearly as out of breath.

"Arhys!" Cattilara cried, and flung herself upon him. "Five gods, five gods! What has that woman done to you?"

"Sorry, Royina," Liss muttered to Ista's ear. "We were in the middle of this field when she suddenly cried that there was something wrong with her lord, ran for her horse, and galloped off. There was no diverting her with anything short of a crossbow bolt."

"Sh. It's all right." Ista quelled a twinge of nausea at her trick on Catti, effective though it had been. "Well—sufficient. Wait by Goram, but do not speak or interrupt. No matter how strange what you hear may sound."

Liss dipped dutifully and went to lean on the wall by the groom, who nodded welcome. She cocked her head dubiously at Lady Cattilara, sobbing in Lord Arhys's enfeebled grip.

Cattilara grasped his hand in turn, tested its weakness, and turned her tear-stained face up to her husband's. "What has she *done* to you?" she demanded.

"What have *you* done to me, Catti?" he asked gently in turn. He glanced at his brother. "To both of us?"

Cattilara looked around, glaring at Ista and at Illvin. "You *tricked* me! Arhys, whatever they say, they lie!"

Illvin's brows went up. "Now, there's a comprehensive indictment," he murmured.

Ista tried to ignore the distracting surfaces for a moment. The demon was as tightly closed as Ista had yet seen it, dense and shiny, as if, all other routes blocked, it was trying to flee inside itself. It seemed to tremble.

As if in terror? Why? *What does it think I can do to it?* More: *What does it know that I don't?* Ista frowned in mystification.

"Catti." Arhys stroked her wild hair, patting it smooth, absorbing her sobs on his shoulder. "It's time to tell the truth. Sh, now. Look at me." He took her chin, turned it to his face, smiled into her wet eyes with a look that would have made Ista's heart, she thought, melt and run down into her shoes. It had an even less useful effect on the hysterical Catti. She slithered out of his weak grip and crouched at his feet, weeping on his knees like a lost child, her only clear words a repeated, *No, no!*

Illvin rolled his eyes ceilingward, and rubbed at his forehead in exasperation with an equally weak swipe. He looked as though he would gladly trade what was left of his soul at this moment for escape from the room. He glanced up to meet Ista's commiserating gaze; she held up two fingers, *Wait . . .*

"Yes, yes," Arhys murmured to his wife. His hand, on her head, gave it a soft little shake from side to side. "I command all here at Porifors; all its lives are in my hands. I have to know all. Yes."

"Good, Arhys," muttered Illvin. "Stand up to her, for once."

Ista pressed her hand to her mouth, for Arhys was speaking. *Yes, better that this should come from him. She will not resist him, or at least, not as much.*

"What happened after you stabbed the . . . sorceress?" Arhys asked. "How did you capture her demon?"

Catti sniffled, swallowed, choked, and coughed. In a rough voice she answered, "It just *came* to me. I didn't do *anything*. It was either me or Illvin, and it was more afraid of Illvin." A grim little smile fleeted across her face. "It promised me anything if I would flee away. But there was only one thing I wanted. I wanted you back. I *made* it put you back. It still wants to escape, but I'll never let it, *never*."

Will against will. The demon, Ista suspected, was experienced, strong with the consumption of more than one life. But on certain narrow issues, Cattilara was more willful. More than willful: obsessed. If the demon had mistaken Catti for a more tractable mount than Illvin, it had been in for an interesting surprise. For all her exasperation with Catti, Ista felt a certain dark satisfaction at the thought of the demon's dismay.

"You do realize," Ista said, "that the demon is stealing life from Illvin to keep Arhys . . . moving?"

Catti's head jerked up. "It's only fair. *He* stabbed Arhys; let *him* pay!"

"Hold hard!" said Illvin. "It wasn't *just* me in that botch-up."

"If you hadn't grabbed my hand, it wouldn't have happened!"

"No, nor if Arhys hadn't tripped, or if Umerue had dodged the other way, or, or any of a hundred other things. But we all did. And it did." His mouth set in a flat line.

"Yes," said Ista slowly. "Four persons combined to effect an outcome desired, I daresay, by none. I am not so sure about the . . . fifth party present."

"It's true," said Illvin, "that demons thrive on misfortune and disorder; it is their nature, and the magic they lend partakes of that nature. Or so the divines always taught me." He turned against his pillows and studied his sister-in-law uneasily.

"Well, *this* demon was sent here," said Cattilara. "*On

purpose. It was supposed to seduce Illvin, or Arhys, or both, and take Castle Porifors from within for the prince of Jokona. I stopped *that* from happening. As much as any soldier pushing back a scaling ladder in a siege." She tossed her hair and glowered, as if daring anyone to criticize *this* achievement.

Illvin's lips pursed in a look of sudden enlightenment. Arhys's brows drew down in dismay.

"And Lord Pechma?" prompted Ista.

"Oh, Pechma was easy. The demon knew all about him." Cattilara sniffed disdain. "All I had to do, after I'd arranged Illvin and walked Arhys back to *our* bed, was find Pechma and accuse him, and convince him he would be hanged out of hand in the morning if he didn't run away. He did the rest himself. He's probably still running."

The young woman had spent a busy night, Ista reflected. The artistic malice of Illvin's naked *arrangement* took her aback. A little revenge, perhaps, upon a man who'd remained steadfastly undazzled by his brother's choice of bride?

"So *none* of this is *Arhys's* fault," Catti continued passionately. "Why should *he* be the only one to suffer?" She turned her angry face to Ista. "So, you—whatever you have done to bind him to this chair—you let him up!"

Ista touched her lips. "Very many people suffer, who are not at fault," she said. "It's not a new condition in the world. I will—as you say—release Arhys in a while, but all must speak freely first. The Temple tells us that demons work their wonders at a terrible cost. Just how long do you imagine you can keep this one going?"

Cattilara's jaw set. "I don't know. As long as I breathe and have will! Because if the demon magic stops, Arhys *dies.*"

"If . . . that is indeed the alternative," Illvin put in suddenly, "perhaps this turn and turnabout is no bad thing. I can stand to share . . . half, say. Suppose half of each day should be Arhys's, and half mine?"

And then he need not be a fratricide? Or even one-quarter of a fratricide? The rising hope was writ plain in his face. Cattilara brightened at the unexpected offer of alliance, and she looked up at Illvin with new speculation.

Ista hesitated, shaken in her certainties. *Uncertainties*, her bleak thought corrected. "I think," she said, "this cannot work, or cannot work for very long. However starved it is, the demon must be slowly consuming Catti, or it should have faded by now, or been unable to maintain its spell. Learned dy Cabon told me that the demon always turns the tables on its mount, given enough time."

"So Arhys is saved, I will take the risk!" said Cattilara.

Arhys drew a sharp breath of protest and shook his head.

"Seems almost worthwhile to me," muttered Illvin darkly.

"But it's not a risk. It's a certainty. And Arhys dies the same, and Cattilara is destroyed."

"But *when*, how long, *that's* the question!" Cattilara argued. "All sorts of other things could happen before . . . then."

"Yes, and I can tell you some of them," said Ista. "Illvin, I am sure, studied the theology of death magic in the Bastard's seminary. I had a closer acquaintance with it, once. Arhys isn't *alive* now. The demon captured his severed spirit and returned it to haunt his own body. A familiar, congenial abode, I suspect, in some ways. But he is cut off from the support of his god, and his spirit is equally torn from the nourishment of matter. He cannot maintain life, except by what is plundered from Illvin, nor increase it, nor *engender* it."

Cattilara flinched, hunching her shoulders in protest.

Ista felt her way further into the dark consequences. "So his fate must be the fate of the lost spirits. Slowly to fade, to blur, to grow unmindful of himself, the world, his memories—his loves and hates—to forget. It is a sort of senility. I have seen the blind ghosts drifting. It is a quiet damnation, and merciful—for them. Less merciful for a man still in his body, I think."

"You mean he'll lose his *wits*?" said Illvin, aghast.

"That's . . . not so good," said Arhys. "I have not so many to spare as you." He attempted to smile at his brother. The attempt failed miserably.

Ista bit her lip and forged on. "I have a guess why the demon gives Illvin so little time, barely enough—no, not even enough—to eat. Why their shares are so very uneven. I think, when Illvin is awake, the demon . . . loses ground, maintaining Arhys's body. For every hour of waking life given to Illvin, the dead body decays a little more. In time, the rot shall start to be evident to the senses of others." It was evident to her heightened sensitivity already, now that she knew how to look. *I do not love my new education.* "Is that the fate you desire for your handsome husband, Lady Cattilara? A senile mind trapped in a decomposing body?"

Cattilara's lips moved, *No, no,* but she did not speak. She hid her face against Arhys's knees.

Gods, why did you give this vile task to me? Ista spoke on, relentlessly. "Illvin is dying too, being slowly drained of more life than he can replace. But if Illvin dies, Arhys will . . . stop, as well. Both their mother's sons lost together. *Not* her wish, I can assure you. Which end will come first in this evil race, I cannot guess. But that is the ultimate arithmetic of demon magic: two lives traded for one, then that one subtracted. Leaving, for all your pains, nothing. Do I have my tally theologically correct, Lord Illvin?"

"Yes," he whispered. He swallowed and found his voice. "Demon magic—the divines say—invariably engenders more chaos than it ever produces order. The cost is always higher than the prize. Some who dabble in demons try to spread the cost to others and keep the prize for themselves. It seldom works for long. Although it is said that some very wise and subtle theologians, Temple sorcerers, can use the demon magic according to its nature, and not against it, and yet effect good. I never quite understood that part."

Ista was very unsure about her next move, but it seemed the logical progression. She had a profound mistrust of logic; it was quite as possible to reason one's way, step by slow step, into a mire of deep sin as it was to fall into it head-long. "I have now heard depositions from all concerned here except one. I think this demon has acquired the gift of speech. One wonders from whom, if it can make . . . bilingual puns, but anyway. I would speak with it. Lady Cattilara, can you let it come up for a time?"

"No!" She frowned at Ista's look, and added, "It's not me that's the problem. It tries to get away. It will try to run off with my body, if it can."

"Hm," said Ista. She didn't greatly trust Cattilara, but this assertion could well be true.

"Tie her to the chair," Liss suggested laconically from her place by the wall. Ista looked over her shoulder at the girl; Liss raised her eyebrows and shrugged. She kept a detached posture, but her eyes were wide and fascinated, as if she were watching a play and wanted to hear the next act.

"You don't understand," said Cattilara. "It won't want to go back in, afterward."

"I will undertake to hold it," said Ista.

Illvin frowned curiously at her. "How?"

"I don't think you can," said Cattilara.

"*It* does. Or it would not fear me so, I think."

"Oh." Cattilara's face screwed up in thought.

"I think," said Arhys slowly, "this prisoner's interrogation could be a most important one. It touches on the defense of Porifors. Will you dare it, dear Catti—for me?"

She sniffed, frowned, set her teeth.

"I know you have the courage," he added, watching her.

"Oh—very well!" She made a face and climbed to her feet. "But I don't think this is going to work."

The young marchess watched with dismay as Goram, with Liss's assistance, dragged the half-paralyzed Arhys out of the chair to sit on the floor propped up against the side of the bed. Cattilara cooperated, though, plopping down in his vacated spot and laying her hands out on the wooden arms. Goram hastened to produce makeshift ties from Illvin's stock of belts and sashes.

"Use the cloths," Arhys advised anxiously. "So they will not cut into her skin."

Ista glanced at the scabs circling her own wrists like bracelets.

"Tie my ankles, too," Cattilara insisted. *"Tighter."*

Goram was overcautious, under the march's worried eye, but Liss finally achieved knots that Cattilara approved. The ties seemed more bundles than bindings by the time Liss finished.

Ista moved her stool over to face Cattilara, very conscious of Arhys's strong, limp body laid out by her skirts. "Go ahead, then, Lady Cattilara. Release the demon, let it up."

Cattilara's eyes closed. Ista half closed hers, trying to see those inner boundaries with her inner eye. It was not so much a case of letting, it seemed, as driving. "Come out, you," Cattilara muttered, sounding like a boy poking a badger out of its hole with a stick. "Up!"

A surge of invisible violet light—Ista summoned all her sensitivity. On the surface, Cattilara's expression changed, the stiff anxiety giving way, briefly, to a languid smile; her tongue ran over her lips, lasciviously. She grimaced, as if stretching the muscles of her face in unaccustomed directions. The violet tinge flowed throughout her body, to the fingertips. Her breath drew in.

Her eyes snapped open, widening in terror at the sight of Ista. "Spare us, Shining One!" she shrieked. Everyone in the room flinched at the sharp cry.

She began to rock and yank at her bindings. "Let us up, untie us! We command you! Let us go, let us go!"

She stopped, and hung panting, then a sly look flashed in her face. She sank back, closed her eyes, opened them again, returning to that stiff, blinking anxiety. "As you see, it's useless. The stupid thing won't come out, even for me. Let me up."

The violet tint, Ista noted, still filled Cattilara's body from edge to edge. She waved back Liss, who had started forward with a disappointed look on her face. "No, the creature lies. It's still right there."

"Oh." Liss returned to the wall.

Cattilara's face changed again, dissolving into rage. "Let us go! You blockheads, you have no idea what you have brought down on Porifors!" She bucked and jerked with terrifying strength, rocking the chair. "Flee, flee! We must flee! All flee! Go while you can. *She* is coming. *She* is coming. Let us go, let us go—" Cattilara's voice rose and broke in a wordless scream. The chair began to topple: Goram caught it and held it as it thumped and scraped.

The frenzied struggles did not diminish, though Cattilara grew scarlet with the effort, and her breath pumped in frightening rasps. Was the demon desperate enough to seek its escape through Cattilara's death, if it could arrange it? Yes, Ista decided. She could well picture it breaking its mount's neck by running madly against a wall, or flinging her headfirst over a balcony. Threatening pain to Cattilara's body was obviously useless, even if Arhys would . . . well, he'd have no choice but to sit still for it. But it was clearly a futile tactic.

"Very well." Ista sighed. "Come back up, Lady Cattilara."

The violet tide seemed to slosh back and forth within the confines of Cattilara's spasming body. The tint receded, but then flooded back. Cattilara unable to regain control? Ista hadn't expected this. *Oh, no. And I promised her I would hold it . . .*

"Stay," said Ista. "I was sent by the god to cut this knot. Release Arhys, and I will release you." Would it believe her? More important, would the threat jolt Catti into ascendancy again?

The demon-Catti froze in its fight, staring through wide eyes. The soul-stuff in the conduit gushed back toward Illvin. Abruptly, the horrified expression drained from Arhys's face, to be replaced with—nothing at all. A slack, pale stillness. He toppled over on his side like a rag doll falling. Like a corpse collapsing. Porifors's brilliant champion turned to a carcass, a mass of dubious meat it would take two men to drag away.

But his spirit was not uprooted in the white fire Ista had seen in the dying before. His ghost merely drifted apart, shifting from the locus of his body but scarcely otherwise changed. A shock of horror raced through Ista. *Five gods. He is sundered already. His god cannot reach him. What have I done?*

"Mmmmmm PUT HIM BACK!" Cattilara raged up to full control of her body like an unleashed mastiff taking down a bull by its nose. The violet light snapped closed into a tight, defensive ball, the channels reappeared, the fire flowed again. Arhys's breath drew in with a jerk; he blinked and opened his jaw to stretch his face, and pushed himself back into a sitting position, looking half stunned.

Ista sat shaken. The ploy had worked on Cattilara as her impulse had guessed, but had revealed . . . something she scarcely understood. *No more ploys. I have not the stomach for them.*

Cattilara hung wheezing in her bindings, staring malignantly at Ista. "You. You horrid old bitch. You tricked me."

"I tricked the demon, too. Are you sorry?" She signed to Goram and Liss, and they began cautiously unwinding the marchess's restraints.

Illvin, who had been peeking worriedly over the side of his bed at his brother, leaned back again and stared in disquiet at Ista. "How are you doing this, lady? Are you perchance a sorceress, too? Are we to trade one demon enemy for a stronger one?"

"No," said Ista. "My unwelcome gifts stem from another source. Ask Catti's . . . pet. *It* knows." *Better than I do, I suspect.* If possession of or by a demon made one a sorcerer, and the hosting of a god made one a saint, what ambiguous hybrid did one become in the hands of the demon-god?

"God-touched, then—you claim?" he asked. Neither believing nor disbelieving yet, but watchful.

"To my everlasting sorrow."

"How came this about?"

"Some suffering bastard prayed to a god too busy to attend to him, and He delegated the task to me. Or so He feigned."

Illvin sank down in his sheets. "Oh," he said very quietly, as her meaning sank in. After a moment, he added, "I would speak more with you on this. In some, um, less busy hour."

"I'll see what I may do."

Arhys moved his nearly nerveless hand to caress his wife's ankle. "Catti. This can't go on."

"But love, what shall we *do*?" She rocked her head to favor Ista with a heartbroken glare. "You cannot take him *now*. It's too soon. I will not give him up *now*." She rubbed at the red marks on her arms as her ties fell away.

"He's already had more time than is given to many men," Ista chided her. "He accepted the risks of his soldier's calling long ago; when you bound yourself to him in marriage, you accepted them, too."

But what of his sundering? Death of the body was grief enough. The slow decay of the ghosts, souls who had refused the gods, was a self-destruction. But Arhys had not chosen this exile; it had been imposed upon him. Not his soul's suicide, but its murder . . .

Ista temporized. "But no, it need not be today, in hasty disarray. There is a little time yet. Enough to put his affairs in order while he can still command his wits, if he does not tarry, enough to write or speak his farewells. Not much more than that, I think." She considered Illvin's dangerously emaciated fragility. *This tangle is far worse than I first guessed. And even second sight does not yet see a way out.*

Arhys shoved himself upright. "You speak sense, madam. I should call the temple's notary to me—review my will—"

"It's not fair!" Cattilara lashed out again. "Illvin slew you, and now he'll gain all your possessions!"

Illvin's head jerked back. "I am not *destitute*. I do not desire the dy Lutez properties. To avoid that taint, I would gladly give up any expectations. Will them to my niece, or to the Temple—or to *her*, even." A twist of his lips indicated his brother's wife. He hesitated. "Except for Porifors."

Arhys smiled, staring down at his boots. "Good boy. We do not yield Porifors. Hold to that, and you shall serve me still, even when my grave has swallowed all vows."

Cattilara burst into tears.

Ista levered her exhausted body upright from her stool. She felt as though she had been beaten with sticks. "Lord Ill-vin, your brother must borrow of you for a little longer. Are you ready?"

"Eh," he grunted, without enthusiasm. "Do what you must." He glanced up at her and added with suppressed urgency, "You will come again, yes?"

"Yes." She moved her hand, released her ligature.

Illvin sank back. Arhys rolled to his feet, a picture of strength again. "Ah!"

He enfolded the weeping Cattilara in his arms and led her out, murmuring comforting endearments.

Yes, Ista thought bitterly. *You caught her—I'll bet you didn't even try to dodge—you deal with her* . . . And he would, she felt sure. What less would one expect from a man with soap in his saddlebags . . . ? Her temples were throbbing.

"Liss, I'm going to go lie down now. I have a headache."

"Oh." Liss came promptly to her side, offering her arm in support. As a lady-in-waiting she had her limits, but Ista had to allow, she was one of the best courtiers she'd ever encountered. "Would you like me to bathe your forehead in lavender water? I saw a lady do that, once."

"Thank you. That would be lovely."

She glanced back at Lord Illvin, lying silently, emptied of life and wit again. "Take care of him, Goram."

He bobbed a bow, gave her a look of inarticulate frustration, and abruptly dropped to his knees and kissed the hem of her skirt. "Bles't One," he mumbled. "Free him. Free us all."

Ista swallowed aggravation, produced an unfelt smile for him, extracted her skirt from his grip, and let Liss usher her out.

15

A PALL WAS CAST OVER PORIFORS THAT EVENING. THE castle's master and mistress withdrew into private conclave, and all the planned entertainments were abruptly canceled. Ista could only be relieved to be left in her chambers. Toward sunset, Liss reported, a few of Arhys's key officers were called to him, and exited much later looking very grim. Ista hoped the march had mustered the wit to leave the original story of Umerue's death intact and devise some other tale to cover his impending—or was that retroactive?—lethal illness. But given that the truth implicated the marchess for the Jokonan princess's murder, Ista couldn't picture Cattilara rushing to, nor Arhys permitting, public confession.

Ista's dreams were untroubled that night by gods or visions, although made unpleasant enough by murky, erratic nightmares involving either disastrous travel on broken-down or dying horses, or confused wandering through crumbling, architecturally bizarre castles for the repair of which she was somehow responsible. She woke poorly rested, and waited impatiently for noon.

She sent Liss to help Goram and warn him of her visit, then watched for the meal tray to be brought up. It was handed in at Lord Illvin's door by the maid; shortly afterward Liss emerged and strolled across the gallery to Ista's chambers.

"Goram will signal by opening the door when he's ready," Liss reported. She was subdued, still unsettled by yesterday's evil wonders and increasingly worried for Foix, for all that Ista had assured her that he must be in the hands of the archdivine of Maradi by now. Liss had been more consoled by Ista's pointing out that Lady Cattilara had hosted a more powerful demon than Foix's for over two months without visible deterioration. Ista only wished her own heart could share in the reassurance she ladled out.

At last the carved door on the gallery opposite swung open, and Liss escorted Ista across.

Illvin was sitting up in bed, dressed in tunic and trousers, hair brushed back and tied at his nape.

"Royina," he said, and bowed his head. He looked both wary and shocked. Goram or Liss or both had presumably finally informed him of Ista's rank and identity, in the little time since he had returned to consciousness. "I'm sorry. I swear I prayed for help, not for you!"

His speech was slurred again. Ista was reminded that while she'd had a day to digest the developments, Illvin had only been granted an hour. She sighed, went to his bedside, and stole the white fire from the lower half of his body to reinforce the upper. He blinked and gulped.

"It's not that—I didn't mean to insult . . ." His words trailed off in embarrassed confusion, not slurred now, just mumbled. He attempted to shift his legs, failed, and eyed them with misgiving.

"I suspect," she said, "that *royina* is not the capacity in which I was called here. The gods do not measure rank as we do. A royina and a chambermaid likely look much the same, from their perspective."

"You must admit, though, chambermaids are more numerous."

She smiled bleakly. "I seem to have a calling. It is not by

my choice. The gods appear attracted to me. Like flies to blood."

He waved one weakened hand in protest at this metaphor. "I confess, I have never thought of the gods as flies."

"Neither have I, really." She remembered staring into those dark infinities. "But dwelling on their real nature hurts my . . . reason, I suppose. Saps my nerve."

"Perhaps the gods know what they are about. How did you know what I dreamed? I saw you three times, when I waked in my dreaming. Twice, you shone with an uncanny light."

"I dreamed those dreams, too."

"Even the third one?"

"Yes." No dream, that, but she was abashed by that rash kiss. Though after Cattilara's performance, it had seemed such a small self-indulgence . . .

He cleared his throat. "My apologies, Royina."

"What for?"

"Ah . . ." He glanced at her lips, and away. "Nothing."

She tried not to think about the taste of his reviving mouth. Goram dragged the somewhat battered chair to Illvin's bedside for her, and put out the stool at the bed's foot for Liss, before retreating to stand at a hunched sort of attention by the far wall. Ista and Illvin were left staring at one another in equal, she was sure, bafflement.

"Supposing," he began again, "that you are not here by chance, but by the prayers of, well"—he cleared his throat in embarrassment—"someone—it must be to solve this tangle. Yes?"

"Say rather, uncover it. Its solution eludes me."

"I thought you had agency over Catti's demon. Will you not banish it?"

"I don't know how," she admitted uneasily. "The Bastard has given me my second sight—given me back, I should say, my second sight, for this is not the first time the gods have troubled me. But the god gave me no instructions, unless they are contained in another man I saw in my dreams." *And vice versa.* Upon consideration . . . was dy Cabon's appearance, on the heels of the Bastard's mysterious second kiss, some sort of intimation of just that? "The god sent me a spiritual conductor, Learned dy Cabon, and I dearly desire his counsel in this before I proceed. He has studied something, I believe, about how demons are properly dispatched back to their Master. I'm certain he is meant to be here. But I have lost him on the road, and I fear for his safety." She hesitated. "I'm not in haste in this matter. I see no merit in releasing Arhys from his body only to doom him to the damnation of a lost ghost."

He grew still. "A ghost? Are you sure?"

"I saw it, when the spell was interrupted here yesterday. Nothing . . . happened, and it should have. There is a white roaring, when the doors of a soul are opened by death to the gods; it is a huge event. Damnation is but a silence, a slow freezing." She rubbed her tired eyes. "And more—even if I knew how he might find his way to his god, I am by no means sure that Arhys can convince his wife to release him. Yet if he does not persuade her, who else could? Not me, I fear. And even if she would let him go . . . the demon she has contracted seems skilled and powerful. If she no longer is sustained by the overmastering will to keep Arhys seemingalive, if she collapses into grief—she will be very vulnerable to it."

He vented a "Hm" of deepening doubt.

"Has she much strength of character, in your observation?"

He frowned. "I would not have said so, before this. Lovely girl, adores Arhys, but I'd swear that if she held up a lighted candle beside one pretty ear, I could blow it out through the other. Arhys doesn't seem to mind." He smiled wryly. "Although if such beauty had worshipped me so ardently, my opinion of her wits might well have risen higher upon the swelling of my head, or whatever, too. Yet—she resisted the cloud of Umerue's sorcery, and I . . . did not."

"I suspect Umerue underestimated her. And that's another thing," said Ista. "How could a princess of Jokona, a devout Quadrene, come by a demon in the first place? And keep it concealed, or otherwise evade accusation? They burn sorcerers there, though how the Quadrene divines keep the demon from jumping to another through the flames, I don't know. They must do something to tie it to its mount before dispatching them both."

"Yes, they do. It involves much ceremony and prayer. An ugly business; worse, it doesn't always work." He hesitated. "Catti said the sorceress was *sent*."

"By whom? The prince her brother? Assuming she had been dumped back into his household by her last late husband's heirs."

"I believe she was, yes. But . . . it's hard to picture Sordso the Sot dabbling in demons for the sake of Jokona."

"Sordso the Sot? Is that what the men of Caribastos call the young prince?"

"That's what everybody calls him, on both sides of the border. He chose to spend the hiatus between his father's death and the end of his mother's regency not in studying statecraft or warfare, but in wine parties and versifying. He's actually quite a pretty poet, in a self-consciously melancholy sort of vein, judging by the samples I've heard. We all hoped he would pursue the calling, which looked to be more rewarding for him than a prince's trade." He grinned briefly. "My lord dy Caribastos would be glad to give him a pension and a palace, and take the burdens of government off his narrow shoulders."

"It seems the prince is not so inattentive now. It was he who sent the raiding party into Ibra, which fled east from Rauma over the mountains and so encountered me. They had tally officers to account the prince's fifth. Did Liss tell you of this?"

"Only in brief." He nodded to the riding girl, who nodded back in confirmation. He paused, his dark brows drawing down. "Rauma? Strange. Why *Rauma*?"

"I guessed that it was to encourage the Fox of Ibra to keep his troops at home, come the fall campaign, instead of sending them in support of his son against Visping."

"Mm, could be. Rauma just seems very deep in Ibran territory to strike at so. Bad lines of retreat, as the raiders apparently found."

"Lord Arhys mentioned that by his reckoning, of the three hundred men who left Jokona, only three returned."

Illvin whistled. "*Good* for Arhys. Costly diversion for Sordso!"

"Except that they came very close to paying for all by carrying me off with them. But that could not have been part of their original plan. They didn't even carry maps of Chalion."

"I know the march of Rauma of old. I can imagine he would give the Jokonans a hot welcome. He used to be one of our better enemies, till we all became in-laws with Ibra. Your daughter's marriage took a great deal of pressure off Porifors's western flank, for which I do thank her, Royina."

"Royse Bergon is a dear boy." Not that Ista could help approving of anyone so plainly smitten with her daughter as Iselle's young Ibran husband.

"His father the roya is a bit of a cactus, though. Dry, spiny, will make your fingers bleed."

"Well, he's our cactus now."

"Indeed."

Ista sat back with a troubled sigh. "The news of this—at least, the news that a highborn lady of Jokona's court harbored a demon and attempted to suborn a Chalionese fortress by sorcery—should not be suppressed. I should write a warning to Archdivine Mendenal at Cardegoss, and to Chancellor dy Cazaril, at least."

"That would be well," he conceded reluctantly, "for all that I am gravely embarrassed by how closely Umerue came to succeeding. And yet—it wasn't the archdivine of Cardegoss who was dragged by chance and his hair here to the hind end of Chalion. It was you. A more unlikely answer to my prayers I can scarcely imagine." His mouth twisted up in puzzlement as he squinted at her.

"*Did* you pray to the Bastard, in your coherent moments?"

"Say, *waking*, rather than *coherent*. It all seems a fog till—yesterday? Yesterday just now. Yes, I prayed desperately. It was the only course left to me by then. I couldn't even form the right words aloud. Just howling in my heart. To my god, whom I had abandoned—I haven't been much for prayer since I became a man. If He'd said, *Boot off, boy, you wanted to be on your own, now eat what you cooked,* I should have thought Him within His rights." He added more slowly, "Why *you*? Unless this tangle has some older roots still, with my brother's father and Cardegoss court politics."

His shrewd guess discomfited her. "I have an old, dry knot of guilt still left to be undone with the late Lord dy Lutez, yes, but it has nothing to do with Arhys. And *no*, Arvol was *not* my lover!"

Illvin looked taken aback at her vehemence. "I did not say so, lady!"

She let out her breath. "No, you didn't. It's Lady Cattilara who thinks the old slander is a *romantic* tale, five gods spare me. Arhys just wants to take me for some spiritual stepmother, I think."

He surprised her by snorting. "He would." His fondly exasperated headshake scarcely enlightened her as to how to interpret this cryptic remark.

She said a little tartly, "Until I heard you two speaking with each other, I had half decided *you* were the jealous murderer. The despised bastard brother, denied father, title, property, pushed over the edge by this last loss."

His dry half laugh did not sound in the least offended. "I have encountered that delusion once or twice before. The truth is exactly the reverse. *I* had a father all my life, or at any rate, all of his. Arhys had—a dream. My father undertook the raising of us both, in all practical matters, and he tried to do well by Arhys, but it was always with that little extra mindful effort. To me, his love flowed without hindrance.

"But Arhys was never jealous or resentful because, you see, someday it would all be made right. Someday, his fine father would call him to court. When he was big enough.

When he was good enough, a good enough swordsman, horseman, officer. The great Lord dy Lutez would place him at his right hand, present him to his glittering retinue, and say to all his powerful friends, *See, this is my son, is he not well?* Arhys would never wear his best things; he kept them packed for the journey. For when the call came. He was ready to leave on an hour's notice. Then Lord dy Lutez died, and . . . the dream stayed a dream."

Ista shook her head in sorrow. "In all the five years I knew him, Arvol dy Lutez scarcely mentioned Arhys. He never spoke of you. If he had not died in the dungeons of the Zangre that night . . . that summons still might never have come, I think."

"I wondered, in retrospect. I pray you, don't tell Arhys that."

"I am not sure yet what I must tell him." *Although I have my fears.* Whatever it was, it was clear she had best not put it off too long.

"Me, I had a live man for a father," Illvin went on. "Cranky betimes—how we fought when I was younger! I am so glad he lived long enough for us to be grown men together. We cared for him here at Porifors after his palsy-stroke—albeit not too long. I think he wished to be gone to look for our mother by then, for a few times we found him out searching for her." His rich voice tightened. "Twenty years dead, she was. His life was so lightly held at the last, his death in the Father's season seemed no sorrow. I held his hand at the end. It felt very cool and dry, almost transparent. Five gods, how did I get on to this subject? You will have me leaking, next." He was leaking now, she thought, but he steadfastly ignored the suspect sheen in his eyes, and, politely, she did, too. "Thus, my experience of bastardy." He hesitated, eyed her. "Do you—you, who say you have seen them face-to-face—believe the gods bring us back to those we loved? When our spirits rise?"

"I do not know," she said, surprised into honesty. Was he thinking forward, to Arhys, as well as back to the elder Ser dy Arbanos, in this moment? "Perhaps I've never loved anyone enough to know. I think . . . it is not a fool's hope."

"Hm."

She looked away from his face, feeling an intruder upon that wistful inward frown. Her eye fell on Goram, rocking and clenching his hands again. Outwardly, a grizzled aging menial. Inwardly . . . stripped, plundered, burned-out like some village ravaged by retreating troops.

"How came you by Goram?" Ista asked Illvin. "And where?"

"I was reconnoitering in Jokona, as is my habit whenever I have a spare week. I collect castle and town plans, for a pastime." The brief smile that flitted across his mouth implied that he collected rather more than this, but he went on. "Having ridden down to Hamavik in the guise of a horse dealer, and having accumulated rather more stock than I'd intended, I found myself in need of an extra groom. As a Roknari merchant, I buy out Chalionese prisoners whenever I have a chance. The men with no family have little hope of ransom. Goram less than most, as he'd plainly lost most of his wits and memory. I'd diagnose a knock to the head in his last battle, though there's no scar, so it might have been some other ill treatment, or fever. Or both. It was clear no one else in the market wanted him that day, so I drove a better bargain than I'd expected. As it proved." The smile flickered again. "When we reached Porifors, and I freed him, he asked to stay in my service, as he no longer was sure where his home lay."

By the wall, Goram nodded endorsement to the tale.

Ista drew breath. "Are you aware that he is demon-gnawed?"

Illvin jolted upright. "No!"

Goram looked equally dumfounded. Liss's head jerked around, and she stared at the groom in wonder.

Illvin's eyes narrowed in rapid thought. "How do you know this, Royina?"

"I can see it. I can see his soul-stuff. It's all in rags and tatters."

Illvin blinked, sank back. After a moment he said, more cautiously, "Can you see mine?"

"Yes. To me, it appears as an attenuated white fire, streaming out of your heart to your brother. *His* soul is gray as a ghost's, beginning to decompose and blur. It is *in* his body, but it is not *attached* to his body. It just . . . floats there. Liss's is bright and colorful, but very centered, very solid and tight within the matter that generates it."

Liss, evidently deciding she had been complimented, smiled cheerfully.

After a reflective silence Illvin said, "That must be very distracting for you."

"Yes," she said shortly.

He cleared his throat. "Are you saying, then, that Goram was a sorcerer?"

Goram shook his head in horrified denial. "I'm not ever so, lady!"

"What *can* you remember, Goram?" Ista asked.

His seamed face worked. "I know I marched with Orico's army. I remember the roya's tents, all red-and-gold silk, shining in the light. I remember . . . marching as a prisoner, with chains on. Working, some field work, hot in the sun."

"Who were your Roknari masters?"

He shook his head. "Don't remember them, much."

"Ships? Were you ever on ships?"

"Don't think so. Horses, yes. There were horses."

Illvin put in, "We've talked before about what he could remember, when I was trying to find out his family. Because he must have been a prisoner for several years, if it was from the time the prince of Borasnen first attempted the fortress of Gotorget, two years before it fell. I think from some things Goram has said that must have been the campaign he was in. But he doesn't remember his captivity either, much. That was why I thought his brains might have been baked by a fever, perhaps just before he came my way."

"Goram, can you remember what has happened to you since Lord Illvin ransomed you?" asked Ista.

"Oh, aye. *That* don't hurt."

"Can you remember anything at all from just before Lord Illvin bought you out?"

Goram shook his head. "There was a dark place. I liked it because it was cool. Stank, though."

"Wits and memories eaten out, the demon jumped, and yet—not dead," mused Ista. "Abandoning a live mount is not easy for a demon, I gather from dy Cabon; they get all tangled together somehow. Killing the person forces the demon out. Like Umerue. Or like the Quadrene burnings."

"Don't burn me!" cried Goram. He shrank down smaller, almost crouching, and stared in dismay at his own chest.

"No one will burn you," Illvin said firmly. "Not in Chalion, in any case, and now there is no need, because she says the demon is gone. All gone. Right?" He shot Ista a compelling glare.

"Very gone." And most of Goram with it, it seemed. She wondered if he *had* been a servant, before—or something more.

"Hamavik . . ." murmured Illvin. "How suggestive. Both Goram and Princess Umerue were there at the same time. Could this . . . damage of Goram's have any relation to Umerue's demon?"

It made an enticing sort of connection. And yet . . . "Catti's demon didn't feel as if it had been dining on soldiers. It felt . . . I'm not sure how to put this. Too womanly. I suppose we can try to get information out of it again. I don't think the way it carried on here yesterday was any more usual for a demon than for a person. Or sorcerers would be far more conspicuous."

Liss, Ista noted, was looking most disturbed. Was she seeing a future Foix in Goram's slack, timid, bewildered face? Where *was* the boy? Ista wasn't desperate enough to pray yet, considering her feelings about prayer, but she thought she might become so if this hideous uncertainty went on much longer.

Ista continued, "Learned dy Cabon told me that demons

were very rare, usually—but not these past few years. That the Temple had not seen an outbreak like this since Roya Fonsa's day, fifty years gone. I cannot imagine what rip in the Bastard's hell can be leaking them back into the world in such numbers, but that's what I am beginning to picture."

"Fonsa's day." Illvin's words were starting to slur. "Strange."

"Your time is almost up," Ista said, eyeing the thickening white rope with disfavor. "I can portion you some more."

"You said Arhys would start to rot, though," Illvin objected muzzily. "High summer. Can't have . . . bits of him falling off into his soup, can we now . . . ?" His voice was fading. He roused himself in a spasm of despair. "No! There must be another way! Have to find another way! Lady—come again . . . ?"

"Yes," she said. On the reassurance, he released his grip on the edge of his counterpane and slid down. His face emptied once more into waxen stillness.

❧

Ista kept to her chambers again that day, waiting impatiently for the sun to run its course and rise again. She penned her new letters to Cardegoss and, when the sun dropped, paced the stone courtyard until even Liss abandoned her side and sat on a bench to watch her circulate. By the following mid-morning she was reduced to mentally composing another sharp letter to the provincar of Tolnoxo, though the first could barely have arrived yet, let alone been acted upon.

Rapid footsteps sounded on the stairs outside; Ista looked up from nibbling on her quill feather to see Liss's braid flash past beyond the grille. She thumped through to Ista's chamber and stuck her head in the door.

"Royina," she said breathlessly. "Something is happening. Lord Arhys has ridden out with a party of armed men—I'm going to the north tower to try to see what I can."

Ista rose so hastily she nearly knocked over her chair. "I'll go with you."

They climbed the winding stone staircase to this vantage behind a hastening crossbowman in Porifors's gray-and-gold tabard. All three went to the northeast edge and peered over the crenellations.

On this side of the castle, opposite the drop to the river, the land rolled away more level with the ridge. A road, pale with dry dust, wound east through the arid, sunny countryside.

"That's the road from Oby," panted Liss.

A pair of horsemen were galloping down it, details blurred by the distance. But even from here, Ista could see that one rider was thick, and the other much thicker. The thicker one wore some brown garment over flashes of white. The stiff gait of a horse attempting to canter under Learned dy Cabon's jouncing weight was distinctive, at least to Ista's experienced eye.

A little way beyond them galloped a dozen other men. An escort . . . ? *No.* Green tabards of Jokona, *here*, under the frowning brow of Porifors itself? Ista gasped. The pursuing soldiers were closing on the lead pair.

With a scuff of slippers and a flutter of silks, Lady Cattilara emerged onto the tower top and ran to look over. She stood on tiptoe and leaned, her pale bosom heaving. "Arhys . . . five gods, oh, the Father of Winter protect you . . ."

Ista followed her gaze. Below Porifors, Arhys on his dappled gray led a troop of mounted men headlong up the road. The lesser horses were hard pressed to keep up with the gray's reaching strides, and Liss muttered approval of its ground-eating action.

Cattilara's lips parted on her panting, and her eyes grew wide and anxious. She vented a little moan.

"What," murmured Ista to her. "You can't be afraid of his being killed, after all."

Cattilara shot her a sulky look, hunched one shoulder, and returned her stare to the road.

Dy Cabon's overburdened horse was laboring, falling behind. The other horseman—yes, it was certainly Foix dy Gura—pulled up his own mount and motioned the divine onward. Foix's horse capered on the road, fighting his reins. Foix held the beast short with his left hand, grasped his sword hilt, and rose in his stirrups to glare at his pursuers.

No, Foix! Ista thought helplessly. Foix was a strong swordsman, but unsubtle, without Lord Arhys's brilliant speed; he might do for one or two of his enemies, maybe three, who would not rise again, but then the rest would overwhelm him. He had not yet seen the rescue riders approaching, out of his sight in a long hollow. He would throw himself away to save the divine, without need . . .

His right hand rose again from his hilt, fingers clenching and stretching. His arm went out, tensely. A faint violet light seemed to flicker from his palm, and Cattilara's breath drew in sharply in astonishment. Liss did not react; was oblivious to this light, Ista realized.

The first horse in the approaching pack stumbled and fell headlong, spilling its rider. Two others fell atop it before they could pull up. Several horses reared, or shied and tried to bolt to the sides. Foix jerked his mount around and began galloping after dy Cabon.

So. Foix still has his pet bear. And it seems he's taught it to dance. Ista's lips pursed in worry at the implications.

But other worries were more immediate. Past the rise and dip in the road, dy Cabon met Arhys. The divine's lathered brown horse staggered to a halt and stood spread-legged; the dappled gray reared beside it. Gesticulations, pointings. Arhys flung his hand in the air, and his troop reined up around him. More hand-waving, and quietly called orders blurred by the breeze to unintelligibility at Ista's apprehensive height and distance. Swords were drawn, bows cocked, lances leveled, and the troop spread out and began to move up behind the brow of the road.

Dy Cabon's failing horse stumbled on at a walk toward Porifors, but he twisted his bulk in the saddle to watch over his shoulder as Foix crested the hill. Foix recoiled briefly at

the sight of the armed troop, but an openhanded wave from
Arhys, and a wilder arm-circling from dy Cabon, beyond,
apparently reassured him. He lashed his horse onward,
spoke briefly with Arhys, turned, and drew his sword.

A breathless pause. Ista could hear her blood thudding in
her ears, and, foolishly, some bird warbling in the brush, a
bright, liquid, indifferent trill, just as if this were some morning of peace and ease. Arhys raised his sword high and swung
it down sharply in signal, and his troop thundered forward.

The men from Porifors crested the rise and fell upon the
Jokonan troop too fast for the leaders to turn and retreat. The
horsemen in both vans were instantly engaged. The Jokonans at the rear yanked their horses around as hard as they
could and spurred away, but not faster than at least a couple
of crossbow bolts. A rider in a green tabard toppled and fell
from his saddle. The range from here was too great for the
bowman sharing Ista's vantage on the tower to waste his
quarrels in the fray, and he swore in frustration at his impotence, then glanced at the royina and mumbled an apology.
Ista waved him full royal dispensation, gripped the hot,
gritty stone, and leaned squinting into the light.

Arhys's sword danced in the sun, a glittering blur. His
dappled gray was crowded up in the middle of a pack of
kicking, squealing horses. A Jokonan soldier who had managed to get his lance unshipped whipped it up over his own
mount's head and jammed it awkwardly, backhanded, across
the haunches of the mount of the man who presently engaged Arhys's sword. Arhys jerked away. Cattilara screamed
as the lance wrenched back again, spattering blood.

"My lord is struck!" cried the bowman, leaning out as
tensely as the women. "Oh—no. His sword arm rises. Five
gods be thanked."

The horsemen disengaged, the Jokonan swordsman reeling in his saddle. The spearman saw an opening and galloped through to pursue his retreating comrades, bending
low over his mount's neck; a crossbow bolt whizzed over his
head to encourage him on his way.

Curse it, that spearpoint *had* found a mark in Arhys's shoulder; Ista had seen the shock of the contact shove the Jokonan's hand back, almost ripping the shaft from his grip. Yet Arhys's sword swung unhindered . . . Her breath drew in sharply, and she whirled away and started for the stairs.

"Liss, attend me!"

"But Royina, don't you want to see how it comes *out*?"

"Attend me."

Not waiting to see if the girl followed, Ista yanked up her lilac skirts and shuffled down the tight, dark stone curve of the tower stairs. She almost fell in her haste, then hugged the outer wall and the wider tread, but did not slow.

Out the door, across another courtyard, under the archway, into the stone court. Up the stairs. Her feet thumped across the gallery. She tugged open Illvin's carved door.

Goram was crouched by Lord Illvin's right side, groaning in fear. Illvin's linen tunic was yanked open and half-down. The groom glanced over his shoulder at her entry and cried, "Lady, help!"

His hands, she saw as she neared, were pressed to Illvin's shoulder, and gory with blood. The tunic sleeve was soaked in scarlet. Ista tore around the room until she found a cloth that might be folded into a pad, bundled it clean side outward, and offered it; Goram snatched his hands away just long enough to grab it and stuff it against the jagged wound in Illvin's shoulder.

"I didn't! I didn't!" cried Goram to her, his eye rolling white-rimmed. "It just *happened*."

"Yes, Goram, I know. It's all right," Ista soothed him. "You're doing well." Almost, she was tempted to squeeze the rope of white fire shut again, returning the ugly gash to its rightful owner. But now was clearly not a good moment to drop Arhys senseless from his saddle. Illvin's closed gray eyelids did not move or flutter or pinch in pain, at least. In his unfeeling state he might be freely tended, washed with brine, jabbed with sewing needles. So, Ista wondered dizzily, if the demon permitted him to wake this noon, would the needle punctures still be there when the wound they held closed fled back to his brother?

The door swung open; Liss at last.

"Liss. Run at once and find some woman used to tending wounds—the Mother's craft must have much practice here—have her bring her soap and salves and needles, and a servant to carry water as well."

"What? Why?" She trod closer in curiosity.

"Lord Illvin is badly cut."

At this point, Liss saw the blood, and she gasped. "Yes, Royina. But—how could . . . ?"

"*You* saw the spear thrust."

"*Oh.*" Her eyes grew very wide indeed, and she turned and ran.

Goram peeked quickly under the pad and clapped it tight again. Ista hung over his shoulder. The puncture was not so deep as she had feared; already the sluggish flow of blood was diminishing. "Good, Goram. Keep pressing."

"Aye, lady."

Ista waited, shifting from foot to foot, until voices sounded again from the gallery outside. Liss opened the door for a woman in an apron bearing a basket, and ushered her in; a male servant followed.

"Lord Illvin . . ." Ista began, and glanced at Goram, "fell out of bed and struck his shoulder." On what? Ista's invention failed her. She passed rapidly on. "Tend to him and bind him. Help Goram clean up. Speak of this to no one but me, Lord Arhys, or Lady Cattilara."

Those of the rescue party from Porifors who hadn't chased after the Jokonans might be escorting their new guests through the gates just about now, Ista guessed. She strode for the door. "Liss, attend me."

16

ISTA HURRIED UNDER THE ARCHWAY INTO THE ENTRY court in time to see the flushed and gasping Learned dy Cabon sag from his horse into the arms of one of Lord Arhys's men. The soldier helped the divine totter a few steps to collapse in the narrow shade of the wall by the almond tree. He held a worried hand to dy Cabon's face and spoke to a servant, who hurried away. Dy Cabon struggled out of his semiconcealing brown vest-cloak, letting it fall around him to the petal-strewn pavement.

Foix, looking almost equally hot and harried, jumped from his horse, threw down the reins, and strode to the divine's side.

"Curse it, Foix," dy Cabon wheezed, staring up at him, "I told you to stop playing with that thing."

"Fine," Foix snarled back. "Ride back and lie down by the side of the road for Jokonan dog meat, if you don't like it. The pack could feast for a month."

The servant arrived, and, at the soldier's gesture, upended a bucket of water slowly over dy Cabon, soaking his dirty white robes. Dy Cabon did not recoil or protest, but just sat limply, raising his chin and opening his mouth.

Foix nodded in gratitude and took a tin cup of water that another servant proffered from a second bucket, gulped it down, then scooped up a second and third and repeated the performance. With a fretful grimace, he ladled up another cupful, squatted by dy Cabon's side, and held it to the divine's lips. Dy Cabon lifted a shaking hand to it, guzzling noisily.

The soldier gave Ista a respectful salute as she approached, and murmured to her, "Very close to the heatstroke, that one. It's a bad sign when a man that big stops sweating. But don't worry, Royina, we'll get him right around."

Foix's head swiveled. "Royina!" he cried. "Five gods be thanked! I kiss your hands, I kiss your feet!" He pushed another cup of water into dy Cabon's grip and lunged over to one knee before her skirts, grasping her hands and planting a hot kiss on the back of each. "Ah!" He pressed them to his sweaty forehead in a less formal but entirely sincere addition. He did not rise immediately, but swung one leg around and sat cross-legged and wheezing, allowing his broad shoulders, for just this moment of safety, to slump.

He grinned up at Liss, flanking Ista. "So, you made it here, too. Might have known."

She grinned back. "Yes, you might."

"Been chasing after your dust since Maradi. The fastest horses were always already taken, for some reason."

Her smile stretched to a cheery smirk.

He squinted. "Pretty dress. Quite a change."

She drew back a little, self-consciously. "It's only loaned."

At a clacking of hooves, Foix looked up and scrambled to his feet. Lord Arhys, flanked by another mounted soldier, trotted through the gate on his dappled gray, swung down, and flung his reins to a groom.

"So, Royina." Arhys turned to her, his smile flickering. "I think your lost ones are returned to you."

Foix bobbed him a bow. "Only by virtue of your succor, sir. I had not time to introduce myself, out there. Foix dy Gura, at your service."

"Even if I had not met your brother, your sword and your enemies were recommendation enough. Arhys dy Lutez. Porifors is mine. I shall welcome you in better style hereafter, but I must first see to my scouts. Those Jokonans should not have been on that road—we took two prisoners alive, so I mean to find out how they came so close unseen." He cast Ista a glum glance. "Now do I doubly miss Illvin—his command of the Roknari tongue is better than any other's, here." Arhys gave a wave to Dedicat Pejar, dashing into the entry court with his tunic half fastened and his sword belt askew to greet his restored officer. "Here is one of your own men, to show you how to go on." He called to a servant, "See that these two have everything they need, till my return. Whatever Pejar or the royina ask."

The servant gave him an acknowledging half bow. Arhys's gaze was wary, sweeping past dy Cabon, still sitting bedraggled on the pavement. The divine made an exhausted hand motion, a truncated blessing, promising greater courtesies later.

Arhys turned for his horse again, but paused as Ista grasped him by the sleeve. She reached upward and touched his tunic, torn and bloody on the right shoulder, felt through the rip, and ran her fingers over his cool, unbroken skin. She turned her hand over before him to silently display the dark carmine smear. "At your earliest spare moment, March, I suggest you come inspect your brother's wound. Your brother's new wound."

His lips parted in dismay; he met her level gaze, and winced. "I see."

"Ride carefully, till then. Wear your mail."

"We were in haste—" He fingered the rip, his frown deepening. "Indeed." He gave her a grim nod and swung up again on his sidling horse. Motioning to his mounted man to follow, he cantered out.

Foix glanced around and back to Pejar, worry in his eyes. "Is Ferda here? Is he well?"

"Well, sir, but gone looking for you," Pejar replied. "He's

probably reached Maradi by now. I expect he'll make the circle and turn up back here in a few days, swearing at the waste of horseshoes."

Foix grimaced. "I trust he won't take the same road we did. Wasn't what the march of Oby led me to expect at all."

Why are you not now in the temple hospital at Maradi? Ista wanted to ask, but decided to wait. Foix's soul was as vigorous and centered as Liss's, but it appeared to her inner eye that a bear-shaped shadow lurked in his gut. It seemed to sense her scrutiny, for it curled tighter, as if attempting to hibernate. She motioned the hovering servant to her side. "See that these men are speedily refreshed, especially the divine, and lodged in rooms near me."

"Yes, Royina."

She added to Foix, "We must speak of—everything, as soon as we may. Have Pejar direct you to me in the stone court as soon as you are both recovered."

"Yes," he said eagerly, "we must hear all your tale. Lord Arhys's ambush was the talk of Oby, yesterday."

Ista sighed. "So much of dire import has happened since then, I had nearly forgot it."

His brows climbed. "Oh? We'll hasten to your side, then."

He bowed and turned away to assist the servant in coaxing dy Cabon back to his feet. Foix seemed very practiced at it, as if hauling the fat man up and forcing him to move had become second nature of late; dy Cabon's grumbles were equally perfunctory. The damp divine did not so much drip as steam, but he seemed to be gaining relief from his initial distress.

Cattilara's light tread echoed in the archway. The men looked around. Despite his overheated debility, dy Cabon smiled in a Cattilara-smitten fashion. Foix blinked, and went rather still.

"Where is my lord?" Cattilara demanded in anxiety.

"He has ridden back out with his scouts," Ista said. "It seems that spear thrust we saw found another target."

Cattilara's eyes widened. Her head turned toward the stone court.

"Yes," said Ista. "He is being cared for now, however."

"Oh. Good."

Cattilara's sigh of relief was premature, in Ista's judgment. The girl had not yet thought it through. But she likely would. "Lord Arhys will return by noon—no doubt."

Cattilara's lips pinched at her, briefly.

Ista went on, "Lady Cattilara dy Lutez, Marchess of Porifors, may I introduce to you my spiritual conductor, Learned Chivar dy Cabon, and Foix dy Gura, officer-dedicat of the Daughter's Order. You have met his captain and brother Ferda."

"Oh, yes." Cattilara managed a distracted curtsey. "Welcome to Porifors." She paused, returning Foix's uncertain look. For a moment, they stood as stiffly as two strange cats just sighting each other. The two demon shadows within them were so tightly closed in Ista's presence, it was hard to guess their reaction to this proximity, but it did not seem one of joyous greeting. Liss, observing Foix's lack of the more usual male response to the lovely marchess, brightened slightly.

Ista gestured to the waiting servant, and added, with deliberate emphasis, "*Lord Arhys* detailed this man to see to their needs. The divine is dangerously fatigued from the heat and should have care at once."

"Oh, yes," agreed Cattilara rather vaguely. "Pray continue. I shall welcome you all more properly . . . later." She dipped a curtsey, Foix produced a bow, and she fluttered away up the staircase. Foix and dy Cabon followed the servant and Pejar through the archway, presumably to where the Daughter's men were quartered.

Seized with unease, Ista watched Cattilara depart. She was suddenly reminded from Lord dy Cazaril's testimony that there were slower ways for demons to slay their mounts. Tumors, for example. Might one be started already? She tried to read for it in Cattilara's soul-stuff, some black blot of disorder and decay. The girl roiled so, it was hard to be sure. Ista could imagine the consequences—the passionate Cattilara, mad with hope, insisting that the symptoms were her longed-for pregnancy, jealously guarding a belly that swelled apace not with life but with death . . . Ista shivered.

Illvin speaks truth. We must find a better way. And soon.

Less than an hour passed before the two strays returned to Ista in the stone court. They both looked much revived, having evidently undergone some rough-and-ready bath involving sloshing buckets and drains. Wet hair combed, in dry clothes that, if not exactly clean, were less sweat-stained, they managed some ragged semblance of a courtly style in her honor.

Ista gestured the divine to a stone bench in the arcade's shade, and sat by his side. Foix and Liss settled themselves at her feet. Liss spent a moment plucking her unaccustomed skirts into a more graceful arrangement.

"Royina, tell us of the battle," Foix began eagerly.

"Your brother had a better view. Get his account, when he returns. I would hear your tale first. What happened after we abandoned you on the road?"

"I would not say, abandoned," objected dy Cabon. "Say *saved*, rather. Your hiding place worked, or else the god heard the prayers from my heart. And bowels. I didn't dare even whisper aloud."

Foix snorted agreement. "Aye. That was an ugly hour, crouching in that cold water—seems more attractive in retrospect—listening to the Jokonans thump by overhead. We finally crawled out of the culvert and took to the brush, trying to stay out of sight of the road but follow after you. *That* was a scramble. It was past dark by the time we reached the village at the crossroads, and the poor villagers were just starting to creep back to their homes. A good bit poorer, after the Jokonan locusts had passed through, but it could have been much worse. They'd evidently thought Liss a madwoman at first, but by that time they were praising her as a saint sent from the Daughter Herself."

Liss grinned. "I no doubt sounded a madwoman when I first rode in shrieking. Thanks be for my chancellery tabard. I'm glad they listened. I didn't wait to see."

"So we learned. The divine was done in by then—"

"You weren't much better," muttered dy Cabon.

"—so we took their charity for the night. Never ceases to amaze me, when people with so little share their bit with strangers. Five gods rain blessings upon 'em, for they'd just had their allotment of bad luck for a year at least.

"I talked them into loaning a mule to the divine, though they sent a boy along to be sure it got back again, and we started for Maradi in the morning, following Liss. I'd have preferred to chase you, Royina, but not unequipped as we were. I wanted an army. The goddess must have heard me, for we found one a few hours later, coming up the road. The provincar of Tolnoxo loaned us mounts, and you can believe I jumped to join his troop. Would have saved steps to let them come to us back at the village, for we passed through there again in the afternoon—returned their mule, at least, which made its owner happy." He glanced at dy Cabon. "I probably should have sent dy Cabon on to the temple at Maradi—he might have caught up with Liss—but he refused to be parted from me."

Dy Cabon growled reluctant agreement under his breath. "I wasted two miserable days in dy Tolnoxo's baggage train. The parts of me that meet a saddle were pounded to bruises by then, but even I could see we were following too slowly."

"Yes, despite all my howling." Foix grimaced. "The Tolnoxans gave up at the border, claiming the Jokonan column would break up into a dozen parts and scatter, and that only the men of Caribastos, who knew their own country, had a chance of netting them. I said we only needed to follow one part. Dy Tolnoxo gave me leave to take my horse and try it, and I almost did just to defy him. Should have; I might have caught up in time for Lord Arhys's welcoming fête. But the divine was mad to get me back to Maradi, for all the good *that* proved to be in the end, and I was worried about Liss, so I let myself be persuaded."

"Not mad," dy Cabon denied. "Justly worried. *I* saw those flies."

Foix huffed in exasperation. "Will you *leave off* about those accursed flies! They were no one's beloved pets. There were a million more in the manure pile they came from. There is no shortage of flies in Tolnoxo. No need to ration 'em!"

"That's not the point, and you know it."

"Flies . . . ?" said Liss, bewildered.

Dy Cabon turned to her in eager, and irate, explication. "It was after we left dy Tolnoxo's troop and came at last to the temple house in Maradi. The next morning. I came into Foix's chamber and found him drilling a dozen flies."

Liss's nose wrinkled. "Ick. Wouldn't they squash?"

"No—not—they were marching around. In a parade array, back and forth across the tabletop, in little ranks."

"File flies," murmured Foix, irrepressibly.

"He was experimenting with his demon, that's what," said dy Cabon. "After I *told* him to leave the thing strictly alone!"

"They were only *flies*." Foix's embarrassed grin twisted. "Granted, they did better than some recruits I've tried to train."

"You were starting to dabble in sorcery." The divine scowled. "And you haven't stopped. What did you do to make that Jokonan's horse stumble?"

"Nothing counter to nature. I understood your lecture perfectly well—your god knows you've repeated it often enough! You can't claim that turmoil and disorder didn't freely flow from the demon—what a splendid pileup! No, nor that it didn't result in good! If your order's sorcerers can do it, why can't I?"

"*They* are properly supervised and instructed!"

"Five gods know, you are certainly supervising and instructing *me*. Or at least, spying and badgering. Comes to much the same thing, I suspect." Foix hunched. "*Anyway*," he returned to his narrative, "they told us in Maradi that Liss had ridden to the fortress of Oby in Caribastos, thinking it the likeliest place to find the royina. Or if not the royina, someone fit to pursue her. So we followed, as fast as I could make dy Cabon ride. We arrived two days after Liss had left, but we heard the royina was rescued and safe at Porifors, so took a day to rest the divine's bruised saddle parts—"

"And yours," muttered dy Cabon.

"And followed on to Porifors," Foix raised his voice over this, "on a road that the march of Oby told us was perfectly safe and impossible to miss. The second part of his assurance proved true. Daughter's tears, I thought the Jokonans had come back for a rematch, and we were going to lose the race this time, within sight of our refuge."

Dy Cabon rubbed his forehead in a weary, worried gesture. Ista wondered if his morning's dangerous parching had left him with a lingering headache.

"I am very concerned about Foix's demon," said Ista.

"I, as well," said dy Cabon. "I thought the Temple could treat him, but it is not to be. The Bastard's Order has lost the saint of Rauma."

"Who?" said Ista.

"The divine of the god in Rauma—it is a town in Ibra, not far from the border mountains—she was the living agent of the god for the miracle of—do you remember that ferret, Royina? And what I told you about it?"

"Yes."

"For weak elementals that have taken up residence in animals, to force the demon into the dying divine who will return it to the god, it is sufficient to slay the animal in his or her presence."

"Thus the end of that ferret," said Ista.

"Poor thing," said Liss.

"It is so," dy Cabon admitted. "Hard on the innocent

beast, but what will you? The occurrences are normally quite rare." He took a breath. "The Quadrenes use a related system to rid themselves of sorcerers. A cure worse than the disease. But, once in a great while, a saint may come along who is gifted by the god with the trick of it."

"The trick of what?" said Ista, with a patience she did not feel.

"The trick of extracting the demon from a human mount and returning it to the god, and yet leaving the person alive. And with the soul and wits intact, or nearly so, if it goes well."

"And . . . what *is* the trick of it?"

He shrugged. "I don't know."

Ista's voice grew edged. "Did you sleep through *all* your classes in that seminary back in Casilchas, dy Cabon? You are supposed to be my spiritual conductor! I swear you could not conduct a quill from one side of a page to the other!"

"It's not a *trick*," he said, harried. "It's a *miracle*. You cannot pull miracles out of a book, by rote."

Ista clenched her teeth, both infuriated and ashamed. "Yes," she said lowly. "I know." She sat back. "So . . . what happened to the saint?"

"Murdered. By that same troop of Jokonan raiders who overtook us on the road in Tolnoxo."

"Ah," breathed Ista. "*That* divine. I heard of her. The march of Rauma's bastard half sister, I was told by one of the women captives." *Raped, tortured, and burned alive in the rubble of the Bastard's Tower. Thus do the gods reward Their servants.*

"Is she?" said dy Cabon in a tone of interest. "I mean . . . was she."

Liss put in indignantly, "What blasphemy, to slay a saint! Lord Arhys said that of the three hundred men who left Jokona, no more than three returned alive. Now we see why!"

"What *waste*." The divine signed himself. "But if it is so, she was surely avenged."

"I would be considerably more impressed with your god, dy Cabon," said Ista through her teeth, "if He could have arranged one life's worth of simple protection in advance, rather than three hundred lives' worth of gaudy vengeance afterward." She drew a long, difficult breath. "My second sight has returned."

His head swiveled, and his arrested gaze flashed to her face. "How did this come about? And when?"

Ista snorted. "You were there, or nearly so. I doubt you have forgot *that* dream."

His overheated pink flushed redder, then paled. Whatever he was trying to say, he could not get it out. He choked and tried again. "That was *real*?"

Ista touched her forehead. "He kissed me on the brow, here, as once His Mother did, and laid an unwelcome burden thereupon. I told you things of dire import have been happening here. That is the least of them. Did you hear any rumor, at Oby, of the murder of Princess Umerue by a jealous courtier of hers, some two or three months ago here at Porifors? And the stabbing of Ser Illvin dy Arbanos?"

"Oh, yes," said Foix. "It was the next greatest gossip there, after your rescue. Lord dy Oby said he was most sorry to hear about Lord Illvin, and that Lord Arhys must miss him greatly. He knew the brothers of old, he said, from long before he became Lord Arhys's father-in-law, and said they always steered together, up and down this corner of Caribastos for going on twenty years, like a man's right and left hands on his reins."

"Well, that was not the true story of the crime."

Foix looked interested, if skeptical; dy Cabon looked interested and extremely worried.

"I have been three days sorting through the lies and misdirections. Umerue may have been a princess once, but by the time she came here, she was a demon-eaten sorceress. *Sent*, I was told, and this part I believe, to suborn Porifors and deliver it to someone in or near the court of Jokona. The effect this might have on the coming Visping campaign, especially if the treachery was not revealed until the most critical possible moment, I leave to your military imagination, Foix."

Foix nodded, slowly. The first part, he had no trouble following, obviously. What was to come . . .

"In a secret scrambling fight, both Umerue and Lord Arhys were slain."

Dy Cabon blinked. "Royina, don't you mean Lord Illvin? We just met Lord Arhys."

"Just so. The demon jumped to Arhys's wife—a mistake from its point of view, it appears, because she promptly seized control of it and forced it to stuff Arhys's severed soul back into his own body, stealing strength from his younger brother Illvin to keep his corpse moving all the same. Some distorted species of death magic—I will ask you, *Learned*, to expound the theology of it at your earliest convenience. And then the marchess feigned it was Illvin injured, and the princess killed, by the princess's Jokonan clerk, whom she terrified into fleeing."

"So *that's* what I felt when I saw her," whispered Foix, sounding much enlightened. "Another demon."

"I witnessed everyone's testimony," avowed Liss loyally. "It's all true. We even questioned the demon, though *that* wasn't much use. When Lord Arhys was struck in the fight this morning by that Jokonan lancer, the cut appeared on Lord Illvin's body. It was dreadfully uncanny." She added reflectively, "Bled like a stuck pig, too. Well, so he would— they do stick pigs with lances, I think."

Ista glanced at the sun and measured the shortening shadows in the stone courtyard. "In a while, you will speak with all concerned, and bear witness as well. But dy Cabon, listen. I do not know why your god has brought me to this house of woe. I do not know what, or who, can be saved out of this ghastly tangle. I do know that at some point, one way or another, that demon has to be driven out of Lady Cattilara. It is wild to escape, with her body by preference, but it will kill her in order to fly in another's if it gains the chance.

Arhys is beginning to deteriorate, body and, I fear, mind as well. Worse—I suspect his soul may already be sundered. Lord Illvin is dying slowly, being drained by this sorcery of more life than his body can replace. When he dies, his brother ends, and Cattilara, I believe, will be swallowed by her demon."

She stopped, drew breath, looked around at the shocked faces staring back at her. Not one, she realized with a chill, was staring at her as though she had gone mad. They were all staring at her as though she was going to tell them what to do next.

Booted footsteps echoed in the archway. Ista looked up to see Lord Arhys enter, observe her and her little court, and approach. He stopped and gave her a bow, then stood taken rather aback by the staggered, searching looks he was collecting from his new guests.

"Lord Arhys." Ista's nod acknowledged the bow. "I have been apprising my escort's acting captain and my spiritual conductor of the true state of affairs here at Porifors. It is necessary that they know, that they may guard and advise me to best effect."

"I see." He forced a grimace into an unfelt smile. He paused a moment as if considering what to say for himself— apologize for being dead, perhaps?—then, apparently defeated by the quandary, passed on to more immediate affairs. "My scouts are dispatched, but not yet returned. Our prisoners were not very cooperative, but it appears their patrol was the screen of some larger force, given the task of cutting communications on the road between Porifors and Oby. And that the attack on dy Gura and the divine was premature in some fashion that we were unable to extract from them, for all the howls we squeezed out. We are taking precautions— topping our cisterns, warning the town, sending riders to alert outlying areas to be on guard. I have heard nothing of such a Jokonan force from my own men along the border, but . . . I have been much distracted from my duties these past few days."

Ista pursed her lips on a worried exhalation. "An attack from Jokona? Why now?"

He shrugged. "A delayed reprisal for the death of their princess? We had expected one before this. Or . . . a much-less-delayed attempt to regain a great prize, lately lost." His gaze on her was grave.

Despite the heat, Ista shivered. "I would not chose to bring down such trouble on any host, least of all you. Perhaps . . . I should remove to Oby." Run away? A beguilingly sensible cowardice, that. Leave this castle, leave this tangle, leave these anguished and benighted souls to sink under the accumulating weight of their misjudgments, misery, and love . . . she could run away. She could.

"Perhaps." He gave her an ambiguous nod. "But only if we can be sure we have secured the road, or else we would just be delivering you into Jokonan hands, a gift already un-wrapped. I must ride out this afternoon—I can't stop now. You must see that," he added with peculiar earnestness. "You must not stop me now."

"Since I know not how," she sighed, "you are safe from that chance for the moment. Other chances, I cannot speak for."

"I shall be forced to take my rest, shortly—"

"Illvin *must* be allowed to eat, especially now," she said, alarmed.

"I do not wish otherwise. But I would see his new wound, first."

"Ah. That would be wise, I think."

As he seemed to expect her company, she rose and fol-lowed him up the stairs, her people trailing in unconcealed curiosity. The entry of so many persons alarmed Goram, whom Ista tried to reassure with a few soft words; he seemed more consoled by Liss's kindly pat on his shoulder. At the march's direction, he unwrapped Illvin's new band-age. Arhys's inspection was brief, experienced, and grim. Foix and dy Cabon peered with diffident interest at the bloody tear in Arhys's tunic as he bent over his silent brother. When the march turned away, they crowded up to the bedside to get a whispered account from Liss.

Arhys's hand clenched and unclenched on his sword hilt. He murmured to Ista, standing with him a little apart, "I confess, I was not altogether sorry to find those Jokonan soldiers out on my road this morning. I think some part of me was starting to hope for a better death. Less . . . ignominious, than the first, less shameful to my father's honor. I see there is a problem with this plan."

"Yes," said Ista.

"I feel as though I am lost in some dark and evil maze, and cannot find my way out."

"Yes," said Ista. "But . . . no longer alone in the labyrinth, at least."

His smile flickered; he squeezed her hand. "Indeed. My good company grows apace since the gods guided you here. That is a greater comfort than I had expected."

The meal tray arrived. Lord Arhys excused himself; Ista trusted he would find the safe harbor of his bed before his midday collapse overtook him. She ushered her own people out again, to give Goram time to do his necessary work, but she directed dy Cabon to stay, assist, and observe.

Leaning on the gallery railing, she watched Lord Arhys stride out of sight below, trailing the subtle smoke of his eroding soul. She rubbed her palm, still tingling where he had gripped it.

I could run away. No one else here can, but I could.

If I chose to.

17

FOIX, DISQUIET IN HIS EYES, LEANED HIS ELBOWS ON THE balustrade by Ista's side to watch Arhys exit. "Remarkable man," he observed. "If that Jokonan sorceress's purpose was to remove Porifors from the strategic map, paralyze its strength as a fortress . . . she may have achieved some success even in her failure, to have crippled such a commander. Or worse than crippled, the Daughter forbid."

Liss came over to rest against the rail on Ista's other side, listening and frowning in worry.

"What did you sense of that demon, when you met Lady Cattilara in the forecourt?" Ista asked Foix.

He shrugged. "Nothing very clearly. I felt . . . prickly. Uneasy."

"You did not see it, riding within her soul like a shadow?"

"No, Royina." He hesitated. "Can you?"

"Yes."

He cleared his throat. "Ah . . . can you see mine?" Absently, his hand rubbed his belly.

"Yes. It looks like the shadow of a bear, hiding in a cave. Does it speak to you?"

"Not . . . exactly. Well, a little. Not in words, but I can

sense it, if I sit quietly and pay attention. It is much calmer and happier than it was at first. Tamer." He managed a lopsided grin. "I have been training it to do some tricks, when the divine does not harass me."

"Yes, I saw the one on the road. Very clever of you both, but very dangerous. Do you have any sense of what it was, or where it was, before it found you?"

"A bear, wandering in the wild. A bird before that, I think, for neither the bear nor I could ever have viewed the mountains from above, and I now seem to have such a memory. Confused, but I do not think I dreamed it. Swallowing huge insects, ugh. Except that they weren't ugh. Ugh! Before that . . . I don't know. I think it does not remember being newborn, any more than I remember being a mewling infant. It had existence, but not wits as such."

Ista straightened, stretching her aching back. "When we return to Lord Illvin's chamber, study his attendant, Goram. I believe he once held a demon, as you now do."

"The *groom* was a sorcerer? Ha. Well, why not? If a demon can lodge in a bear, why not in a simpleton?"

"I do not think he was always a simpleton. I suspect he may have once been a cavalry officer of Roya Orico's army, before he was taken prisoner and enslaved unransomed. Study Goram closely, Foix. He may be your mirror."

"Oh," said Foix, and shrank a little. Liss's frown deepened.

At length the carved door opened, and Goram gestured them all back inside. The sheets had been changed, the bloodied linen robe whisked away, and Illvin dressed for company in his tunic and trousers, his hair tied back. Ista was obscurely grateful that he was made so presentable before her companions. Goram fetched the chair for her, and with little bobbing bows seated her by Illvin's bedside.

Dy Cabon reported to Ista in an awed whisper, "I watched the wounds close up, just now. Extraordinary."

Lord Illvin gingerly rubbed his right shoulder and smiled across at Ista. "I seem to have missed a busy morning, Royina, except not quite. Learned dy Cabon has been telling me of his alarming ride. I am glad your lost company is returned to you. I hope your heart is eased."

"Much eased."

Dy Cabon took the stool at the foot of the bed, a precarious perch for his bulk. Ista introduced Foix, and gave a short, blunt précis of his encounter with the bear, by way of preamble to describing his performance on the road. Goram hovered anxiously on the bed's other side, putting bites to Illvin's mouth while he listened.

Illvin, frowning, fended off a piece of bread, and said, "That such a raiding party should come so close to Porifors indicates either a young Jokonan hothead swaggering for show, or something moving behind. What say our scouts?"

"Dispatched, not yet returned," said Ista. "Lord Arhys prepares, he tells us, and has sent out warnings to the countryside."

"Good." Illvin eased back against his pillows. "Five gods help me, the days flit past me like hours. I would be out there riding now!"

She added, "I told your brother to wear his mail."

"Ah," he said. "Yes." His mouth set, his left hand going again to probe his elusively wounded shoulder. He stared down at his feet, absorbed in who-knew-what reflections. Ista wondered if his mind circled as dizzily as her own.

She drew a long breath. "Goram."

He paused in his spooning. "Lady?"

"Were you ever in Rauma?"

He blinked in bewilderment. "Don't know the place."

"It's a town in Ibra."

He shook his head. "We were at war with Ibra, before. Weren't we? I know I was in Hamavik," he offered as if in compensation. "Lord Illvin found me there."

"Your soul shows demon scars, dreadful ones. And yet . . . if you had been a sorcerer during your captivity, commanding the resources of a demon, you ought to have been able to escape, or otherwise improve your lot."

Goram looked daunted, as though being chastised for some lapse.

Ista opened a palm to soothe him, and continued, "There are . . . too many demons about. As if some great outbreak had occurred, the divine told me, is that not so, Learned?"

Dy Cabon rubbed his chins. "It's surely beginning to appear so."

"Has the Temple mapped the sightings? Are they coming from one place, or from every place at once?"

A thoughtful look came over his suety face. "I have not heard from every place, but of the reports I have heard, there do seem to have been more toward the north, yes."

"Hm." Ista stretched her tight shoulders again. "Lord Illvin, dy Cabon has also told me that the divine of the Bastard in Rauma was a saint of his order, gifted with the ability to draw demons from their mounts and return them, somehow, miraculously, to the god. The Jokonan raiders slew her."

Illvin breathed out through pursed lips. "*That's* an unfortunate loss just now."

"Yes. Else he would have hauled Foix straight to her, and not come here instead. But now I'm wondering if it may have been more than a mischance. When I was captive, riding in the Jokonan column's baggage train, I saw a strange sight. A high-ranking officer, perhaps the commander himself, rode along tied to his saddle like a prisoner, or a fainting wounded man. His face was slack . . . he could not control his drooling, and he mumbled, without words, or sometimes cried out as if in fear, or wept. I thought perhaps a head blow had destroyed his reason, but he bore no bandages or bloodstains whatsoever. I now wonder, if I'd had my second sight then—what great gouges I might have seen within his soul."

Illvin blinked at the disturbing word-picture. His wits leapt ahead to the conclusion Ista had not yet stated aloud. "Might he have been another sorcerer in the service of Jokona, do you think? Commanding that column?"

"Perhaps. What if the saint of Rauma did not die without a fight, or wholly in vain? What if it was she who'd ripped his demonic powers out by the roots, even as she fell to common violence? At the start of a campaign, do we not burn the enemy's crops, fill their wells, deny them their resources? I think a saint who could banish demons at will would be a powerful resource, against an enemy who commanded, perhaps, more such sorcerers. Maybe more than those two. Why Rauma, you asked me yesterday. What if the saint's murder, which we took for an incidental evil of the raid, was instead its main purpose?"

"But demons do not readily work together," objected dy Cabon. "One sorcerer, high in the Jokonan court, could do much damage, were he of evil bent. Well, or of loyal bent," he conceded fairly. "To Jokona, that is. But to call up or command a legion of demons—that is the vocation of the Bastard alone. Unimaginable hubris in a man, and doubly so for a Quadrene. Also, such a perilous concentration of demons would generate chaos all around it."

"War gathers on these borders," said Ista. "A greater concentration of chaos I can hardly imagine." She rubbed her forehead. "Lord Illvin, you have studied the court of Jokona, I suspect. Tell me something of it. What are Prince Sordso's principal advisors and commanders like?"

He eyed her with shrewd interest. "It's mostly still the cadre of older men he inherited from his father. His first chancellor was his paternal uncle, though he's lately died. The present general of Jokona has served for years. Sordso's own friends and boon companions are a much younger lot, but he hasn't had a chance to put any into positions of power. Too soon to tell if any of them will prove fitted for war or government, though they seem to run largely to rich men's sons with too little chance, or drive, to learn their own trades. Arhys and I have speculated which will move up when the old men finally start to die off.

"Oh, and his mother, Princess Joen—Dowager Princess Joen. She was Sordso's regent, along with his uncle and the general, until he came of age. I wanted to probe down that way when she took the reins a few years ago, but Arhys was seized with a fit of deference for her sex and sad widowhood. And anyway, in the midst of what proved to be Roya Orico's final illness and death, we feared Cardegoss might not be able to rescue us from our mistakes. Or worse, might fail to support a victory."

"Tell me more of Joen," said Ista slowly. "Did you ever meet her? If Umerue had held to her initial plan, she would have become your mother-in-law."

"Daunting thought. It is a measure of Umerue's powers that such a drawback never troubled my mind. I've never met Joen face-to-face. She is some ten or fifteen years older than I am, and had more or less disappeared into the women's quarters by the time I was old enough to notice the politics of the princedom. I will say, she was the most continually pregnant princess in recent Jokonan history—certainly did her duty by her husband. Though she was not entirely fortunate in her children, for all her efforts. Out of a dozen or so, only three sons, and two of those died young. Some miscarriages and stillbirths, too, I think. Seven girls lived to marry—Sordso has family alliances all over the Five Princedoms. Oh, and she takes her descent from the Golden General most seriously. Makes up for the disappointments of her husband and son, I suppose—or maybe it creates them, I don't know."

The Golden General, the Lion of Roknar. For a time, back in Roya Fonsa's reign, the brilliant Quadrene leader had looked to unite the Five Princedoms for the first time in centuries, and roll like a tide over the weak Quintarian royacies. But he had died untimely at the age of thirty, destroyed by aging Roya Fonsa in a work of death magic, during a night of towering self-immolation. The rite that killed both leaders had saved Chalion from the Roknari threat, but also spilled the curse that would haunt Fonsa's heirs down to Ista's day, and beyond. The Golden General had left only renewed political disorder in the princedoms for legacy, and a few young children, Joen the least and youngest.

No surprise, that she might grow up regarding him as a lost hero. But if Joen could not follow in her great father's striding steps, barred by her sex from war and politics, might she have at least sought to re-create him in a son? All those pregnancies . . . Ista, who had experienced two, did not underestimate their brutal drain on a woman's body and energy.

Ista frowned. "I was thinking about what Catti's demon said. *She* is coming, it cried, as if this were some dire event. I had taken it to refer to me, for I believe my god-touched state is a consternation to demons, but—I wasn't coming. I was already there. So that makes no sense, really. Not that much of what it had to say made sense."

Illvin remarked thoughtfully, "If someone in the court of Jokona is indeed dipping into sorcery for the purpose of moving against Chalion, I must say, it is not going all that well for him. Both his demon-agents—sad Umerue *and* the column's commander—were lost in the first two trials of their prowess, if your guess is good."

"Perhaps," said Ista. "Yet not without advancing Jokonan goals. The saint of Rauma is dead, and Porifors . . . is much distracted."

He glanced up sharply at this. "Arhys still leads us—does he not?"

"For the moment. It's clear his reserves are drawing down."

Illvin, reminded, took another bite of bread and dutifully chewed. His face screwed up in thought. He swallowed, and said, "It occurs to me that we do have one here who must know all the inward plans, if such exist, of whoever in Sordso's court is behind this. The demon itself. We should question it again. More firmly." He added after a reflective moment, "It might be better if Arhys were not present this time."

"I . . . quite see your point. Here, perhaps, tomorrow?"

"If it may be arranged. Not sure if Catti will agree, without Arhys persuading her."

"She must be made to," said Ista.

"I will have to leave that part to you."

With some relief, if Ista read him right. She said, "But were these losses all of Jokona's sorcerers, or two of many? If all the elementals that have lately been found in Chalion are lost or escaped from the same source, how many more were captured as intended? And how? Perhaps these two were sacrificed, as a commander with many men would send some into a breach, knowing he will bear losses, but counting the gain to himself worth the cost. But not if he has few men. Unless he is very desperate . . ." She tapped her fingers on her chair arm. "No, it cannot be Joen. She would not put a demon into her own daughter." She glanced at Goram. "Unless she were terribly ignorant of their nature and effects, and in that case I can hardly see how she could control one sorcerer, let alone many."

Illvin cast her an odd look. "You love your own daughter very much, I take it."

"Who would not?" Ista's smile softened. "She is the bright star of Chalion. Beyond my hope and my deserving, for I could do little enough for her during my dark times."

"Hm." He smiled curiously at her. "And yet you said you'd never loved anyone enough to guess at heaven's hope."

She made a little excusing gesture. "I think the gods may give us children to teach us what true love really is, that we may be fitted for Their company at the last. A lesson for those of us whose hearts are too dull and inert to learn any other way."

"Inert? Or merely . . ."

The rope of white fire was beginning to attenuate; his hand fell back weakly to his coverlet. Goram glanced with dismay at the amount of food still left on the tray. Ista watched Illvin sink back, his eyes closing, and clenched her teeth with frustration. She wanted that mind in her service against this conundrum, but Arhys's body seemed equally needed today. She wished it were winter, that she might steal another hour for Illvin. But it was too beastly hot to let the march start to rot.

"Come again, shining Ista," he breathed with a fading sigh. "Bring Catti . . ."

Gone. It was like watching him die, every day. She did not desire the practice.

❦

Ista turned aside at the stairs down to the stone court. "Learned, please attend upon me. We must talk."

"And I, Royina?" said Liss hopefully.

"You may . . . make yourself comfortable within call."

Taking the hint, Liss strolled away to a bench on the court's far end. After an uncertain moment, Foix followed after her, looking not displeased. They put their heads together the moment they sat down.

Ista led dy Cabon back to the bench in the cloister walk's shade and gestured him to a seat. He settled himself with a tired grunt. The days of riding and anxiety had told on him; his stained white robes hung loosely, and his belt was cinched in a few new notches. Ista, remembering the god's immense girth and overflowing abundance in dy Cabon's dream-borrowed body, could not, on the whole, regard this shrinking as an improvement.

She sat beside him, and began, "You say you witnessed the banishing of an elemental, when the ferret's rider was discharged from the world. How exactly was it accomplished? What did you see?"

He shrugged his thick shoulders. "There was not a great deal to see with my poor eyes. The archdivine of Taryoon led me into the presence of the divine who had volunteered for the task. A very elderly woman, she was, frail as paper in the temple hospital bed. She seemed three-fourths detached from the world already. There is so much to delight us in the world of matter—to tire of it seems ungrateful to me, but she told me she'd had all the pain she could eat and would pass from this banquet to a better one. She genuinely desired her god, as a weary sojourner desires his own bed."

Ista said, "A man I know who had a mystic vision, under the most extraordinary circumstances, once told me he saw the dying souls rising up like flowers in the goddess's garden. But he was a devotee of the Lady of Spring. I think each god may have some different metaphor—fine animals for the Son of Autumn, I have heard, strong men and beautiful women for the Father and the Mother. For the Bastard—what?"

"He takes us as we are. I hope."

"Hm."

"But no," dy Cabon continued, "there were no special tricks or even prayers. The divine said she did not need them. As she was the one doing the dying, I didn't argue. I asked her what it was like, dying. She gave me such a look out of the corner of her eye, and told me, pretty tartly, that when she found out she'd be sure to let me know. The arch-divine signed me to cut the ferret's throat then, which I did, into a basin. The old woman sighed, and snorted, as if at some other foolish remark like mine, which we could not hear. And then she stopped. It took her only a moment to pass from life to death, but it was unmistakable. Not a sleep. An emptying out. And that was that. Except for the cleaning up after."

"That . . . is not especially helpful," sighed Ista.

"It was what I saw. I suspect she saw more. But I can scarcely imagine what."

"In my dream—the dream you entered into—the god kissed me twice. The first time on the brow"—she touched the spot—"as His Mother once did, and so I recognized it as the gift of second sight, of seeing the world of spirit directly as the gods do, for I had received it so before. But then he kissed me a second time, on—in—my mouth. More deeply and disturbingly. Learned, tell me, what was the meaning of that second kiss? You *must* know—you were right there."

He gulped and blushed. "Royina, I cannot guess. The mouth *is* the Bastard's own theological sign and signifier upon our bodies, as the thumbs are upon our hands. Did He give you no other clues but me?"

She shook her head. "The next day, Goram, with some very confused notion about a royina—even if only a dowager royina—being able to undo what a princess had done, invited me in to kiss his master. And for an elated moment, I thought I'd solved the riddle—that it was to be a kiss of life, as in the children's story. But it didn't work. Nor on Lord Arhys, when I attempted him, later. I did not take the trial further afield, fortunately for my reputation in this castle. The kiss was clearly something else, some other gift or burden."

Ista drew breath. "I face a three-way knot. Two parts may be loosed together; if I could find some way to banish Cattilara's demon, Illvin would be freed, and the marchess saved. But what hope may be found for Arhys? I saw his soul, Learned. He is surely sundered, or my inner eyes are blind. It would be bad enough to complete his death, and lose him to his god. It would be worse to secure his damnation, and lose him to nothingness."

"I . . . um . . . know that some souls, suffering especially disrupted deaths, have lingered for a few days, to be helped on their way by the prayers and ceremonies of their funerals. Slipped through the doors of their deaths before they quite shut."

"Might the rites of the Temple help him find his way to his god, then?" It was a bizarre image; would Arhys walk to his own funeral, lie down on his bier?

He grimaced. "Three months seems very late. Choice is the trial of all who are trapped in time; and *that* choice is the last one time imposes. If his moment for decision still lingered, through some habit of the body, could your second sight tell?"

"Yes," said Ista lowly. "It can. But I want another answer. I do not like this one. I had hopes of that kiss, but it failed."

He scratched his nose in puzzlement. "You said the god spoke to you. What did He say?"

"That I was sent here, in answer to prayers, Illvin's among others, probably. The Bastard *dared* me, by my own son's god-neglected death, not to turn aside." She frowned fiercely in memory, and dy Cabon edged a little back from her. "I asked Him what the gods, having taken Teidez, could give me that I would trade spit for. He answered, *Work*. His blandishments were all decorated about with annoying endearments that would have bought a human suitor a short trip to the nearest mud puddle by the hands of my servants. His kiss on my brow burned like a brand. His kiss on my mouth"—she hesitated, went on doggedly—"aroused me like a lover, which I most certainly am *not*."

Dy Cabon edged farther back, smiling in anxious placation, and made little agreeing-denying motions, his hands like flippers. "Indeed not, Royina. No one could mistake you for such."

She glowered at him, then went on. "Then He disappeared, leaving you holding the sack. So to speak. If this was prophecy, it bodes you ill, Learned."

He signed himself. "Right, right. Um. If the first kiss was a spiritual gift, so ought the second to be. Yes, I quite see that."

"Yes, but He didn't say what it *was*. Bastard. One of his little jokes, it seems."

Dy Cabon glanced up as if trying to decide if that were prayer or expletive, guessed correctly, and took a breath, marshaling his thoughts. "All right. But He *did* say. He said, *Work*. If it sounds like a joke, it was probably quite serious." He added more cautiously, "It seems you are made saint again, will or nil."

"Oh, I can still nil." She scowled. "That's what we *all* are, you know. Hybrids, of both matter and spirit. The gods' agents in the world of matter, to which they have no other entrée. Doorways. He knocks on my door, demanding entry. He probes with his tongue like a lover, mimicking above what is desired below. Nothing so simple as a lover, he, yet he desires that I open myself and surrender as if to one. And let me tell you, I *despise* his choice of metaphors!"

Dy Cabon flippered frantically at her again. It made her want to bite him. "You are a very fortress of a woman, it is true!"

She stifled a growl, ashamed to have let her rage with his god spill over onto his humble head. "If you don't know the other half of the riddle, why were you put there?"

"Royina, I know not!" He hesitated. "Maybe we should all sleep on it." He cringed at her blistering look, and tried again. "I will endeavor to think."

"Do."

At the other end of the courtyard, Foix and Liss were now sitting closer together. Foix held Liss's hand, which she did not draw back, and spoke earnestly over it. She was listening to him, in Ista's jaundiced view, with entirely too credulous an expression on her face. Ista rose abruptly, and called her to attend. She had to call twice to summon her notice. The girl scrambled up hastily, but her smile lingered like perfume in the air.

❧

Lady Cattilara, in some desperate attempt to sustain her role of chatelaine before her new guests, held a dinner that afternoon in the same chamber where she and her ladies had entertained Ista on the second night. Arhys was again out; a very few of his officers attended, clearly more to make a convenient hasty meal than to play courtier. Cattilara had seated Foix as far from herself at the high table as she could, given his claim to Ista's side as her present guard captain. Despite the distance, it seemed to Ista that the two remained highly aware of each other throughout the strained meal. Aware, but plainly not attracted.

Learned dy Cabon, nervous, nevertheless led the prayers with admirable discretion, keeping his pleas for godly blessings safely vague. The conversations that commenced as the food was passed limped along; the divine took refuge from them in industrious chewing. He did not neglect to listen, however, Ista noted with approval.

Ista found one of Arhys's senior officers on her right hand, buffering Liss and Foix down at the end. He was polite, undaunted by her rank, but preoccupied. After a few pragmatic exchanges about the food and wine, he abruptly said to her, "My lord has told us that he is very ill. Had you heard?"

"Yes. I am aware. We have discussed it."

"Indeed, I had marked that he was pale, and not eating or sleeping well, but I had not expected . . . if he is that ill, should he not be made to rest?" He glanced across at Cattilara as if considering a potential alliance against his forceful commander, for Arhys's good.

"Rest will bring no cure for what he has," said Ista.

"I fear his riding about in this weather may worsen his sickness."

"I don't see how it can."

Cattilara, on Ista's left, glowered at her.

"I did not know you for a physician, Royina." He let his tone trail off invitingly.

"I'm not. Alas."

"Quite the reverse," murmured Cattilara resentfully.

The officer blinked uncertainly, but finally mustered the perception to veer from a subject so clearly unpalatable to the marchess. "Brigands from the princedoms do not normally ride so close to Porifors, I assure you, Royina. But we chewed them well enough this morning, I think they will be discouraged from new attempts."

"They were rather more than brigands, I thought," said Ista. "Troops, or so their tabards proclaimed, though I suppose real brigands wouldn't hesitate to so disguise themselves. Has Sordso the Sot roused himself to some more military posture than heretofore, or do you think someone else in his court may be probing your defenses?"

"I should never have thought it of Sordso, but indeed, since the unfortunate death of his sister Umerue, I have heard that a great change has come over him. We shall have to find him another nickname if this keeps on."

"Oh?"

Thus encouraged, he turned eagerly to a safer court gossip than his own. "It is said that he has bestirred himself about his army, which he never did before. And given up drinking. *And* dismissed all his boon companions. And, quite abruptly, he has married, to an heiress of Borsasnen. *And* taken two official concubines as well, which the Roknari name as wives so as to avoid the stigma of bastardy there. Which he had not troubled to before, for all one hears that his advisors had long urged him to wed. He sounds quite a reformed soul. Not to mention energized, though perhaps the new wives will prove the cure for that. We rather hope this extreme virtue will not last. His poetry was not bad; it would be a shame to lose it." He grinned briefly.

Ista's brows rose. "This sounds not at all as Lord Illvin described the man, but I suppose Illvin has not had much chance to follow developments in Jokona, or indeed, anywhere else, in the past few months."

His head jerked around. "*Illvin* described—does he speak, now? Did he speak to you, Royina? Oh, that is hopeful news!"

Ista glanced back at Cattilara, listening with her jaw clamped shut. "He has brief periods of lucidity. I have spoken with him almost daily since I came here. There is no doubt that his wits are intact, but he remains very weak. I think he is by no means out of danger yet." She returned Cattilara's glower.

"Still—still—we feared his wits were gone for good, when he did not awaken. They were as great a loss to Porifors as Arhys's sword arm . . . would be." He caught the marchess's scowl and covered his confusion in a bite, and another.

The ordeal of dinner was not dragged out with more than

a perfunctory musical interlude, to Ista's relief. Dy Cabon went to his room for some much-needed rest, and Foix accompanied Arhys's officer to see what help his little troop might lend to Porifors in exchange for their board. And, if Ista's estimation of Foix held true, to decant from the man most of the pertinent defensive information about the fortress and its denizens. Foix's next letter to Cardegoss was likely to be very informative. She wondered if he'd yet confessed his new pet to Chancellor dy Cazaril, or if that gap might be smoothly concealed in the very abundance of his tidings.

18

LISS WAS BRUSHING OUT ISTA'S HAIR BEFORE BED, A TASK
the girl seemed to enjoy—Ista suspected it brought back
happy memories of the stables—when a diffident knock
sounded at the door of the outer chamber. Liss went to answer it and returned a moment later.

"It's one of Lord Arhys's pages. He says his lord waits
below, and would beg a word with you."

Ista's brows went up. "At this hour? Very well. Tell him I
will be down directly."

Liss went to convey the message, and Ista slipped out of
her wrapper and back into the lavender linen shift and black
silk overrobe. Her hand hesitated over the mourning brooch,
lying on the table, then fastened the soft black fabric beneath
her breasts with it as before. Inadvertently appropriate garb,
for Arhys's presence, she reflected. With Liss carrying a
candle in a glass vase to light their steps, she went out on the
gallery.

Lord Arhys stood at the foot of the stairs, holding a torch
aloft, looking up intently. He still wore his sword and boots,
as if just returned from riding out. Ista was glad to see a coat
of mail beneath his gray-and-gold tabard. The night air was

soft and still from the day's heat, and the flame gave a steady light, cast down over his pale features.

"Royina, I would speak with you. Apart."

Ista gestured toward the bench at the courtyard's far end, and he nodded.

"Wait here," Ista said quietly to Liss, and the girl nodded and plunked down at the top of the steps. Ista descended and paced across the pavement at Arhys's side. He handed his torch to his page, but the boy could not reach the bracket high on a carved pillar, and Arhys smiled briefly and took it back to set therein. He dismissed the page to keep Liss company. Ista and he settled themselves on either end of the stone slab, still not wholly cooled from its day's baking. The starry depths of the sky, bounded above by the roofs' rectangle, seemed to swallow the golden glow of Liss's candle and the torch, and give back nothing. Arhys's face was a gilded shadow against the deeper shadows, but his eyes gleamed.

"A busy day, your restored companions and their Jokonan tailpiece have brought us," he began. "Two of my patrols, to the south and the west, have returned with nothing to report. Two have not yet come back, and they concern me." He hesitated. "Cattilara did not greet my return. She is angry with me, I think."

"For riding out on your duties? She will surely forgive you."

"She will not forgive my dying. I am become her enemy in this, as well as her prize."

Have you, now? "She still thinks she can get you back. Or at least prevent you from going. She does not, I think, perceive the wasting effect of this delay upon you, being blinded by the surfaces of things. If she sees the disintegrating ghosts at all, I do not think she understands the nature of their damnation."

"Damnation," he breathed. "Is that what my state is. That explains much."

"Theologically, I do believe that is precisely what it is, although perhaps Learned dy Cabon could refine the term. I do not know the scholars' language, but I have seen the thing itself. You are cut off from the nourishment of matter, but blocked from the sustenance of your god. And yet, not by your own will, as the true and mercifully sundered spirits are. By another's interference. This is . . . wrong."

He stretched and clenched his hands. "It can't go on. I don't even bother to pretend to eat, now. I drink only sips. My hands and face and feet are growing numb. Just within the past ten days I've noticed it, faintly at first, but it's getting worse."

"That does not sound good," she agreed. She hesitated. "Have you prayed?"

His hand went to his left sleeve, and Ista remembered the black-and-gray prayer cord bound secretly there. "Need for the gods comes and goes in a man's life. Cattilara longed for a child, I made my obeisances . . . but if the Father of Winter ever heard me, He gave me no sign. I was never the sort to receive portents, or to delude myself that I had. Silence was always my portion, in return for my prayers. But of late it seems to me the silence has grown . . . emptier. Royina"—his gaze, sparking out of the shadows, seemed to pierce her—"how much longer do I have?"

She was about to say, *I don't know*. But the evasion smacked of cowardice. No Mother's physician could answer him with any better knowledge than hers. *What do I know?* She studied him, with both outer and inner sights. "Of ghosts, I have seen many, but more old than new. They accumulate, you see. Most still hold the form of life, of their bodies, for some two or three months after death, but drained of color, and of caring. They slowly erode. By a year after, second sight can usually no longer distinguish human features, though they still have the form of a body. By several years old, they are a white blur, then a fainter blur, then gone. But the time varies greatly, I suspect, depending on the strength of character the person had to begin with." And the stresses of their dwindling existence? Arhys was unique in her experience. The demands upon his spirit would be huge for a living man. How could his starveling desolate ghost sustain them?

The great-souled give greatly, from their abundance. But even they must come to the end of themselves, without the upholding hands of . . . Her mind shied from completing the thought. She reined it round. *Their god.*

"So what is my appearance now?"

"Almost wholly colorless." She added reluctantly, "You are beginning to blur about the extremities."

He rubbed his face with an exploring hand and murmured, "Ah. Much comes clear." He sat silent for a little, then tapped his knee. "You once told me you had promised Ias not to speak of my father's true fate to any living soul. Um. Well. Here am I, before you now. Royina, I would know."

Ista was surprised into a snort. "You are a most excellent lawyer, for a dead man. This counterthrust would be a very good, sharp point, if it weren't that I'd lied to you in the first place. Ias never asked me for any such promise. He was scarcely speaking to me by then. The tale I told you was but a shield, to hide my cravenness."

"*Craven* is not how I'd describe you, lady."

"One learns better than to hand one's choices to fear. With age, with every wound and scar, one learns."

"Then I ask the truth of you now, as my bier gift. More desirable to me than flowers."

"Ah." She let out her breath in a long sigh. "Yes." Her fingers traced over the smooth, cool amethysts and silver filigree of the brooch beneath her breast. *Dy Lutez wore it in his hat. He wore it there on his last day, I do recall.* "This will be but the third time in my life to make this confession."

"Third time pays for all, they say."

"What do they know?" She snorted again, more softly. "I think not. Still, my auditors have been of the best, as befits my rank and crime. A living saint, an honest divine, the dead man's dead son . . . so." She had told it over in her mind enough times; it needed no further rehearsal. She straightened her back, and began.

"All men know that Ias's father, Roya Fonsa, in despair at the loss of his sons and his royacy before the onslaught of the Golden General's alliance, slew his enemy by a rite of death magic, giving up his own life in the balance."

"That is history, yes."

"Fewer men know that the rite spilled a residue, a subtle curse afflicting Fonsa's heirs, and all their works. First Ias, then his son Orico. Teidez. Iselle. Orico's barren wife, Sara. And me," she breathed. "And me."

"Ias's was not noted as a fortunate reign for Chalion," he conceded warily. "Nor Orico's."

"Ias the Unlucky. Orico the Impotent. The nicknames given by the vulgar do not touch the half of it. Ias knew of his curse, knew its origin and its nature, though he did not tell even Orico until he lay on his deathbed. But he shared the knowledge with Arvol dy Lutez, his companion from boyhood, marshal, chancellor, right arm. Possibly, as Orico did later with his own favorites, Ias was trying to use Arvol as a tongs by which to handle the affairs of Chalion without spilling his evil geas upon them. Not that the ploy worked. But it suited Arvol dy Lutez's ambitions and huge energies well enough. And his arrogance. I grant, your father did love Ias in his way. Ias worshipped him, and was utterly dependent upon his judgment. Arvol even selected me for him."

Arhys pulled on his close-trimmed beard. "The rumor I have heard bruited by the envious that they were, ah, more intimate than boon companions, I take to be political slander?"

"No," she said simply. "They were lovers for years, as all Cardegoss knew but did not speak of outside the capital walls. My own mother told me, just before I wed, so I would not step into it unawares. I thought her callous, then. Now I think her wise. And worried. Looking back, I think it also was an offer to let me back out, though I missed that implication entirely at the time. Yet for all her candid warnings—

which, I found later, Lord dy Lutez had insisted she give me—to prevent trouble for him, mostly, I suspect, though also for Ias—I did not understand what it meant. How could I—a romantic virgin, overwhelmed by what seemed a great victory on the field of love, to be chosen as bride by the roya himself? I nodded and agreed, anxious to seem sophisticated and sensible."

"Oh," he said, very quietly.

"So if ever you thought your mother untrue to her vows, to take Illvin's father to her bed, be assured she was not the first dy Lutez to break them. I suspect her mother was less shrewd and honest than mine, preparing her for her high marriage. Or less informed."

His brows climbed in reflection. "That accounts for . . . much, that I did not understand as a boy. I thought my father had cast her off, in anger and humiliation, and that was why he never came here. I never thought that she had cast him off."

"Oh, I'm quite sure that Lord dy Lutez was thoroughly offended by her defection," Ista said. "No matter how justi-fied. His pride would keep him from returning, but his sense of justice, to give him credit, likely also kept him from pur-suing any vengeance. Or perhaps it was shame. I can hope." She added dryly, "In any case, he still had her property to add to his vast holdings, for compensation of his wounds."

He eyed her. "You thought him greedy."

"No man accumulates all that he did by chance. Yet I would not call it greed, exactly, for he scarcely knew all he held, and a greedy man numbers each coin."

"What would you call it, then?"

Ista's brows pinched in. "Consolation," she tried at last. "His possessions were a magic mirror, to reflect him the size he wished to be."

"That," he said after a moment, "is a fearsome judgment, Royina."

She bent her head in an acknowledging nod. "He was a very complex man." She drew breath, began again. "Arvol and Ias did not betray me by concealing their love. They betrayed me by concealing the curse. I entered into marriage with Ias unaware of my danger, or the danger to my children-to-be. The visions started when I became pregnant with Iselle. The gods, trying to break in upon me. I thought I was going mad. And Ias and dy Lutez let me go on thinking that. For *two years.*"

He jerked a little at the sudden fierceness in her voice. "That seems . . . most unkind."

"*That* was cowardice. *And* contempt for my wits and spine. They mired me in the consequences of their secret, then refused to trust me with its cause. I was a mere girl, you see, unfit to bear such a burden. Though not unfit to bear Ias's children into that darkness. Except the gods did not seem to regard me as unfit. For it was *me* They came to. Not Ias. Not dy Lutez. Me."

Her lips twisted. "I wonder—in retrospect—how put out Arvol was by that? He would have been the sole shining hero to save Ias, if he could. It was his accustomed role. And indeed, for a while it did appear that the gods had assigned it to him.

"At last—do even the gods grow impatient with our obtuseness?—the Mother of Summer Herself appeared to me, not in dream but in waking vision. I was prostrated—I had not yet learned to be suspicious of the gods. She told me that the curse might be broken and carried out of the world by a man who would lay down his life three times for the blighted House of Chalion. Being young, and frenzied with anxiety for my babies, I took Her words too literally, and concluded that She meant me to devise a perilous rite to accomplish this paradox."

"Perilous indeed. And, um . . ." His brow wrinkled. "Paradoxical."

"I told all to Ias and Arvol, and we took counsel together. Arvol, afflicted by our weeping, volunteered to attempt the hero's role. We hit upon drowning as the method, for men were known to come back from that death, sometimes. And it does not disfigure. Arvol studied it, collected tales, investigated victims both lost and saved. In a cavern beneath the Zangre, we set up the cask, the ropes, the winch. The altars to all the gods. Arvol let himself be stripped, bound, lowered upside down, until his struggles ceased, until the light of his soul went out to my inner eye."

He began to speak; she held up her hand, to block the misunderstanding. "No. Not yet. We drew him out—pressed the water from his throat, pounded on his heart, cried out our prayers, until he choked and breathed again. *And I could see the crack in the curse.*

"We had planned the ritual three nights in succession. On the second night, all went the same, until his hair brushed the surface of the water, and he gasped out to stop, he could not bear it. He cried I was trying to assassinate him, for jealousy's sake. Ias hesitated. I was shaken, sick in my stomach—but I let reason compel me. It was Arvol's own chosen method, it had worked once . . . I wailed for fear for my children, and for the frustration of coming so close, to miss saving them by a handbreadth. For rage at his slander. And for raising my hopes so high upon his pride, then dashing them so low upon his frailty." She added simply, "I'd believed in his account of himself, you see."

In the night, in some hollow below the castle walls, insects sang, a thin, high keening. It was the only sound. Arhys had forgotten to breathe. His body, perhaps, was losing the habit. She wondered how long it would take him to notice.

"When we drew him out the second time, he was dead indeed, and not all our tears and prayers, regrets and recriminations, and oh, there were many of those last, brought him back again. Ias half decided, later, that Arvol's accusation of jealousy was true; half the time, I agreed myself. The fault was . . . Ias's, for weakness, and mine, for impatience and unwisdom. For if Ias had stood against me, I would have yielded, or if I had listened to my heart and not my head, and allowed Arvol more time, who is to say that after another day, or week, or month, he might have recovered his nerve?

I'll never know, now. The gods forsook me. The curse remained, unbroken, worse in its effects than ever. Until another generation threw up another man, more fitted to lift it from the world." She drew breath. "And that is how I came to murder your father. If you really want to know."

He was silent for a long time, remembered to inhale, and said, "Lady, I think this is not a confession. This is an indictment."

She rocked back. "Of Arvol? Yes," she said slowly, "that, too. If he had never volunteered, I'd have thought no less of him. If he had died on the first attempt, well, I would have thought the task beyond any man, or my design mistaken. But to demonstrate the true possibility, and *then* fail . . . shattered my heart. It was not, I came later to learn, death by rote that the gods required. One cannot force another's soul to grow wide enough to admit a god to the world, but that dilation, not the mere dying, was what was wanted. Arvol dy Lutez was a great man. But . . . not quite great enough."

He stared into the darkness. The torch had almost burned out, though at the top of the stairs Liss's candle still glowed. She sat with her chin propped in her hands, eyelids drooping; the page had fallen asleep, curled up against her skirts.

"If my father had lived," he said at last, "do you think he would ever have called me to his side?"

"If he had wrenched open his soul wide enough to succeed, I think it would thereafter have been more than wide enough to encompass you. Those who have admitted a god do not shrink back to their former size, in my experience. If he had never made the attempt . . . well, he was never quite small enough to turn aside from hazard, either. So, I do not know."

"Mm." It was a little noise, but contained a cache of pain nonetheless. He glanced up at the sky, reading the clock of the stars. "Royina, I keep you from your bed."

But not the reverse. In the long, lonely watches of his unsleeping nights, what did he now think about? She took the hint nonetheless and rose. He stood with her, his war gear creaking.

He took her hand, half bowed, briefly pressed his cool forehead against its back. "Royina, I do thank you for these garlands of truth. I know they cost you dear."

"They are dry and bitter thorns. I wish I could give you some better bier gift." *With all my cracking heart, I do wish it.*

"I do not desire any softer wreath."

Liss, seeing them pace once more across the court, prodded the page awake and came to the foot of the stairs to receive Ista back from Arhys's arm. Arhys saluted them solemnly and turned away, his sleepy page pattering after. The echoes of his receding footfalls in the archway sounded like muffled drums in Ista's ears.

❧

It was long before Ista slept. In the gray of dawn, she seemed to hear thumping and low voices in the distance, but her exhaustion drew her back down into her pillow. She fell into an evil dream where she sat at a high table with Lady Cattilara. The marchess, glowing faintly violet, plied her guest with food until Ista's belly strained, and drowned her wits in drink until Ista lay back in her chair unable to rise for the paralysis in her limbs.

Only a much louder thumping at the door to the outer chamber roused her from this bizarre dream imprisonment. She exhaled in relief to find herself in her own bed, her body normally proportioned and mobile again, if feeling anything but well rested. By the bright lines seeping through her shutters, it was broad day.

Liss's steps sounded, then voices: Foix's, deep and urgent, dy Cabon's, sharp and excited. Ista had already swung out of bed and pulled her black robe about herself when the door between the chambers opened and Liss poked her head in.

"Royina, something very strange has happened . . ."

Ista pushed past her. Foix was dressed for the day in blue tunic, trousers, boots and sword, his face flushed with exertion; dy Cabon's white undertunic was on askew, its front buttons mismatched with their buttonholes, his feet yet bare.

"Royina." Foix ducked his head. "Did you see or hear anything, at Lord Illvin's chambers or on the gallery, along about dawn? Your room is closer than ours."

"No—maybe. I fell back to sleep." She grimaced in memory of the unpleasant dream. "I was very tired. *Was* there something?"

"Lady Cattilara came at dawn with some servants and carried off Lord Illvin on a pallet. To take him down to the temple to pray over, and consult with the temple physicians, she said."

"The temple physicians should come up to attend upon him in Porifors, I would think," said Ista, disturbed. "Did Lord Arhys go with them?"

"The march is nowhere to be found this morning. I first learned of all this when one of his officers asked *me* if I'd seen him."

"I last saw Arhys last night. He came to speak with me down in the courtyard, around midnight. Liss was there."

The girl nodded. She had evidently wakened before Ista—she was dressed and had a tray with morning tea and fresh bread sitting ready on a table—but not much before, for this all seemed news to her as well.

"Well," Foix continued, "I felt strangely uneasy—probably left over from the bad dreams I'd had last night, which really made me wonder about the castle food, but anyway, I made an excuse to walk down to the temple to see what was happening. Lady Cattilara had never come there. I asked around. I finally discovered that she had commandeered a supply wagon and a team of dray horses from the garrison's stable down there. No one knew what had been loaded aboard, but the wagon, with Goram driving and one of the servants sitting beside him, was seen leaving the town gate at least an hour ago, on the road south."

Ista's breath drew in. "Has she or Arhys been seen since?"

"No, Royina."

"Then she has stolen them away. Taken Arhys, and abducted Illvin to maintain him."

Foix's gaze upon her sharpened. "This is the marchess's doing, do you think? Not Lord Arhys's?"

"Lord Arhys would never abandon Porifors and his post. Not for all his wife's weeping," said Ista with certainty. *Being a stronger-minded man than Ias. But then, a dy Lutez always was.*

"But her demon wanted to flee, you told us," said dy Cabon. "Suppose it has gained the upper hand?"

"Then why take the baggage?" asked Liss logically. "Lady Cattilara's body and her jewel case, and one fast horse, would serve it better."

Foix eyed her with a flash of respect.

"Not, I think, the upper hand," said Ista slowly. "But suppose her demon had persuaded her that both their goals could be better served by flight? She would have all its cooperation, then."

"She desires her husband's life restored, or at least, his strange half death continued indefinitely," said Foix. "How is that served by heaving him and poor Lord Illvin into a wagon and driving off?"

"Er," said dy Cabon.

All the faces in the room turned toward him. "What?" said Ista sharply.

"Ah, um . . . I'm wondering if something I might have said . . . Lady Cattilara came to me last evening after dinner. For spiritual guidance, I thought. We talked about this dire knot. Poor chick, her tears glittered down like little jewels of sorrow across her cheeks."

Ista rolled her eyes. "No doubt. And then?"

"I tried to counsel as well as console, to bring her to some sense of what a theological danger she had placed her husband in. As well as the physical danger inflicted upon his brother, and her own soul's peril. I said, more demon magic was no cure. Nothing but a miracle could alter the inevitable course of events. She asked me, where were miracles to be had, for all the world as if they came from some holy emporium. I said, only saints could channel them to us from the gods. She asked, where were saints to be found? I said, all sorts of strange and unexpected places, both high and low. I said, I thought *you*, Royina, were the saint into whose hands this tangle had been given for unraveling. She said, um, well, some wild and unconsidered things—she seems to think you are her enemy. I assured her that could not be so. She suggested any other saint in the world would be better suited for the task, and asked me to send for one, as though saints were physicians, to be obtained from the Temple by draft. Well, some saints *are* physicians, but it's not like . . . I suggested that she wasn't likely to get any other answer from the gods; most people don't even get *one*. I'm afraid she is not very interested in the subtler truths of theology."

"She wants a rite by rote," said Ista. *As I did, once.* "A merchant's bargain. Pay the coin, get the goods. She just can't find the peddler."

He shrugged. "I fear it is so."

"So now she has taken her quick and her dead and gone on pilgrimage. To look for a miracle. To order."

"The roads here are very unsafe, as we found yesterday," said Foix in a voice of worry. "Lord Arhys would surely not permit his wife to go out on them now, no matter what her hope."

"Do you think he had a choice? Is there one pallet in that wagon, or two—the brothers lying side by side like bundles of cordwood? The demon could help her to it—the dual inactivity would likely be a relief to it."

Dy Cabon scratched his head. "She has a better right to seek healing for Lord Arhys than any other person. He *is* her husband."

"Illvin isn't," said Ista shortly. "And what Arhys needs

goes beyond healing. They must be brought back. Foix, muster your troop and their horses. Liss, wrap my knees for riding, I don't want to tear open these scabs."

Dy Cabon said, "Royina, you should not be out on the road either!"

"I agree with you, but Foix has not the authority to command Cattilara's servants against her own wishes. And someone must handle her demon."

"I think I might do that, Royina," said Foix. He glanced warily at dy Cabon.

"Can you, simultaneously, handle a screaming, weeping, distraught woman?"

"Ah," he said, contemplating this unpalatable vision. "Can you?"

"I think so." *In fact, I think I'm looking forward to it.* .

"I would, um, appreciate that, Royina."

"Good. Warn Arhys's officers . . . hm." Her eyes narrowed. "I suspect Arhys would not want this tale bruited about. Dy Cabon. If we're not back in—how long, Foix? Two hours?"

"They had four horses hitched, and an hour's start—two or three hours."

"If we're not back in three hours, tell Arhys's senior officers what we have done, and have them send men after us." Ista turned to Foix. "Hurry. We'll meet you in the forecourt as soon as the horses are saddled."

He saluted her and was gone. Liss was already stripping out of her fine dress and kicking off her slippers. Ista pushed the protesting dy Cabon out the door.

"But I should ride with you, Royina!" cried the divine. "And Foix should not be left unguided!"

"No. I need you here. And if Foix's dancing bear requires a collar, I am better fitted to supply it."

"And you're too fat and you ride too slow," Liss's unsympathetic voice floated through the window, accompanied by a thump of boots being lined up.

Dy Cabon reddened.

Ista rested her hand on his shoulder. "This is a dry country, and culverts are hard to come by. You will be one less terror for my heart to worry about, safe in here."

His color deepened, but he bowed in unhappy obedience nonetheless. Ista shut the door on him and hurried to don her riding clothes.

19

IN THE FORECOURT, ISTA WAS STARTLED BY THE HORSE Liss led out for her. Tall, shimmering white with a soft gray nose, mane and tail like silk banners—Ferda would have waxed poetic. The stall stains were carefully washed off its coat, with only a few faint yellow traces that reminded her inescapably of the blotches on dy Cabon's white robes. It snuffled and nudged at her, big dark eyes liquid and amiable.

"What's this?" Ista asked, as Liss led it to the mounting block.

"They tell me his name is Feather. Short for Featherwits. I asked for the best-trained horse in the stable for you, and they begged me to take him out, because since Lord Illvin fell sick he's done little but laze in his stall and eat and get fat."

"Is this Lord Illvin's own mount, then?" asked Ista, throwing a leg over the broad back. The horse stood perfectly still for her as she disposed her padded knees gingerly against its sides and found her stirrups. "Surely it isn't a warhorse."

"No, he has another stallion for that—evil-tempered scarred red brute that no one else will go near." Liss threw herself up on her courier palomino, which sidled uncooperatively and seemed inclined to buck, but settled under her stern hand. "It's savaged any number of grooms. They showed me their injuries. Very impressive."

Foix's hand rose and fell, and he and Pejar on their mounts led the way out the gate, followed by Liss and Ista and then the half dozen remaining men of the Daughter's company. They sorted themselves into single file to descend the narrow switchback road past the village. Beyond its walls, they turned onto the road from Tolnoxo that Ista had arrived down so many crowded days ago. Foix set a brisk but not killing pace, walking up slopes, trotting down, cantering on the flat. *Featherwit* seemed a slander, for the horse was so responsive to Ista's lightest command of rein or heel that it seemed she had only to think her desire. Its trot was a long smooth ripple, its canter like being rocked along in a sedan chair. She was relieved by its gentleness, for it seemed a long way to the hard ground from her perch. Lord Illvin would need a tall horse, certainly.

Riding through a moist wooded area by the river, they stirred up a plague of large buzzing horseflies. Ista grimaced and slapped at the ones she could reach as they settled hungrily on Feather's silky sides. They crunched disgustingly, leaving blood streaks on her palm. Liss's palomino bucked and squealed. Foix glanced back over his shoulder; only Ista saw the little violet flicker from his hand, but the ugly flies lifted from Liss's mount. Since they then collected on Ista's, this seemed little improvement, but the cavalcade broke into the sunlight and left the flies behind before she could complain.

They made the long climb up the valley's steeper side and stopped to water the horses at the village with the olive grove, some five miles out from Porifors. This shade was mercifully free of bloodsucking insects. Pejar went off to inquire of the villagers for word of the wagon they pursued. Ista found herself standing and stretching next to Foix in the shadow of a huge olive bole as the sweaty horses gulped from the stream.

"Still playing with flies?" she inquired softly. "I saw that trick. No more, please, or I shall report you to the divine."

He blushed. "It was a good deed. Besides, I wanted to please Liss."

"Hm." She hesitated. "Take my advice, and do not use magic to court her. Most especially, do not yield to the temptation to use it *directly* to induce her favor."

By his embarrassed grin, he knew precisely what she implied—and this wasn't the first time the notion of some sort of aphrodisiac spell had crossed his mind. "Mm."

Ista's voice dropped further. "For if you do, and she finds out, it will destroy her trust not only in you, but in her own mind. She would never again be sure if a thought or a feeling were truly her own. She would be constantly halting, second-guessing, turning about inside her head. Madness lies down that road. It would be less crippling and more loving if you should take a war hammer and break both her legs."

His smile had grown fixed. "As you command. Royina."

"I do not speak as your royina. I do not even speak as one god-touched. I speak as a woman, who has walked to the end of that road and returns to report the hazards. If you still possess half the wits you started with—and if it is indeed love you seek and not just your gratification—you will listen as a man."

His little bow, this time, was visibly more thoughtful, his smirk wiped clean.

Pejar came back with the news that a wagon and team had indeed stopped at the grove earlier, lingering in the shade long enough to unhitch and water both pairs of horses; the wagon had left again not half an hour before. Foix grimaced satisfaction and cut their own rest short.

Another four miles of trotting brought them to the top of a long rise. They at last saw their quarry rumbling down the road, small in the distance, the wagon's canvas top, painted with the sigil of Porifors's garrison, bright in the sunlight. Foix waved his troop onward. They had largely closed the gap before someone from the wagon spotted them. The invisible driver whipped up the team, but the lumbering dray horses, burdened by the load they towed, were no match for the pursuers' faster mounts.

Men of Foix's company galloped up on either side of the noisily bouncing vehicle to lean over and seize the lead pair's reins. As she in turn urged her horse up and around, Ista could hear Cattilara's voice crying out in protest. The wagon slowed to a halt.

Cattilara, dressed in an elegant traveling costume of gray and gold, was crouched on the driver's box berating a terrified Goram, who hunched down with his eyes nearly shut, clutching his team's reins in clenched and shaking hands. Ista narrowed her eyes against the light of the world and tried to extend her inner vision to its fullest sensitivity, to directly perceive not spirits hidden in matter, but spirits alone. Was this how the gods saw the world? Cattilara's demon was not, to Ista's relief, expanded and dominant, but curled in on itself within her again. Another male servant, one of Cattilara's younger ladies, and Arhys's page cowered together in the wagon's back.

Two nearly extinguished forms lay side by side within. With the blockage of Ista's corporeal vision by the canvas and wood, it became almost easier to see what she was actually looking for. A wispy line of white fire, sluggishly drifting from one body to another; at a level of perception even below that, a net of violet light running three ways, the spell-channel.

She tightened her fingers, and Feather stopped and stood in a placid obedience. She let the reins fall to his withers and stretched her hands, letting her spirit follow along with her body. And then, for the first time, flow beyond her body. *Bastard, help me. Curse You.* She did not, did not dare, try to break the underlying lines of the demon's spell yet, but she set her ligatures and summoned soul-fire. The white line from Illvin to Arhys blazed up like a thatch catching alight in a distant dark.

Arhys's deep voice sounded from within, irritable as a man waking from sleep: "What *is* this? Illvin . . . ?"

Cattilara's screaming abuse abruptly stopped. Her head drew in, and she shrank in her seat. Panting, she glowered at Ista.

Movement sounded within the wagon: a creak, bootsteps on the floorboards. Arhys poked his head out and stared around. "Bastard's hell! Where *are* we?" A glance at the familiar landscape evidently answered the question to his satisfaction, for he turned his frown on his weeping wife. "Cattilara, *what have you done?*"

On the wagon's other side, the tensed Foix breathed relief and sent a small salute of thanks in Ista's direction. The mauve flicker waiting in his palm died away.

Cattilara turned in her seat and threw her arms around her husband's thighs in wild supplication. Goram ducked out of her way. "My lord, my lord, no! Order these people away! Tell Goram to drive on! We must escape! She is evil, she wants to encompass your death!"

Automatically, he patted her hair. His rolling eye fell on Ista, watching grimly. "Royina? What is this?"

"What is the last thing you remember, Lord Arhys?"

His brows drew in. "Cattilara sent me an urgent message to attend upon her at the garrison's stable yard. I walked in and found this wagon standing at the ready there, then— nothing after that." His frown deepened.

"Your wife took it into her head to carry you off and seek healing for you elsewhere than Porifors. To what extent she was encouraged in this by her demon, I know not, but it certainly *assisted* her in it. Illvin was brought along principally, I suppose, as your commissary."

Arhys winced. "Desert my post? Desert *Porifors? Now?*"

Cattilara flinched at the iron in his voice. Her collapse in tears before him failed, for once, to have any softening effect. When he turned her face up to his, Ista could see the tension in the tendons of his hands, standing out like cords beneath his pale skin.

"Cattilara. Think. This desertion dishonors my trust and my sworn oaths. To the provincar of Caribastos, to the Royina Iselle and Royse-Consort Bergon—to my own men. It is impossible."

"It is *not* impossible. Suppose you were sick of, oh, any other illness. Someone else would have to take over then all the same. You *are* ill. Another officer must take your post for now."

"The only one I would trust to take over at a moment's notice in this present uncertainty is Illvin." He hesitated. "Would be Illvin," he corrected himself.

"No, no, no—!" She fairly beat on him with her fists in a paroxysm of frustration and rage.

Ista studied the pulsating lines of light. *Can I do this*? She wasn't sure. *Well, I am sure that I can try. So.* She folded her fleshly hands quietly in her lap and reached again with her spirit hands. Again leaving the demon's underlying channels undisturbed, she tightened the ligature between Illvin and Arhys nearly to closure.

Arhys fell to his knees; his lips parted in shock.

"If you want him upright and moving," said Ista to Cattilara, "you must keep him so yourself, now. No more stealing."

"No!" screamed Cattilara as Arhys half collapsed across her. Goram grabbed at him to keep his heavy body from toppling from the seat. Cattilara stared down at Arhys's pale confused face in horrified denial. The fire of her soul roiled up from her body and collected at her heart.

Yes! Ista thought. *You can. Do it, girl!*

Then, with a wail and a white rush, Cattilara fainted away. The disorderly fire burst from her heart, splashing irregularly in the spell-banks. Ista extended a transparent hand again. The flow steadied, settled. Not too swift, lest it drain its reservoirs altogether, nor too slow, lest it fail its purpose. Just . . . there. Her inner eye rechecked the lines. A tiny trickle of life still flowed from Illvin, just enough to maintain contact. She dared not touch the demon's subtle net, not that she was at all sure she could break it even if she tried. Arhys blinked, flexed his jaw, shakily stood up, one hand braced on Goram's shoulder.

"Oh, *thank* you," muttered Foix into the blessed silence.

"I used to carry on not unlike that, from time to time, in my first grief," murmured Ista across to him, in uncomfortable reminiscence. "Why in five gods' names did no one ever smother me and put themselves out of my misery? I may never know."

A rasping voice from within the wagon said, "Bastard's demons, *now* what?"

A flash of relief crossed Arhys's features. "Illvin! Out here!"

A padding of bare feet; Illvin, wearing only his linen robe and looking much like a man wakened too early after a night of too much revelry, stumbled out and stood blinking into the bright morning, one lean hand grasping the canvas frame for balance.

His eye fell on Ista, and his face lit. "Witless!" he cried in delight. This odd greeting, Ista concluded belatedly, was actually addressed to his horse, who flicked its ears and snuffed, flaring its gray nostrils, and almost, but not quite, moved from the spot on which its rider had bade it stand. "Royina," Illvin continued, giving her a nod. "I trust Feathers-for-Wits here has gone well for you? Five gods, did no one think to cut his feed?"

"He is a most perfect gentleman," Ista assured him. "I find him very shapely."

Illvin looked down at Catti, now slumped over against Goram's shrinking shoulder. "What's this? Is she all right?"

"For the moment," Ista assured both him and Arhys, who was eyeing his wife even more uncertainly. "I, ah . . . required that she change chairs with you for a little while."

"I did not know you could do that," said Illvin cautiously.

"Neither did I, till I tried it a moment ago. The demon's spell is unbroken, just . . . reapportioned."

Arhys, his face rigid with his discomfiture, nevertheless

knelt and gathered Cattilara up in his arms. Illvin felt his right shoulder and frowned; his frown deepened as his glance took in a slow red leak starting on Cattilara's shoulder. He leaned aside for his burdened brother to duck back into the wagon. Ista handed her reins to Liss and scrambled from her saddle across to the wagon seat; Illvin extended a hand to swing her safely aboard.

"We must talk," she told him.

He nodded in heartfelt agreement. "Goram," he added. His groom looked up with open relief in his face. "Get this wagon turned around and headed back to Porifors."

"Yes, my lord," said Goram happily.

Ista ducked after Arhys and Illvin as Foix began calling instructions to his men to help back and turn the team. Arhys laid Cattilara, her head lolling, down on the pallet he had just vacated. It was dim and musty under the canvas after the bright light outside, but Ista's eyes quickly adjusted. The other servant, Cattilara's woman, and the page squatted fearfully at the back of the wagon among three or four small trunks. It seemed modest provision for the journey, though the marchess's jewel case no doubt reposed somewhere within the baggage.

Arhys sent the manservant and the woman forward to sit with Goram. His page, round-eyed with worry, settled near him; he gave the boy a reassuring ruffle of the hair. Arhys sat cross-legged by his wife's head. Illvin handed Ista down onto the pallet opposite; she felt her scabs crack under their pads as she folded her knees. Illvin started to settle cross-legged next to her, realized the inadequacy of his narrow robe for that position, and sat instead on his knees.

Arhys glowered down at his wife. "I can't believe she'd think I would desert Porifors."

"I don't imagine she did," said Ista. "Hence this deceit." She hesitated. "It's a hard thing, when all your life rides on the decisions of others, and you can do nothing to affect the outcome."

The wagon finished its turn and started off at a walking

pace. The team would be tired enough by the time they'd retraced the ten or so miles to the castle.

Arhys touched Cattilara's shoulder, now showing a dark red stain from the slow ooze beneath. "This won't do."

"It must, till we get back to Porifors," said Illvin uneasily. He stretched his arms and hands and hitched his shoulders, as if settling back into a body grown unused to him. He tested his own grip, and frowned.

"I can only hope the garrison hasn't fallen into an uproar over my disappearance," said Arhys.

"As soon as we arrive," said Ista, "we must make another attempt to question Cattilara's demon. It must know what is afoot in Jokona and, most of all, who dispatched it." She repeated to Illvin the officer's tale of the sudden reform of Sordso the Sot.

"How very strange," mused Illvin. "Sordso never showed any sign of such family feeling before."

"But—will we be able to question the creature, Royina?" asked Arhys, still staring down at Cattilara. "We had little enough luck the last time."

Ista shook her head in equal doubt. "I did not have Learned dy Cabon's advice, before. Nor the assistance of Foix dy Gura. We may be able to set one demon upon the other, to some good effect. Or . . . to some effect. I shall take counsel of the divine when we return."

"I would take counsel of my brother, while I can," said Arhys.

"*I* would take counsel of some food," said Illvin. "Is there any in this wagon?"

Arhys bade his page search; the boy emerged from rooting among the supplies with a loaf of bread, a sack of leathery dried apricots, and a skin of water. Illvin settled and began conscientiously gnawing, while Arhys detailed the reports from Porifors's scouts.

"We are missing news from the north road altogether," Illvin observed as Arhys wound up his rapid account. "I mislike this."

"Yes. I am most troubled for the two parties that have not yet returned or sent any courier. I was about to send another patrol after them, when my morning duties were so unexpectedly interrupted." Arhys glanced in exasperation at his unconscious wife. "Or possibly go myself."

"I beg you will not," said Illvin, rubbing his shoulder.

"Well . . . no. Perhaps that would not be wise, under the circumstances." His gaze upon Cattilara grew, if possible, more worried. She looked terribly defenseless, curled up on her side. Without the underlying strain of subterfuge in her face, her striking natural beauty reasserted itself.

He glanced up and managed a brief smile for Ista's sake. "Do not be alarmed, Royina. Even if some unseen force approaches from that direction, there is little they can do against Porifors. The walls are stout, the garrison loyal, the approaches for siege engines difficult in the extreme, and the fortress stands upon solid rock. It cannot be undermined. Support from Oby would arrive before our assailants had time to finish making camp."

"If Oby is not itself attacked at the same time," muttered Illvin.

Arhys glanced away. "I have spoken at length with the temple notary in the past few days, and placed my will in writing under his care. The castle warder has charge of all my other papers. I have appointed you my executor, and joint guardian of little Liviana."

"Arhys," said Illvin, his voice drawn with doubt. "I would point out that there is no guarantee that I will get out of this alive either."

His brother nodded. "Liviana's grandfather becomes her sole sponsor in that case, and guardian of all her dy Lutez properties. In all events—given the lack of any child between Catti and me—I mean to return Cattilara with her jointure to the guardianship of Lord dy Oby."

"Cattilara would care as little for my rule as I would care to exert it," said Illvin. "Thank you from us both."

Arhys nodded in wry understanding. "If you—if—if you

cannot undertake it in Liviana's name, Poriforts's military command must revert to the provincar of Caribastos, to be assigned to a man he judges able to carry out its tasks. I have written him to warn him . . . well, only that I am ill, and that he may wish to look about him just in case."

"You take care of every duty. No matter how distasteful." Illvin smiled bleakly. "You have always sought to take a father's care of us all. Is there any doubt which god waits to take you up? But let Him wait a little longer, I say." He glanced aside at Ista.

But no god awaits him, Ista thought. *That's what sundered* means.

Arhys shrugged. "The days gnaw at me as rats gnaw a corpse. I can feel it now, more and more. I have already overstayed, most grievously. Royina . . ." His eyes upon her were uncomfortably penetrating. "*Can* you release me? *Is* that why you were tumbled down here?"

Ista hesitated. "I scarcely know what I can do and what I cannot. If I am meant to channel miracles, that one would not be my first choice. Yet it is the nature of miracles that their human conduit may not choose them, except to cry them *yes* or *no*. It is only demon sorcery that we may bend to our own wills. No one bends a god."

"And yet," said Illvin thoughtfully, "the Bastard is half a demon himself, they say. I think his nature is not wholly as the rest of his family's. Perhaps his miracles are not either?"

Ista frowned in confusion. "I . . . don't know. He seemed just as much beyond me in my dream as his Mother did in my vision of her, nigh on twenty years ago. In any case, I have only tried to rearrange the strength that flows among you three. I have not tried to break the bindings beneath, or force the demon to do so against its mistress's will, though it is clear enough that it would abandon all and fly if it could."

"Try now," said Arhys.

Both Ista and Illvin made simultaneous noises of protest, and glanced at each other.

"Because if you *cannot* do this, I must also know," said Arhys patiently.

"But—there is no way to test it but to do it. And then I would not know how to undo it."

"I did not suggest that you then seek to undo it."

"I would fear to leave you damned."

"More than I am now?"

Ista looked away, discomfited. She read a soul-deep exhaustion in his face; as if he grew hourly less loath to end his travails, even into the dwindling silence of nothingness. "But—what if this is *not* the task I was sent for? What if I am wrong in my reasoning—again? I should have been ecstatic if it had been given me to heal you. I do not wish to murder another dy Lutez."

"You did once."

"Yes, but not by sorcery. By drowning. The method would not work on you. You haven't taken a breath in the last fifteen minutes."

"Oh. Yes." He looked embarrassed and made an effort to inhale.

Illvin's eyes had grown wide. "*What* tale is this?"

Ista glanced at him, gritted her teeth, and said, "Arvol dy Lutez did not die in the Zangre under questioning. Ias and I drowned him by mistake in the course of an attempt among the three of us to call down a miracle for Chalion's sake. The treason accusation was entirely false." Well. That was certainly getting more succinct with practice.

Illvin's mouth hung open for a moment longer. He finally said, "Ah. I always did think that treason charge was oddly handled."

"The rite failed because Arvol's courage failed." She stopped. Then blurted out, "And yet I might have saved the hour even at the last, if I could have called down a miracle of healing. Even as he lay drowned dead at our feet. The Mother, the very goddess of remedy, stood at my right hand, just around some . . . corner of perception. If my soul had not been so knotted with rage and fear and grief that there was no room in it for any god to enter." Three prior confessions had all evaded this codicil, she realized. She glanced aside again at Illvin. "Or if I had loved him instead of hated him. Or if—I don't know."

Illvin cleared his throat. "Most people fail to work miracles most of the time. Such a dereliction scarcely needs accounting for."

"Mine does. I was called." She brooded, as the wagon creaked along. *Now I am called again. But what for?* She glanced up at Arhys. "I wonder how our lives would have been different if your father *had* brought you to court? Maybe we put the wrong dy Lutez in that barrel." Now, *there* was a vision. "What was he like at twenty, Illvin?"

"Oh, quite as he is now," Illvin responded. "Not as polished or practiced, perhaps. Not as broad in the shoulder." A smile of memory flickered over his mouth. "Not as level-headed."

"Not as dead," growled Arhys, frowning at his hands, which he was stretching and clenching again. Testing for numbness? For increasing numbness?

"When I was young and beautiful, at court in Cardegoss . . ." When Arhys had not yet been married even once. When all things were still possible. Might she then have taken a dy Lutez as a lover after all, and made the false slander true? And yet Fonsa's dark curse had blighted all budding hopes in that court—to what horrors might it have bent *that* sweet dream, to what disasters drawn Arhys's youthful brilliance? Would it be true or false comfort to suggest to Arhys that Arvol had kept him away for his own safety? She suppressed a shudder. "It was still too late."

Arhys blinked at her, missing the implications, but Illvin grunted a pained laugh. "Imagine you'd met him before you'd married Ias, then, as long as you're spinning might-have-beens," he advised dryly. He cast her an odd look. "All my might-have-beens come out the same either way."

The wagon bumped and rocked, marking a turn off the road. Ista peeked out to discover that they had returned to the walled village, and were stopping in the olive grove again to water the horses. The sun had climbed to noon, and the day was growing very hot.

Ista clambered down for a moment to stretch her half-healed legs and get a drink. Liss still had Lord Illvin's white horse in tow, watering it at the stream. Illvin looked out longingly at it, then abruptly disappeared back inside the wagon. Voices came from behind the canvas, some sort of argument involving Illvin, Goram, and the manservant. Illvin emerged a few minutes later smiling in satisfaction, wearing his groom's leather trousers and the manservant's boots below his light linen robe. The trousers were cinched in around his waist and barely reached his calves, but the boots made up the difference.

Illvin reclaimed his horse and grinned as he mounted it. Appreciation for a body up and moving at will through the bright world again was plain in his face, perhaps the more keenly felt for the fragility of the stolen moment. He let Liss help lengthen his stirrups, spoke a word of thanks, settled in his saddle, and gave Ista a cheery salute.

Goram, Ista was relieved to see, now wore a pair of ill-fitting linen trousers evidently borrowed from the wagon's scanty store, though the hapless manservant was left barefoot. The Daughter's men helped roll up the wagon's canvas sides partway, as the heat of the day was making the suffocating stuffiness a greater trial than the dust of the road. Not, Ista conceded, that Lord Arhys was likely to notice either one. They started off again. Foix disposed four of his men before and two behind the lumbering wagon, and Illvin and Liss rode along at either side, within easy speaking distance.

A few miles from the village they topped the rise, swung right along the slope, and began their drop into the broad valley that Porifors guarded. They rounded a stand of trees; abruptly, Foix flung up a hand. Their little party ground to a halt.

Illvin rose in his stirrups, his eyes widening. Ista and Arhys scrambled to the front of the wagon and looked out.

Arhys's lips drew back, and his teeth clenched, though only Ista's breath drew in, harsh as a rasp down her dry throat.

Turning onto the road just ahead of them from some cross-country push was a large column of cavalry. The white pelicans of Jokona glowed on their sea-green tabards. Their armor glinted. Their spearpoints winked in the light in a long line, stitched like jewels across a courtier's cloak in the descending folds of the land.

20

A LOW MOAN BROKE FROM GORAM'S LIPS AS HE CROUCHED, gray with fear, over his team's reins.

"Get back, get back," Arhys hissed to the manservant and Cattilara's woman, shoving them behind him to stumble and crouch in the bed of the wagon. His hand clapped down on Goram's shoulder. "Drive on! Drive through them, if we can." He stood up and signaled to Foix, sitting his skittering horse and staring frantically forward and back. "Go on!"

Foix gave him a salute, drew his sword, and wheeled his horse around. The forward four men from the Daughter's Order drew their weapons and fell in to either side of him, preparing to clear the way for the wagon behind them. It was not possible to see how much of the Jokonan column had already debouched onto the curving road ahead, though the number still to come, strung back through the brush on the valley's steep side to their left, seemed to go on and on. Goram whipped up his team. The wagon groaned and began to rumble forward.

The Jokonans nearest them looked over their shoulders to see what was bearing down on them from behind. Shouts, the ring of weapons being drawn, the squeals of horses jerked around and spurred forward.

Arhys grabbed Ista by the upper arm and hustled her back to relative cover in the wagon's center. The wagon bed bumped and rocked, and Ista dropped to her knees before she was pitched onto them. Illvin's parade horse trotted beside the wagon, breaking into its rocking canter as the dray horses picked up speed. Illvin leaned over and shouted, "Arhys! I need a weapon!" His empty hand extended in demand toward his brother, who looked frantically around. Illvin glanced ahead. "Quickly!"

With a curse, Arhys snatched up the only pointed object in view, a pitchfork that had been fastened along the wagon bed's inner wall. He swung it out to Illvin, who glared at his brother in extreme exasperation but grabbed it anyway, sweeping it around prongs forward. "I was *thinking* of a *sword*."

"Sorry," said Arhys, drawing his. "It's taken. *I* need a horse." His head swiveled to Liss, cantering along the opposite side.

"No, Arhys!" Illvin shouted over the rumbling of the wagon, the quickening hoofbeats, and the yells rising ahead. "Stay back! Have some sense!" He pointed to the unconscious Cattilara.

Arhys's head jerked back, and he drew breath through his teeth not for air but for anguish, as he realized just whose body must now bear his battle risks.

"Stay by the royina! Ah. Here comes my sword—!" Illvin clapped his borrowed boots to his white horse's sides; the beast's broad haunches bunched, and it sprang forward with a startling bound. Illvin's linen bed robe flapped open on his bare torso and fluttered in his wake. His tied-back hair streamed out behind him.

Ista clutched the side boards and stared out open-mouthed. Wrong horse, wrong weapon, wrong armor—half naked qualified as *wrong armor*, did it not?—yelling like a madman . . . Illvin wrapped his right arm around the pitchfork and pointed it like a lance at the Jokonan soldier bearing down upon him, sword upraised. At the last moment, at some hidden pressure from Illvin's knee, the heavy white horse swerved, caroming into the Jokonan's mount. The pitchfork tines slid up on either side of the enemy's descending sword wrist. A twist, a yank, a snatch, and Illvin was riding onward with the hilt clutched in his other hand while the Jokonan tumbled from his saddle and was half trampled by the horses of Foix's two rear guards galloping after them. Illvin gave a whoop of triumph and brandished the sword, but, with a thoughtful glance at the humble tool gripped under his other arm, also hung on to the pitchfork.

Although their noisy charge succeeded in driving the Jokonans immediately ahead of them off the road and scattering them to the sides, the enemy cavalrymen formed up rapidly again behind and began to give chase. There seemed nothing aboard to throw at them but four trunks and some hard bread crusts, though Arhys's page groped frantically through the gear for some better missiles. Cattilara's woman clutched her mistress's flaccid body and wailed. Galloping along on the wagon's right, Liss had drawn her new dagger, but it seemed an inequitable match for the mounted men's swords. Arhys lunged over and dragged Ista back to the center, then waited tensely, swaying on one knee, sword unsheathed, ready to dart to whatever side an enemy first tried to climb through.

The white horse shimmered by, heading to the rear; with a sun glitter, a sword spun into the wagon and clanged on the floorboards. Arhys kicked it over to the barefoot manservant, who snatched it up gratefully and took up a guard position on the wagon's end. A few minutes later, the white horse overtook them at a gallop on the other side, and Illvin leaned in to toss yet another sword aboard. His grin flashed past like a streak of light as he brandished the pitchfork and hurtled onward once more.

From the driver's box, Goram cried out. Arhys plunged forward. Ista could see only the back of Arhys's legs as he braced himself and swung at some unseen assailant riding alongside. He moved with power, speed, and utmost sureness. But the white line of soul-fire pouring out of Cattilara and into him seemed to have doubled in speed and density. *Too fast*, thought Ista frantically. *She cannot sustain this rate for long. It will empty her . . .*

The wagon rumbled around a tight curve. Ista slid across the rough boards on hands and knees, collecting splinters in her palms, tumbling into Cattilara on her pallet. The waiting girl's tear-streaked face was mottled red and white with heat and terror. Beyond Liss, one of the men of the Daughter's Order fell back along the roadside, bleeding and toppling from his saddle, his horse limping and slowing. Ista tried to spin around and mark his fate, but she was bounced again as a wheel smacked through a pothole, and by the time she found her balance and looked up again, he was lost to her view. A galloping Jokonan was poking his sword rather clumsily through the space between the wagon's side and the half-rolled-up canvas top, and being parried equally clumsily by Arhys's page, fighting from his knees with Illvin's captured sword.

Louder cries and curses came from ahead, in two languages. A flash of red-violet demon light seared across Ista's inner vision as she crouched, staring downward. A scream of tortured metal sounded from beneath the wagon. The wagon wobbled, then jerked down on the left rear side. The three women slithered across the wagon bed in a heap; even Ista yelped. She heard the snap of the rear axle, then the back end dropped altogether and began dragging. With a cry, the manservant fell out. Arhys slid back in from the driver's box, barely avoiding spearing the weeping waiting woman on the point of his blade.

Arhys stared around wildly. "Liss!" he called.

"Here!" The palomino had held to its position on the wagon's right side and was now slowing with them.

More cries rose from up ahead, along with crashing noises and a scream of a horse. The lurching wagon slewed off the crown of the road and grated to a tilted stop. Arhys dropped his sword and snatched up his wife's limp body, heaving her out and across into startled Liss's arms. "Take her, take her! Ride, if you can. On to Porifors."

"Yes, yes!" Ista endorsed this. Foix's horse flashed into Ista's view, sliding to a rearing halt. Ista pointed downward. "Foix, did your demon do that?"

"No, Royina!" He leaned over his pommel to stare in at her; his eyes were very wide. The bear shadow was not curled tight within him, but on its seeming-feet, its head swinging dizzily from side to side.

"Royina . . . ?" Liss's hoarse voice called uncertainly, as she struggled to get a better grip on her limp load.

"Yes, take Cattilara and ride, or all are lost together! Foix, go with her, get them through!"

"Royina, I can't—"

"Go!" Ista's scream nearly burst her lungs. Both horses wheeled away. Foix's sword, swinging past, shed a spatter of dark wet drops. Cries, scraping metal, the twang of a crossbow, and the *thunk* of a heavy blade biting flesh—whose?— echoed back to Ista's ears. But the dual echo of their horses' hooves dwindled in the distance without slowing or diverting.

Ista climbed forward to grab the rear edge of the driver's seat and peek over. Dropped across the road in front of them was a large palanquin with green cloth hangings and gold trim. One of the foremost dray horses plunged and kicked, its front legs tangled with the palanquin's rear boards and braces. The splintered wood had ripped its skin. The other lead horse was down in its traces, bleeding and making dreadful noises. A dozen bearers in heavily embroidered green uniforms were scattered about, shouting and screaming, the ones who could still walk trying to help their injured comrades. Three of them tried to control the rearing horse and drag a moaning fourth man out from under the wreckage.

They had descended perhaps half the height of the slope to the river bottom, where the road made its last turn for Porifors. If not for this ghastly obstruction, Ista realized, they might well have burst through the front of the column, though whether they could have outdistanced the enemy thereafter was an open question.

Goram sat frozen, his hands in the air; Ista followed his frightened gaze to a Jokonan soldier standing in the road with a cocked crossbow, trained upon the groom. Another and another ran up, until the wagon was surrounded by a dozen tense men, their fingers tight, and sometimes trembling, on the release catches.

A Jokonan soldier sidled up cautiously and pulled Goram down off his box. Goram stumbled onto the road and stood with his arms wrapped tightly around his torso, sniveling uncontrollably. The soldier returned to grab at Ista and manhandle her down. She went unresisting, the better to keep to her feet. Arhys emerged upon the box and stood a moment, sword out but held still. His jaw tightened as his gaze swept over the bowmen. One corner of his mouth turned up in a weird smile, as it apparently crossed his mind just how little those gleaming quarrels might affect him, should he choose to leap in an attack, to the consternation—truncated consternation—of his enemies. But the smile grew sour, and his teeth set, as he followed out the rest of the inevitable consequences. Very slowly, he lowered the tip of his blade.

A crossbowman motioned him to throw down his weapon. Arhys's eyes coolly considered the quarrels aimed at Ista, and he did so. The blade clanged on the gravel. A Jokonan snatched it up, and Arhys stepped deliberately down off the box. For just a moment longer, the Jokonan soldiery forbore—or feared—to seize him.

Two more green-uniformed bearers assisted a small, shaken-looking woman clad in dark green silks out from under the drunkenly angled canopy of the palanquin. Ista's breath drew in.

Her inner vision revealed a soul the like of which Ista had never seen before. It roiled and boiled with violent colors in the confines of the woman's body, but darkened toward the center, till Ista seemed to be looking down a black well at midnight. Black, yet not empty. Faint colored lines radiated out from the bottomless pit in all directions, a tangled web that writhed and pulsed and knotted. Ista had to forcibly blink away the overpowering second sight in order to take in the surface of the woman.

On the outside, the woman was a bizarre mix of delicately decorated and aged and drab. She was only a little taller than Ista herself. Dull, gray-brown curling hair was braided up in an interlaced Roknari court style, bound with strings of glittering jewels in the shapes of tiny flowers. Her face was sallow and lined, without paint or powder. Her dress was many-layered, embroidered with thread of gold and brilliant silks picturing interlocking birds. The body it covered was slight, with slack breasts and sagging belly. Her mouth was pursed and angry. Her pale blue eyes, when they turned at last on Ista, burned. Seared.

A young officer on a nervously capering horse rode near; he pulled it to a halt and swung down beside the woman, abandoning his reins, which were snatched up at once by a soldier hurrying to assist him. The officer stared at Ista as if transfixed. His high rank was signaled more by the gold and jewels decorating his horse's gear than by elaborations on his own clothing, but he bore a gold-trimmed green sash across his chest decorated with a string of flying white pelicans. High cheekbones graced a handsome, sensitive face, and the hair braided tightly to his scalp was bright crinkled gold in the blazing noon. His soul . . . was lost in an intense violet haze that extended to the margins of his body.

They have a sorcerer. The origin of the flash of chaotic power that had popped the wagon's axle pins and burst the rear wheels off seemed revealed to Ista's inner eye, for the color in his body still pulsed and shivered as if in some aching reaction or echo. Yet even as she stared across at him, the demon light seemed to shrink in on itself, retreating.

The page and the waiting woman, clinging to each other, were prodded out of the back of the wagon at sword's point and made to stand near Arhys. The march's eyes flicked to

them, half closed as if in some attempt at reassurance, and
returned to the old woman and the officer. Illvin and the
Daughter's men had all disappeared from sight. Scattered?
Captured? Slain?

Ista grew conscious of her plain riding costume, stripped
of decoration or marks of rank, of her flushed face and sweat
and dirt. Too-familiar calculations raced through her mind.
Might she pass for a waiting lady or a servant? Conceal from
her captors the value of their prize, effect some escape from
their inattention? Or would they just throw her to their
troops for a cheap tidbit, to be tormented and discarded like
that unfortunate maidservant of the rich woman from
Rauma?

The sorcerer-officer's eye took in Goram, and widened
briefly, then narrowed in thought. Or even . . . recognition?
Thought, but not confusion. *He sees Goram's ravaged soul.
Yet it does not surprise him.* His eyes traveled on to Arhys,
and his lips parted in true astonishment.

~Mother, she shines with a terrible light, and her guardian
is a dead man!~ he said in Roknari to the woman at his side.
His stare at Ista intensified, grew fearful, as if he wondered
if *she* were performing Arhys's appalling marvel of revivifi-
cation. As if he imagined she concealed some further body-
guard of walking corpses, about to erupt from the dirt of the
road beneath their feet.

This must be the Dowager Princess Joen herself, Ista realized with a shock. *And Prince Sordso.* The erect, slender
young man looked anything but a sot right now. And yet—
was it Sordso, in that alert body? The demon light seemed
utterly ascendant. He took a step backward; the woman
grabbed his arm, her fingers pinching fiercely.

~She bears a god, we are undone!~ he cried in rising terror.

~She does no such thing~ the woman hissed in his ear.
~Those are nothing but smears. She has barely enough capacity to channel a little sight. Her soul is choked with scars
and disruption. She is afraid of *you.*~

That much was surely true. Ista's mouth was dry, her

head pounding; she seemed to float on a rocking sea of panic.

The woman's blue eyes narrowed, flared with triumph. ~Sordso, look at her! This is Ista herself, just as she was described! Half the prize we came for, delivered into our hands! This is a gift from the gods Themselves!~

~She hurts to look upon!~

~No, she is nothing. You can take her. I'll show you. Take her now!~ The clawed grip shook the young man's arm. ~Undo her.~ One of the coiling strings of light writhing from her dark belly seemed to brighten, blaze. Its distal end, Ista saw, terminated in Sordso's body like some obscene umbilicus.

The young man moistened his lips; the violet light returned to the margins of his body, and intensified. He raised a hand, using the dense habits of matter to direct a force that had nothing to do with matter at all. A purple glare boiled off his palm and wound around Ista like a coiling snake.

Her knees went first, buckling beneath her, dropping her into the dust. Her cracked scabs split open altogether, and she could feel the blood trickle and soak, slick beneath the battered, sweat-stained, loosening bandages. Her spine seemed to unhook itself, bone from bone, and she bent forward helplessly. Hideous knots of spasming pain began beneath each shoulder blade. Almost, her bowels seemed loosened as well, if that was not just by her own horror. She had a glimpse of Arhys's bearded lips parting, of his eyes darkening with dismay, as she sank down before all assembled here for no cause that fleshly eyes could see. Her hands went out to catch herself, then her arms grew limp as well. Her head grew heavier still, and she was barely able to turn it aside so that her soft cheek and not her slackening mouth smeared into the sharp-edged gravel and the dirt.

~You see? So will all Chalion and Ibra bow before us.~ Joen's voice dripped with satisfaction. Ista could see her green silk slippers, peeping from beneath her skirts, and Sordso's polished boots. The boots shifted uneasily. In some dizzied distance, Ista could hear Goram's low, choked, liquid sobbing. Blessedly, the injured horse's screams had stopped; perhaps some merciful man had cut its throat. *Perhaps some merciful man will cut mine.*

~I admit,~ Princess Joen's voice went on above Ista's head, ~I do not understand the dead man . . . ~ The slippered footsteps shuffled through the gravel, approaching Arhys. Ista found herself unable to even moan. She could barely blink; a drop spun from one eyelash to plop into the dust before her nose.

From the slope above echoed sudden shouts. Ista's head was turned the wrong way, looking out over the brim of the road into the valley beyond. Around and behind her, men's booted feet suddenly scuffled. She heard a crossbow twang, and caught her breath in fear for Arhys. Hoofbeats. *Many* hoofbeats, pounding, scrambling, sliding down from the ridge above. A lunatic whoop in a suddenly dearly familiar voice.

Sordso gasped. His boots crunched across the gravel; grunting, he swung those green slippers up out of sight. The boots staggered past Ista's face; nearby hooves scraped. Ista managed to turn her head a little more. The prince's horse, with Joen in her elaborate dress clinging awkwardly to its saddle, was being towed forward at a sudden trot by a running bearer, who shot a look of fear over his shoulder, up-slope.

A thump sounded. The invisible weight like a huge hand pressing Ista to the earth lessened. The rasp of Sordso's sword being drawn from its scabbard sliced across her hearing, and she flinched, and at last jerked her head around the other way. Some crossbowman had been careless enough to take his eyes off Arhys for a moment, and the march was now locked in struggle with him. Several nearby bowmen had fired upward, and were frantically recocking. Arhys yanked a dagger from the sheath of the man he wrestled and flung him aside just in time to parry Sordso's thrust. The thrust of steel, that is. A violet light collected in Sordso's palm. He shoved it forward.

The searing purple line passed through Arhys's body without effect, to bury itself in the soil beyond. Sordso yipped with surprise and scrambled frantically backward as a riposte from the dagger nearly swept his sword from his grip. The scramble became a run.

What seemed a very avalanche of horses overwhelmed them. The Jokonan bowmen were knocked aside, ridden down. Swords clanged and spears thrust, fiercely wielded by yelling men in gray-and-gold tabards. In front of Ista's face, a set of hooves that seemed the size of dinner plates suddenly materialized, and danced. Three long equine legs were silk-white, the fourth soaked scarlet with blood.

"Got you that horse you were wanting," Illvin's voice, would-be laconic but for its gasping, sounded from above. Beyond the dinner plates, another set of hooves crunched and slid. And, more sharply, "Five gods! *Is she hurt?*"

"Ensorcelled, I think," Arhys gasped back. He knelt beside Ista, gathered her up in cool, unliving, welcome hands. Heaved to his feet, and boosted her upward still farther, into his brother's arms. She landed with a limp grunt, stomach down across Illvin's lap.

Illvin cursed, and grabbed a thigh through her skirt to hold her there. He bellowed over his shoulder to someone, not Arhys, "Get Goram!"

"They're re-forming!" shouted Arhys. "Go!" The loud slap of his hand across the white horse's rump was scarcely needed to speed them on their way; the animal was already pirouetting. They plunged downslope, away from the road.

The source of the terrifying gore was revealed, before Ista's bouncing nose, as an ugly cut across Feather's right shoulder, bleeding freely. The ground swept past dizzily. The horse hesitated, its body bunching; Illvin leaned far back in his saddle, his clutch on her leg tightening to a vise. Abruptly, they were sliding straight down the steep hillside in a spray of dirt and stones, the horse's front legs braced; it seemed nearly to squat on its broad haunches behind. Illvin whooped again. Whipping bushes slapped and scratched

Ista's face. The least loss of balance, and they would all three be tumbling heads over tails together, bones shattering and guts smashed . . .

The endless slide terminated not in disaster, but in a wild splash across Porifors's little river. Other horses were galloping up around them now. Illvin released his death grip on her thigh and gave her buttocks a distracted, reassuring pat.

Ista found her control of her body returning, and she spat out a mixture of bloody river water and dirt. What had happened to the sorcerer prince? His attention had been diverted altogether from her, evidently. *For the moment.* Along with control, unfortunately, came sensation. "I think I'm about to vomit," she mumbled into the horse's red-lathered shoulder.

For a blissful instant, they came to a halt. Illvin bent and wrapped his long arms around her, and heaved her upright and over, to sit across his lap. Weakly, she wrapped her arms around that bony sweat-slick torso, itself laboring for breath. His bed robe had been lost somewhere along the route, along with the pitchfork. His mouth was bloodied. His streaked dark hair was a wild tangle across his face. His live body was hot with exertion. But he bore no serious wounds, her testing hands reassured her.

His own shaking hand rose to her face, gently wiping at whatever ungodly mixture of horse blood, sweat, and dirt smeared it. "Dear Is'—Royina, are you hurt?"

"No, that's all from your poor horse," she assured him, guessing it was the blood that alarmed him. "I am a little shaken."

"A little. Ah." His brows arched, and his lips grew less thin, curling up once more.

"I think I am going to have bruises on my stomach from that ride."

"Oh." His hand, across her belly, gave it an awkward little rub. "Indeed, I am sorry."

"Don't apologize. What happened to your mouth?" She reached up with one finger to touch the lacerated edge.

"Spear butt."

"Ouch."

"Better than a spearpoint, trust me." They started forward once more. He glanced over his shoulder. They were on a minor road, hardly more than a track, that ran along the opposite side of the river from the main one. Other gray-tabarded soldiers now rode all around them. "This is a bad time to linger out-of-doors. That Jokonan column we overtook is one of three closing in on the castle just at the moment, the scouts say. No siege engines sighted in their baggage trains yet, though. Can you hang on to me if we canter?"

"Certainly." Ista sat up straighter and brushed hair out of her mouth, she wasn't quite sure whose. She felt his legs tighten beneath her, and the white horse broke without transition into its long, rocking gait.

"Where did you find the troop?" she gasped, clinging harder to his slippery skin against the jouncing.

"You sent them to me, thank you very much. Are you a seeress, as well? I met them coming down the road even as I was galloping back to Porifors to raise them."

Ah. Dy Cabon had carried out his orders, then. A little early, but Ista was not inclined to chide him for it. "Only prudence rewarded. For a change. Did you see Liss and Cattilara, and Foix? We tried to send them on."

"Yes, they passed through us as we were making for the ridge to flank the Jokonan column. They should be safe within the walls by now." He twisted to glance back over his shoulder, but he did not kick his horse to greater speed, by which Ista concluded that they had, for the moment, shaken off their pursuit. The great horse's stride was shortening, its bellows-breath growing more strained; Illvin eased back in the saddle and allowed it to drop to a slow lope.

"What happened up there on the road?" he asked. "What struck you to the ground? Sorcery, truly?"

"Truly. Sordso the Sot is now Sordso the Sorcerer, it seems. How he came by his demon, I know not. But I agree with you—his dead sister's old demon must know. If we must face Sordso in battle . . . does demon magic have a *range*, do you know? Never mind, I'll ask dy Cabon. I wonder if Foix knows by experiment? I wouldn't put it past him."

"Three sorcerers, Foix reported. At least," said Illvin. "Or so he thought he perceived, among the Jokonan officers."

"What?" Ista's eyes widened. She thought of the tangle of strange lines emanating like a nest of snakes from Dowager Princess Joen's belly. One had held its jaws clamped into Sordso, no question. "Then there may be more than three." A dozen? Twenty?

"You saw more sorcerers?"

"I saw something. Something very uncanny."

He twisted again to look over his shoulder.

"What do you see now?" Ista asked.

"Not Arhys, yet. Blast the man. He always has to be the last one out ali—the last one out. I've told him such bravado has no place in a responsible commander. It works on the boys, though, I admit it does. Bastard's hell, it works on *me*, and I *know* better . . . ah." He turned again, a grim smile of temporary relief tweaking up one corner of his bleeding mouth. He let his mount slow to a walk, and frowned; the horse was distinctly limping, now. But Castle Porifors loomed up almost overhead. A few last stragglers were streaming into the town gates from the country round about. The refugees' shouting sounded strained, but not panicked.

Arhys trotted up beside them on a Jokonan horse, presumably obtained by Illvin from the same convenient store as his sword collection. His white-faced page sat up behind, bravely not crying. Ista's inner eye checked the line of pale soul-fire pouring into the march's heart; clearly, Catti still lived, wherever she was. The flow was reduced from its earlier terrifying rush, but still very heavy.

Goram, Ista was glad to see, clung on behind another soldier, and Cattilara's distraught young woman behind a third. Of the barefoot manservant, she saw no sign. Arhys saluted his brother with a casual wave, as casually returned; his eyes upon Ista were grave and worried.

"Time to go in," said Illvin suggestively.

"You'll get no argument from me," returned Arhys.

"Good."

Their tired horses clambered up the switchback road to the castle gate and into the forecourt.

Liss bounded to receive Ista as Illvin lowered her to the ground; Foix followed, to offer her his arm. She leaned on it thankfully, as the alternative was to fall down in a heap.

"Royina, let us take you to your chamber—" he began.

"Where did you take Lady Cattilara?"

"Laid down in her bedchamber, with her women to take care of her."

"Good. Foix, find dy Cabon and attend upon me there. Now."

"I must look to our defenses," said Arhys. "I'll join you as soon as I can. If I can. Illvin . . . ?"

Illvin looked up from instructing a groom in the care of his injured horse.

Arhys's gaze flicked briefly toward the inner court, where his and his wife's chambers lay. "Do what you must."

"Oh, aye." Illvin grimaced, and turned to follow Ista. The wild excitement that had sustained him through the clash on the road was passing off. He limped like his horse, stiff and weary, as they passed under the archway to the fountain court.

21

CATTILARA'S CHAMBER HAD MUCH THE SAME AIR OF FEM-
inine refuge as when Ista had entered it on her first day at
Porifors. Now, however, the marchess's women were upset
rather than welcoming: either anxious and outraged or
frightened and guilty, depending on whether they had been
privy to the escape plan. They stared at the royina's present
bloody, breathless, tight-lipped disarray with horror. Ista
ruthlessly dismissed them all, though with orders for wash
water, drinks, and food for Lord Illvin—and for the rest of
her party, who had all tumbled out onto the road a lifetime
ago this morning with no more breakfast than a swallow of
tea and bread, or less.

Illvin went to Cattilara's basin and wrung out a wet
towel; he glanced at Ista and politely handed it to her first.
The red grime she rubbed off her face was startling. Nor was
all of the blood from the horse, she realized as she dabbed
gingerly at her scratches. Illvin rinsed and wrung out the
cloth again and rubbed down his own bloody face and dirt-
streaked torso, and accepted a cup of drinking water from
Liss, draining it in a gulp. He then trod over to Ista's side to
stare at Cattilara, laid down on her bed still in her traveling

dress. The right sleeve had been removed, and a compress bound about the ambiguous wound in her shoulder.

She was lovely as a sleeping child, unmarred but for a smudge on her cheek. On her, it looked an elegant decoration. But Illvin's finger uneasily traced the new sunken quality around her eyes. "Surely her body is too slight to support Arhys's as well as her own."

And he ought to know. Ista glanced at Illvin's hollow cheeks and ridged ribs. "For weeks or months, no. For hours or days . . . I think it is her turn. And I know who Porifors can least spare right now."

Illvin grimaced, and glanced over his shoulder at the opening door. Foix escorted an anxious dy Cabon within.

"Five gods be thanked, you are saved, Royina!" the divine said in heartfelt tones. "The Lady Cattilara as well!"

"I thank you, too, Learned," said Ista, "for abiding by my instructions."

He regarded the marchess's silent form with alarm. "She was not injured, was she?"

"No, she is not hurt." Ista added reluctantly, "Yet. But I have induced her to lend her own soul's strength to Arhys for a time, in place of Lord Illvin. Now we must somehow compel her demon to speak. I don't know if it was master or servant to Princess Umerue, but I am certain it was witness to—more, a product of—Dowager Princess Joen's demonic machinations. Illvin was right, yesterday: it has to know what she was doing, because it was part of what she was doing. Although it seems to have escaped her . . . leash." Upon reflection, an encouraging realization. "Joen's control is evidently not inviolable."

Dy Cabon gazed at her in blank alarm, and Ista realized belatedly that this must seem gibberish to him. Illvin's high brow wrinkled in nearly equal puzzlement; he said cautiously, "You said Joen seemed more uncanny than Sordso. How so?"

Haltingly, Ista tried to describe her inner vision of the dowager princess, glimpsed so briefly and terrifyingly beside her wrecked palanquin, and of the demon-ridden Prince Sordso. Of how Sordso's demon fire had seemed to unknit her very bones. "Demons have always cringed before me up till now, though I do not know why. I did not know I was so vulnerable to them." She glanced uneasily at Foix.

"This array you describe is very strange," mused dy Cabon, rubbing his chins. "One demon battening on one soul is the rule. There is no room for more. And demons do not usually tolerate each other even in the same general vicinity, let alone in the same body. I do not know what force could harness them all together like that, apart from the god Himself."

Ista bit her lip in thought. "What Joen contained did not look like what Sordso contained. Sordso seemed possessed of a common demon, like Cattilara's or Foix's, except ascendant instead of subordinate—like Catti's when she let it up for questioning, before, and we could barely force it back down again. It was the demon, not her son, who was answering to Joen."

Dy Cabon's face bunched in distaste as he took this in.

Ista glanced at Foix, standing behind him and looking even less pleased. He was as sweat-soaked and grimed from the morning's work as any of them, but he, at least, seemed to have escaped any bloody wound. "Foix."

He jerked. "Royina?"

"Can you help me? I wish to push Cattilara's soul-fire down into her body, and the demon light up into her head, that it may speak and answer and yet not seize her. Without allowing it to break the net by which it sustains Arhys. This not being a convenient moment to drop Porifors's commander down dead. . . . More dead."

"Are you just waiting till Lord Arhys is ready, then, Royina, to release his soul?" asked Foix curiously.

Ista shook her head. "I don't know if that is my task, or even if I could if I tried. I fear to leave him a ghost, irrevocably cut off from the gods. Yet he hangs by a thread now."

"Waiting till *we* are ready, more like," muttered Illvin.

Foix frowned down at Cattilara. "Royina, I stand prepared at your command to do anything I can, but I don't understand what you want of me. I see no fires, no lights. Do you?"

"I did not at first. My sensitivity was but a confused wash of feelings, chills, intuitions, and dreams." Ista stretched her fingers, closed her fist. "Then the god opened my eyes to His realm. Whatever the reality may be, my inner eye now sees it as patterns of light and shadow, color and line. Some lights hang like a net, some flow like a powerful stream."

Foix shook his head in bewilderment.

"Then how did you work the flies, and the stumbling horse?" asked Ista patiently. "Do you not perceive anything, perhaps by some other metaphor? Do you hear, instead? Or touch?"

"I"—he shrugged—"I just wished them. No—*willed* them. I pictured the events clearly in my mind, and commanded the demon, and they just happened. It felt . . . odd, though."

Ista bit her finger, studying him. Then on impulse, stepped in front of him. "Bend your head," she commanded.

Looking surprised, he did so. She grasped his tunic and pulled him down yet farther.

Lord Bastard, let Your gift be shared. Or not. Curse your Eyes. She pressed her lips to Foix's sweaty brow. *Ah. Yes.*

The bear whined in pain. Briefly, a deep violet light seemed to flare in Foix's widening eyes. She released him and stepped back; he staggered upright. A barely perceptible white fire faded on his brow.

"*Oh*." He touched the spot and stared around the room, at all his company, openmouthed. "*This* is what you see? All the time?"

"Yes."

"How is it that you do not fall down when you try to walk?"

"One grows used to it. The inner eye learns, just as the outer ones do, to sort out the unusual and ignore the rest.

There is seeing without observing, and then there is *attending*. I need you to attend with me to Cattilara now."

Dy Cabon's mouth pursed in awe and alarm; his hands rubbed one another uncertainly. "Royina, this is potentially very bad for him . . ."

"So are the several hundred Jokonan soldiers moving in around Castle Porifors, Learned. I leave it to your reason to decide which danger is more pressing just now. Foix, can you see—" She turned back to find him staring down at his own belly in a sort of horrified fascination. "Foix, attend!"

He gulped and looked up. "Um, yes, Royina." He squinted at her. "Can you see yourself?"

"No."

"Just as well, maybe. You have these odd little sputtering flashes flaring off your body—all sharp edges, I can see why the demons cringe . . ."

She took him by the hand and led him firmly to Cattilara's bedside. "Look, now. Can you see the light of the demon, all knotted in her torso? And the white fire that streams from her heart to her husband's?"

Foix's hand hesitantly traced the white line, proof enough of his perceptions.

"Now look beneath that stream to its channel that the demon maintains."

He glanced along the line of white fire, then to the trickle still leading from Lord Illvin, and back to Cattilara. "Royina, isn't it coming out rather *fast*?"

"Yes. So we haven't a lot of time. Come, see what you can do." As before, she made passes with her hands over Cattilara's body; then, for curiosity's sake, dropped her hands to her sides and just willed. It was easier to make the white fire obey using the habits of dense matter, but her material hands were actually not necessary to the task, she found. Cattilara's soul-fire collected at her heart, pouring outward as before. Ista made no attempt to interfere with the rate that Arhys was drawing on it. At least while it continued she knew he was still . . . functional, wherever he was.

"Now, Foix. Try to drive her demon to her head."

Looking very uncertain, Foix moved around the bed and grasped Cattilara's bare feet. The light within him flared; Ista seemed to hear the bear growl menacingly. Within Cattilara, the violet demon light fled upward. Ista's inner eye checked for the continued maintenance of Arhys's life-net, and she tried setting a ligature around Cattilara's neck. It worked for the soul-fire as before, but for the demon?

Evidently, it did, because Cattilara's eyes suddenly opened, glittering with a sharpness alien to the marchess. The very shape of her face seemed to change, as the underlying muscles altered their tension. "Fools!" she gasped out. "We told you to flee, and now it is too late! She is come upon you. We shall all be taken back, weeping in vain!"

Her voice was breathy and disrupted, for the pumping of the body's lungs was not coordinated with the mouth's speech.

"She?" said Ista. "Princess Joen?"

The demon tried to nod, found it could not, and lowered Cattilara's eyelashes in assent instead. Illvin quietly brought a chair to the bed's other side and settled himself in it, leaning forward on one elbow, eyes intent. Liss withdrew uneasily to seat herself on a chest by the far wall.

"I saw Joen standing in the road," said Ista. "From a black pit in her belly seemed to swarm a dozen or more snakes of light. At the end of every snake, is there a sorcerer?"

"Yes," whispered the demon. "That is how she harnessed us all to her will. All, to her will alone. How it hurt!"

"One such band of light ended in Prince Sordso. Are you saying this woman placed a demon in her *own son*?"

Unexpectedly, the demon vented a bitter laugh. The shape it gave Cattilara's face seemed to shift again. ~At last!~ it cried in Roknari. ~He would be the last to go. She always favored her sons. We daughters were useless disappointments. The Golden General could not live again in *us*, to be sure. At best we were bargaining counters, at worst drudges—or fodder . . .~

"That is Umerue's voice," whispered Illvin in grim dismay. "Not as she came to us in Porifors, but as I glimpsed her once before, back in Hamavik."

"From where is Joen collecting these elementals?" asked Ista.

The demon's voice shifted again, back to the Ibran tongue. "Stolen from hell, of course."

"How?" Dy Cabon asked. He hung over Foix's shoulder at the foot of the bed, eyes wide.

The demon managed to indicate a shrug with a lift of Catti's eyebrows. "The old demon did the trick for her. We were filched from hell all mindless and confused, chained to her leashes, fed and trained up . . ."

"Fed how?" asked Illvin, his voice growing apprehensive.

"On souls. It is part of how she manages so many; she farms them out to feed on other souls than her own. At first animals, servants, slaves, prisoners. Then as Joen learned the subtleties of it, on others purpose-taken for their knowledge or gifts. She would place us in their bodies till we had eaten up the things she wanted us to know, then yank us out again. Until we grew fit to become riders upon her best sorcerer-slaves. Fit even to mate with a princess! If she were a sufficiently scorned princess."

"Goram," said Illvin urgently. "Was my groom Goram such a one? Made demon fodder?"

"Him? Oh, yes. He was a Chalionese captain of horse, we think. Never any food of ours, though. She gave us a finch, first, and then the little servant girl. Then that Chalionese scholar, the tutor. She let us eat him all up, as he was only to be executed for following the ways of the Bastard anyway. And then the Jokonan courtesan. She got along better with the tutor than we would have expected, being similarly fascinated by men. Joen despised her for the very expertise she sought to steal, so let her go alive and witless, to find her fate in the streets."

Dy Cabon and Illvin looked equally sick; Foix had hardly

any expression at all. Dy Cabon said, "You mean Princess Joen somehow pulls demons from their mounts while the mounts still live? Separates them from the victim souls as the saint of Rauma did?"

The demon's lips curved up in an unpleasant smile. "Exactly the reverse. For Joen, the purpose was binding, not separation. When we'd fed enough, she pulled us out, tearing the souls apart. Taking what she desired for us, leaving the rest as waste. A process equally painful to both parties, we can assure you, though it helped keep us off-balance and servile, we suppose."

Ista was uncertain why the demon had suddenly grown so forthcoming, but she determined to press on while its mood lasted. "The *old* demon," she repeated. "What is this?"

"Ah. Joen's legacy," said the demon. It spoke now, Ista thought, in the scholar's voice, precise and dry, its Ibran of a pure native accent from somewhere in central Chalion, not at all like Cattilara's softer northern speech. Nor did the young marchess speak in quite such rounded periods. "Shall we tell you all the tale of it? The enemies of our enemy are no friends to us. And yet, why not? We know what awaits us, why shouldn't you? Fools." This last was delivered in an oddly dispassionate tone.

It waited for the body to supply it with breath again, and continued, "In the days of the Golden General's glory, men swarmed in from the Archipelago, seeking advancement in his court and spoils on his battlefields. Among them was an old, old sorcerer, who had long plied his demon magic in the islands among the Quadrenes, passing among them subtly and uncaught. His demon was older still, dozens of lives old. The chaos and disorder of the promised war attracted them like perfume. It was a vast mistake, for the Lion of Roknar was beloved of the Father Himself, and possessed many god-gifts, among them the inner sight.

"The old sorcerer was perceived, accused, convicted, and burned. In its immense accumulated craft, the ancient demon jumped from its dying mount and evaded the Quadrene divines' precautions. Yet it could not jump so far as to reach safety, so it chose for its new mount a person whom the Golden General would not burn—his three-year-old daughter, Joen."

"Princess Joen has been a sorceress all these years?" cried dy Cabon in astonishment.

"Not quite." The demon smiled briefly, bitterly, with Cattilara's lips. "The Golden General was wild with rage and grief. He turned to his god in prayer, and yet another gift was granted to him. The Father gave it to him to encapsulate the demon, to put it to sleep within the little girl. It was the Lion's intention, then, when Chalion was conquered, to secretly seize and bring back a saint of the Bastard, if any such could be found, to excise the demon safely from his daughter according to the forbidden Quintarian rites. And then he rode off to his war.

"But by Roya Fonsa's great work of sacrifice, the Lion of Roknar died before he could accomplish his aims, or return. The disunited princedoms settled into another generation of border war with the Quintarian royacies. And the sealed demon waited for its mount's death, that it might be released again into the world of men. For fifty years, it waited.

"Then, some three years past, something *happened*. The capsule broke open, releasing the demon into Joen. But not into the malleable child the demon had chosen. Into the harsh, determined, embittered, and embattled woman."

"How?" asked dy Cabon.

"Yes," said Illvin. "Why hold fifty years, then fail? Unless it was set so . . ."

"I know how," said Ista, her mind burning with cold satisfaction. "I believe I could name the very day and hour. I will tell you in a moment. But hush, let it go on. Then what?"

The demon's eyes narrowed at her in something like respect. "Joen was in a desperate quandary, then. She was co-regent for Prince Sordso with her two closest enemies, the general of Jokona and her late husband's brother. Sordso was a surly young sot who hated them all. The general and his uncle were conspiring to seize Sordso and put his uncle on the throne of Jokona in his place."

"Ah," said Illvin in a disconsolate tone. "*That* was when I'd wanted to strike at Jokona. What excellent timing it might have been, just as their palace coup began . . . oh, well."

"Joen was frantic," said the demon. "She believed—or convinced herself—that the old demon was a legacy from her great father, given to her in secret to rise up in just such an unhappy hour and save his grandson from traitors. So she kept it in secret and began learning from it. The old demon was pleased to have such an apt pupil, and taught her everything, thinking it would soon turn the tables and mount her. It underestimated the iron strength of her will, tempered through four decades of swallowed rage. It became even more her slave."

"Yes," whispered Ista. "I follow that."

"Joen's co-regents were her first enemies to earn her attention. Easy because so intimate, we suppose. The uncle, well, he died quietly. The general underwent a subtler fate, and soon became Joen's fondest supporter in all things."

"Joen is a Quadrene, if fallen into blasphemy by their lights," said dy Cabon, his face knotting with consternation. "But a bad Quadrene is not the same thing as a good Quintarian. She can't possess the correct theological background to handle *any* elemental safely, let alone a troop of them."

"Indeed," breathed Ista, "not."

The demon-Catti continued, "Her leashed demons soon became more to her than salvation for Sordso; they became her joy. At last, at last, she could exert her will and force a compliance that smiled as it hurried to obey. Her family was not last, but first to fall to her binding. Except for Sordso."

The demon's voice and language changed again. ~She took *me* when I refused to be wed to a Quintarian bastard lord, and her eyes shone with triumph as she did so. All, all to do exactly as she said, always, down to the smallest detail. Except for Sordso, her golden cub. Oh, it cheers my heart even in this living death to know that she finally took my brother Sordso.~ Catti's—Umerue's—lips drew back in a fierce grin. ~I warned him not to defy her. Did he listen? Of course not. Hah!~

"Cattilara said you were sent to suborn Porifors," said Ista to the demon. "Hence, I suppose, the inclusion of the courtesan . . ."

Illvin's expression, across the bed from her, was a study in surmise, a complicated amalgam of memory, regret, and horror. Ista wondered if these half-digested souls would all run together into one mind, in time—or would they always be a little separate?

"Was it Illvin or Arhys whom your mother instructed you to bind to yourself?" Ista asked. "Or both?"

The Umerue-lips' smile softened. ~Lord Illvin. He seemed pretty enough at first. But then we saw Arhys . . . Why settle for second-best, for second-in-command, and all that complicated plot of usurpation and revolt to follow, when we might so simply and pleasantly take Porifors from the top down?~ It added in Ibran, "Lord Arhys, yes," and "Arhys. Yes. Mm." And, sighing in no identifiable tongue, "*Ah.*"

"It seems it was unanimous," murmured Illvin dryly. "The servant girl, the princess, the courtesan, and I doubt not the scholar, too. All up in smoke at the first sight of him. I wonder if that bird was female as well? If so, it would probably have flown to his finger. And so Joen's plot was put in disarray by an altogether older sorcery than demon magic." His brow wrinkled half in amusement, half in pain. "Fortunately for me." All pain, now. For a moment, his deep underlying exhaustion floated very near his surface, as if the pull of the whole world bowed his back. Then his dark eyes glittered, and he straightened. "So how was this master demon released from its long prison? You said you knew, Royina."

"I guess, at least. It was the timing—do you not see it?

Three years ago on the Daughter's Day, the Golden General's death curse was pulled from Chalion, and from my House: all his spilled, perverted god-gifts swept up and taken back by the gods through their chosen saint. And if all was retrieved that day—it must have included the power of the encapsulation."

Illvin met dy Cabon's eyes; the divine gave a reflective nod.

Ista mused, "I wonder, if Arvol and Ias and I had succeeded in breaking the curse twenty years ago, would Joen have been granted her demon two decades sooner? And which of them would have been ascendant then?"

Dy Cabon stared down at Cattilara with an expression of arrested theological curiosity. "*I* wonder if the actions of this same Roknari master sorcerer would account for the outbreak of elementals that Chalion suffered in Fonsa's day . . . ?" He shook off the distractions of historical theory, as it perhaps occurred to him that the outbreak they faced now was suddenly all too present and practical.

Why is the creature telling us all this? Ista wondered. To create fear and disorder among her little company? To spread its own distress? She glanced around at Foix's stolidity, dy Cabon's thoughtfulness, Illvin's shrewd concentration. If that was the plan, it wasn't working. Maybe it had simply stolen enough humanity by now to enjoy complaining to an attentive audience. Maybe, with all hope of flight lost, at some last gasp and despite its preferred solitary nature, it sought allies.

The door opened; startled, Ista snapped around. Lord Arhys entered and gave her a respectful nod. She was glad to see he was mail-clad again. He, at least, would not be overheated by his armor. He was followed by maids with trays, a welcome sight, and Goram, considerably recovered, with a pile of Illvin's clothing and war gear.

Ista's party seized on the contents of the trays without ceremony. Arhys strode to the bedside and stared down at his wife, his face bleak. The demon looked back, but said nothing. Ista hoped that wasn't Cattilara's longing leaking into its eyes. Then she wondered if her own eyes had looked like that, resting on him.

"Is she awake?" Arhys flexed his hand in puzzlement. "How then do I . . . ?"

"Cattilara sleeps," Ista told him. "We gave her demon access to her mouth, that it might speak. Which it has."

"What's arrived out there, Arhys?" demanded Illvin. He alternated downing bites of meat wrapped in bread and swallowing gulps of cold tea with being dressed by his groom.

"About fifteen hundred Jokonan soldiers, my scouts estimate. Five hundred in each column. My two scouts who made it back, that is. Since the ring of besiegers is now closed around Porifors, I despair of the other dozen. I have never lost so many scouts before."

"Siege engines?" Illvin asked around a mouthful of bread, thrusting a leg into a boot of his own held by the kneeling Goram. The lost manservant's boots were tossed aside. Dead man's shoes? No telling now.

"None reported. Supply wagons, yes, but no more."

"Huh."

Arhys glanced at Ista. She did not know what expression was on her face, but he attempted reassurance. "Porifors has withstood sieges before, Royina. The town walls are secured as well—I have two hundred men of my own down there, and half the townsmen are former garrison soldiers. There are tunnels between us to shift reinforcements. What was it, Illvin, fifteen years ago that the Fox of Ibra sent up an assault of three thousands? We held them for half a month, till dy Caribastos and dy Tolnoxo—the present provincar's father—relieved us."

"I don't think it's siege engines that Jokona sends against us now," said Illvin. "I think it's sorcerers." He supplied his brother with a blunt synopsis of the demon's testimony. As he spoke, Goram, pale but resolute, expertly combed back his hair and bound it in a tight knot at his nape, then shook out his mail coat ready to don.

"If this madwoman Joen truly drags a dozen or more sorcerers on leashes," Illvin concluded, ducking into his mail, "you may be sure she means to let them slip against us. If not for revenge for her lost daughter, then for a blow against Chalion to turn the whole line of attack that Marshal dy Palliar plans against Borasnen. An early strike, and hard; and if successful, to be followed by a sweep into north-central Chalion before Iselle and Bergon's forces are properly mustered . . . that's the way *I'd* do it, if I were the Jokonans. I mean, if I were only mad, and not *stupid*."

Arhys grinned briefly. "I can scarcely guess what Sordso's staff officers are like at present."

"Cooperative," said Ista blackly. "Of one mind."

Illvin grimaced, and at Goram's silent tap held out a forearm for the groom to buckle on his vambrace.

"Arhys," Ista continued urgently. "Despite your strange state, you have no inner sight, correct?"

"Nothing like what you describe, no, Royina. If anything, my sight seems less than before. Not blurred or dimmed, but drained of color. Except that now I see better at night; almost the same as in the day."

"So you did not see, did not perceive, the strike that Prince Sordso made upon you, when you clashed on the road?"

"No . . . what did *you* see?"

"That deep light that marks demon magic to my inner eye. A searing bolt of something. Or anyway, it was clear that Sordso thought it was going to be a searing bolt of something. But it passed through you harmlessly, as though you weren't even there."

They both looked to dy Cabon, who opened his plump hands in uncertainty. "In a sense, he isn't there. Not as live souls are, nor even as demons are. The true sundered ghosts are divorced from all realities, the world of matter and the world of spirit both."

"Is he, then, immune to sorcery?" began Ista. "And yet it is sorcery that sustains him now . . . Learned, I do not understand."

"I will give it thought—"

A tangled mess of violet lines of light abruptly appeared throughout the room, flared, and vanished. Foix jumped. A moment later, so did everyone else, as vessels of tea or wine or wash water tipped or cracked or shattered. Illvin's clay cup cleaved in his hand as he was lifting it to his lips, and he danced backward to avoid the splash down his gray-and-gold tabard.

"Joen's sorcerers are now in place, it seems," said Ista flatly.

Foix swung around in wide-eyed dismay; within him, his bear shadow was on its feet, snarling. "What was the purpose of *that*? A warning? If they can do *that*, why not burst our bellies or our skulls and have it over with?"

Dy Cabon raised a shaking hand. "Free demons cannot slay *directly*—"

"The Bastard's own death demon does," said Ista. "I have seen it do so."

"That is a very special case. *Free* demons, those escaped into the realm of matter . . . well, they *might* try to slay directly, but—death opens a soul to the gods. Whether the soul chooses to advance through that door at that moment or not is a matter of will, but in that instant it opens both ways. And the demon is vulnerable to recapture."

"And so they jump away when their *mount* is slain . . ." said Foix.

"Yes, but using magic to slay also creates a link between sorcerer and victim. The effort and the backwash are supposed to be very hard on the sorcerer, as well." He paused thoughtfully. "Of course, if a sorcerer uses magic to stampede your horse over a cliff, or any other indirect method of accomplishing your death, the risk does not apply."

A panting soldier in a gray-and-gold tabard burst through the door. "Lord Arhys! There is a Jokonan herald at the gate, demanding parley."

Arhys drew in his breath between his teeth. "Warning indeed. Notice. Well, they have all my attention now. Illvin,

Foix, Learned dy Cabon—Royina—will you attend upon me? I want your sight and your counsel. But stay back below the battlement, out of view, as much as you may."

"Yes." Ista paused to release her ligature from Cattilara's neck and be certain the demon would remain quiescent. Foix watched silently, taking up station at Ista's shoulder as if to guard her. Liss had not been named in Arhys's roll, but she rose anyway, arms crossed and shoulders tucked as if trying to make herself small and unnoticed.

Illvin, striding for the door in Arhys's wake, suddenly stopped and swore. "The cisterns!"

Arhys's head swiveled; the two looked at each other. Illvin clapped his brother on the shoulder. "I'll check, and meet you above the gate."

"Hurry, Illvin." Arhys motioned all within to follow him out; Illvin turned aside on the gallery and ran.

22

THEY CROSSED THE COURT OF THE FLOWERS AND CLIMBED
the inner stairs after Arhys. Above the gate a projecting parapet thrust out. Arhys shouldered past his archers spread out
along the sentry-walk, mounted to the top of the battlement,
and stood spread-legged, staring down. Ista peeked out between the toothed stones.

To the right, where the road turned away toward Oby, she
could see the Jokonans settling into camp in a grove of walnut trees, just out of bowshot or catapult range. Tents were
being set up, and horse lines arranged. On the far side of the
grove, some especially large tents of green cloth were rising
at the hands of servants, some wearing the uniforms of the
palanquin bearers. To the left, down in the valley along the
river, another column was pouring in, threatening the town
walls. At its rear, some soldiers were already driving a few
plundered sheep and cattle into the arms of their camp followers, dinner on the hoof.

Beyond, the countryside looked deceptively peaceful—
emptied out, Ista hoped; only one or two barns or distant
outbuildings seemed to be on fire, presumably sites of some
temporary, desperate resistance. The enemy had not—or not

yet—fired the fields and crops. Did they anticipate being in secure possession of them by harvesttime? The third column presumably was taking up position behind the castle, along the ridge.

The drawbridge was up, the castle gates closed. On the other side of the deep dry cleft that fronted the wall, the Jokonan parley officer stood, bareheaded. The blue pennant of his office hung limply from the javelin in his hand in the afternoon heat. He was flanked by two tense guards, sea-green tabards over their mail.

As the parley officer turned his face upward, Ista's breath drew in. He was the same translator she had met in the raiding column retreating from Rauma. So, was his new duty a reward or a punishment? He did not notice her, half concealed in the embrasure; but it was quite clear by the alarmed widening of his eyes that he recognized Arhys as the sword-wielding madman who had nearly taken his head off in that ravine. Arhys's stony expression gave no clue if the recognition was returned.

The Jokonan moistened his lips, cleared his throat. "I come under the flag of parley from Prince Sordso to Castle Porifors," he began, in loud, clear Ibran. He gripped the shaft of his blue pennant as a man might clutch a shield, and ground the butt a little harder into the dry soil by his boot. It was considered very bad form to shoot a messenger, likely to be coldly criticized by an officer's peers and commanders, later. Rather too belated a consolation from the messenger's point of view, to be sure. "These are the demands of the prince of Jokona—"

"Doesn't it worry you, Quadrene," Arhys overrode him in a carrying drawl, "that your prince has become a demon-ridden sorcerer? As a pious man, shouldn't you be burning him rather than obeying him?"

The guards did not react, and Ista wondered if they had been chosen for their lack of Ibran. By the grimace that flashed over the parley officer's face, he might have felt that his enemy had a point, but he returned sharply, "They say *you* are a man dead three months. Does it not worry your troops to be following a walking corpse?"

"Not notably," said Arhys. He ignored the slight murmur of his archers, clustered behind him. The looks they exchanged covered a range of expressions, from disbelief to alarm to revelation, plus one fellow who vented an impressed *Ooh*. "I can see how it might pose a problem for *you*. How, after all, can you kill me? Even a sorcerer must find it a troublesome paradox."

With a visible effort, the parley officer wrenched himself back to his script. "These are the terms of the prince of Jokona. You will surrender the Dowager Royina Ista at once, as hostage for your cooperation. All officers and soldiers of the garrison will lay down their arms and march out your gate in surrender. Do this, and your lives will be spared."

"To be corralled as demon fodder, perchance?" muttered dy Cabon, crouched looking through an embrasure farther down the walkway. A rather more merciful fate, Ista couldn't help reflecting, than what a divine of the Bastard caught in such a conflict might normally expect from overexcited Quadrene troops.

"Come, come, Jokonan, would you trouble me to spit upon you?" asked Arhys.

"Pray save your spit, Lord Arhys. I hear such liquids will be hard to come by in there soon."

Lord Illvin had climbed up behind the parapet in time to hear this exchange, and smiled sourly. He cast a quick look out over Ista's head, taking in the enemy's arrangements in a sweeping pass. Arhys glanced down at him; Illvin leaned his shoulders against the wall below his brother's feet and gazed back out over the forecourt. In a voice pitched not to carry to the Jokonans, he reported, "They got both cisterns. Leaking like sieves. I have men bailing with every intact vessel they can find, and trying to line the tanks with canvas to slow the outflow. But it's not good."

"Right," Arhys murmured back. He raised his voice again to the parley officer. "We refuse, of course."

The parley officer looked up with grim satisfaction at what was obviously the expected answer. "Prince Sordso and Dowager Princess Joen are merciful beyond your deserving. They will give you one day to reconsider your stance. I will come again tomorrow to hear your new answer. Unless you send to us first—of course." With a bow, he began to back away, inadequately covered by his two guardsmen. He retreated quite a distance before he dared to turn his back.

Not just the expected answer: the desired outcome, apparently.

"What happens next?" asked dy Cabon in worry. "An assault? Will they really wait a day?"

"I wouldn't trust them to," said Arhys, jumping down onto the walk again.

"An assault, yes," said Ista. "But not, I think, by their troops. I would wager anything you please that Joen wishes to play with her new toys. Porifors is her very first chance to test her array of sorcerers in open war. If the results satisfy her . . ." A purple line, though only one this time, flashed across Ista's inner vision.

Most of the stretched bowstrings along the sentry walk snapped at once, twanging. A couple of men yelped from the sting of the recoiling cords. An exception was a cocked crossbow that let loose. Its quarrel shot into the thigh of the man standing next to its bearer; the man screamed and fell backward off the walk to smack onto the stones of the court and lie still. His horrified comrade gaped at his bow, flung it from himself as though it burned his hand, and hurried after his fallen mate.

Another, darker flash crackled past.

"Now what?" muttered Foix uneasily, staring up and down the line of appalled archers. Some, already fishing in their belts for replacement strings, found them shredding in their hands.

A few moments later, across the rooftops of the castle's inner courts, a plume of smoke billowed into the air.

"Fire in the stable," said Illvin, his laconic voice at odds with his sudden lunge forward. "Foix, I want you, please." He sped away down the stairs, long legs taking them three at a time.

Now it begins in earnest, thought Ista, her stomach clenching.

Liss's eyes were huge. "Royina, may I go with them?" she gasped.

"Yes, go," Ista released her. She bolted away. Every competent hand would be needed . . . *And then there is me.* She took herself down off the wall, at least.

Arhys, running past her, called, "Lady, will you look to Cattilara?"

"Of course." A task of sorts. Or maybe Arhys, a prudent commander, merely wanted to get all the useless deadwood stored in one safe place.

Ista found Cattilara's ladies in hysterics; when she had finished with them, their noise was at least muted to well-suppressed hysterics. Cattilara lay unchanged, except for an already visible shrinking of the soft flesh of her face, tightening across her bones. The demon light was knotted tensely within her, making no attempt—yet—to fight for ascendance. Ista blew out her breath in unease, but made sure that the soul-fire continued to pour out toward Arhys without impediment.

❧

Through the endless afternoon, Ista made frequent forays from the marchess's chambers to check the effect of the various ripples of sorcery light that scraped through her perceptions. Only that first great assault on the water supply seemed fully coordinated. After that the attack broke into a disorder mirrored by its effects. People fell and broke bones. The horses saved from the burning stable block, let loose in the star court, knocked down a gallery in their squealing and plunging. A wasp nest fell with it, and three men died screaming, choking, and convulsing from the stings; more men were knocked about and injured by the sting-maddened horses.

Other, smaller fires started in other courts. The little remaining water dwindled rapidly. Most of the stored meat, no matter how preserved, was found to be starting to rot and stink; bread and fruit grew green mold that seemed to spread even as one watched. Weevil larvae burgeoned in the flour supply. Leather straps and fiber ropes rotted and came apart in people's hands. Pottery cracked. Boards broke. Mail and swords began to rust with the speed of a maiden's blush.

Any men with histories of tertiary fever began violent relapses; Cattilara's pleasant dining hall was soon filled with men on pallets, moaning, burning, shivering, and hallucinating. Dy Cabon was pressed into service to help tend the sick and, unbelievably soon, the dying. By evening, the faces of the soldiers and servants that Ista passed had gone beyond edgy and frightened to a pale, deadened, bewildered shock.

At sunset, Ista climbed the north tower, the highest, to take stock. Liss, stinking with smoke and limping from being stepped on by frantic hooves, mounted slowly after her. A man in a gray-and-gold tabard clumped up behind to drop an armload of stones onto a growing pile by the battlement, exchange uneasy grunts with two comrades whose unstrung warped bows were flung aside into a corner, then turn and clump back down the winding stairs.

In the level light of the westering sun, the unpeopled countryside appeared weirdly beautiful and serene. In the grove of walnut trees, the Jokonans' well-ordered camp seemed to be enjoying a feast; the only smokes were thin aromatic trails rising from cooking fires. Little clusters of horsemen rode about, patrolling, delivering messages—out for an evening jaunt, for all Ista could tell. All abroad wore sea-green tabards.

The town, behind its walls in the valley, also sent up plumes of smoke, but ugly and black. With better access to water than the castle crowning the hill, the townsmen had

kept most of their blazes from spreading out of control, so
far. But the few tiny figures Ista could see moving fearfully
through its streets and alleys were stiff with fatigue. The
men behind its walls crouched, or sat barely moving, or lay
as if in exhausted naps. Or dead.

Leaden bootsteps scuffed on the stone stairs, and Ista
looked around to see Lord Illvin emerge onto the tower platform carrying a small, greasy cloth sack. Even the flushed
light of sunset failed to make his face look anything but
filthy and pale. Soot and sweat had melted together, to be
rubbed in odd streaks by whatever swipe of his hand had
dashed the grime from his eyes. He had abandoned chain
mail and scorched tabard hours ago, and his plain linen shirt,
dotted with small black spark holes, was half stuck to his
torso.

"Ah," he said in a voice that sounded as though it came
from the bottom of a mine shaft. "There you are."

She nodded greetings; he came to her shoulder, and together they stared down into the disaster of Porifors, behind
its deceptively blank and solid outer walls.

The whole stable block was burned-out. Blackened tim-
bers were strewn across it, and messes of broken roof tiles
spilled over them like blood. Temporarily, no other smoke
was rising, but one corner of the kitchen block was also
blackened and fallen in. The star court was a mess—one
gallery knocked down, the fountain empty and choked with
filth. Horses were tethered along one side; their backs
looked odd and lozenge-shaped from this high angle of
view. What people who could be seen scuttled about bent
and anxious.

"Have you seen Learned dy Cabon lately?" Ista asked Illvin.

He nodded. "Still holding up in the sickrooms. We have
pallets strewn through three chambers now. Half a dozen fellows just came down with dysentery. With no wash water
left, it won't even take demons to spread *that* all over the
fortress. Bastard's hell. At this rate, Sordso will be able to

take Porifors by assault tomorrow with six ponies, a rope ladder, and a Quadrene temple children's choir." His teeth gritted, white against his blackened face. "Oh." He held out the sack. "Would you like some baked horsemeat? It's not rotted. Yet."

Ista eyed it dubiously. "I don't know. Is it Feather?"

"No. Happily."

"Not . . . right now, thank you."

"You should keep up your strength. Five gods know when we'll eat again." He dug out a chunk and dutifully munched it. "Liss?" He held out the bag to her.

"No, thank you," she echoed Ista thinly.

Failing to take his own advice, he passed the bag on to the former archers, now stone-throwers, who accepted it with murmured thanks and somewhat less revulsion. A crack sounded, as another timber in the stable block gave way and fell in a cloud of soot. Illvin returned to the inner side of the tower to stare down into the debacle again.

"That was one day. Less. Bastard's tears, what will we be reduced to in one week?"

Ista leaned on the sun-warmed stone with arms that shook, past prayer. "I have brought this down upon you all," she said in a low voice. "I am sorry."

His brows flicked up; he rested on one elbow beside her, looking across at her. "I'm not so sure you can claim that honor, lady. The situation here was well along this road before you ever arrived in our midst. If your presence had not baited the Jokonans into attack now, you may be sure they would have struck within another month or so—against a fortress with both of its most experienced commanders dead and rotted, or worse, and none even to explain the horrors pouring down out of nowhere upon it."

Ista rubbed her aching brow. "So we're actually not sure if I make any difference, except this way I hand myself as hostage and pawn to Joen." Perhaps. She stared down at the patterned paving stones, far below her. *There are other ways to avoid becoming a hostage.*

He followed her gaze, and his eyes narrowed in a penetrating frown. He reached out with two fingers and gently turned her chin toward him. "You made a difference to *me*," he said. "Any woman who can wake a man from a sleep of death with a kiss deserves a second glance, I think."

Ista snorted bitterly. "I didn't wake you with a kiss. I only disrupted and redirected the flow of your soul-fire, as I did later with Cattilara. The kiss was just . . . self-indulgence."

A little smile curved his lips. "I thought you said it was a dream."

"Uh . . ." *Oh.* So she had. His lips curved up farther, maddeningly. She said, "A stupid impulse, then."

"Come, I thought it was a brilliant impulse. You underestimate yourself, lady."

Ista flushed. "I am afraid I have no talent for"—she swallowed—"dalliance. When I was young I was too stupid. Now I'm old, I am too drab." *Too stupid then too mad then too drab then too late.* "I'm just not the sort."

"Really?" He turned around, leaned against the battlement, and took up her hand with an air of great curiosity. One sooty finger began to trace the dirt-streaked lines within her palm. "I wonder why not? They say I am a man of wit. I should be able to figure it out, with a little study. Map the ground plan of Castle Ista, mark the defenses . . ."

"Find the weaknesses?" Firmly, she took her hand back.

"All right, a deal of study."

"Lord Illvin, this is not the time or place for this!"

"Truly. I'm so tired I could hardly stand up. Nor climb to my feet, either."

There was a short silence.

His lips peeled back on a flash of teeth. "Ha. I saw your mouth twitch, then."

"It did not." It did now, helplessly, as she was reminded of the bird in its nest.

"Oh, better—she smirks!"

"I do *not*."

"Poets speak of hope in ladies' smiles, but give me a

smirk any day, *I* say." Somehow, his thumb was massaging her palm again, tracing the subtle muscles of her hand. It felt wonderful. She wished he would rub her shoulders, her feet, her neck, her everything-that-hurt. And everything hurt.

"I thought you said Arhys was the great seducer in the family." She tried to muster the energy to take her hand back again, and failed.

"Not at all. He's never seduced a woman in his life. They leapt on him from ambush all by themselves. Not without cause, I grant you." He smiled, briefly. "There is this, about being the sparring partner of the best swordsman in Caribastos. I always lost. But if ever I meet the *third* best swordsman in Caribastos, he's going to be in very deep trouble. Arhys was always better at all things we turned our hands to. But there is one thing that I am quite certain I can do that he cannot."

It was the fault of the hand massage; it lulled her. She said unthinkingly, "What?"

"Fall in love with you. Sweet Ista."

She jerked back. She had heard that endearment before, but not on *those* lips. "Don't call me that."

"Bitter Ista?" His brows climbed. "Cranky Ista? Cross, ill-tempered, cantankerous Ista?"

She snorted; he relaxed, and his lips quirked again. "Well, I can no doubt learn to adjust my vocabulary."

"Lord Illvin, be serious."

"Certainly," he said at once. "As you command, Royina." He bowed slightly. "I am old enough to have many regrets. I've made my share of mistakes, some"—he grimaced—"hideous indeed, as you well know. But it was the little, easy things—the kisses I did not give, and the love I did not speak, because there was no time, no place—and then, no chance . . . Surprisingly sharp sorrows those are, for their size. I think all our chances grow narrow, tonight. So I shall reduce my regrets—however brief—by one, at least . . ."

He leaned closer. Fascinated, she did not retreat. Somehow, that long arm had found its way around her aching shoulders. He folded her in. He was quite tall, she reflected; if she didn't bend her head back, she was going to end up with her nose squashed to his breastbone. She looked up.

His lips tasted of soot, and salt sweat, and the longest day of her life. Well, and horsemeat, but at least it was fresh horsemeat. His dark eyes glittered between narrowed lids as her arms found their way around that ridged torso and pressed him inward. What was it she had snarled to dy Cabon—*mimicking above what is desired below . . . ?*

Some minutes later—too many? too few?—he lifted his head again and set her a little from him, as though to look upon her without having to cross his eyes. His slight smile was altogether drained of irony now, though not of satisfaction. She blinked and stepped back.

Liss, sitting cross-legged against the parapet on the opposite side of the platform, was staring up with her mouth open. The two soldiers weren't even pretending to be watching Jokonans. Their riveted expressions were of men contemplating a daunting feat they had no desire to emulate, such as swallowing fire, or being the first to charge up a scaling ladder.

"Time," Illvin murmured, "is where you take it. It will not linger for you."

"That is so," whispered Ista.

She had to give his dalliance this much credit; the stones seemed suddenly a much less attractive solution to her plight. That had been his intent, she had no doubt.

A dark violet splash of light sparked past her inner vision, and Ista's head turned to follow it. From somewhere below, an outraged cry rang out. She sighed, too wearied to pursue the mystery. "I don't even want to look."

Illvin's head, too, had turned at the cry. By his lack of further craning, he also shared her surfeit of horrors. But then he looked back at her, his eyes narrowing. "You looked around before we heard anything," he noted.

"Yes. I see the sorcerous attacks as flashes of light in my inner vision. Like little bolts of lightning, flying from source to target, or like streaking fire-arrows. I can't tell what their effect will be just by seeing them, though; they all look much the same."

"Can you tell sorcerers from ordinary men just by looking? I can't."

"Oh, yes. Both Cattilara's demon and Foix's appear to me as shapes of shadow and light within the boundaries of their own souls, which, since they are both living persons, are bounded by their bodies. Foix's demon still retains the shape of a bear. Arhys's ragged soul trails him, as though it struggles to keep up."

"How far *away* can you tell if a person is a sorcerer?"

She shrugged. "As far as my eye can see, I suppose. No, farther than that: for my inner eye sees spirit shapes right through matter, if I pay attention, and concentrate, and perhaps close my outer eyes to reduce the confusion. Tents, walls, bodies, all are transparent to the gods, and to god-sight."

"What about a sorcerer's sight?"

"I am not sure. Foix seemed not to have much, before I shared mine, but his elemental is an inexperienced one."

"Huh." He stood a moment, looking increasingly abstracted. "Come over here." He took her hand and towed her to the western side of the tower, overlooking the walnut grove. "Do you suppose that you could give an exact tally of Joen's sorcerers, if you tried? In her camp, from here?"

Ista blinked. "I don't know. I could try."

The trees' feet were now wading in gray shadow, though their very tops still glowed golden green in the last of the light. Campfires twinkled through the leaves, and a suggestion of the pale squares of many tents. Men's voices carried enough to be heard up on the battlements, although not well enough to make out what they said in the Roknari tongue. On the far side of the grove, the cluster of big green tents, gaudy with pennants, began to glow like verdant lanterns from the lamps being set within them.

Ista took a long breath to try to compose her mind. She extended her perceptions, closing her eyes. If she could sense Joen or Sordso from here, could they sense her? And if Joen could sense her . . . she took another breath, banished the frightening thought, and determinedly uncurled her soul once more.

Upwards of five hundred faint soul-lights moved like fireflies among the trees, the Jokonan soldiers and camp followers busy about their ordinary tasks. A smattering of souls glowed with a stronger, much more violent and disrupted light. Yes, there were the threads, the snakes, wavering through the air from those scattered whorls to converge all in one dark, disturbing spot. Even as she watched, one line crossed another as their possessors moved in space, passing like two strands of insubstantial yarn that did not knot or tangle.

"Yes, I can see them," she told Illvin. "Some are snubbed up near to Joen, some are all spread out across the camp." Her lips moved as she made her count. "Six hug the command tents, twelve are arranged near the front of the grove, nearest to Porifors. Eighteen altogether."

She peeked, turned half around toward the river and the Jokonans' second camp investing the town, and closed her eyes once more. Then turned fully around, toward the bivouac of the third column that had set up along the ridge to the east of the castle, cutting the road to Oby and commanding the valley upstream. "All the sorcerers seem to be in the main camp near Joen. I see no ribbons reaching to the other two camps. Yes, of course. She would want all her sorcerers as close under her eye as possible."

She completed her turn and opened her eyes again. "Most of the sorcerers seem to be sheltered in tents. One is standing under a tree, looking this way." She could not see his physical body, through the leaves, but she could tell which tree it was.

"Hm," said Illvin, staring over her shoulder. "Can *Foix* tell which is which? What man is a sorcerer, what man is not?"

"Oh, yes. I mean, he can now. He saw the sorcery light with me when the cups broke—and again, standing on the wall when the rest of it began." She glanced warily back over her shoulder at Illvin's tense, closed expression. His eyes were tight with thought, some notion that did not seem to give him much pleasure. "What are you thinking?"

"I am thinking . . . that by your testimony Arhys appears to be immune to sorcery, but sorcerers do not appear to be immune to steel. As Cattilara proved upon poor Umerue. If Arhys could close with them, just them, and yet somehow avoid the other fifteen hundred Jokonans around Porifors . . ." He drew a breath, and wheeled. "Liss."

She jerked upright. "Lord Illvin?"

"Go and find my lord brother, and ask him to attend upon us here. Fetch Foix, too, if he is to be found."

She nodded, a bit wide-eyed, scrambled up, and scuffed rapidly down the tower's turning stairs. Illvin stared out over Prince Sordso and Princess Joen's camp as if memorizing every detail. Ista leaned uneasily by his side, studying that profile suddenly gone distant and cool.

He looked back and smiled down at her in apology. "I am seized by a thought. I fear you will find me a rather distractible man."

It wasn't how *she* would describe him, but she smiled briefly back in attempted reassurance.

All too soon, footsteps sounded on the stairs. Arhys emerged into the luminous twilight, followed by Liss and Foix. Arhys looked scarcely more corpselike than anyone else in Porifors at present, but his face was spared the usual smears of sweat. Foix's stolidity masked a deep depletion. He had spent the afternoon clumsily trying to undo sorceries all over the castle, to little effect. Dy Cabon had named the effort fundamentally futile, for various theological reasons that no one stayed to listen to, and yet had begged Foix's aid himself when faced with the rising demands of the sick.

"Arhys, come here," said Illvin. "Look at this." His brother joined him at the western parapet. "Five gods attest we know this ground. Royina Ista says there are but eighteen sorcerers in Joen's pack altogether. A dozen lie in the front

of the camp, along there . . ."—his hand swept in an arc—
"six more in the command tents, a rather better guarded
area, I suspect. One big circle could pass round them all, if
it were rapid enough. How many sorcerers do you think you
could excise with steel?"

Arhys's brows rose. "As many as I could close with, I
suppose. But I doubt they would just stand there while we
galloped up to them. As soon as they thought to drop our
horses, we'd be afoot."

"What if we attacked in the dark? You said you see better
in the dark these days than other men."

"Hm." Arhys's gaze upon the grove intensified.

"Royina Ista." Illvin turned urgently to her—and where
was all that *Sweet Ista* now? "What happens when a leashed
sorcerer is slain?"

Ista frowned. Surely the question was rhetorical. "You've
seen it yourself. The demon, together with whatever pieces
of its mount's soul it has digested, jumps to whatever new
host it can reach. The body dies. What the fate of the remaining parts of the person's soul may be, I do not know."

"And one other thing," Illvin said, excitement leaking
into his voice. "The leash is broken. Or at least—Cattilara's
demon broke from control at Umerue's death. More: at that
moment, the free demon became Joen's rebellious enemy,
dedicated to flight from her as fast as possible. How many
demons could Joen suffer to have cut away from her array—
jumping randomly into unprepared hosts, or even turning on
her—before she was forced to retreat in disorder?"

"If she doesn't have others in reserve, ready to harness
like a fresh team of horses," said Arhys.

"No," said Ista slowly, "I don't think she can. All must be
there, tied in her net, or they will fly—away from each other
if not from her. By Umerue's testimony, it took Joen three
years to develop this array, to bring each sorcerer-slave to
some apex of carefully selected, stolen skills. Without another visit to whatever back door of hell her master demon
can unlock, I doubt she can replace them. And all she'll get

at first is a spate of mindless, formless, ignorant elementals. We know she spills them, too; it cannot be a well-controlled process, not when dealing with the essence of disorder itself. Although . . . Cattilara's demon fears recapture; if that is not just some filial obsession of Umerue's, it implies recapture is possible. I don't know how quickly Joen might effect it."

"With several freed demons flying in all directions, it would be more difficult, I should guess," said Illvin.

Arhys leaned his elbow on the stone wall and eyed his brother. "You are thinking of a sortie. A sorcerer-hunt."

"Aye."

"It cannot be done. I am certain to take wounds—which Catti would be forced to bear."

Illvin looked away. "I was thinking the royina could switch you back to me. For the occasion, as it were."

Ista gasped protest. "Do you realize what that would mean? Arhys's injuries would be yours."

"Yes, well . . ." Illvin swallowed. "But then Arhys could go on for quite a bit more than his enemies would guess. Perhaps physicians or women could stay at my side, binding up the leaks as they spring. Buying extra minutes."

Arhys frowned. "And then . . . what? At your last gasp, break the link? Return all my wounds to me at once?"

Ista tried not to let her voice emerge as a shriek. "Leaving you trapped in a hacked-apart body that can neither die nor heal?"

Arhys said vaguely, "I really don't have all that much feeling in my body anymore. . . . Maybe I might not be trapped. Maybe"—his ravishing gray eyes rose to meet Ista's, and the sudden light in them terrified her down to her bones—"I might be released."

"To the death of nothingness? No!" said Ista.

"Indeed not!" said Illvin. "I mean the sortie to swing round and return to Porifors. The others would ride to guard you, and clear your way to the sorcerers. *And* make sure you got back."

"Mm." Arhys stared down into the dusk. "How many men do you think it would take?"

"A hundred would be best, but we do not have a hundred. Fifty might make it."

"We do not have fifty, either. Illvin, we do not have twenty, not mounted."

Illvin straightened up from the parapet. The excitement drained from his face. "Twenty is too few."

"Too few to ride out? Or to ride back?"

"If too few to ride back, then too few to ride out. I could not ask it of any man if I were not riding myself, and I would perforce be detained in here."

"Only in a sense," said Arhys. He was looking increasingly, disturbingly, intent. "We are dying here by the hour. Worse—Lord dy Oby will ride apace to our relief. He was never laggard, but for the sake of his daughter he will brook no delay. Without warning of Joen's demonic deceits, he will race his troops into this trap."

"He cannot be here before day after tomorrow, at the soonest," said Illvin.

"I wouldn't be so sure. If today's courier was taken by the Jokonan screen and failed to arrive at Oby, he'll know at once, for I know the warnings about the ambush of Foix and the divine reached him. The fortress of Oby is already well aroused." Arhys's frown deepened. "Also, the longer we wait, the worse condition we will all be in."

"That would certainly appear to be true," Illvin conceded.

"And," his voice lowered, "the worse condition I will be in. Our men are dying now without a blade being lifted or a quarrel being fired. By nightfall tomorrow, at this rate, Sordso's forces will be able to walk unopposed into a castle manned only by corpses, unmoving save for one. And I will be left facing the same enemy—alone and unsupported."

"Ah," said Illvin, sounding shaken.

"Had you not thought it through? I'm surprised. Royina"—he turned to Ista—"I am sundered now. Freeing me from this body will not change that state. Let it be done while . . . while there is still some honor in it. Some use."

"Arhys, you cannot ask this of me."

"Yes. I can." His voice fell further. "And you cannot refuse me."

Ista was trembling, both at what he proposed and at what he envisioned. That solitary fate was, she had to admit, the logical progression of events.

"Arhys, no, this is too fey," protested Illvin.

"Fey is a man who looks forward to death. I look back upon mine. I am beyond fey, I think. If this hazard is to be cast at all, it must be soon. In the dark before dawn."

"*This* night?" said Illvin. Even he, who had advanced the plan, sounded appalled at its sudden acceleration.

"This very night. We've been shoved most forcefully onto the defensive, and the Jokonans do not look to us, in our present shock, to turn it about. If ever the gods gave me the gift for finding the moment on the field, I swear to you, this is one."

Illvin's lips parted, but no sound came out.

Arhys smiled slightly and turned again to view the walnut grove in the fading light. Though perhaps not fading for him, Ista was reminded. "So, how would I find these sorcerers and not waste time butchering ordinary men?"

Foix cleared his throat. "I can see them."

Behind them, sitting small and cross-legged by the wall again, Liss caught her breath.

Arhys looked across at Foix. "Would you ride out with me, dy Gura? It's a good pairing. I think you are less vulnerable to these sorcerous attacks than any other man here."

"I . . . let me look at the ground." Foix, too, advanced to the battlement and leaned upon it, staring down at the camp. Ista saw by the way his eyes opened and closed that he marshaled his second sight to study this challenge.

Arhys turned to Ista. "Royina, can you manage this thing? Neither Illvin nor I will be able to speak to you—we must rely on your judgment when to make or break our links."

I am every kind of afraid. Physically. Magically. Morally. But mostly the last. "I think I could cut Illvin free of you, yes. What about Cattilara?"

"I would spare her," said Arhys. "Let her sleep."

"To wake a widow? I am not sure that is a betrayal she could ever forgive. She may be young and foolish, but she is not a child now, and will never be a child again. In any case, she must be allowed to wake and eat, that she may lend you strength, and not fail through no fault of her own."

Illvin said, "I fear if she has any hint of this, she will grow quite frenzied. And I doubt her demon will be on our side either."

The stars were coming out, overhead. On the western horizon, glowing pink feathers of cloud were fading to gray. So much indifferent beauty, in the world of matter . . .

"I must take thought for Cattilara," said Ista. *It seems no one else is willing to.*

From the deepening shadows, Foix spoke: "Lord Arhys, if you decide to ride out, I will go with you. If the royina will release me to your command."

Ista hesitated for three sick heartbeats. "I release you."

"Thank you, Royina, for this honor," Foix said formally.

"Come," said Arhys to Illvin. "Let us go see if there is enough unbroken gear left in Castle Porifors to outfit this curious hunt. Foix, attend." He turned for the stairs.

Illvin strode back to grasp Ista's hand and lift it to his lips. "I shall see you shortly."

"Yes," whispered Ista. The grip tightened, and was gone.

23

IT WAS CLOSE TO MIDNIGHT BEFORE LORD ARHYS WENT
to rest in his chambers, so that Cattilara, on the other side of
the door, might be roused to eat. His page removed his
boots, but no more, and settled by the foot of the bed to
guard his repose. Ista thought the exhausted boy would be
asleep on the floor before five minutes had passed. Arhys lay
back on his bed, eyes wide and dark in the light of the
room's sole candle.

"Be tender with her," he pleaded to Ista. "She has had to
endure far too much."

"I will use my very best judgment," Ista returned. Arhys accepted her words with a nod. It was Illvin, overseeing the dis-
positions before returning to the night's too-eventful watch,
who cocked a curious eyebrow at her as they turned away.

"Be as careful of her as of her demon, and I don't mean
it the way Arhys does," he muttered to Ista. "After that accursed escapade with the wagon, I believe there is no limit
to what she would do in pursuit of her ends."

"I will use," said Ista neutrally, "my very best judgment."
She let Foix and Liss pass before her into Lady Cattilara's
chamber and closed the door upon him, gently but firmly.

The most levelheaded of Cattilara's ladies was just arriving with the meal tray. The haggard look on her face, as well as the care she took setting the food down, told Ista she recognized the cost of it. Ista dismissed her only as far as a seat on a chest. Liss stayed by Ista's elbow as she approached Cattilara's bed.

"Foix, stand by her feet. Keep an eye on her demon," Ista directed. Foix nodded and did so. Ista was unhappy to be demanding yet one more duty of him, when he was so plainly drained to the point of swaying on his feet. He desperately needed to rest for a few hours before the sortie. But Joen had taught her greater caution of demons.

Ista called up her inner sight and closed her hands around the flow of soul-fire from Catti's heart, reducing it to the tiniest trickle of contact with Arhys. Ista imagined the look of life flowing from his face in the next room, and her chest tightened. The demon shadow squirmed in agitation, but did not challenge Ista's control. Cattilara's eyes flew open, and her breath drew in. She sat up abruptly, then swayed, dizzy. Liss pressed a tin cup of water into her hand. By the way she guzzled, pressing it to her dry lips, Ista thought they were none too soon with this sustenance. Liss transferred the tray to a small table by the bedside and drew off the linen cover. Plain fare, and stale, presented on a miscellany of battered old plates.

Catti glared over the cup at Ista and glowered down at the tray. "What is this? Servants' food? Or a prisoner's? Is the mistress of Porifors so dethroned by her usurper, now?"

"It is the last and best untainted food in the keep, reserved for you. We are now surrounded by a Jokonan army and besieged by a troop of sorcerers. Their demon magic is chewing everything within these walls to pieces and spitting it out upon us. All the water is gone. The meat seethes with maggots. Half the courts are burned, and a third of the horses lie dead. Men are dying tonight below us of disease and injury without ever having come within bowshot of Joen and Sordso's troops. Joen's new way of making war is ingenious, cruel, and effective. Extraordinarily effective. So eat, because it is the only meal Arhys will have tonight."

Cattilara gritted her teeth, but at least she gritted them on her first bite of dry bread. "We could have fled. We should have fled! I could have had Arhys forty miles from here by now, and out of this. Curse you for a lack-witted bitch!"

Foix and Liss stirred at the insult, but Ista's raised hand stayed them. "Arhys would not have thanked you. And who is *we*? Are you even certain whose voice speaks from inside your head right now? Eat."

Catti gnawed, gracelessly, but too driven by her ferocious waking hunger to spurn the proffered meal. Liss kept the water coming, for Cattilara's sunken features betrayed how dangerously parched she had grown. Ista let her chew and swallow for several minutes, until she began visibly to slow.

"Later tonight," Ista began again, "Arhys rides out on a hazardous sortie, a gamble to save us all. Or die trying."

"You mean him to die," Catti mumbled. "You hate him. You hate me."

"You are twice mistaken, though I admit to a strong desire to slap you at times. Now, for instance. Lady Cattilara, you are the wife of a soldier-commander and the daughter of a soldier-commander. You cannot possibly have been raised, here in this dire borderland, to such wild self-indulgence."

Cattilara looked away, perhaps to conceal a flash of shame in her face. "This stupid war has always dragged on. It will always drag on. But once Arhys is gone, he's gone *forever*. And all the good in the world goes with him. The gods would take him and leave me bereft, and I curse them!"

"I have cursed them for years," said Ista dryly. "Turnabout being fair." Cattilara was furious, distraught, writhing in overwhelming pain. But was she divorced altogether from reason?

So what is reality now, here in this waking nightmare? Where is reason? Absurd, that I of all women should insist on reason.

"Keep chewing." Ista straightened her weary back, crossed her arms. "I have a proposition for you."

Cattilara glowered in suspicion.

"You may accept or refuse, but you may not have other choices. It quite resembles a miracle, in that regard. Arhys rides out tonight against Joen's sorcerers. Illvin has volunteered to accept his wounds, to the point of death. It seems to me that *two* bodies, both nourishing Arhys's sword arm and bearing his hurts, would carry him farther than one. Perhaps just the needed edge, that little difference between almost succeeding, and almost failing. You can be a part of his ride, or you can be shut out of it."

Foix, startled, said, "Royina, Lord Arhys would not desire this!"

"Quite," said Ista coolly. "No one else here will offer you this choice, Cattilara."

"You cannot do this behind his back!" said Foix.

"I am the appointed executor of this rite. This is women's business now, Foix. Be silent. Cattilara"—Ista drew breath—"widow you are and shall be, but the grief you will carry into the rest of your life will be different depending on the choices you make tonight."

"How better?" snarled Cattilara. Tears were leaking from her eyes now. "Without Arhys, all is ashes."

"I didn't say better. I said, different. You may accept the part apportioned to you, or you may lie down and be passed over. If you do not take your part, and he fails, you will never, ever know whether you might have made the difference. If you accept the part, and he still falls—then you will know that, too.

"Arhys would have protected you from this choice, as a father would a beloved child. Arhys is wrong in this. I give you a woman's choice, here, at the last gasp. He looks to spare you pain this night. I look to your nights for the next twenty years. There is neither right nor wrong in this, precisely. But the time to amend all choices runs out like Porifors's water."

"You think he will die in this fight," grated Cattilara.

"He's been dead for three months. I did not war against

his death, but against his damnation. I have lost. In my life-time, I have looked two gods in the eye, and it has seared me, till I am afraid of almost nothing in the world of matter. But I am afraid of this, for him. He stands this night on the edge of the true death, the death that lasts forever, and there is none to pull him back from that precipice. Not even the gods can save him if he falls now."

"Your choice is no choice. It's death all ways."

"No: death in different ways. You had more of him than any woman alive. Now the wheel turns. Be assured, some-day it will turn for you. All are equal in this. He goes first, but not uniquely. Nor alone, for he will have a large Jokonan escort, I do think."

"He will if I have anything to do with it," growled Foix.

"Yes. Do you imagine not one of them is also beloved, as Arhys is? You have a chance to let Arhys go out in serenity, with his mind clear and unimpeded, concentrated as the sword which is his symbol. I will not give you leave to send him off harassed and dismayed, distracted and grieved."

Cattilara snarled, "Why should I give him up to death—or to the gods, or to you, or to anyone? He's *mine*. All my life is his."

"Then you shall be hollow and echoing indeed, when he is gone."

"This disaster is not my doing! If people had just done things my way, this all could have been averted. Everyone is against me—"

The food on the tray was all gone. Sighing, Ista touched her ligature, and opened the channel wide once more. Catti-lara sank back, cursing. The flow of soul-fire from Catti's heart was slow and surly, but it would suffice for the next few hours.

"I would have liked to give her a chance to say good-bye," said Ista sadly. "Lord Illvin's remarks on kisses with-held and words unspoken weigh much on my mind."

Foix, his face appalled, said, "*Her* remarks were better left unspoken to Lord Arhys just now, I think."

"So I judged. Five gods, why was I appointed to this court? Go, Foix, get what rest you may. It is your most urgent duty now."

"Aye, Royina." He glanced at Liss. "Will you come down to see us off? Later on?"

"Yes," whispered Liss.

Foix started to speak, seemed to find his throat strangely uncooperative, nodded thanks, and bowed his way out.

❧

Ista, too, eventually went to lie down in her chambers for a few hours. She longed for a dreamless slumber, feared the sleep of dreams, but in any case merely dozed, disquieted by the occasional agonized noises that filtered in through her lattice from a castle disintegrating, it seemed, about all their ears. At length Liss, drawn face candlelit by a stub in a brass holder whose glass vase lay in shards somewhere, came to rouse her. Ista was already awake and dressed. The bleak mourning garb was growing dirty and frayed, but its black robe suited her mood and the shadows of this hour.

Liss followed her, holding up the meager light, as Ista eased out the door onto the gallery. She took three steps down the empty stairs, and stopped. Her breath caught.

A tall, somber man stood on the treads two below her, so that his face was level with hers, in precisely the position she had kissed and challenged the dead Arhys, half a lifetime ago here. His face and form were uncertain in outline; she thought he looked a bit like Arhys, a bit like Arvol, and more than a little like her own dead father, though dy Baocia had been a shorter, thicker man. He was not much, she thought, like Ias.

He was dressed as an officer of Porifors, in mail and a gray-and-gold tabard; but the mail gleamed, and the tabard was pressed and perfect, its embroidery bright as fire. His hair and beard were pure gray, cut short as Arhys's were, clean and fine. The wavering candlelight did not reflect from his upturned face, nor from the endless depths of his eyes; they shone instead with their own effulgent light.

Ista swallowed, raised her chin. Stiffened her knees. "I wasn't expecting *You* here."

The Father of Winter favored her with a grave nod. "All gods attend on all battlefields. What parents would not wait as anxiously by their door, looking again and again up the road, when their child was due home from a long and dangerous journey? You have waited by that door yourself, both fruitfully and in vain. Multiply that anguish by ten thousands, and pity me, sweet Ista. For my great-souled child is very late, and lost upon his road."

The deep resonance of his voice seemed to make her chest vibrate, her bones ring. She could barely breathe. Water clouded her vision and fell from her unblinking eyes. "I know it, Sire," she whispered.

"My calling voice cannot reach him. He cannot see the light in my window, for he is sundered from me, blind and deaf and stumbling, with none to take his hand and guide him. Yet you may touch him, in his darkness. And I may touch you, in yours. Then take you this thread to draw him through the maze, where I cannot go."

He leaned forward and kissed her on the brow. His lips burned like cold metal. Fearfully, she reached up and touched his beard, as she had Arhys's that day, tickling strange and soft beneath her palm. As he bent his head, a tear fell as a snowflake upon the back of her hand, melted, and vanished.

"Am I to be a spiritual conductor on Your behalf, now?" she asked, dazed.

"No; my doorway." He smiled enigmatically at her, a white streak in the night like lightning across her senses, and her reeling mind slipped from dazed to dazzled. "I will wait there for him, for a little while." He stepped backward, and the stair was empty again.

Ista stood, shaken. The spot on the back of her left hand where his tear had splashed was icy cold.

"Royina?" said Liss, very cautiously, stopped behind her. "Who are you talking to?"

"Did you see a man?"

"Um . . . no?"

"I am sorry."

Liss held up her candle. "You're crying."

"Yes. I know. It's all right. Let us go on now. I think perhaps you had better hold my arm till we get down the stairs."

The stone court, the archway, the star court with its restive horse line, and the gate into the forecourt passed in a dark blur. Liss held her arm the whole way, and frowned at its fierce trembling.

The torchlit forecourt was crowded with men and horses. Most of the flowerpots were broken, fallen from the walls or tipped, spilling their dry soil. The succulents were smashed, the more tender flowers wilted and limp like cooked greens. The two espaliered trees on the far wall shed dry leaves in the breathless night heat, falling one by one atop a drift of rotting petals.

Foix was the first to notice her arrival; his head turned, and his mouth opened. No doubt she moved in a cloud of god light, just at present, being so recently touched. *And I bear a burden that I am most gravely charged to deliver.* Her eye swept the court, found Arhys and Illvin, but her attention was temporarily distracted by the horse they both studied. From a distance.

It was a tall, long-nosed chestnut stallion, held by three sweating grooms. A blindfold covered its eyes beneath its bridle, which was fitted with a deep curb bit. One groom held its upper lip tightly in a twitch. Its ears were back flat, and it squealed angrily, showing long yellow teeth, and kicked out. Illvin was standing well back from it, looking aggrieved.

Ista came up beside him and said, "Lord Illvin, do you know that stallion is possessed of an elemental?"

"So Foix has just informed me, Royina. It explains a *lot* about that horse."

Ista peered through half-closed eyes at the writhing mauve shadow within the animal. "Grant you, it appears to be a small, unformed, stupid one."

"That explains yet more. Bastard's hell. I was going to lend the accursed beast to Arhys. His good dappled gray has gone lame, along with half the horses that remain to us—an outbreak of thrush, developing with unnatural speed, and I hope Arhys can soon deliver our thanks to whichever Jokonan sorcerer thought of *that* one."

"Is this an especially good warhorse?"

"No, but no one will care if Arhys rides it to death. In fact, I think the grooms are hoping he will. Five gods know I've tried to, without success."

"Hm," said Ista. She walked forward; the two grooms holding the beast's head squeaked protest. Her eyes narrowed, and she reached up and placed her god-splashed hand upon the stallion's forehead. A tiny six-pointed mark burned upon her skin, snow-white to her outer vision, a fierce spark to her inner eye. "Remove its blindfold."

The groom glanced somewhat desperately at Illvin, who nodded permission but drew his sword and held it with the flat out, watching tensely.

The horse's eyes were dark brown, with purple centers. Most horses' eyes had purple centers, Ista reminded herself, but they didn't usually have quite so deep a glow. The eyes fixed on her, and rolled whitely. She stared back. The animal suddenly grew very still. Ista stood on tiptoe, grabbed one ear, and whispered toward it, "Behave for Lord Arhys. Or I will make you *wish* I'd merely ripped your guts out, strangled you with them, and fed you to the gods."

"Dogs," corrected the nervous groom holding the twitch.

"Them, too," said Ista. "Take off the twitch and stand away."

"Lady . . . ?"

"It's all right."

The groom backed away. The horse, shivering, flicked its ears up to strict attention and arched its neck to bring its face, submissively, flat to Ista's torso. It gave a brief nudge, leaving a trail of red horsehairs across her black silk robe, and stood perfectly quietly.

"Do you do that sort of thing often?" Illvin inquired, strolling over. With extreme caution, he reached out to give the beast an experimental pat on the neck.

"No," sighed Ista. "It has been a day for unique experiences."

Illvin was simply dressed in light linen trousers and his spark-spotted shirt, in preparation for his role to come. Arhys looked so much as he had when Ista had seen him for the very first time that she caught her breath. Except that his mail and tabard were not blood-spattered. Yet. He smiled soberly at her as he came to her side.

"A word, Royina, before I go. Two words."

"As many as you please."

He lowered his voice. "First, I thank you for bearing me up to a better death. One less shameful, small, and stupid than my first."

"Our men may yet surprise you on that score," said Illvin gruffly. On the far side of the forecourt, a mere dozen soldiers were also preparing their mounts. Pejar was among them; his face was flushed with fever, Ista noted. He should have been lying on a pallet, not attempting this. Then she wondered how few men in Porifors were still able to walk at all, at this hour.

Arhys smiled briefly at his brother and forbore to argue or correct, or pull that thin hope from his hands. He turned back to Ista. "Second, I beg a boon."

"Anything within my power."

His clear eyes fixed on her with penetrating intensity; she felt targeted. "If this dy Lutez manages to die well tonight, let it complete the set that was left undone so long ago. Let what victory I may gain swallow up forever the old, cold dereliction. And be you healed of the long wound that another dy Lutez dealt you."

"*Oh*," said Ista. *Oh.* She dared not let her voice break; she had still an office to perform. "I was given a message for you, too."

His brows rose; he looked a little taken aback. "No courier has penetrated the Jokonan blockade for a day. What messenger was this?"

"I met Him on the stairs but now. It is this." She swallowed to clear her voice.

"Your Father calls you to His Court. You need not pack; you go garbed in glory as you stand. He waits eagerly by His palace doors to welcome you, and has prepared a place at His high table by His side, in the company of the great-souled, honored, and best-beloved. In this I speak true. Bend your head."

Wide-eyed, astonished, he did so. She pressed her lips to his brow, the pale skin neither hot nor cold, unsheened with sweat. Her mouth seemed to leave a brief ring of frost that steamed in the heavy night air. A new line appeared in her second sight, a fine thread of gray light, strung from him to her. *It is a life-line.* It could, she somehow knew, stretch to the ends of the earth without breaking. *Oh.*

Moved, she completed the full formal rite, kissing the back of each hand, then bending to his feet and touching her lips to each boot as well. He jerked a little, as if to dissuade her, but then stood still and allowed the gesture. He recaptured her hands and helped pull her back to her feet. Her knees felt like water.

"Surely," he whispered in awe, "we are blessed."

"Yes. For we bless each other. Be at rest in your heart. It will be very well."

She backed away to let Illvin embrace his brother. Illvin held Arhys away by his shoulders, after, and gazed with smiling puzzlement into those strange exultant eyes, which seemed to look back from some great and receding distance. The cool lips smiled kindly, though. Illvin turned to give him a leg up on the painfully obedient red stallion, check his girths and stirrups and gear one last time, and slap his leather-clad leg in some habitual gesture. He stood away.

Ista looked around through blurred and stinging eyes to find Liss, standing at the shoulder of Foix's horse. Foix was already mounted. He saluted Liss in the gesture of the Daughter's Order, touching his forehead. She returned a courier's salute, fist tapped over her heart. Foix, meeting Ista's eyes, saluted her as well; she gave back the sign of the fivefold blessing.

The dozen men of Arhys's forlorn little company mounted up at his quiet word. No one spoke much.

"Liss," Ista choked, and cleared her throat. "Liss," she began again. "Attend on me. We must get to the tower."

Both Liss and Illvin fell in beside her, and they started back through the archway. Behind them, Ista could hear Porifors's gates begin to creak open, the iron ratcheting of the drawbridge chains echoing among the dying flowers. Illvin walked backward a moment, staring into the fire-streaked dark, but Ista schooled herself not to turn around.

24

ISTA'S ACHING LEGS PUSHED HER UP THE NARROW TOWER
stairs, the curving stone wall harsh beneath her groping
hand, into a square of unexpected radiance. Rows of candles
were lined up at the base of the parapet walls on the north
and south sides, stuck into blobs of their own wax, burning
clear and unwavering in the breezeless night air. The heat
seemed to stream upward into the starry night sky, but withal
the air of the tower was much less close and stale than that
of the forecourt.

With their arrival, the platform seemed crowded. Ista surveyed the arrangements she'd ordered and breathed satisfaction. At one side Lady Cattilara, dressed in a robe, lay
silently upon a straw pallet that was covered with a sheet.
Another pallet, also covered with old linens, lay empty beside her. The sewing woman with her basket, Goram, and
Learned dy Cabon, his robes now very stained indeed, all
waited anxiously. The little company would have to suffice;
the few physicians and acolytes of the Mother left alive in
the beleaguered town were felled by fevers, or worse, and in
any case could not be smuggled up the collapsed tunnels to
their castle's aid.

Illvin, emerging from the stair's blackness, shielded his eyes against the candle glow. "Royina, will you be able to see out, to track my brother's progress?"

"It won't be these eyes I use to follow him. And your attendants must be able to see you." Her material hand reached to touch the invisible reassurance of the gray thread, which seemed to spin out from her heart into the darkness below. "I will not lose him now."

He grunted somewhat disconsolate acquiescence, drew a breath, and seated himself upon the empty pallet. Laying his sword aside, he peeled out of his speckled and sweat-stained shirt and rolled up his loose trouser legs. Goram helped pull off his boots. He swung his long legs out straight and lay back, face not so much composed as rigid, his dark dilated eyes looking up at the stars. Wisps of cloud, moisture out of reach, crossed the spangled vault in gray feathers. "I am ready." His voice sounded parched, but not, Ista thought, just from lack of water.

From the castle below, she heard the faint ratchet of the drawbridge chains being pulled up again very slowly, and a jingle of harness and thump of hooves passing away from the walls, fading with distance. The gray thread was moving in the pool of darkness below, very like a fishing line taken by a pike. "We have not much time. We must begin." She dropped to her knees between the two pallets.

Illvin took her hand and pressed it to his lips. She caressed his slick brow as she took it back. Composed herself. Shut out the confusing sight of her eyes and brought up the tangle of lights and shadows by which the realm of spirit represented itself to her now. She suspected the gods simplified it for her, and that the reality beneath this was stranger and more complex still. But this was what she was given; it must do.

She undid her ligature around the white trickle coming from Illvin's heart, opening the channel wide. Soul-fire poured out, joined the sluggish, sullen stream from Cattilara, and flowed away into the night, winding around the gray thread but not touching it. The life drained from Illvin's face, leaving it stiff and waxen, and she shuddered.

She turned away and studied the sleeping Cattilara. The demon swirled in agitation beneath her thin breastbone. Enormous stresses propagated here, straining toward some cataclysmic breakage. Ista's next task was dangerous indeed, dangerous to them all, but she could not shirk from it. So many souls were at risk in this ride . . .

She tightened Cattilara's ligature, pushing the soul-fire up from her heart toward her head. The demon tried to follow it. She laid her snow-spangled left hand upon Cattilara's collarbone, stared in fascination at the gray glow her fingers suddenly shed. The demon shrank again, crying with new terror. Cattilara's eyes opened.

She tried to surge upright, only to find her body still paralyzed. "You!" she cried to Ista. "Curse you, let me *go*!"

Ista let out her tight breath. "Arhys rides out now. Pity his enemies, for death on a demon horse descends upon them out of the darkness, bringing sword and fire. Many will bear him company on his journey to his Father's keep tonight, their souls like ragged banners borne before his echoing feet. You must choose now. Will you aid him or impede him, in his last journey?"

Cattilara's head yanked back and forth in an agony of denial. "No! No! No!"

"The god himself awaits his coming, His own holy breath held in the balance of the moment. Arhys's heart flies ahead to his Father's hand like a messenger bird. Even if he could be dragged back now, he would spend the rest of his life, and I think it would not be long, hanging at that window, longing for his last home. He would not thank you. He could not love you, with all his heart anchored in that other realm. I think he might even grow to hate you, knowing what glory you denied to him. For one last moment, the last instant of time and choice, think not of what you desire, but of what he does; not of your good, but of his greatest good."

"No!" screamed Cattilara.

"Very well." Ista reached to open the ligature, one eye on the restive, mutinous demon.

Cattilara turned her head away, and whispered, "Yes."

Ista paused, exhaled. Murmured, "So I pray the gods may hear even me, and let my whispered *yes* tower above my shouted *no* and mount all the way to their fivefold realm. As I would be heard, so I hear you." She swallowed hard. "Hold your demon on its course. It will not be an easy one."

"Will I feel much pain?" asked Cattilara. Her eyes met Ista's at last. Her voice would have been almost inaudible, but for the silence on the platform. Not even cloth rustled, from the people standing watching.

Yes, no, I have no idea. "Yes, I think so. All births have some."

"Oh. Good." She turned her head away again, but not in denial. Her eyes were wet, but her face was as still as carved ivory.

Ista lifted her hand, but her intervention was not needed. As Cattilara's face went slack, the white fire burst redoubled from her heart, to join the flow from Illvin in a torrent, roaring down over the parapet. *So, you do not ride alone, Arhys. The hearts of the two who love you best go with you now.* She hoped his body received their outpouring as an exaltation, at the other end of that white line.

She rose and hurried to the parapet, motioning the others to make ready with pads, cloths, and tourniquets. She stared out into the darkness, the roads like gray ribbons, the open spaces rucked like mist-shrouded blankets across an unmade bed, the trees of the grove black and silent. A few watch fires burned in the enemy camp, and Jokonan horsemen slowly patrolled back and forth out of bowshot. A clot of moving shadows reached the trees, slipping between the patrols.

She glared out with all the strength of her other eyes, following the white flood and thin gray thread to where a dozen soul-sparks moved, atop the lesser life-blurs of their horses. Arhys's gray glow was distinctive, Foix's violet-tinged double shadow even more so. She could see clearly through all the moving masses that lay between, when Arhys kicked the demon-lit shape of his horse into a canter. He closed rapidly on a quiescent, colored thread of sorcerer light, like a hawk swooping on unsuspecting prey.

"Can you see Foix?" Liss's breathless voice sounded by her ear.

"Yes. He rides by Arhys's side."

The shouts of alarm didn't go up till the first tent went down. As more cries and a ring of steel split the night, the mounted patrols wheeled about and began galloping back toward the camp. Abruptly, the snake of sorcerer fire stretched and snapped. A bluish gout of soul-fire shot aloft, separating even as Ista watched from a violent purple streak, which sped away trailing soul shreds in torn-off, fluttering rags. The bluish gout writhed in agony, and faded into *elsewhere*. The purple streak grounded itself in a moving soul-spark somewhere beneath the trees; both the recipient and the demon dropped flat in the shock of that arrival. But the snake did not renew itself.

"That's one," said Ista aloud.

The attackers made no cries or calls at all, moving in grim, determined silence. The pale blur of another tent, sheltering the head of another colored snake, swayed, shook, and collapsed. The Jokonan sorcerer gathered energy for some strike at his attacker; Ista could see the flash of a bolt of demon magic pass through Arhys, and hear the wail of the sorcerer's surprise and woe, cut off. She rather thought that faint, distant, liquid *thunk* might have been a beheading. Another violet streak separated from another white gout. Shocked and tumbling, the violet blur fell helter-skelter into a horse being ridden toward the fray by a Jokonan cavalryman. The animal stumbled, jerked sideways, dumped its rider, and wheeled to run at a hard gallop away down the Oby road. The loose snake head seemed to quest after it as if seeking to strike, but then fell back in on itself, disintegrating in a stream of sparks.

"That's two," said Ista.

From the trees a wavering glow blazed up, yellow and bright, as a tent caught fire. Beyond the grove, lights were being lit in the big green command tents. Ista had no doubt that those sorcerers asleep when the first blow fell were now astir, yanked awake by Joen if they'd slept through the noise. How quickly could the surprised Jokonans coordinate their defenses? Their counterattack? Another spurt of soul-fire, without a demon this time, seared past her eye. An ordinary enemy soldier slain, or one of Arhys's defiant volunteers? From a god's-eye view, she realized, it made no difference. All death-births were accepted equally into that realm.

"Three," she counted, as the attack pressed forward.

"Are we winning?" gasped Liss.

"It depends on what you think is the prize."

At the fourth tent the attackers began to come to grief at last. Three sorcerer snakes had somehow combined there. Possibly Arhys was weirdly invisible to them, for they chose to concentrate on Foix. Of course—they must imagine another sorcerer as the greatest danger to them, mistake Foix for the heart or head of the enemy strike. Soul-lights swayed, jerked, spun in Ista's dizzied perceptions. The bear went down, roaring, under a net of fire. But the fourth and fifth snakes were beheaded, ribbon-bodies lashing furiously in their death throes before shredding apart in a streaming aurora. From that far green-glowing tent, Ista could hear a woman fiercely screaming, but the Roknari words were blurred to unintelligibility by distance and rage.

"I think they have taken Foix," said Ista.

Behind her, a triple gasp. "Help!" cried the sewing woman. White-faced, Liss whirled and dropped back to her post by Cattilara's side.

On both Cattilara's right thigh and on Illvin's, long dark slices had opened up. A brief glimpse of the red-brown of pulsing muscle, a pale streak of tendon, then both the twin wounds were flooded with red. The sewing woman and Liss, and Goram and dy Cabon, hastened to pad and bind each cut and slow the stream.

Yes. Yes, thought Ista. Her strategy was good. On one recipient, that sword cut would have gone to the core. The half wounds were half as dire. She almost laughed aloud, if blackly, imagining the dismay of Arhys's assailant, knowing from the shock of contact, the jerk of blade from the bone, the ringing up his arm, how hard he'd struck, yet seeing that wound close up again before his eyes . . . Indeed, the wild wail that echoed up now from the grove might well be the very man. *You thought you'd dropped all the horrors of nightmare down upon Porifors, while you sat safe. Now, watch Porifors return the favor. We hold, we hold.*

For a very little while longer.

She turned again to try to peer beneath the trees. She could mark Arhys's striding progress across the camp by the sounds of terror, she thought, as his enemies flew screaming before his pale face and deadly blade. And by the streams of white fire rising in his wake. He was unhorsed; she was uncertain when that had happened. She hoped he was not yet alone, without one comrade left to guard his back.

I think he is alone now.

A weird wet *thunk* sounded behind her. She glanced back to see her helpers rushing to press pads to Illvin's and Cattilara's stomachs. *That was a crossbow bolt.* She wondered if Arhys had plucked it out to throw back at his dazed enemies, or left it in place like a badge. It would have been a killing strike, on any other man, at any other time. *Soon there will be more. By the gods, a dy Lutez does know how to die three times, and three times three if needed.*

She fell to her knees behind the parapet, clinging to the stone.

It seemed to her that some great black glacier, some ice dam in her soul, was melting, as if a hundred summers' heat had fallen on it in an hour. Cracking, coming apart. And that in the mile-deep, mile-long lake of icy green water backing it up, an expectant surge rippled from bank to bank, from the surface to the uttermost depths, troubling the waters. *I passed blessing to you in the forecourt. But you passed blessing back to me, too. Trading rescues. Five gods watch us ride out together in this breaking dawn.*

You Five may awe us. But I think we must awe You, too.

"Seven," she whispered aloud.

Then something went wrong. A hesitation, a turning away. Too many, far too many, soul-sparks swirled around that gray flame. *Now he is surrounded, cut off. Dozens who ran away now run toward, encouraged by their own numbers, daring to take him down.*

In the midst of your enemies, your Father has prepared a feast for you, on a table your father set long ago. Here it comes . . .

Another *thunk*, and another. From behind her, Liss's sharp voice cried, "Lady, there are too many wounds splitting open! You must stop this!"

Dy Cabon's strained rumble, "Royina, remember you promised Arhys that Lady Cattilara would live—!"

And a certain fat white god has promised Illvin to me, if I did not mistake Him. If we both live. A god-given lover, importunate and bold as a scarred stray cat, rubbing past my guard into my good graces. If I can keep him fed.

She glanced over her shoulder. Illvin's body jerked upward with the transferred force of some massive blow to Arhys's back, and Goram, his face frantic, rolled him over to reach the red rent. Cattilara's white hand half split from its wrist, and Liss pounced to staunch the spurting.

Now. Oh yes, now. Ista clenched her hand about the torrent of white fire running past her shoulder. The flow stopped abruptly. Wild shocks pulsed back in both directions from her grip. The violet channel shattered. The white fire, the constant companion of her inner eye for days, winked out.

A hushed hesitation: then, in the shadowed grove, a grotesque roar of hysteria-tinged triumph went up from half a hundred Jokonan throats.

The ice dam exploded. A wall of water towered, bent, and broke, thundering forward, bursting its banks, blasting her soul wide, wider, scouring and flushing a lifetime of stones, rubble, rotted and clotted trash before it. Boiling, roaring outward. Ista spread her arms wide, and opened her mouth, and let it go.

The gray thread, almost lost to view in the violent blazes, stiffened to a taut rope. It began to move back through her new dilation, faster and faster, until it seemed to smoke with the heat of its passage, like an overstrained fiber rope about to char and burst into flame. For an instant, Arhys's astonished, agonized, ecstatic soul moved *through* hers.

Yes. We are all, every living one of us, doorways between the two realms, that of matter that gives us birth, and that of spirit into which we are born in death. Arhys was sundered from his own gate, and lost the way back to it forever. So it was given to me to lend him mine, for a little time. But so great a soul does need a wide portal; so knock down my gates and breach my walls and burst them wide, and pour through freely, by my leave. And farewell. "Yes," Ista whispered. "Yes."

He did not look back. Given what he must be looking on toward, Ista was not in the least surprised.

It is done, Sire. I hope You find it was done well.

She heard no voice, saw no radiant figure. But it seemed to her she felt a caress upon her brow, and the ache there, which had throbbed for hours as though her head were bound in a tight iron band, stopped. The end of the pain was like a morning birdsong.

There was a real morning birdsong, she realized muzzily, here in matter's lovely realm, a cheery, brainless warble from the bushes below the castle walls. The gray cloud-feathers among the fading stars were just beginning to blush a faint, fiery pink, color creeping from east to west. A little thread of lemon light lined the eastern horizon.

Illvin groaned. Ista turned to find him sitting up in dy Cabon's grip, pulling blood-soaked bandages from his unmarked body. His lips parted with dismay as he took in the extent of the mess, starting to glow scarlet as color seeped back into the world. "Five gods." He swallowed against a surge of bile. "That was bad, at the end. Wasn't it." It was no question.

"Yes," said Ista. "But he's gone, now. Safe and gone." In the grove below, the fear-crazed Jokonans, she somehow knew, were hacking Arhys's body to bits, pulling it apart, terrified that it might yet reassemble and rise once more against them. She did not see any merit in mentioning this to Illvin just now.

Cattilara lay on her side, curled up. She cried in quiet, stuttering sobs, almost unable to breathe, clutching the sponge that had stanched her stomach so hard that the blood bubbled through her fingers. The sewing woman patted her clumsily and uselessly on the shoulder.

The world darkened around Ista, as if dawn, appalled by the scene, retreated again over the horizon. Strolling into her mind like some casual wayfarer, a Voice spoke: familiar, ironic, and immense.

My Word. Spacious in here all of a sudden, is it not?

"What are *You* doing here now? I thought this was become your Step-father's battlefield."

You invited Me. Come, come, you can't deny it: I heard you whispering over in that corner.

She was not sure she had any emotions left for this. Not rage, in any case. Her disembodied quietude might be either serenity or shock. But the Bastard was surely a god to be approached with caution. "Why do you not appear in front of me?"

Because I am behind you, now. The Voice grew warm and amused. The press of an enormous belly seemed to heat her back, along with an obscene implication of loins against her buttocks, and a pressure of wide hands upon her shoulders.

"You have a vile sense of humor," she said weakly.

Yes, and you catch every one of My jokes, too. I love a woman with a keen ear. He seemed to breathe into hers. *You should have a keen tongue to go with them, I vow.*

Her mouth filled with fire.

"Why am *I* here?"

To complete Arhys's victory. If you can.

The Voice was gone. The darkness faded into a streaked pale dawnlight. She found herself fallen on her knees on the tower platform, leaning into Illvin's alarmed grip.

"Ista? Ista!" he was saying into her ear. "Royina, dear, don't frighten a poor naked cavalier. Speak to me, yes?"

She blinked open blurry eyes. He was only a nearly naked cavalier, she discovered to her disappointment. The bloodstained rags of his linen trousers were still rucked up around his loins. He was a most magnificent mess otherwise, true, dark matted hair falling in a wild tangle over his face and shoulders, sweaty and soot-smeared and smelly and striped with red. But all his scars were old ones, healed and pale. He huffed with relief when he saw her looking back at him and bent his neck to kiss her. She fended off his lips with her palm. "Wait, not yet."

"What *was* that?" he asked.

"Did you hear anything? Or see anyone?"

"No, but I'll swear you did."

"What, would you not swear instead that I am mad?"

"No."

"And yet you see no god lights, hear no voices. How do you know?"

"I saw my brother's face when you blessed him. And yours when he blessed you. If that is madness, I would run down the road after it dressed as I am, and barefoot."

"I will walk slowly."

". . . Good."

He helped her to her feet.

Liss said anxiously, "Royina, what of Foix?"

Ista sighed. "Foix went down beneath many soldiers and sorcerers. I did not see his soul arise, nor his demon flee. I fear he is taken, perhaps wounded as well."

"That's . . . not good," said dy Cabon, still kneeling by Illvin's pallet. His teeth grated in a little, nervous gesture. "Do you think . . . do you think Joen can bind him into her array?"

"I think yes, given time. What I do not know is how long he can resist her." *Five gods, I do not wish to lose another boy.*

"Not good at all," Illvin agreed.

He had barely exhaled, steadying himself upright, when a shout rang out, Goram's voice: "Lady Catti! No!"

Ista twisted around. Cattilara was on her feet, her bloody robe falling wide about her. Her eyes were huge, her mouth open. The demon light within her had expanded to the margins of her body, and pulsed violently.

"The demon is ascendant!" Ista cried. "It is taking her. Seize her, do not let her run!"

Goram, closest, attempted to take her arm. A violet light appeared in her palm, and she shoved it toward him. He fell, retching. Ista staggered toward her, stepping between her and the opening of the stairs. Cattilara started forward, then shied away, her hands raised as if to shield her eyes. She looked around frantically. Her knees bunched, and she lunged for the wall.

Liss sprang forward and grabbed her ankle. She twisted, snarling, and yanked at Liss's hair. Illvin danced forward, hesitated for an instant of calculation, and clipped her precisely across the side of the head. She flipped backward, half-stunned.

Ista tottered over and fell to her knees beside her. She seemed to see the demon like a tumor spreading tendrils throughout Cattilara's body. Winding like a parasitical vine around the tree of her spirit, sapping strength, and life, and light. Stealing the high complexities of personality, language, knowledge, and memory that it could not, in the fundamental disorder of its nature, ever make for itself.

Oh. Now I see how to do this.

She reached out with her spirit hands and lifted the demon, trailing recoiling tendrils, from Cattilara's soul. It came unwillingly, flopping in panic like some sea creature drawn out of the water. Ista held out a material hand, fingers spread for a screen, and pushed back the trailing shreds of

Cattilara's soul, like carding wool, until only the demon was left in her hand. She held it up dubiously before her face.

Yes, said the Voice. *That's right. Go ahead.*

She shrugged, popped the demon in her mouth, and swallowed it.

"Now what? Are You going to extend this metaphor to its logical conclusion? It would be just like You, I think."

I shall spare you that, sweet Ista, said the Voice, highly amused. *But I do like your vile sense of humor. I think we shall get along well, don't you?*

There was no cranny in her armored spirit for the demon to wedge itself within, to clutch, to hold; and it wasn't only that she was filled by the god. She felt the demon, knotted up in terror, pass out the other side of her soul. Into the realm of the spirit. Into the hands of the god its Master. Gone.

"What will happen to the pieces of the other souls who are tangled up in it?" she asked in worry. But the Voice had vanished again or, at least, didn't choose to answer.

Cattilara was crouched on the tower platform, panting and hiccuping in little short sobs.

Illvin cleared his throat apologetically, and shook out his hand. "The demon tried to fling you to your death, and its freedom," he told her.

She stared up at him with a ravaged face. In a ragged voice she said, "I know. I wish it had succeeded."

Ista motioned the sewing woman, Goram, and Liss to her. "Get her to a bed, a real bed, and call her women to her. Find her what comforts this castle can yet yield. Don't let her be left alone. I'll come to her when I can." She saw them down the spiral stairs, Cattilara, weary beyond weeping, leaning on the sewing woman and shrugging away from Liss.

Ista turned back to find Illvin and dy Cabon slumping worriedly on the eastern parapet, staring down at the Jokonan camp in the growing light. It roiled with activity, half hidden beneath the trees. Wisps of smoke still rose from the tents that had been burned. A stray saddled horse trotted away from a man trying to catch it; his Roknari curses carried faintly through the moist dawn air. Ista craned her neck in hope, but it did not appear to be Illvin's red stallion.

"So what has happened, Royina?" asked dy Cabon, gazing down in perplexity. "Have we won or lost?"

"It was a very great hunt. Arhys slew seven sorcerers before they brought him down. He stumbled at the eighth. I think it was a sorceress. I wonder if she was young and beautiful, and he could not force his hand swiftly enough to the task?"

"Ah," said Illvin sadly. "That would be Arhys's downfall, wouldn't it."

"Perhaps. The Jokonans had realized how few were his numbers and were combining against him by then, anyway. But the freed demons are fled away in all directions; Joen did not recover any."

"Alas that we do not have two more Arhyses to complete the task," said Illvin. "Perhaps ordinary men must try now." He hitched his shoulders and frowned.

Ista shook her head. "Joen has hurt us, and now we have hurt her back. But we have not defeated her. She still holds eleven sorcerers on her strings and an army barely scratched. She is in a rage; her assault will redouble, without mercy."

Dy Cabon slumped on the parapet, thick shoulders bowed. "Then Arhys rode in vain. We are lost."

"No. Arhys has won us everything. We have only to reach out our hands to collect it. You didn't ask me what I did with Cattilara's demon, Learned."

His brows went up, and he turned toward her. "Did you not bind it in her, as before?"

"No." Ista's lips drew back on a smile that made him recoil. "I ate it."

"What?"

"Don't look at me; it's your god's metaphor. I have finally penetrated the mystery of the Bastard's second kiss. I know how the saint of Rauma accomplished her task of booting demons out of the world and back to their holy commander. Because it seems the trick of it has now fallen to me. Arhys's parting gift, or rather, something he made possible." She shivered with a sorrow to which she dared not yet give way. "Illvin."

Her voice was sharp, urgent; it jerked him from the grieving lassitude that seemed to be overtaking him, as he leaned all his weight on the wall and stared into nothing. He had lost, she reminded herself, a worrisome amount of his own blood in the past hour, for such an already-depleted man. Muddled with Cattilara's, it was spread out in clotting pools across half the tower platform. His wounds had all closed as if they had never been, except for the row of scabbed needle holes bound with thread across his shoulder. He looked back at her and blinked owlishly.

"What is the swiftest, most efficient possible way by which I might come face-to-face with Joen?"

With unthinking brilliance, he replied simply, "Surrender." Then stared at her aghast, and clapped his hand to his mouth as if a toad had just fallen from his lips.

25

ISTA HAD JUST FINISHED WASHING, OR AT LEAST, CLEAN-ing, her body with a half cup of water and some rags when Liss returned to their chambers. She clutched a pile of white garments in her arms, pushing open the inner door with a twist of her hips. "These are the best Cattilara's women could find in a hurry," she announced.

"Good. Put them on the bed." Ista closed the dirty black robe back about herself and came over to examine them. It had not been, by any definition, a bath, but at least the touch of her less-sticky skin against clean clothing might not feel like some violation. "How fares the marchess?"

"She is asleep now. Or unconscious. I really couldn't be quite sure, looking at her. She was very pale and gray."

"Just as well, either way. The blood she spent on the tower buys her a favor, perhaps, in this drained slumber." Ista sorted through the piles. A linen shift the color of new cream, bordered with elaborate cutwork, looked as though it had a hem short enough that she would not trip over it. A delicate white overrobe, embroidered in shining white thread that lent it weight and swing, was a Bastard's Day festival garment. The unknown needlewoman had somehow endowed the friezes of tiny dancing rats and crows with considerable charm. "Perfect," Ista murmured, holding it up. The spark, she noticed, was gone from her left hand, though the frost mark on her skin remained.

"My lady, um . . . isn't it a little *provocative* to place yourself in Quadrene hands wearing the Bastard's own color?"

Ista smiled grimly. "Let them imagine so. Its real message is one I do not expect them to read. Haste, now. Tie the ribbons of the shift in back straightly, please."

Liss did so, cinching in the graceful waist. Ista pulled on the overrobe, shook out the wide sleeves, and fastened it closed beneath her breasts with the amethyst-and-silver mourning brooch. The meaning of the heirloom had shifted, it seemed to her, half a dozen times since it had come into her possession. All its old woes had drained out utterly, last night. Today she wore it new-filled with stern sorrow for Arhys, and for those who had ridden with him. All about her must be renewed, in this hour.

"The hair next," she instructed, sitting on the bench. "Something quick and neat. I do not mean to go out to them looking like a madwoman dragged through a hedge, or a haystack hit by lightning." She smiled in memory. "Put it in one braid."

Liss swallowed hard and began brushing. And said, for the fourth or fifth time since dawn on the tower, "I wish you would take me with you."

"No," said Ista with regret. "Ordinarily, you would be much safer as the servant of a valuable hostage than left in a crumbling fortress about to fall. But if I should fail in what I attempt, Joen would make demon fodder of you, steal your mind and memories and courage for her own. Or take you in trade for her sorcerer-slaves that Arhys killed last night, and set you on me not as my servant but as her guard. Or worse."

And if Ista succeeded . . . she had no idea what might happen after that. Saints were no more immune to steel than sorcerers, as her predecessor the late saint of Rauma—was no longer able to testify.

"What could be worse?" The long strokes of the brush faltered. "Do you think she has enslaved Foix and his bear? Yet?"

"I'll know in an hour." What *worse* might be, should Liss fall into Joen's hands, suddenly occurred to Ista. Now *that* would be the perfect, unholy union of two hearts: to feed Liss to Foix's bear, and let Foix's own caring drive him mad with horror and woe as their souls mixed . . . Then she wondered whose mind was blacker, Joen's, to do such a thing, or her own, to impute such a course to Joen. *It seems I am not a nice person, either.*

Good.

"There are some white ribbons here. Should I braid them in?"

"Yes, please." The pleasant, familiar yank of the plaiting went on swiftly, behind Ista's back. "If you see any chance of it at all, I want you to escape. *That* is your highest duty to me now, my courier. To carry away the word of all that has happened here, though they call you mad for it. Lord dy Cazaril will believe you. At all costs, get you to him."

Silence, behind her.

"Say, '*I promise, Royina,*'" she instructed firmly.

A little mulish hesitation, then a whisper: "I promise, Royina."

"Good." Liss pulled the last bowknot tight; Ista rose. Lady Cattilara's white silk slippers did not fit Ista, but Liss knelt and tied on a pair of pretty white sandals that did well enough, binding the ribbons around Ista's ankles.

Liss led the way to the outer chamber, opening the door to the gallery for Ista to step through.

Lord Illvin was leaning against the wall outside, arms folded. It seemed he had also found half a cup of water to bathe in, for though he still reeked more than slightly, his hands and fresh-shaved face were clean of blood and dirt. He was dressed in the colors of court mourning, in the light fabrics of this northern summer: black boots, black linen trousers, a sleeveless black tunic set off with thin lines of lavender piping, a lilac brocade sash with black tassels wrapped about his waist. In the hot noon, he had dispensed with the weight of the lavender vest-cloak, though an anxious Goram hovered with the garment folded over his arm. Goram had arranged his master's hair in the pulled-back, elegant braiding in which Ista had first seen it; the frosted black queue down the back was tied with a lavender cord. Illvin straightened as he saw her and gave her a sketch of a courtier's bow, truncated, she suspected, by bloodless dizziness.

"What is this?" she asked suspiciously.

"What, I had not thought you slow of wit, dear Royina. What does it look like?"

"You are not going with me."

He smiled down at her. "It would reflect exceedingly oddly upon the honor of Porifors to send the dowager royina of all Chalion-Ibra into captivity without even one attendant."

"That's what *I* said," grumbled Liss.

"The command of the fortress has fallen to you," Ista protested. "Surely you cannot leave it now."

"Porifors is a shambles. There is little in here left to defend, and not enough men left standing to defend it with, though I would prefer to conceal that fact from Sordso for a while yet. The parley for your transfer this morning has bought us hours of precious delay, which we could not have purchased with blood. So if this is to be Porifors's last sortie, I claim it by right. By the unfortunate logic of the situation, in my *last* bad idea, I could not ride along to correct my strategy in midleap. But such logic does not prevail here."

"Your riding would not have changed the outcome."

"I know."

Disconcerted, she studied him. "Do you, in some fey mood, seek to outdo your brother?"

"I never could before; I see no need to try now. No." He took her hand and made little soothing circles on her palm with his thumb. "In my youth, I was apprenticed to my god's order, but I missed the whisper of my calling. I will not miss that calling twice. Well, I scarcely see how I can, when it smacks me on the side of the head and bellows, *Attend!* in a voice to bring down the rafters. I spent the years of my manhood aimlessly, though well enough in my brother's service, for the lack of a better direction. I have a better direction now."

"For an hour, perhaps."

"An hour will suffice. If it is the right hour."

Arhys's forlorn page padded into the stone court, and cried from the foot of the stairs, "Royina? They are come for you now at the postern gate."

"I come," she called down gently to him. She hesitated, frowning at Illvin. "Will the Jokonans even let you go along with me?"

"They will be glad enough to have another prisoner of rank, at no further cost to themselves. It is also the perfect disguise by which I might scout their camp and number their forces."

"How much scouting do you think you can do as a prisoner?" She squinted at him. "What are you disguised *as*?"

His lips twitched. "A coward, dear Ista. As they believe we betray you in terror to save our property, so they will think I have attached myself to you to save my skin."

"I don't think they are going to think any such thing."

"So much the better for my poor reputation, then."

She blinked, beginning to feel light-headed. "If I fail, they will make demon food of you. A very banquet for some Jokonan officer-sorcerer. Maybe Sordso himself."

"Ah, but if you succeed, Royina! Have you given thought to what you will do after?"

She looked away uncomfortably from that dark, intent gaze. "After is not my task."

"Just as I thought," he said in a tone of triumph. "And you accuse *me* of being fey! I rest my argument. Shall we go?"

She found her hand disposed upon his arm while she was still trying to decide if she was convinced or just confused.

He handed her down the stairs as though they advanced together in some procession, a wedding or a coronation or a feast day, or onto a dance floor in a roya's palace.

The illusion ended soon enough as they picked their way across the charnel wreckage of the star court—two more horses lay dead and swelling there this morning—through the shadow of the archway, and into the disorder of the entry court. A dozen men clustered on the walls in view of whatever Jokonan embassy waited without, very nearly the whole of the garrison who *could* stand.

Two short, round towers bulged outward on either end of the front wall of the forecourt, allowing a covering cross fire upon the outer gate. A few more soldiers, and a broad, familiar figure in unfamiliar clothes, waited by the leftward tower that harbored the postern door. Ista and Illvin, trailed by Goram and Liss, came to a halt there.

"Learned." Ista favored dy Cabon with a nod. He had shed his order's distinctive robes, not that his filthy whites hadn't been ripe enough to burn by now, and was dressed in a hodgepodge of borrowed gear that mostly failed to fit him. In any color but white, Ista noted.

"Royina." He swallowed. "Before you go . . . I meant to beg your blessing."

"We are well met, then; before I went, I meant to beg yours."

She stood on tiptoe, leaned over his sadly reduced belly, and kissed his forehead. If the god light passed any message to him, it was too subtle even for her inner eye to read. He swallowed and placed his hand upon her brow. Whatever ceremonious benediction he'd mustered escaped him as he burst into tears: he managed only a choked "Bastard help us!"

"Sh, sh," Ista soothed his agitation. "It is well." Or as well as might be, under the circumstances. She studied him narrowly. His sleepless hours with the spell-sickened, with their impossible demands made upon skills he didn't even possess, had shaken him badly. The bloody rite on the north tower had been even more harrowing. His god, she thought, had sapped and mined his soul very nearly to the point of breakthrough, stressing him close to cracking open, little though he realized it. The gods had either been unusually lucky in driving two such mules down the road to Their task at Porifors, or else had been trying exceptionally hard . . . *I wonder if dy Cabon is Their second sortie?*

Five gods—was it possible to pray that her burden might pass to him instead? The notion shook her, and she blinked to clear her vision. She had a hideous conviction that the answer was *yes. Yes. Yes!* Let the responsibility for disaster pass to another, not to her, not to her *again* . . .

Except that dy Cabon's chances of surviving success, let alone failure, seemed to her even less than her own. She fought back an impulse to fling herself upon him and beg him to take her place. *No.*

I have paid for this place. I am emptied out with the cost of it. I will not give it up for any man.

"Buck up, dy Cabon, or else take yourself off," Illvin muttered, scowling. "Your weeping is unnerving her."

Dy Cabon swallowed again, marshaling his self-control. "Sorry. Sorry. I am so sorry that my mistakes brought you here, Royina. I should never have stolen your pilgrimage. It was presumption."

"Yes, well, if not you, the gods would have just had to send someone else to make the mistakes." *Who might have failed upon the road.* "If you would serve *me*, live to testify. Your order will need to know all the truth of this, one way or another."

He nodded eagerly, then paused, as if finding her offer of release harder to digest than he'd expected. He bowed and stood back, brow wrinkled.

Illvin removed his sword and passed it to Goram. "Hold this for me till I return. No point in handing my father's blade to Sordso for a present, unless it be point first." Goram ducked a nod and tried to look stern, but his features just came out looking contorted.

Ista embraced Liss, who, with a glower at dy Cabon, managed not to cry at her. Then Illvin was handing her through the dark, close space under the tower. The door opened to the light, and a soldier grunted and heaved at something that fell with a muffled thump, then turned aside to let the two of them pass.

The object turned out to be a narrow board, which he had thrown across the sharp cleft before the castle wall. Illvin hesitated, and Ista wondered if he thought of all the random breakage Porifors had suffered in the day past, and if this makeshift bridge was likewise vilely ensorcelled. But he cast her a quick, encouraging smile over his shoulder and stepped briskly across it. It bent disturbingly, in the center of its span, but held.

Ista glanced across at the Jokonan embassy drawn up before the gate to accept her surrender. Some dozen horsemen were assembled—mostly soldiers, together with three officers. Ista recognized Prince Sordso instantly. The translator-officer rode nervously by his side. The other officer, a heavy, leathery, bronze-skinned man with gray-bronze hair, was also a sorcerer-slave, Ista saw by the ascendant demon light that filled his skin. As with Sordso, a twisting ribbon of light floated from his belly back toward the distant green tents.

Also tethered thus was the one horsewoman, or rather, a woman who rode pillion Roknari-style behind a servant, sitting sideways on a padded chair atop the horse's haunches with her feet demurely disposed on a little shelf. The sorceress wore courtly, trailing garments, and a broad-brimmed hat tied below her chin with dark green ribbons. She was a much younger woman than Joen, though neither maidenly nor beautiful. She stared intently at Ista.

Ista stepped out after Illvin, keeping her eyes upon his face and not the dark drop below, which was deliberately lined at the bottom with sharp rocks and glinting broken glass. Cattilara's sandals slipped on her sweating feet. Illvin reached to clasp her hand, a hard grip, and pulled her to stand upon the dusty ground beyond. Instantly, the board was jerked back, scraping through the postern door, which was then clapped shut.

The woman rode closer. Even as Ista looked up to return her glower, the demon light within her faded, until Ista only saw skin and clothing. The mere expression of a face, not the colors of a soul. Ista's breath caught, and she looked again at Sordso. Now he appeared no more than a golden-haired young man upon a prancing black horse. Not one of the sorcerers flung up their hands, wincing at the glare of Ista's god light, nor did the demons cringe within them—she *could not see* the demons within them.

My inner sight is stolen. I am blinded.

Something else was missing. The pressure of the god upon her back, which had borne her forward floating as if in a dream since that bloodstained dawn upon the north tower, was gone as well. Behind her, only an empty silence loomed. Infinitely empty, since so infinitely filled just moments before. She tried frantically to think when she had last felt the god's hands upon her shoulders. She was certain He had been with her in the forecourt, when she had spoken with dy Cabon. She *thought* He had been with her when she'd stepped onto the board across the cleft.

He was not with me when I stepped off.

Her useless outer eyes blurred with terror and loss. She could barely breathe, as though her chest was bound tight with heavy cords. *What have I done wrong?*

~Who is this?~ asked Prince Sordso, pointing at Illvin.

The bronze-skinned sorcerer pushed his horse up next to the prince's and stared down in surprise at Illvin, who looked back coolly. ~I believe it is Ser Illvin dy Arbanos himself, Your Highness—Lord Arhys's bastard brother, the bane of our borders.~

Sordso's blond eyebrows went up. ~The new commander of Porifors! What does he here? Ask him where is the other woman.~ He gestured at his translator.

The officer rode nearer to Illvin. "You, dy Arbanos! The agreement was for the dowager royina and the daughter of the march of Oby," he said in Ibran. "Where is Lady Catti-lara dy Lutez?"

Illvin favored him with a slight, ironic bow. His eyes were icy black. "Gone to join her husband. When, watching last night from the tower, she felt him die, she flung herself from the parapet and gave her grief to the stones below. She lies now waiting to be buried, when you withdraw as you agreed and we can again reach our graveyards. I come in her place, and to serve Royina Ista as warder and attendant. Since, having seen your armies and their dubious discipline once before, the royina did not desire to bring her hand-maidens among you."

The translator's brows drew down, and not only at the oblique trailing insult. He repeated the news to Sordso and the others. The sorceress nudged her rider to bring her closer. ~Is this true?~ she demanded.

~Look yourselves for what you really seek, then,~ said Ill-vin, with a bow in her direction. ~I should think Prince Sor-dso could recognize the remnants of his own sister Umerue from this distance, if she were still . . . well, *alive* is not quite the right term, now, is it? If she were still residing within Lady Cattilara behind those walls.~

The translator jerked in his saddle, though whether in surprise at Illvin's message or at the tongue in which it was spoken, Ista was not sure. Sordso, the bronze-skinned offi-cer, and the sorceress all turned their heads toward Porifors, their expressions growing intent and inward.

~Nothing,~ breathed Sordso after a moment. ~It is gone.~

The sorceress eyed Illvin. ~That one knows too much.~

~My poor sister-in-law is dead, and the creature *you* lost is fled beyond your reach,~ said Illvin. ~Shall we get this over with?~

At a nod from the prince, two soldiers dismounted. They first took the precaution of checking Illvin for concealed blades in his sash and boots; he suffered their hands with a look of bored displeasure. Tension flowed into his long body when one of the soldiers approached Ista, relaxing only slightly when the man knelt by her white skirts.

"You are to take off your shoes," the translator called to

her. "You will walk barefoot and bareheaded into the presence of the August Mother, as befitting a lesser woman and a Quintarian heretic."

Illvin's chin went up and his jaw set. Whatever objections he had been about to voice, though, he closed his teeth upon. It was an interesting subtlety, Ista thought, that they did not also demand Illvin's boots. The disparity only drove home his impotence to protect her.

The man's hot hands pawed at the ribbons Liss had so lately tied around Ista's ankles. She stood rigidly, but did not resist. He pulled the light sandals away from her feet and threw them aside. He stood, backed away, and remounted his horse.

Sordso rode up to her, his eyes searching her from head to foot. He smiled grimly at what he saw—or possibly at what he didn't see. In any case, he did not fear to turn his back on her, for he gestured her sharply to take position directly behind his horse in the procession forming up. Illvin tried to offer her his arm, but the bronze-skinned officer pulled his sword and pointed with it for him to walk behind her. Sordso's hand rose and fell in signal, and they started off across the dry, uneven ground.

Ista was barely conscious of the brass-bright noon through which she stumbled. She groped inside her mind, within an echoing darkness. Called silent curses to the Bastard. Then, silent prayers. Nothing came back.

Were the Jokonan sorcerers doing this? Defeating a god in the realm of matter? Surely *these* opponents could not overwhelm *this* god . . . ?

Not the god's failure, then, but hers; her spirit gates had somehow been shut again, broken and tumbled in, choked with stones of fear, anger, or humiliation, denying the new-dilated passage . . .

She had made a mistake, some monstrous mistake, somewhere in the past few fleeting minutes. Maybe she had been supposed to give this task, to give the god, to dy Cabon after all. Maybe keeping it for herself had been the great presumption, a huge and fatal presumption. Overweening arrogance, to imagine such a task was given to *her*. Who would be stupid enough to give such a task to *her*?

The gods. Twice. It was a puzzle, how beings so vast could be so vastly mistaken. *I knew better than to trust them. Yet here I am—again* . . .

Sharp stones bit her feet along the road. The procession turned aside toward the grove, angling through a low space of dark muck that sucked at the horses' hooves and stank of stagnant water and horse piss. They scrambled up a slight rise. She could hear Illvin's long footfalls behind her, and his quickening breath, his uneven puffing revealing more of his debilitation than his face ever would. The grove loomed before her, its shade a blessed relief from the hammering sun overhead.

Ah. Not so blessed after all, nor any relief. They marched up past an aisle of the dead. Laid quite deliberately along the left side of their route, as if made witnesses to this procession, were the bodies of the men of Porifors killed last night in Arhys's sortie. All were stripped naked, their wounds exposed to feed the iridescent green flies that buzzed about them.

She glanced up the row of pale forms, counted. Eight. Eight, of the fourteen who had ridden out against fifteen hundreds. Six must still live somewhere in the Jokonan camp, then, wounded and taken. Foix's muscular body was not among the still forms. Pejar's was.

She looked again, and recalculated: *five still live*.

There was a ninth here, but not a body. More of a . . . pile. A spear was driven into the ground behind the shambles, with Arhys's disfigured head displayed atop the shaft, peering out sightlessly over the Jokonan camp. The once-ravishing eyes had been cut out by whatever fear-maddened soldier had sought revenge upon the emptied form.

Too late. He was gone before you got there, Jokonan. Her bare feet faltered over some root, and she gasped in pain.

Illvin, striding forward, caught her arm before she tripped and fell headlong.

"They bait us. Look away," he instructed through clenched teeth. "Do not faint. Or vomit."

He looked ready to do both, she thought. His countenance was as gray as any of the corpses', though his eyes burned like nothing she had ever seen in a man's face.

"It's not that," she whispered back. "I have lost the god."

His brows flickered in consternation and confusion. The bronze-skinned officer, his sword out, gestured them along toward the far edge of the grove, though he did not force Illvin from her side. Maybe she, too, looked as though she were about to faint.

She thought Illvin's judgment of *baiting* to be precise. If either of them had still concealed any uncanny power—or any strength at all—that display might well have drawn it out of them, in some furious, futile lashing at their complacent enemies. If she had been either a sorceress or a swordsman, she swore the prince would not have survived the smirk he had cast over his shoulder as she'd stumbled past Arhys's remains. From a failed saint, the Jokonans were quite safe, it seemed.

"They meant to march Catti past that," Illvin muttered under his breath. "Add it to their tally, and five gods grant I may be the one to come collect . . ." His eyes didn't stop glancing from tent to tent, tracing the path of last night's destruction, summing the condition of the men and horses that they passed. Thin silver tracks slid down his face, but his hand scorned to wipe at them, under the gaze of the few dozen jeering soldiers crowded up to watch their little parade. Ista did not know enough vile Roknari to translate the insults, though Illvin no doubt did. His dogged mutter continued, "They're not preparing to strike camp. They're preparing an assault. Are we surprised? Ha. One thing shows—they don't know how weak we've grown. Or they'd be preparing for a romp . . ."

Was he trying to distract his senses from the Jokonan desecration of his brother's corpse? She prayed the ploy might serve him. She tried to extend her own blinded senses for any breath of the god, anywhere. Nothing. Joen and Sordso had placed Arhys's head along her path to be a symbol of her failure, a hammerblow of despair. *I wonder if Arvol dy Lutez felt as bereft as this, when his dangling hair touched the water for the second time?*

And yet the symbol turned beneath her enemies' feet, for the reminder of defeat was also a reminder of triumph. A presence in an absence. *Strange.*

The god may be absent, but I am still present. Maybe this is a task for dense matter, to do what matter does best: persist. So. She took a breath and kept on walking.

They arrived before the largest of the green tents. One side was rolled up, revealing what appeared to be nothing so much as a portable throne room. Rugs were strewn thickly across the ground. A dais ran along the back, supporting a pair of carved chairs decorated in gold leaf, and a scattering of cushions for lesser haunches. The pious dark green of staid and stern maternal widowhood was everywhere, overpowering even the sea-green of Jokonan arms, and never had Ista loathed the color more.

Dowager Princess Joen, dressed in a different but equally elaborate layering of stiff gowns from when they had—five gods, was it only this time yesterday that they had met upon the road?—sat in the smaller, lower of the two chairs. Her woman attendants knelt upon the cushions, and a drab, moonfaced young woman who might be another daughter crouched at her feet. Ista could not tell how many of them were sorceresses. A dozen officers stood at painful attention along each side. Ista wondered if all eleven of Joen's surviving leashed demons were present for this . . . demonstration.

Twelve. Foix stood rigidly among the Jokonan officers. His face was bruised and cut, but cleaned, and he was dressed anew in Jokonan garb and a green tabard with white pelicans flying. His expression was dazed, his weird smile forced and unnatural. Ista didn't even need her lost sight to be certain that a glittering new snake floated from the woman on the dais to him, and that its fangs were sunk deeply into his belly. Illvin's eyes, too, passed across Foix; and his jaw set, if possible, even more tightly.

The possibilities for more cruel baiting were endless. Fortunately, perhaps, time was not. The bronze-haired officer gestured Ista forward to the middle of the carpets, to the center of this brief set piece of power, facing Joen. Illvin was stopped at sword's point a few paces back, behind Ista's right shoulder, and she was more sorry that she could not see him than that he could see her. She wondered what final stamp of humiliation had been prepared for her.

Oh. Of course. Not humiliation. Control. The humiliation out there had been to gratify Sordso's sortie-stung troops. The woman in here was more practical.

Ista blinked, seeing Joen for the first time without inner sight, without the vast dark menace of the demon glowering from her belly like some pitch-black pit into which one might fall forever. Without her demon, she was just . . . a little, sour, aging woman. Unable to command respect or compel loyalty; easy to escape. Small. Five gods, but she was small, all her possibilities shrunken in upon herself: her only recourse, force. Stubborn will without scope of mind.

Ista's mother had once filled her household with her authority from wall to wall. The Provincara's husband had ruled Baocia, but within his own castle even he had lived on her sufferance. Ista's eldest brother, upon inheriting his father's seat, had found it easier to move his capital to escape the permanent childhood that awaited him in his mother's house than to attempt to claim rule there. Yet even at her direst, the old Provincara had known her limits, and had chosen no space larger than what she could fill.

Joen, it seemed to Ista, was trying to fill Jokona with her authority as a woman filled a household, and by the same techniques; and *no one* could stretch herself that far. In an unbounded world of infinite space, one might move at will, but perforce must leave room for the wills of others. Not even the gods controlled it all. Men enslaved each other's bodies, but the silent will of the soul was sacred and inviolable to the gods if anything was. Joen was seizing her slaves from the inside out. What Joen did to her enemies might be named war; what she did to her own people was sacrilege.

Prince Sordso took his high seat, flinging himself into the chair with a habit of body not yet eradicated by his new demonic discipline. He grimaced around the chamber. His mother's gaze fell on him, and he sat up straight, attentive.

Ista's eye was drawn again to the moonfaced princess at Joen's feet. The girl seemed to be about fourteen, but stunted for her age, with the stubby fingers and odd eyes of one of those late-life children born sadly lack-witted, and who often did not live long. She was one princess who would not escape her mother's household via marriage to some distant country. Joen's hand fell upon her head, although not in a caress, and it came to Ista: *She's using the girl for a demon repository. Her own disdained daughter's soul is made a stall for it.*

The demon that she intends next to set in me.

Joen stood up, facing Ista. In heavily accented Ibran, she said, "Welcome to my gates, Ista dy Chalion. I am the Mother of Jokona." Her hand lifted from the girl's head, flicked out, fingers spreading.

Within Ista, the god unfolded.

Her second sight burst anew upon Ista's mind like a dazzling lightning stroke, brilliant beyond hope, revealing an eerie landscape. She saw it all, at one glance: the dozen demons, the swirling, crackling lines of power, the agonized souls, Joen's dark, dense, writhing passenger. The thirteenth demon, spinning wildly through the air toward her, trailing its evil umbilicus.

Ista opened her jaws in a fierce grin, and took it in a gulp.

"Welcome to mine, Joen of Jokona," said Ista. "I am the Mouth of Hell."

26

A WAVE OF LIGHT PASSED ALONG THE DEEP VIOLET CORD between Joen and Ista, and its color and brilliance seemed to intensify. Was Joen's first shocked impulse to strengthen her line? For a dizzy instant, Ista wondered who was the fisherwoman and who the fish. Then she felt the struggling, panicked young demon pass firmly into the Bastard's hands, within her.

You have hooked a god, Joen. Now what shall you do? It was as though a galley had thrown a grappling hook onto a continent, thinking to tow it away.

"She bears the demon-god!" Joen screamed. "Kill her now!"

Yes. That would do . . .

Yet even as Joen cried out, time seemed to stretch in Ista's perceptions like cold honey spinning off a spoon on a winter morning. She did not think it would stretch indefinitely.

Where should I begin? Ista asked the Presence within her.

Begin at the center, It replied. *The rest will follow perforce.*

She opened her material hands and let her spirit hands

flow out along the violet cable. Enter Joen's body through that channel. Wrap the dark mass, and pull it out toward her. It came resisting, surging and spitting, streaming corrosive violet shadows like water spilling. It burned her spirit hands like vitriol, and she gasped with the unexpected pain, which seemed to strike down into the center of her being and pulse back out to every extremity, the way the shock of a great wound reverberated in a body. The creature was very dense, and ugly. And large. And old, centuries old, rotten with time.

It is hideous.

Yes, said the god. *Go on anyway. Finish Arhys's ride.*

Ista's material hands were too sluggish to keep up with her streaming will. With her spirit hands alone, she combed back the strands of Joen's soul tangled with the demon. Yet as fast as she did so, Joen flung out tendrils of cold white fire to wrap the demon round again and pull it back. The demon shrieked.

Let go, Ista urged. *Let it go, and turn to some better task. Even now, you have a choice.*

No! Joen's mind returned. *It is my gift, my great chance! No one shall wrest it from me, least of all you! You were so feckless, you couldn't even keep your own son alive! Mine shall have his place; I have promised it!*

Ista flinched, but the Presence sustained her. *If she will not stay, she must come,* It said. *Continue.*

Your wrongful attempts to impose order create yet vaster destruction, said Ista to Joen. *You torment and demolish the very souls you most desire to make grow and love you. You possess truer gifts, stunted though they have been. Let go, find them instead, and live.*

The whipping white fire was a visible scream of denial. In it Ista could discern not the faintest whisper of assent.

So.

Ista brought the great violet-black demon to her lips, and pulled it inward. It seemed to stretch and distort in its passage, its screeching becoming pain in her mouth, fire in her gullet. *There are souls inside it,* she realized. *Many pieces of old souls, all digested and smeared together. Souls of the dead, and the long dead. What is to be done about them?*

The dead belong to Us; sorting them is beyond your calling. The souls of the yet living, torn apart untimely while still trapped in the realm of matter, those are your care on Our behalf.

And this? Ista asked. Joen's live white soul-fire, tangled with the demon, was passing into her now. It clawed and burned.

Comes out of your hands and into Mine.

This is not the quiet damnation of sundering. Indeed, the white fire seemed to howl, splitting Ista's ears from within. *Neither is this heaven's healing.*

No, said the Voice regretfully. *This is will-not. So it shall pass with its demon to the place of be-not.*

Ista had a vision of a strange, dimensionless void, the picture leaked, perhaps, from His mind to hers: a roiling pool of demon energy, without form, without personas, without minds or wills or song or speech or memories or any gift of higher order—the Bastard's hell. Reservoir of pure destruction. Spilling from that pool into the world of matter, a thin controlled flow. Returning to it, an erratic stream. Balancing the life of the world exactly midway between the hot death that is chaos and the chill death that is stasis. She realized at last why the concatenation of Joen's demons had made her edgy, on a level separate from their direct threat to Porifors. Was it possible that such a vortex of disorder might create its own rip between the two realms, one that even the gods might be hard-pressed to mend again? So much divine attention in one small place . . .

Some human attention now would gratify Me greatly, the Voice murmured. It did not, Ista noticed, either confirm or deny her guess. *Bring me in the rest of my little brethren, sweet Ista, as swiftly as you may. It will no doubt take practice before it comes easily.*

So therefore my first trial is a dozen at once? The pain flaring in her stomach felt as though she had been forced to swallow molten lead. *Along with that sickening, twisted thing?*

Well, said the Voice affably, *there is this; if you survive this, no other demon astray in the realm of matter should pose too onerous a challenge to you hereafter . . .*

Ista considered a wealth of objections starting with *What do you mean, if?* but abandoned the impulse. Starting an argument with this Presence was likely to do nothing but spin her in endless circles till she was dizzy, and make Him laugh.

You will not abandon me again? she asked suspiciously.

I did not abandon you before. . . . nor you Me, as I have marked. Persistent Ista.

She turned her second sight outward again. Trying to see the god with it had been as futile as trying to see the back of her own head. Joen's mouth was open, her eyes rolling back, her body slumping. Somewhere under Ista's breastbone, the first burst of pain was diminishing, as the god drew the ancient demon and its clawing mistress back into His realm. Following after it, but now running to her and not to Joen, a dozen tangled, writhing cords of light jerked and yanked, as the demons fettered upon them tried to flee the feared presence of their god. The human bodies in which they were lodged were only just beginning to move under their riders' frantic lashings.

One at a time or all together? Ista reached out with her spirit hands and plucked one cord at random, and slid her light-palms along it to the demon within one of Joen's attendant women. This one was well cultivated, with parts of three or four different souls whirling within it. The white soul-fire of the living host was more readily discernible, and she combed it back toward the woman, imperfectly. Ista swallowed the demon. The woman's back arched, and she began to collapse. The demon passed through into the god's hands more easily this time, almost immediately.

These cords. I recognize them. I pulled Arhys safe to shore last night with something very like one.

They were stolen from Us, long ago. The demon could not have created them, you know. The Voice was edged with wrath, though only the faintest reflection of it glimmered through to Ista, else she would have been crushed flat.

Ista reached for another cord, repeating the gesture of plucking and combing. It was a man, one of the officers; his mouth opened on a beginning scream. *I'm not getting it all sorted,* she worried. *I'm not getting it right.*

You are brilliant, the Voice reassured her.

It is imperfect.

So are all things trapped in time. You are brilliant, nonetheless. How fortunate for Us that We thirst for glorious souls rather than faultless ones, or We should be parched indeed, and most lonely in Our perfect righteousness. Carry on imperfectly, shining Ista.

Another, then, and another. The demons flowed to her, through her, faster, but it was an undeniably sloppy process. The next demon was Sordso's, and it was the most complex construct Ista had yet encountered. Layer upon layer of souls and their talents were interpenetrated with the young man's agonized, constricted soul-fire. It was a weirdly loving fabrication. Ista thought she perceived bits of soldiers, scholars, judges, swordsmen, and ascetics. All the Golden General's public virtues, collected and concentrated: the purified pattern of perfect manliness. It was horrifying. How could something made of souls be so coldly soulless?

No poets, though. None at all.

This dark piece of soul here is different, she realized, as one fragment began to flow through her fingers.

Yes, said the god. *The man still lives, in the realm of matter.*

Where? Is it . . . ? Should I attempt to . . . ?

Yes, if you think you can endure it. It will be uncomfortable.

Ista rolled up the patch of darkness and bundled it aside in her mind. It pulsed there, hot and thick. Somewhere off the edge of her material vision, the bronze-skinned Jokonan officer was lifting his sword, beginning to turn. A motion in black was Illvin, beginning to move with—no, after—him.

Ista ignored it all and kept on combing. Sordso's mouth was
opening on a wordless howl, but not, she thought, of a man
bereaved by his dispossession. It might be rage. It might be
triumph. It might be madness.

Then the next cord, then . . . the last.

She glanced upward with both material and inner sight at
the ashen Foix in his green tabard, standing among the startled Jokonan officers. The violet shadow within him was no
longer bear-shaped, but distributed unevenly throughout his
body. It seemed both to cringe from her, and stare in fascination.

She considered the final cord in her spirit hand. Lifted it
to her lips. Bit it through.

Good, said the Voice.

Oh. Should I have asked?

*You are my Door-ward in the realm of matter. A lord's ap-
pointed porter does not run to him to ask if each beggar,
whether in rags or silks, should be admitted or turned away,
else he might as well stand at his gates himself. The porter
is expected to use his judgment.*

My judgment? She let the end of the cord go. It snapped
back into Foix, and he was free. Or . . . whatever Foix was
now, was free.

Foix's face flickered; his lips parted, firmed. Then, after
a bare second, stretched again in that horrible strained smile
of perfect assent. False falseness; treachery turning in air. *He
is much less simple than he looks.*

Ista was barely aware of the cries and turmoil erupting
throughout the tent. The voices grew faint and far off, diminishing, the figures dimmer and dimmer. She turned to
follow the entrancing Voice.

❧

She seemed to come to the door of herself, and look through.
An overwhelming impression of color and beauty, pattern
and complexity, music and song, all endlessly elaborated,

bewildered her senses. She wondered how confusing the world looked to a newborn infant, who had neither names for what she saw nor even the concept of names. The child began, Ista supposed, with her mother's face and breast, and from there worked outward—and in a lifetime could not come to the end of it all.

This is a world greater and stranger than the one of matter that gave my soul birth, and even the world of matter was beyond my comprehension. How now shall I begin?

Well, Ista, said the Voice. *Do you stay or go? You cannot hang forever in My doorway like a cat, you know.*

I have not words for this. I would see Your face.

Abruptly, she was standing in an airy room, very like a chamber in Porifors. She quickly glanced down, and was relieved to discover she was granted not only a body, healed and light and free of pain, but clothes as well—much as she had been wearing but cleansed of stains and mended of rips. She looked up, and rocked back.

This time, He wore Illvin's body and face. It was a healthy, full-fleshed version, if still tall and lean. His courtier's garb was silver embroidered on white, his baldric silk, his sword hilt and signet ring gleaming. His hair, pulled back in Roknari braids and a long, thick queue, was pure white. The infinite depths of His eyes destroyed the illusion of humanity, though, even as their darkness recalled the man.

"I should have liked," she admitted faintly, "to see what Illvin looked like with white hair."

"Then you will have to go back and wait a while," the Bastard replied. His voice was scarcely deeper or richer than the original's; it even adopted those northern cadences. "You would take your chances, of course; by the time all his hair is white, will there be any left?"

His body and face shifted through a hundred possible Illvins at a hundred possible ages, straight or bent, thin or fat, bald or not. The laughter on His lips remained the same, though.

"I desire . . . this." It was unclear even to Ista if her hand gesture indicated the god or the man. "May I come in?"

His smile softened. "The choice is yours, my Ista. As you do not deny Me, I will not deny you. Yet I would still await you, if you chose the long way home."

"I might become lost upon the road." She looked away. A great calm filled her. No pain, no terror, no regret. Their immense absences seemed to leave room for . . . something. Something new, something never dreamed of before. If this was what Arhys had experienced, it was no wonder he'd never looked back. "So this is my death. Why did I ever fear it?"

"Speaking as an expert, you never seemed to Me to fear it all that much," He said dryly.

She looked back. "There may be more to paradise than the cessation of pain, but, oh, it seems almost paradise enough. Might a next time . . . hurt?"

He shrugged. "Once you return to the realm of matter, the protection I can offer you is limited, and its bounds, alas, do not exclude pain. This death is for you to choose. The next may not be."

Her lips curved up despite themselves. "Are you saying I might find myself back at this same gate in another quarter of an hour?"

He sighed. "I do hope not. I should have to train another porter. I quite fancied a royina for a time." The eyes glittered. "So does my great-souled Illvin. He's prayed to Me for you, after all. Consider my reputation."

Ista considered His reputation. "It's dreadful," she observed.

He merely grinned, that familiar, stolen, heart-stopping flash of teeth.

"What training?" she added, feeling suddenly cantankerous. "You never explained anything."

"Instructing you, sweet Ista, would be like teaching a falcon to walk up to its prey. It might with great effort be done, but one would end with a very footsore and cranky bird, and a tedious wait for dinner. With a wingspan like yours, it's ever so much easier just to shake you from my wrist and let you fly."

"Plummet," Ista growled.

"No. Not you. Granted, you tumble and complain halfway down the abyss, but eventually you do spread your wings and soar."

"Not always." Her voice went lower. "Not the first time."

He tilted his head in a sliver of acknowledgment. "But I was not your falconer then. We do suit, you know."

She glanced away, and around the strange, perfect, unreal room. Antechamber, she thought, boundary between the inside and the outside. But which door was which? "My task. Is it done?"

"Done and well-done, my, true, foster, laggard child."

"I have come very late to everything. To forgiveness. To love. To my god. Even to my own life." But she bowed her head in relief. *Done* was good. It meant one could stop. "Did the Jokonans slay me, as Joen ordered?"

"No. Not yet."

Smiling, He stepped up to her and tilted her chin up. He lowered His mouth to hers as boldly as Illvin had, that afternoon—yesterday?—on the tower. Except that His mouth tasted not of horsemeat but of perfume, and there was no uncertainty in His eyes.

His eyes, the world, her perceptions, began to flicker.

Infinite depths became dark eyes reddened with frenzied weeping. Perfume became parched, salt flesh, then fragrance, then flesh. Sweet silence became noise and cries, and then silence, and then din again. Painless floating turned to a crushing pressure, headache, thirst, which melted in turn to bliss.

I think He takes His foot to his cat and pushes her to decision. She had no doubt she might yet dodge around that boot in either direction. But just what direction He desired was plain. The unsettling *Not yet* did at least suggest He did not guide her back toward a body pierced with sword thrusts. *The Bastard maneuvers me into this, blast Him.* It felt very comfortable, cursing her god. He was a god she might always curse, and the more inventive the invective, the more He would grin. Well suited, indeed, to true Ista.

The flickering slowed, stopped, on parched mouth, weight and pressure, din and pain. On dear, distraught, blinking, merely human eyes. *Yes.*

And furthermore, my god cheats. He set out this bowl of cream before ever He held the door, and He knew it well. She smiled, and tried to inhale.

Illvin pulled his frantically questing tongue from her mouth, and gasped, "She lives, oh, five gods, she breathes again!"

The crushing pressure, Ista discovered, was Illvin's arms, wrapped around her torso. She stared up into tree branches, blue sky, and his face, bent over hers. His face was flushed with heat and furrowed with terror, and a thin spattering of blood droplets marked it in an angled track from side to side. She raised a weak hand and dabbed at the red beads, and was relieved to find they did not appear to be his.

She whispered through dry, bruised lips. "What has happened?"

"That is what I prayed you might tell me," said Foix's hoarse voice. She looked up to see him looming over them. He still wore his Jokonan mail and tabard, and stood in a convincingly menacing guard stance above his apparent prisoners. She and Illvin were seated on the ground not far from the green command tents. Foix's eyes were white-rimmed, but it seemed not to be the surrounding Jokonans that disquieted him.

"You were marched into the tent," Foix continued in a lower tone. "You looked . . . ordinary. Helpless. Then suddenly the god light blazed from you, so brightly I was blinded for a breath. I heard Joen cry for your death."

Upon her arm, Illvin's tight clutch tightened further.

"When I could see again," continued Foix, gazing away in guard-pretense, "all the demons in the tent seemed to be rushing into you, like hot metal being drawn through a form. I saw you swallow them all down, Joen's soul as well. It was all over in an instant."

"Save one," murmured Ista.

"Eh. Ur. Yes, there was that. I felt when you freed me from Joen's geas. I almost bolted from the tent then, but I got my wits back just in time. Prince Sordso and some other officers were drawing their swords—five gods, but the scraping seemed to go on forever. Sordso's knuckles were white."

"I tried to get between them and you," Illvin said huskily to Ista. He rubbed at his nose and blinked.

"Yes," said Foix. "Bare-handed. I saw you lunge—a lot of good *that* was going to do. But instead Sordso whirled around and hacked at Joen."

"She was already dead by then," murmured Ista.

"I saw. She was starting to topple, but his edge caught her just in . . . time. Or something. He struck so hard, he spun around and fell backward off the dais. Half the freed sorcerers were running away, but I swear half the rest had the same idea Sordso did. There was one of Joen's women had a dagger out, and was going at the body even as it fell. I'm not sure she knew or cared that it was dead—she just wanted to get in her stroke. Everyone was jostling and yelling and starting in every direction. So I jumped in front of Illvin and you and shouted, 'Back, prisoners!' and brandished my sword."

"Cursed convincingly," muttered Illvin. "I just about tried to leap on you. Except that I had my hands full."

"You fell, Royina. You just . . . turned gray and stopped breathing and crumpled up. I thought you had died, for your soul was gone from my sight, like a lantern blown out. Illvin tried to lift you up, fell down, then scrambled up again—I dared not help—I let him drag you out, pretending to stand guard over him. Most of the Jokonans thought you were dead, too, I think. Slain in your sorcery, some kind of death magic like Fonsa and the Golden General all over again. So, um . . . lie still for a minute, there, till we think what to do next."

It was not a difficult suggestion to follow. Following any other instruction, now that would have been hard. Illvin was staring down into her face, looking like a man whose kisses had just brought his beloved back from the dead and was now too terrified to move least he shed unexpected miracles in all directions. Ista smiled up muzzily at his delicious confusion.

"The demons are all gone," she reported in a vague, dreamy voice, in case they still harbored doubts. "It was what I was sent to do, and I did it. But the Bastard let me come back." To where she was now, it occurred to her—sitting on the hard ground in the midst of an enemy camp surrounded by several hundred very live and agitated Jokonans. *Vile sense of humor.* Hers had been a timeless interlude, but for everyone else, she realized, bare minutes had passed since Joen's sanguinary end. But however dismasted their high command, not all of the enemy officers were going to stay confused for long. It was hard to summon fear of anything, in her lingering bliss, but she managed a flash of mild prudence. "I think we should leave now. Right now."

"Can you walk?" asked Illvin uncertainly.

"Can you?" she asked, curious. Crawling, now, she would believe crawling of him, in his present interestingly debilitated state. He should be in bed, she decided. Hers, by preference.

"No," muttered Foix. "Got to drag her again. Or carry her. Can you go on pretending to be a corpse for a little longer, Royina?"

"Oh, yes," she assured him, and sank back gratefully into Illvin's grip.

Illvin flatly refused to drag her, on the grounds that it would scrape her already-bleeding legs and feet further, but carrying her in his arms proved still beyond his strength. A short argument, in which Ista, as a corpse, declined to participate, resulted in Foix helping Illvin rise to his shaking legs with her butt-upward over his shoulder, her arms and legs dangling down in an appropriately lifeless manner. It reminded her of the ride on Feather. She tried not to smile in memory, on the grounds that it would be out of character for her part. Her white gown was even splashed with blood, a continuation, she suspected, of the same spray that had crossed Illvin's face. She could guess its source, and shuddered.

They staggered away. "Turn left," Foix directed. "Keep walking." More Jokonan soldiers ran up to them; Foix pointed backward with his sword toward the command tents and cried, -Hurry! You are needed!- The soldiers sped away as their apparent-officer directed.

Illvin muttered through his teeth, "Foix, you may speak a glib camp Roknari, but I beg you will leave sentences of more than one syllable to me. That tabard can't cover everything."

"Gladly," Foix returned under his breath. "Go right here. We're almost to the horse lines."

"Do you think they're just going to let us walk up and steal horses?" asked Illvin. His wheeze sounded more curious than objecting. Ista peered upside down through slitted eyes to take in the guards loitering in the shade. Some of the men were standing and staring toward the uproar around the green tents.

"Yes." Foix tapped his green tabard. "I'm a Jokonan officer."

"You're relying on more than that," observed Ista, her tone almost as detached as Illvin's.

"Yes, *why* are you so certain they will not stop and question us?" asked Illvin, a hint of nervousness entering his voice as a few heads turned to follow their progress.

"Did you stop and question Princess Umerue?"

"No, not at first. What has that to do with anything?"

Ista mumbled from Illvin's hip, "I spoke imprecisely, before. There is one sorcerer left in this camp. He's on our side, however. Seemed a good idea. The god did not object."

Illvin tensed, turning to stare, presumably, at Foix.

"Two left," said Foix. "Or a sorcerer and a sorceress. If that is your proper classification, Royina. I am not sure."

"Neither am I. We'll have to ask dy Cabon," she returned agreeably.

"Right," said Foix. "Don't do anything that looks too exciting, though. I'd rather not attempt anything gaudier, and there are limits to mild misdirection."

"Indeed," murmured Illvin.

They trod on for a few more steps.

"Well," said Foix, stopping before the lines, "have you a preference, horse-master?"

"Anything already saddled and bridled."

One choice was made for them. At the end of the line, a tall, ugly chestnut stallion suddenly lifted its head and nickered in excitement. It began shifting its haunches from side to side, disturbing the horses tied not-too-closely to it. Ears pricked, it practically danced as they neared, and raised and lowered its head, snorting.

"Bastard's eyes, Royina, can you shut that stupid monster up?" Foix muttered. "Men are starting to stare."

"Me?"

"It's you it wants."

"Set me down, then."

Illvin did so, letting her slide through his arms to her feet, gazing into her face with a searching look that was, for an instant, as good as a kiss, and holding her upright on his arm. She was very glad for the arm.

She approached the possessed animal, who lowered its head again and laid its face flat to her bloody bodice in what might be submission, love, or dementia. She looked it over in fascination. It still wore the bridle with the deep curb bit. A dozen cuts scored its body, but they were already starting to heal with unnatural speed. "Yes, yes," she murmured soothingly. "It's all right. Where he went, you could not follow. You did what you could. It's all right now." She tried to shake off her dreamy lassitude, saying to Illvin, "I believe I had better ride this one. If you don't want it following after us whinnying its heart out." She stood on tiptoe and glanced along the serrated ridge of its backbone. "Find a saddle, though," she added.

Foix filched a saddle from a pile farther down the line, and Illvin tightened the girths while Foix picked out two more horses.

"What is he called?" she asked Illvin as he cupped his hands to give her a leg up. It seemed a very long way to the ground, typical of his mounts. She disposed her skirts awkwardly in the military saddle, and let Illvin's warm hands guide her ankles to the stirrups. His fingers lingered unhappily over the bruises and cuts on her feet.

Illvin cleared his throat. "I'd really rather not say. It's, um . . . crude. He was never a lady's mount. Actually, he was never any sane person's mount."

"Oh? *You* rode him." She patted the snaky neck; the horse turned its head around and nuzzled her bare foot. "Well, if he is to be a lady's mount from now on, he'd probably better have another name, then. Demon will do."

Illvin cocked his brows up at her, and a little grin flashed across his tense mouth. "Nicely."

He turned to take his own horse in hand, hesitating briefly in order to gather his strength before swinging himself up into the saddle. He settled himself with a betraying grunt of exhaustion. By mutual, unspoken assent, they started off across the bordering field together at a staid walk. Somewhere back in the grove, something had caught fire; Ista could hear the muted roar of flames and men's cries for water. How much pent-up chaos, both natural and unnatural, had been released upon the Jokonans by Joen's death? She did not look back.

"Turn left," Illvin told Foix.

"Don't we want to circle out of sight over that rise to the north?"

"Eventually. There's a gully along here that will hide us sooner. Go slowly, though, it's likely to be patrolled. That's where I'd put men, anyway."

The counterfeit calm held. The sharpening noise of the camp fell behind them, and the empty countryside began to feign the air of some other quiet, drowsy, overwarm afternoon, one not given over to war, sorcery, gods, and madness.

"At the earliest chance," Ista told Illvin, "you must bring Goram to me."

"Whatever you desire, Royina." Illvin looked over the ground they traversed, turning in his saddle.

"Shall we attempt to circle back to Porifors?" asked Foix, following his gaze back over the treetops to the distant stone pile. A curl of dirty smoke still rose from somewhere in it. "I think I might be able to get us in, under cover of darkness."

"No. If we clear the gully, I am going to try to win through to the march of Oby."

"I do not know if the royina can ride that far," said Foix, clearly picturing not just Ista but the pair of them falling from their saddles at any moment. "Or do you think to meet him on the road?"

"He won't be on the road. If he's where I suspect, we've less than ten miles to cover. And if he's not there yet, his scouts will be along soon."

They dropped into the gully, where they found Illvin's predicted Jokonan patrol almost immediately. Between the unexpected direction of their passage, Foix's officer's garb and wit-fogging sorcery, their horses' Jokonan gear, and Illvin's crisp, arrogant court Roknari, they soon left the pickets bowing and scraping in their wake. Illvin returned the hapless soldiers the fourfold Quadrene sign, touching his thumb to his tongue in secret apology to the fifth god as soon as they turned again out of sight. They pressed their horses to a faster pace.

Illvin led them onward, finding what cover the country afforded in low places, little watercourses, spinneys, and groves, angling ever north and east. They had gone some four or five miles before they even stopped to water themselves and the horses. Though multiple columns of smoke still smudged the clear blue air behind them, Porifors had disappeared from sight beyond some low, rolling ridges.

"Can you still feel your bear?" Ista asked Foix, when he'd finished dipping his head in the stream.

He sat back on his haunches and frowned. "Not quite as I did before. Joen did something to us. I hope it was not vile."

"It is my impression," said Ista carefully, "that you two have been pressed together by all these events more quickly than you would have grown on your own. Without either of you becoming ascendant or enslaved, you have merged. Because, I think, your demon did not steal your soul, nor did you plunder its power. You both shared freely."

Foix looked embarrassed. "Always did enjoy feeding the animals . . ."

"Drawing you apart is beyond my present skills—or your present need. You have achieved a curious theological state, but not, I suspect, a unique one. I have occasionally wondered where Temple sorcerers came from. Now I know. I expect it was one of the saint of Rauma's tasks to judge who might carry this power without succumbing to it. You will need to take training from the Bastard's Order, probably. I am sure your own order will spare you, if I request it."

Foix's face screwed up. "Me, a Bastard's acolyte? Don't think my father will be best pleased. Or my mother. I can just see her, explaining it to her lady friends. Ouch." He grinned despite himself. "Can't wait to see the look on *Ferda's* face, though . . ." He glanced shrewdly at her. "And will you take training, too, Royina?"

She smiled. "Tutors, Foix. A woman of my rank can demand tutors, to wait on me at my convenience. I think my convenience will be very soon, and possibly not too convenient to them."

The reminder of Ferda and the hope of finding news of his brother overcame Foix's initial urge to coddle Ista, and it was he who marshaled the horses and boosted his companions back aboard.

"Roll up that tabard and stuff it in a saddlebag," Illvin advised, settling into his saddle. "Bastard willing, the next scouts we encounter may well be dy Oby's. Baby Temple sorcerer or no, a mistaken crossbow bolt would not be good for your health."

"Ah. Yes," said Foix, and hastened to do so.

Illvin eyed his red stallion, carrying Ista with such exquisite care that she might hold a cup of water without spilling it, and shook his head in wonder, as if of all the marvels he had lately witnessed this was the most inexplicable. "Can you endure?" he asked her. "It's not much farther now."

"After walking *that* mile, riding a few more is nothing," she assured him. "I feared the god had abandoned me, but it seems He'd only hid Himself within." *And left me to carry Him.* It was one of the Bastard's little jokes, she decided, that He had appeared to her before then as such an enormous man. Had He known? Even she, who had now met three face-to-face, could not guess the limits of the gods' foreknowledge.

"All dark, you were," Foix said. "Makes sense. The Jokonan sorcerers would hardly have towed you into Joen's presence looking like some holy fire ship. They weren't that stupid. But when you lit up . . ." He fell silent. Foix was not, Ista thought, an inarticulate man; but she began to see why Lord dy Cazaril said only poetry could come to grips with the gods. Foix finally managed, "I have never seen anything like it. I'm glad that I did. But if I never see anything like it again, that will be all right."

"I could not see it," said Illvin, in a tone of deep regret. "But I could see when things begin to happen, well enough."

"*I* am glad you were there," said Ista.

"I did little enough," he sighed.

"You bore witness. That means the world to me. And there was that kiss. It did not seem such a small thing."

He blushed. "My apologies, Royina. I was distraught. I thought to draw you back from death, as you once seemed to do for me."

"Illvin?"

"Yes, Royina?"

"You did draw me back."

"Oh." He rode along very quietly for a time. But a strange smile crept across his face, and would not go away again.

At length he looked up and rose in his stirrups, summoning some unimaginable reserve of energy. "Hah," he whispered. Ista followed his glance. It took her a moment to discern the faint clear smokes of careful fires, marking a camp concealed in the watercourse that opened below them. The fires were not few. They followed the ridge around a slight bend, and yet more of the camp came into view. Hundreds of men and horses, more than hundreds—she could not count their numbers, half-hidden as they were.

"Oby," said Illvin in satisfaction. "He made excellent time. Though I thank the gods he was no faster."

"Good," breathed Ista in relief. "I'm done."

"Indeed, and we do thank you for your work, without which we would all be dead in some hideous and uncanny fashion by now. I, on the other hand, still have fifteen hundred ordinary Jokonans to remove from around Porifors. I don't know if Oby meant to wait for dawn, but if we struck more quickly . . ." His eyes glazed over in a familiar fashion, alternating shrewd glances summing the men below with staring off at nothing; Ista forbore to interrupt.

A patrol galloped up to them. "Ser dy Arbanos!" cried its astonished officer, waving wildly at Illvin. "Five gods, you're alive!" The riders formed around them in excited escort and swept them into the part of the camp, marked by tents in the shade, where their commanders had no doubt set up their headquarters.

A voice rang from the trees, and a familiar form shot from the green shadows. "Foix! Foix! The Daughter be thanked!" Ferda ran toward them; Foix swung from his saddle to embrace his eager brother.

"What are these men?" Illvin inquired of dy Oby's officer, nodding toward an unfamiliar company of horsemen in

black and green. The riders opened out to reveal a crowd of
people approaching on foot, some running, some lumbering,
some proceeding more slowly and decorously, all calling out
to Ista.

Ista stared, torn between joy and dismay. "Bastard spare
me, it is my brother dy Baocia," she said in a stunned voice.
"And dy Ferrej, and Lady dy Hueltar, and Divine Tovia, and
all."

27

LORD DY BAOCIA AND SER DY FERREJ LED THE RUSH TO Ista's side. The red stallion laid his ears back, squealed, and snapped his teeth, and both men recoiled several feet.

"Five gods, Ista," dy Baocia cried, temporarily diverted, "that *horse*! Who was mad enough to put you up on such a beast?"

Ista patted Demon's neck. "He suits me very well. He belongs to Lord Illvin, in part, but I suspect he may become a permanent loan."

"From both his masters, it seems," murmured Illvin. He glanced across the camp. "Royina—Ista—love, I must report first to March dy Oby." His expression grew grim. "His daughter is still trapped in Castle Porifors, if the walls hold as I pray."

Along with Liss and dy Cabon, Ista reflected, and added her silent prayers to his. She felt the walls yet held, but in truth her only certainty was that Goram still lived; and she'd been mistaken before.

"With the news we bring," Illvin continued, "I expect his troop will ride within the hour. I cringe to think what rumors have come to him by now of my brother's fate. There is much to do."

"Five gods speed you. Of your many burdens, I am one the less now. These people here will cosset me to distraction, if I know them." She added sternly, "You spare some care for yourself, too. Don't make me come after you again."

A grin ghosted across his mouth. "Would you follow me to the Bastard's hell, dear sorceress?"

"Without hesitation, now that I know the road."

He leaned across his saddlebow and caught her hand, and raised it to his lips. She gripped his hand in turn and bore it to her own lips, and nipped his knuckle secretly, which made his eyes glint. With reluctance, they released each other.

"Foix," Illvin called, "attend upon me. Your testimony is urgently required."

Dy Baocia turned eagerly to Foix. "Do I have you to thank, young man, for the rescue of my sister?"

"No, Provincar," said Foix, giving him a polite salute. "She rescued me."

Dy Baocia and dy Ferrej stared at him rather blankly. Ista became conscious of the bizarre picture they must present: Foix, gray with exhaustion, wearing Jokonan gear; Illvin a hollow-eyed, reeking scarecrow in the most elegant of court mourning; herself in rumpled white festival dress splashed with brown blood, barefoot, bruised, and scratched, her escaping hair completing the impression of general dementia.

"Look after the royina," Foix said to Ferda, "then come to Oby's tent. We have strange and great tales to tell." He clapped his brother on the shoulder and turned to follow Illvin.

Temporarily unmenaced by Ista's erratic steed, Ferda came to Demon's shoulder to help her down. Ista was dizzy with fatigue, but she stayed determinedly upright.

"See that this dreadful horse is well cared for. He bore Lord Arhys faithfully last night. Your brother rode in that great sortie as well, and endured capture and grievous use. He needs rest, if you can make him take it in this uproar. We have all of us been up since dawn yesterday, through flight and siege and . . . and worse. Lord Illvin lost a great deal of blood last night. Make sure he gets drink and food immediately, at the least." She added, after a thoughtful pause, "And if he attempts to ride into battle in his present state, knock him down and sit on him. Although I trust he has more sense."

As soon as her horse was led out of range by a soldier of Oby, dy Ferrej pounced on Ista, practically wresting her from Ferda. "Royina! We have been in terror for your safety!"

And not without cause, in truth. "Well, I am safe now." Soothingly, she patted his hand gripping her arm.

Lady dy Hueltar tottered up, arm in arm with Divine Tovia. "Ista, Ista, lovie!"

Dy Baocia was looking intently after Illvin. "Now that you are all delivered to each other, I think I'd better attend on dy Oby as well." He managed a distracted smile at Ista. "Yes, yes, good."

"Did you bring troops of your own, brother?" Ista asked.

"Yes, five hundred of horse, all that I could muster in a hurry when these people descended upon me waving your alarming letter."

"Then by all means, attend upon Oby. Your guard may well have a chance to earn the coin you pay them. Chalion owes the garrison of Castle Porifors . . . much, but certainly relief above all, and that as soon as may be."

"Ah." He collected Ferda and dy Ferrej and hurried off after the other men, half in curiosity, half, Ista suspected, in eagerness to escape his importunate entourage.

The problem of explaining her own adventures to them without sounding like a raving madwoman, she discovered, could be put off—possibly indefinitely—by asking after their own journey. A mere query of "How did you come here so timely?" induced an answer that ran on until they reached dy Baocia's tents, and longer. The five hundred of horse, Ista found, had been trailed by what seemed a hundred more servants, grooms, and maids, in support of the dozen ladies from the courts of both Valenda and Taryoon who had accompanied Lady dy Hueltar on her self-appointed mission to bring Ista home. Dy Ferrej, more or less in charge of shifting them all, was justly punished, Ista decided. That he had moved them such a distance in a week, instead of a month, was a near miracle in itself, and her respect for him, never low, rose another notch.

Ista cut though a plethora of plans by requesting a wash, food, and bed, in that order; Divine Tovia, always more practical than most of Ista's attendants, and with an eye to the blood on her gown, backed her up. The elderly physician managed to run off all but two maids, her own acolyte-assistant, and Lady dy Hueltar from the tent where she guided Ista for a bath and treatment. Ista had to admit, it was both comfortable and comforting to have those familiar hands about her, applying salve and bandages to her hurts. Tovia's curved sewing needle, too, was very fine and sharp, and her hands were quick about the wincing task of mending flesh where it was required.

"What in the world are *these* bruises?" Divine Tovia inquired.

Ista craned to see the back of her own thigh where the physician was pointing. Five dark purple spots were spaced around it. Her lips curved up, and she twisted about to spread her own fingers between them.

"Five gods, Ista," cried Lady dy Hueltar in horror, "who has dared to handle you so?"

"Those are from . . . yesterday. When Lord Illvin rescued me from the Jokonan column on the road. What excellent long fingers he does have! I wonder if he plays any musical instruments. I shall have to find out."

"Is Lord Illvin that odd tall fellow who rode in with you?" asked Lady dy Hueltar suspiciously. "I must say, I did not like the very forward way he kissed your hand."

"No? Well, he was pressed for time. I shall make him practice, later, until his technique improves."

Lady dy Hueltar looked offended, but Divine Tovia, at least, snorted a little.

Ista was laid down in a tent under a guard of ladies, but rose again to peek out, despite her nightgown, at the sound of many horses thundering out of the camp. It was only late afternoon; on this long summer day Oby's cavalry would be descending on Porifors with hours of light still left for their work. The timing, Ista thought, was excellent. Maximum confusion, disorder, and dismay would have spread through the Jokonan forces from the dire events of noon, and the chances that competent leadership had yet reemerged—especially from the habits of sullen mindless obedience extracted by Joen—were slight.

She let herself be coaxed back to bed by those who loved her. Though the Ista they thought they loved, she supposed, was an imaginary one, a woman who existed only in their own minds, part icon, part habit.

The reflection did not depress her unduly, now that she knew someone who loved the Ista who was real. She fell asleep thinking of him.

❦

Ista awoke from ugly dreams not, she thought, entirely her own, to the sound of female voices arguing.

"Lady Ista wants to sleep, after her ordeal," said Lady dy Hueltar firmly. "I will not have her troubled further."

"No," said Liss in a puzzled tone, "the royina will want the report from Porifors. We started before dawn to bring it to her as swiftly as we could."

Ista lumbered up from her sheets. "Liss!" she cried. "In here!" It appeared she had slept the short summer night through; it sufficed.

"*Now* see what you've done!" said Lady dy Hueltar in aggravation.

"What?" Liss's bafflement was genuine; she had not Ista's years of training in deciphering her now-senior lady-in-waiting's oblique locutions. Ista translated it handily as *I didn't want to travel again today, and now I'll have to, drat you, girl.*

A leap from her cot, Ista discovered, wasn't going to

occur. She did manage to lever herself painfully to her feet before the tent flap was thrown back, admitting a level golden light and a grinning Liss. Ista embraced her; she embraced Ista back. The grin and Liss's presence seemed almost all the report she needed. *Porifors is relieved. There were no more devastating deaths last night.* The rest might be learned in order, or no order, as it came.

"Sit," said Ista, not releasing Liss's hands. "Tell me everything."

"Lady Ista needs to be dressed before receiving petitioners," said Lady dy Hueltar sternly.

"Excellent notion," said Ista. "Do go and find me some clothing to wear. Riding dress."

"Oh, Ista, you won't be riding anywhere *today*, after all you've been through! You need to rest."

"Actually," Liss put in, "March dy Oby has sent some officers to see the camp is broken down and shifted to Porifors as quick as may be. Ferda is waiting with some of your brother's men to guard you on the way, Royina, as soon as you are ready. Unless you prefer to ride in a cart with the baggage train."

"She will surely want to ride in the wagons with us," said Lady dy Hueltar.

"Tempting," Ista lied, "but no. I'll ride my horse."

Lady dy Hueltar sniffed balefully and withdrew.

Ista continued eagerly to Liss, "Oh, you will laugh at my new horse. It has come to me as the spoils of war, I think, though I may persuade Illvin to make it a court gift, which would amuse him. It's Illvin's vile red stallion."

"The one that possessed the stray elemental?"

"Yes; it has conceived a sudden adoration for me, and abases itself in the most appalling unhorselike fashion. You will find it quite reformed, or if you don't, let me know, and I'll put the fear of its god in it again. But say on, dear Liss."

"Well, the castle and town are secured, and the Jokonans driven off or taken—most of them fled north, but there may be some stragglers still lurking."

"Or just plain lost," said Ista dryly. "It wouldn't be the first time."

Liss snickered. "We have captured Prince Sordso and his whole retinue, which has pleased Lord Illvin and March dy Oby no end. They say the prince has gone mad. Is it true you ensorcelled him to hack up the dowager princess?"

"No," said Ista. "All I did was remove the sorcery that was preventing him from doing so. I rather think it was a wild impulse on his part, soon regretted. Joen was dead before his sword struck her; the Bastard took her soul. I wonder if it would be a relief or a regret to Sordso to know that? I should probably tell him in any case. Go on. What of Lady Cattilara, and our stalwart divine?"

"Well, we all watched from the walls as the Jokonans marched you off. And then it got all quiet for a little, and then we could hear some terrible uproar at those big green tents, but we could not make out what was happening. Lady Cattilara surprised us all. After you and Lord Illvin were made hostage, or so we all thought, she rose from her bed. She drove her ladies to defend the walls, since almost all of the men were too sick to stand by then—it seems they make a game of archery here, and the Jokonan sorcerers' spells had not destroyed their sporting bows. Some of the ladies proved quite good shots. They had not the power to penetrate mail, but I saw Lady Catti herself put an arrow right through a rude Jokonan officer's eye. Learned dy Cabon stood with her—she swore that Porifors would not fall while she was still its chatelaine. Me, I threw rocks—if you fling one from a high enough tower, it hits quite hard by the time it lands on its target, even if you don't have a strong throwing arm.

"We could see the Jokonans were just probing, but we bit them till they bled nonetheless. I think we could not have held for long against a determined assault, but we discouraged them from attempting the walls at once—and then it was too late, for the march of Oby's forces struck and swept them away. Lady Catti was quite splendid when she opened the gates to her father. I thought she would break down and weep when he embraced her, for he did, but instead she was very stern."

"What of Goram?"

"He helped hold the walls with us. He was exhausted and feverish this morning, which is why Lord Illvin did not dispatch him to you, he told me to tell you. Since if you are riding to Porifors this morning, it made no sense to send Goram twice ten miles to meet you at almost the same time anyway."

"Excellent thinking. Yes. I will ride at once." She looked around; Lady dy Hueltar was bustling back into the tent leading a maid carrying an armload of clothing. "Ah, good."

Ista's satisfaction died as she saw the dress the maid was shaking out for her; a fine layered silk, suitable for a court function, in widow's dark green. "This is not riding dress."

"Of course not, dear Ista," said Lady dy Hueltar. "It is for you to wear to breakfast with us all."

"I shall take a cup of tea and a bite of bread, if such may be had in this camp, and ride at once."

"Oh, *no*," said Lady dy Hueltar, in a tone of earnest correction. "The meal is being prepared. We are all so looking forward to celebrating having you with us again, just as it should be."

The feast would take two hours, Ista estimated, maybe three. "One mouth the less will not be missed. You all must eat anyway before you break camp; it will not be wasted."

"Now, Lady Ista, do have sense."

Ista's voice dropped. "I ride. If you will not bring me the clothing I asked for, I will send Liss through the camp to beg me some. And if none is to be had, I'll ride in my nightgown. Or naked, if I must."

"I'd share my clothes with you, Royina," Liss offered at once, clearly bemused by that last image.

"I know you would, Liss." Ista patted her shoulder.

Lady dy Hueltar drew herself up in offense, or possibly defense. "Lady Ista, you mustn't be so wild!" Her voice grew hushed. "You wouldn't want people thinking you had been overtaken by your *old troubles* again, after all."

Ista was tempted, for a dangerous moment, to test just how much sorcerous power the Bastard had endowed her with. But the target was too small and unworthy, pitiable in her way. A natural sycophant, Lady dy Hueltar had made her way in the world most comfortably for the past two decades as companion to the old Provincara, enjoying an imagined indispensability and the status lent her by her august patron. It was clear she wished that pleasant existence to continue; and it could, if only Ista would move into her mother's place and take up her mother's life. All just as before, indeed.

Ista turned to the maid. "You, girl—fetch me some riding clothes. White if they may be had, or whatever color, but in any case, not green."

The girl's mouth opened in panic; she glanced back and forth between Ista and Lady dy Hueltar, torn between conflicting authorities. Ista's eyes narrowed.

"*Why* must you even *go* to Porifors?" asked Lady dy Hueltar. Her seamed face worked with distress, close to tears. "With your brother's troop to escort us, we could surely start back to Valenda right from here!"

She must take deeper thought for Lady dy Hueltar, Ista decided, for in truth her years of service had earned her some consideration. But for the moment, Ista meant to ride. She unclenched her teeth and said mildly, "Funerals, dear Lady dy Hueltar. They will be burying the dead today at Porifors. It is my solemn duty to attend. I will wish you to bring me the proper attire when you follow on."

"Oh, *funerals*," said Lady dy Hueltar, in a tone of relieved enlightenment. "Funerals, oh, of course." She had accompanied the old Provincara to a multitude of such ceremonies. It only *seemed* their primary entertainment in late years, Ista supposed dryly, though she'd be hard-pressed to name a commoner one. But Lady dy Hueltar understood funerals.

She won't understand these. But it wouldn't matter. For

the moment, at least, her customary role seemed safely confirmed to her. The old lady brightened instantly.

She actually unbent so far as to go find Ista riding dress,
while Liss went to saddle Demon and Ista gulped tea and
bread. The costume's pale tan color even looked good atop
the chestnut stallion, Ista fancied, settling at last into the saddle. The ride would limber her stiff body, at least. She had a
lingering headache, but she knew its cause; and its cure lay
in Porifors. Ferda waved on his Baocian troop, and Liss fell
in at her side. They pressed forward through the bright
morning air.

❧

A relay of dy Oby's men were hauling out rubble from the
gates of Porifors as Ista's party rode in. Ista watched them
work with glad approval. The rebuilding would be a longer
project, but with so many hands, at least the clearing and
cleaning would be swiftly accomplished.

The forecourt was already swept out. The limp flowers in
the two or three pots left intact on the wall even seemed to
be lifting their heads again; Ista was obscurely grateful, in
all the noisy confusion, that someone had spared a bit of
water for them, and she wondered whose hand it had been.
The apricot and the almond trees, though half-denuded, had
also stopped dropping leaves. She hoped they would recover.

We can do better than hope, she realized, and thought to
them, *Live. By the Bastard's blessing, I command you.* If this
lent the trees any special vigor, it was not instantly apparent;
she trusted the ultimate results would not prove peculiar.

Ista's heart lifted to see Lord Illvin striding through the
archway. He was cleaned up, hair rebraided, freshly dressed
as an officer of Porifors; it even seemed possible that he
might have snatched a few hours of sleep. The shorter,
stouter Lord dy Baocia pattered by his side, puffing to keep
pace. At dy Baocia's other shoulder Learned dy Cabon trod,

waving eagerly at her. To her relief, a tired-looking Goram trailed immediately after them.

Cautiously, Goram took her horse's head, eyeing the beast's new docility askance. Ista slipped from her saddle into Illvin's upreaching arms, returning his secret embrace on her way to the ground.

"Greetings, Ista," said Lord dy Baocia. "Are you, um, all right now?" He bore a slightly dazed expression, as might any commander touring the inside of Castle Porifors this morning. His smile upon her was not nearly so vague as Ista was used to; in fact, she suspected she had all his attention. It felt very odd.

"Thank you, brother, I am well; a little tired, but doubtless less fatigued than many here." She glanced at dy Cabon. "How do the sick men fare?"

"We've had no more deaths since yesterday noon, five gods be thanked." He signed himself in heartfelt gratitude. "A few are even back on their feet, though I judge the rest will be as long recovering as from less uncanny illnesses. Most have been moved down to town, into the care of the temple or their relatives."

"That is good to hear."

"Foix and Lord Illvin have told us of the great deeds and miracles you performed yesterday in the Jokonans' tents, by the grace of the Bastard. Is it true you died?"

"I . . . am not sure."

"I am," muttered Illvin. His hand had somehow neglected to release hers; they both tightened.

"I did have a very odd vision, which I promise I will recount to you at some less hurried moment, Learned." Well, parts of it, anyway.

"For all my terror, how I wish I, too, could have been there to bear witness, Royina! I should have counted myself blessed above all in my order."

"Oh? Well, stay a moment, then. I have another task, which presses on me. Liss, please take my horse. Goram, come here."

Looking puzzled and wary, Goram obeyed, trudging up
to her and giving her a daunted bob of his head. "Royina."
His hands clenched each other nervously, and he shot a look
of supplication at his master. Illvin's eyes narrowed in concern, and his glance at Ista sharpened.

Ista stared one last time at the hollow gaps in Goram's
soul, placed her palms upon his forehead, and poured a sudden flood of white fire out of her spirit hands into those dark
and empty reservoirs. The fire splashed wildly in its new
confines, then slowly settled, as if seeking its proper level.
She breathed relief as the unpleasant pressure in her head
vanished.

Goram thumped down cross-legged on the cobbles, his
mouth open. He buried his face in his hands. After a moment, his shoulders began to shake. "Oh," he said in a far-
away voice. He started to weep—in shock, Ista supposed,
and in other, more complicated reactions. Her last night's
dreams had given her some intimations.

"Lord Illvin, brother, may I introduce Captain Goram dy
Hixar, late of Roya Orico's cavalry via the service of Lord
Dondo dy Jironal. More recently of service, if an involuntary one, to Sordso of Jokona, as swordmaster and horseman. In a sense."

Goram looked up from his sobbing, his face stunned.
Stunned, but not slack: its shape seemed to tighten along
with the mending mind underneath.

"You have returned his memories and his wits? But Ista,
this is wonderful!" cried Illvin. "Now he may find his family and his home at last!"

"Just what it is, remains to be seen," murmured Ista. "But
his soul is now his own, and complete."

Goram's steel-gray eyes met hers, and for a moment, did
not look away. They were filled with amazement, and a roil
of other emotions; she rather thought one of them was anguish. She gave him a grave nod, acknowledging it all. He
returned a shaken jerk of his head.

"Learned," she continued, "you begged a gift of witness,

and you have it. Please help Captain dy Hixar back to his chamber. He needs to rest quietly, for until he has time to put them back in order, his mind and memories will be very unsettled. Some spiritual comfort . . . may not come amiss, when he is ready."

"Indeed, Royina," said dy Cabon, signing himself joyously. "It will be my honor." He helped Goram—dy Hixar—to his feet, and led him off through the archway. Illvin stared after, then turned his dark eyes thoughtfully on her.

Dy Baocia inquired in a small voice, "Ista, what just happened?"

"Princess Joen, through her demon, was in the habit of stealing useful bits of other people's souls for her sorcerers. From, among others, prisoners of war. Prince Sordso was her greatest construct, and full of such fragments. When Sordso's demon passed through me yesterday, the god gave it to me to recognize and retain the portion of Captain dy Hixar woven among the rest, and to return it to him here. It is part of the task the Bastard has laid on me, to hunt demons in the world, pluck them from their mounts, and relay them to His hell."

"This task . . . is now done, yes?" he said hopefully. Or, possibly, worriedly. He glanced around the shambles of Porifors. "Yesterday, right?"

"No, I expect it is only beginning. In the past three years Joen released a very plague of elementals. They have escaped all over the Five Princedoms and the royacies, though their greatest concentration is likely still in Jokona. The woman who had this calling before me was killed in Rauma. It is not an easy, not an easy . . . duty to train for. If I read the god aright—He delights in obscurity and riddles—I think He wanted a successor who would be rather better guarded, through what promises to be a, ah, theologically difficult period."

Illvin's eyes glinted, listening to this. He murmured, "Much becomes clear."

"He told me He did not want to train another porter," Ista

added, "and that He fancied a royina for a time. His exact
words." She let her slight pause emphasize this last. "I am
called. I come." *And you may either help, brother, or get out
of my way.* "I expect to form a traveling court, small and
adaptable; the god's duties are likely to continue physically
wearing. My clerk—as soon as I appoint one—and yours
must deal shortly with forwarding my dower income, as I
doubt my tasks will take me back to Valenda."

Dy Baocia digested it all for a moment, then cleared his
throat and said cautiously, "My men are setting up our camp
by the spring to the east of the castle; will you take your ease
there, Ista, or return to your rooms in here?"

Ista glanced up at Illvin. "That will be for Porifors's
chatelaine to decide. But until this fortress has had more
time to recover, I would not burden it with my expanded
household. I will rest in your camp for a while."

Illvin gave her a short nod in appreciation of her delicacy,
and all that went unspoken in it: *until after the dead are
buried.*

Her brother offered to escort her to his tents, as he was
going in that direction, and Illvin gave her a formal bow of
temporary farewell.

"My duties today are relentless," Illvin murmured, "but
later I must discuss with you the matter of an appropriate
guard company for this traveling court of yours."

"Indeed," she returned. "And other appointments as
well."

"And callings."

"Those, too."

❧

Pejar and his two slain comrades of the Daughter's order
were buried outside the walls of Porifors that afternoon. Ista
and all her company attended upon them. Learned dy Cabon
had come to Ista in distress, earlier, for while he might offi-
ciate—none better, in Ista's view—he had no sacred animals

to sign the gods' acceptances; those belonging to Porifors's own temple were overburdened and reported close to frenzied with the day's demands.

"Learned," she had chided him gently. "We do not need the animals. We have me."

"Ah," he said, rocking back. "Oh. As you are made saint again—of course."

She knelt, now, in the sunlight by each wrapped form in turn, laid her hand upon its brow, and prayed for their signs. In rites at major temples like the one in Cardegoss, each order proffered a sacred animal, appropriate in color and sex to the god or goddess it represented, with an acolyte-groom to handle it. The creatures were led in turn to the bier, and by their behavior the divines interpreted to the mourners which god had taken in their lost one's soul, and therefore where to direct their prayers—and, not incidentally, upon which order's altar to lay their more material offerings. The rite brought consolation to the living, support to the Temple, and occasionally some surprises.

She had often wondered what the animals trained to this duty felt. She was relieved when she experienced no holy hallucinations: merely a silent certainty. Pejar and the first of his comrades were taken up by the Daughter of Spring, Whom they had served so faithfully, she felt at once, and so she reported. The last man, she discovered, was different.

"Curious," she said to Ferda and Foix. "The Father of Winter has taken Laonin. I wonder if it is for the sake of his courage on Arhys's ride—or if he has a child somewhere? He was not married, was he?"

"Um, no," said Ferda. He glanced at dy Cabon's whites and swallowed whatever embarrassment he might have felt on the dead dedicat's behalf.

Ista rose from the graveside. "Then I charge you to find out, and see that the child, if it lives, is cared for. I will write to Holy General dy Yarrin as well. It shall have a purse from me to maintain its infancy, and a claim on a place in my household when it comes of age, if it desires."

"Yes, Royina," said Ferda. Surreptitiously, he wiped his eyes with the back of his hand.

Ista nodded satisfaction. As a conscientious officer, he would not fail in this task, she was sure.

The shaded grove reserved for the castle's dead overlooked the pleasant river; many graves were still being dug, and other grieving people, comrades and relatives of the slain, had watched their company's rites. What rumors were circulating about her in Porifors Ista hardly knew, but within the hour humble petitioners had descended upon dy Cabon to beg the royal saint's indulgence for their dead.

As a result Ista spent the day until darkness fell being conducted by dy Cabon and Liss from graveside to graveside, reporting the fates of souls. There were too many, but the task was not so endless as the devastation Joen's sorcerers would have left across Chalion if not stopped by Porifors's sacrifices. Ista refused none who asked her aid, for most surely, these had not refused her. Every mourner seemed to have some story to tell her of their dead; not, she realized at length, in the expectation that she would do anything, except listen. Attend. *Royina, see this man; make him real in your mind, as in ours; for in the realm of matter, he lives now only in our memories.* She listened till her ears and heart both ached.

Returning to her brother's tents after nightfall, she fell onto her cot like a corpse herself. As the night drew on, she told over the names, faces, fragments of men's lives in her thoughts. How could the gods' minds hold all these tales in full? *For They remember us perfectly.*

At length, exhausted, she rolled over and slept.

28

ARHYS'S FUNERAL TOOK PLACE THE NEXT MORNING IN
the little temple in the town of Porifors, as if an ordinary
border lord had died in an ordinary battle. The provincar of
Caribastos had ridden in with a troop too late to bear arms,
but in time to help bear up the sealed coffin, together with
dy Oby, dy Baocia, Illvin, Foix, and one of Arhys's senior
officers. It was as honorable an escort as might be had.

The sacred animal of the Father of Winter here was a fine
old gray deerhound, his coat brushed to a silvery sheen for
the occasion; he sat at once by the bier when his acolyte-
groom led him up, and would not be moved from his guard-
place thereafter. The normally articulate Illvin was pallid
and close-throated. He managed only a simple *He was a
great-souled man*, in a voice that slid, then stepped back to
Ista's side. It was plain that any further demand for speech
would have cracked him. To spare him, dy Oby and dy
Caribastos stepped forward to deliver all the proper orations,
listing their late relative's and liegeman's public achieve-
ments.

Lady Cattilara, too, was pale and quiet. She did not speak
much to Illvin, or vice versa, just the necessary practical ex-

changes. There would never be friendship between them, exactly; but the blood they'd mingled on the tower, Ista judged,
had bought them enough mutual respect to survive upon.
Cattilara, jaw tight, even managed a polite nod to Ista. For
the three of them, the morning's rite was a redundant
farewell, more a social burden to be endured than an hour of
parting.

After the interment and the funeral meal, the military
men dragged Illvin off for conclave. Lady Cattilara made
scant work of packing, left her ladies to deal with the rest,
and rode out under the escort of one of her brothers, bound
for Oby. It would be after nightfall before she reached it; but
Ista, remembering her own horror of the Zangre after Ias's
death, had no trouble understanding Cattilara's desire not to
sleep another night in her emptied marriage bed. Cattilara
bore away great grief in her heart, down that eastern road,
but not, Ista thought, a crippling burden of hatred, rage, or
guilt along with it. What would eventually grow to fill that
emptiness, Ista did not know—but she felt that it would not
be stunted.

❧

Early the next afternoon, Lord Illvin came to Ista in dy Baocia's camp. They climbed the path above the spring, partly
for the view, which took in both Castle Porifors and the valley it guarded, partly to shed any of Ista's would-be attendants less athletic than Liss. Illvin gallantly spread his
vest-cloak upon a rock for Ista to seat herself. Liss wandered
nearby, looking longingly at an enticing cork-oak tree that
her dress prevented her from climbing.

Ista nodded to Illvin's belt, where both Arhys's and Cattilara's keys now hung. "Provincar dy Caribastos has confirmed your command of Porifors, I see."

"For the moment, at least," said Illvin.

"For the moment?"

He stared thoughtfully along the ridge to where the

stronghold's walls rose from the rocks. "It's odd. I was born in Porifors—lived here almost all of my life—yet I've never owned it, nor expected to. It belongs today to my niece Liviana—a nine-year-old girl who lives half a province away. Yet it is my home, if anyplace is. I own half a dozen little estates in Caribastos, unentailed scatterings from my mother—but they are mere possessions, barely visited. Still, necessarily, Porifors must be defended."

"By you—necessarily?"

He shrugged. "It is the key fortress, along this border."

"I think this border may be about to shift."

He grinned briefly. "Indeed. Things are stirring, in our counsels. I'm stirring 'em. I don't need Arhys's gifts to tell that this is a boon of timing and chance not to be wasted."

"I trust so. I expect Marshal dy Palliar and Chancellor dy Cazaril to ride into the gates of Porifors within the week. If my brother's and dy Caribastos's and Foix's letters"—*and mine*—"do not fetch them, they are not the men I take them for."

"Will they see it, do you think? Here, now, is the moment to turn Joen's strategy about—to sweep down, all unexpected, into Jokona while it is so disrupted, and turn Visping's flank—and the campaign could be done before it was even expected to start."

"It does not take second sight to foresee that outcome," said Ista. "If it works, dy Palliar will doubtless be showered with the acclaim for his grand strategy."

Illvin smiled grimly. "Poor Joen, she even loses that credit. She should have been a general."

"Anything but the frustrated puppeteer she was constrained to be," Ista agreed. "What will become of Sordso? I think he is not quite mad, for all that he sniveled and kissed my skirt hem when I passed him in the forecourt yesterday. His soul is his own now, though it will be long before his nerves are anything but shattered."

"Yes, one scarcely knows if he would be of more use to us as a hostage, or set loose to be a very bad enemy leader."

"He spoke of a religious vocation, and conversion to the Quintarian faith, actually. I've no idea how long the fit will last."

Illvin snorted. "Perhaps his poetry will grow better hereafter."

"I shouldn't be surprised." The castle's battlements stood stark and pale in the bright light, concealing the damage being repaired within; Ista could hear a faint echo of hammering. "By the time Liviana's future husband succeeds to the command of Porifors, it will have become a quiet backwater, like Valenda. This place has earned its peace, I think." She glanced at Illvin, who was smiling down at her. "There are two thoughts in my mind just now."

"Only two?"

"Two thousand, but these are uppermost. One is that my roving court needs a royal seneschal: a competent and experienced officer, preferably one who knows this area, to direct my travels and secure my person."

His brows twitched up, encouragingly.

"The other is that Marshal dy Palliar will need an experienced intelligencer, an officer who knows Jokona and the Jokonans better than any other, who speaks and writes both court and vile Roknari, possessing trunks full of maps and charts and ground plans, to advise his strategies in this region. I greatly fear that these are two mutually exclusive posts."

He touched one finger thoughtfully to his lips. "I might mention, it has occurred independently to several military minds here that any army presently wishing to march north would be very, very happy to possess a cure for sorcerers, to carry close at hand. Should any further enemy sorcerers be encountered on this campaign. Resources devoted to the protection of such a sorceress-saint would not be considered wasted. So the saint's seneschal and the marshal's intelligencer might not find themselves working so far apart as all that."

Ista's brows rose. "Hm? Perhaps . . . If it is clearly understood that the saint serves not Chalion, not even the Temple, but the god, and must go as the god directs. Alongside the marshal's tents for a time, but not in them. Well, well, dy Cazaril will understand that part; and I think he could drill it into dy Palliar's head if anyone could."

He stared thoughtfully up the valley road. "A week, you think, till they arrive?"

"Ten days at most."

"Huh." His long fingers rattled the keys at his belt. "Meantime . . . I actually walked over here to invite you to take rooms within Castle Porifors again, now we are in slightly better order. If you wish. The weather's due to change, judging by the wind; we may have a bit of welcome rain by tomorrow night."

"Not Umerue's old chamber, I trust."

"No, we've lodged Prince Sordso and his watchers there."

"Nor Cattilara's."

"Dy Caribastos and his retinue have taken over that whole gallery." He cleared his throat. "I was thinking of the ones you had before. Across from mine. Although . . . I fear there is not enough space to also house all of your ladies."

Ista managed not to grin, or at least not too broadly. "Thank you, Lord Illvin; I should be pleased."

His dark eyes sparked. His hand-kissing technique was definitely improving with practice, she thought.

❦

Ista sent her restored raiment from Valenda on ahead; even minus all the staid selections in widow's green that she left in her brother's tents, she would be spared living in borrowed clothing henceforth. A little later, dy Baocia escorted her from his camp. Foix attended, guardsman handily making a smooth transition to courtier.

Dy Baocia's transition was a little less smooth, but on the whole he seemed to be managing the leap to the new Ista reasonably well, she thought. He avoided discussing the disturbing part about eating demons, seldom mentioned the god, but he'd entered into the material practicalities of her new vocation with gratifying attention to detail.

"We must determine the size of your personal guard," he remarked as they passed under Porifors's gates. "Too many will be a drain on your purse, but too few could prove a false economy."

"Very true. My needs will, I expect, vary with my locale. Add it to your list to discuss with my seneschal; he'll be the best judge of what this region requires."

"Will your seneschal also serve as your master of horse, as he did for his late brother? Or shall I recommend you a man?"

"Ser dy Arbanos's duties will be too demanding. I have another man in mind, though I'm not sure yet if he will accept. I may return for your recommendation, if not."

"What, not dy Gura, here?" dy Baocia inquired. Foix gave a little agreeable bow. "Or his good brother?"

"Ferda is claimed for the coming campaign by his cousin, Marshal dy Palliar, and must be off to join him shortly. Even as an officer of my household, Foix will likely do considerable traveling back and forth on Temple business; but a horse-master's tasks are daily. I am not sure what title I shall offer Foix. Royal Sorcerer? Master of Demons?"

"I should be perfectly content to retain *officer-dedicat*, Royina," Foix put in hastily, sounding slightly alarmed, then narrowing his eyes in suspicion at her primly pursed lips.

"I shall find you the work first, and the title later, then," she said. "You'll need something to swagger with, when we visit other courts, to keep up the expected royal hauteur on my behalf."

A grin flitted over his mouth. "As you command, Royina."

They turned into the stone court and mounted to the gallery; Ista controlled a shiver, passing up the steps on which she'd once faced a god. From the open door of her double chamber, a familiar but unexpected voice floated.

"She doesn't *want* you," Lady dy Hueltar said severely. "She doesn't *need* you. *I* am here now, and I assure you, I am far better acquainted with all her requirements than you will ever be. So just you run along back to the stables, or wherever you came from. Out, out!"

"Madam, it cannot be so," said Liss in a puzzled tone.

Foix's brows climbed, then drew back down, darkly. Ista motioned him to patience and shouldered within, the men following.

"What is this argument?" Ista inquired.

Colored spots flared on Lady dy Hueltar's cheeks; she hesitated, then drew in her breath. "I was just explaining to this rude girl here that now you are done with that rash pilgrimage, dear Ista, you will be requiring a more befitting lady-in-waiting again. Not a girl groom."

"On the contrary, I need Liss very much."

"She isn't suited to be lady-in-waiting to a royina. She's not even a lady!"

Liss scratched her head. "Well, that's true enough. I'm not much good at waiting, either. I'm better at riding very fast."

Ista smiled. "Indeed." Her smile tightened a little, as she considered the scene she'd interrupted. Had Lady dy Hueltar actually imagined she might trick or drive Liss off, send her away believing herself dismissed?

Lady dy Hueltar made a little nervous gesture, under Ista's cool gaze. "Now that you are *calmer*, Lady Ista, surely it is time we began to think of returning safely to Valenda. Your good brother here will lend us a more adequate escort for the return journey, I'm sure."

"I'm not going back to Valenda. I'm going to follow the army into Jokona to hunt demons for the Bastard," said Ista. "*Safety* has little to do with the god's chores." Her lips curved up, but it was scarcely a smile anymore. "Has no one explained anything to you yet, dear Lady dy Hueltar?"

"*I* did," said Liss. "Several times." She lowered her voice to Ista. "It's all right. I had a great-aunt who grew very confused in her age like this, poor thing."

"I am *not*," Lady dy Hueltar began in rising tones, then stopped. She started again. "It's much too dangerous. I beg you to reconsider, dear Ista. My lord dy Baocia—as the head of the family now, it's your place to insist she be more sensible!"

"Actually," Ista noted, "he's been head of the family for a decade and a half."

Dy Baocia snorted, and muttered under his breath, "Aye—anyplace in Baocia but Valenda . . ."

Ista took Lady dy Hueltar's hand and set it firmly on her brother's arm. "I'm sure you're very tired, dear lady, to have ridden so far, so fast, for so little need. But my brother will see you safely on your way back home tomorrow—or possibly tonight."

"I have already moved my things here—"

Ista cast an eye at the piles of luggage. "The servants will move them back. I will speak with you more later, dy Baocia." With a few more not terribly gentle hints, Ista maneuvered them both out the door. Her last hope of support from dy Baocia failing, Lady dy Hueltar moved off with him in a cloud of mutual exasperation, looking very crushed.

"*Where* did that woman *come* from?" Foix asked, shaking his head in wonder.

"I inherited her."

"My condolences."

"She'll be all right. My brother will find some other corner of the family to tuck her into; it won't please her as well as a higher household, but perhaps she'll get some satisfaction out of parading her former glories. She doesn't batten, you know; in certain narrow ways, she makes herself quite useful. It is sad, though, that she herself destroys the gratitude that ought to be her reward."

Foix glanced at Liss, whose face was a trifle set. He said, "I find my gratitude quite limited, I'm afraid."

Liss tossed her braid. "It doesn't matter."

"*Was* she trying to convince you that I'd dismissed you?" asked Ista.

"Oh, yes. It made her quite cross when I played the fool and failed to take her hints." Liss's mouth twitched up, then down. "It's true, though. I'm not a proper highborn lady."

Ista smiled. "I expect we shall rendezvous with Iselle and Bergon's court before the year is up—in Visping, if not sooner. At which point, by my request and your valiancy, a lady you shall be made in fact—Sera Annaliss dy . . . what was the name of that sheep-infested village, again?"

Liss breathed, "Teneret, Royina."

"Sera Annaliss dy Teneret, lady-in-waiting to the Dowager Royina Ista. Sounds very dignified, don't you think, Foix?"

He grinned. "Aye—I think m'mother will like it quite well. Well, Bastard knows I've got to offer something, now, to make it up to her for, er, the Bastard."

"Ah, you aspire to some social climbing, do you? Well, it's not impossible; this year will offer young officers many opportunities for advancement, I suspect."

Foix swept Liss a courtier's bow. "May I aspire, lady?"

Liss eyed him with smiling speculation, and drifted across the chamber to start putting Ista's things in order. "Ask again in Visping, dedicat."

"I shall."

❧

Ista had dy Cabon bring Goram to her in the stone court. She sat in the colonnade's shade on the bench where they had first spoken, and studied the differences.

Goram dy Hixar's clothing was still that of the groom, his figure still short, his legs still bowed, his beard still grizzled. But he had lost the turtle hunch; he moved now with a swordsman's balance. And tension. His polite bow was supple enough for any provincial court.

"Learned dy Cabon has told you, I think, of my need for a master of horse, yes?" Ista began.

"Yes, Royina." Dy Hixar cleared his throat, uncomfortably, and swallowed his spit in her presence. Goram, she thought, would have let the gobbet fly.

"Can you undertake the task?"

He grimaced. "The work, aye. But Royina . . . I'm not sure if you understand who I was. Am. Why I was not ransomed."

She shrugged. "Captain of horse, swordsman, bravo, quondam murderer, destroyer of lives—not just of enemies', but friends'—shall I go on? The sort of fellow whose funeral's orations are all on the theme of *Well, that's a relief.*"

He winced. "I see I need not confess to you."

"No. I saw."

He looked away. "All my sins delivered . . . it's a strange, strange thing, Royina. The lifting of one's sins is usually considered a miracle of the gods. But your god has brought all mine back to me. Goram the groom . . . was a hundred times better a man than Goram dy Hixar will ever be. I was a blank slate, brought—saved, for no merit of mine—to live for three years with the two best men in Caribastos. Not just best swordsmen—best men, you understand?"

She nodded.

"I scarcely knew such lives were possible, before. Nor wanted to know. I would have mocked their virtues, and laughed. Lord Illvin thought I was overwhelmed with joy when I fell to my knees before you in the forecourt. It wasn't joy that knocked me down. It was shame."

"I know."

"I don't want to be . . . who I am. I was happier before, Royina. But everyone thinks I should be praying my thanks."

She returned him an ironic smile. "Be sure, I am not one of them. But—your soul is your own, now, to make of what you will. We are all of us, every one, our own works; we present our souls to our Patrons at the ends of our lives as an artisan presents the works of his hands."

"If it is so, I am too marred, Royina."

"You are unfinished. They are discerning Patrons, but

not, I think, impossible to please. The Bastard said to me, from His own lips—"

Dy Cabon's breath drew in.

"—that the gods did not desire flawless souls, but great ones. I think that very darkness is where the greatness grows from, as flowers from the soil. I am not sure, in fact, if greatness can bloom without it. You have been as god-touched as any here; do not despair of yourself, for I think the gods have not."

The dim gray eyes reddened, edged with water's gleam. "I am too old to start over."

"You have more years ahead of you now than Pejar, half your age, whom we buried outside these walls these two days past. Stand before his grave and use your gift of breath to complain of your limited time. If you dare."

He jerked a little at the steel in her voice.

"I offer you an honorable new beginning. I do not guarantee its ending. Attempts fail, but not as certainly as tasks never attempted."

He vented a long exhalation. "Then . . . that being so, and knowing what you know of me—which is, I think, more than ever I confessed to anyone, living or dead—I am your man if you will have me, Royina."

"Thank you, Captain: I shall. As my master of horse, you will take your instructions from my seneschal. I think you will find him a tolerable commander."

Goram smiled a little at that, and saluted her farewell.

Dy Cabon stood by her a moment, watching him exit the court. His face was troubled.

"Well, Learned? How do you feel about your witnessing now?"

He sighed. "You know, this god-touched business wasn't as much . . . um . . . as much *pleasure* as I thought it would be, back in Valenda when we started. I was terribly excited, in secret, to be picked out to do the god's work."

"I did try to tell you, back in Casilchas."

"Yes. I think I understand better, now."

"My court is going to need a divine, too, you know. As I am to become a lay dedicat of the Bastard's Order, of a sort, I think you might suit me very well. We will likely be riding into the Five Princedoms. If you truly aspire to martyrdom, as your early sermons to me implied, you may still have a chance."

He blushed deeply. "Five gods, but those were stupid sermons." He took a deep breath. "I'll be glad to forgo the martyr part. As for the rest, though—I will say you *yes*, Royina, with a glad heart. Even though I've had no dreams directing me. Well, *especially* as I've had no dreams directing me. Not so sure I want them, anymore." He hesitated, and added with a wholly inconsistent longing in his voice, "You did say— you *did* see Him face-to-face, in your dreams? Your real dreams?"

"Yes." Ista smiled. "Once, He borrowed your face to speak through. It appears that *Someone* thinks you not unworthy to wear His colors, Learned, to wear in turn the semblance of your flesh."

"Oh." Dy Cabon blinked, taking this in. "Is that so? Really? My goodness." He blinked some more. When he took his leave of her, his mouth was still tugging up.

❧

In the evening after supper, when the sun had set and white stars were coming out in the cobalt sky above the stone court, Lord Illvin climbed the stairs and knocked on Ista's door. Liss admitted him to the outer chamber with a friendly dip of her knees. With a look of extreme bemusement on his face, he held out his hands to Ista.

"Look. I found these growing on the apricot tree in the forecourt, as I was passing through just now."

Liss peered. "They're apricots. Makes sense that's where they'd be . . . doesn't it?" She hesitated.

The fruits were large and deeply colored, with a faint red blush upon their dark golden skins. Ista, bending to look, flared her nostrils at their heavy perfume. "They smell lovely."

"Yes, but . . . it is not the season. My mother planted that tree when I was born, and the almond for Arhys. I know when they're supposed to come ripe, I've watched them all my life. Not for months yet. There are still a few blossoms that haven't fallen, though half the leaves are gone. These two were hiding amongst the few that held on—I saw them by chance."

"How do they taste?"

"I was a little afraid to bite into them."

Ista smiled. "Out of season they may be, but I think they are not a disaster. I think they may be a gift. It will be all right." She pushed open the door of her inner chamber with one foot. "Come in. Let us try them."

"Um," said Liss. "I can stay in sight, if you leave the door open, but I don't think I can get out of earshot."

Ista gave Illvin a tilt of her head, toward the inner door. "Excuse us a moment."

A little smile turning his mouth, he gave her a courtly nod and passed within. Ista pulled the door shut behind him, briefly, and turned to Liss. "I don't think I have explained to you yet about the *other* set of rules for discreet ladies-in-waiting . . ."

She did so, in clear, succinct, but on the whole polite terms. Liss's eyes grew bright as the stars outside, as she listened attentively. Ista was relieved, though not surprised, that Liss seemed neither confused nor shocked. Ista hadn't quite expected *enthusiastic*, however. She found herself swept within, and the door firmly closed behind her, almost before she'd finished speaking.

"I think I shall go sit on the steps a while, dear Royina," Liss's voice called back faintly through the wood. "It's cooler. I think I shall like to sit out for *quite* a *long time*." Ista heard the outer door close, as well.

Illvin's eyes were crinkling with silent laughter. He held out one of the fruits to her; she took it, her hand jerking a little when her fingers accidentally brushed his. "Well," he said, raising his to his lips. "Let us both be brave, then . . ."

She matched his bite. The apricot tasted as wonderful as it looked and smelled, and despite her attempts at daintiness, she ended with juice dribbling down her chin. She dabbed at it. "Oh, dear . . ."

"Here," he said, moving closer, "let me help you . . ."

The kiss lasted quite a long time, with his apricot-scented fingers winding pleasurably in her hair. When they paused for breath, she remarked, "I always feared it would take divine intervention to find *me* a lover . . . I do believe I was right."

"Tch, tch, look at yourself, bittersweet Ista. Saint, sorceress, dowager royina of all Chalion-Ibra, converses with gods, when not cursing them—a man would have to be maniacally intrepid to even *think* of you in that rude way. . . . This is good. It will cut down on my rivals."

She couldn't help it; she giggled. She heard herself, and laughed, in wonder, in joy, in huge surprise. He tasted her laughter, too, as though it were miraculous apricots.

And I was afraid I wouldn't know how to do this.

He'd looked tall and splendid, in the long sweep of black tunic and trousers and boots, but he looked even better out of them, she thought, as she pulled him down beside her on her bed. The warm night demanded neither sheets nor blankets. She left a brace of candles burning, the better to see the god's gifts.

Look for the latest fantasy novel from
award-winning author
Lois McMaster Bujold,
coming soon in hardcover

THE HALLOWED HUNT

Turn the page for a sneak preview!

THE PRINCE WAS DEAD.

Since the king was not, no unseemly rejoicing dared show in the faces of the man atop the castle gate. Merely, Ingrey thought, a furtive relief. Even that was extinguished as they watched Ingrey's troop of riders clatter under the gate's vaulting into the narrow courtyard. They recognized who he was—and, therefore, who must have sent him.

Ingrey's sweat grew clammy under his leather jerkin in the damp dullness of the autumn morning. The chill seemed cupped within the cobbled yard, funneled down by the whitewashed walls. The lightly armed courier bearing the news had raced from the prince's hunting seat here at Boar's Head Castle to the hallow king's hall at Easthome in just two days. Ingrey and his men, though more heavily equipped, had made the return journey in scarcely more time. As a castle groom scurried to take his horse's bridle, Ingrey swung down and straightened his scabbard, fingers lingering only briefly on the reassuring coolness of his sword hilt.

The late Prince Boleso's housemaster, Rider Ulkra, appeared around the keep from wherever he'd been lurking when Ingrey's troop had been spied climbing the road.

Stout, usually stolid, he was breathless now with apprehension and hurry. He bowed. "Lord Ingrey. Welcome. Will you take drink and meat?"

"I've no need. See to these, though." He gestured to the half dozen men who followed him. The troop's lieutenant, Rider Gesca, gave him an acknowledging nod of thanks, and Ulkra delivered men and horses into the hands of the castle servants.

Ingrey followed Ulkra up the short flight of steps to the thick-planked main doors. "What have you done so far?"

Ulkra lowered his voice. "Waited for instructions." Worry scored his face; the men in Boleso's service were not long on initiative at the best of times. "Well, we moved the body into the cool. We could not leave it where it was. And we secured the prisoner."

What sequence, for this unpleasant inspection? "I'll see the body first," Ingrey decided.

"Yes, my lord. This way. We cleared one of the butteries."

They passed through the cluttered hall, the fire in its cavernous fieldstone fireplace allowed to burn low, the few red coals half-hidden in the ashes doing nothing to improve the discomfort of the chamber. A shaggy deer hound, gnawing a bone on the hearth, growled at them from the shadows. Down a staircase, through a kitchen where a cook and scullions fell silent and made themselves small as they passed, down again into a chilly chamber ill lit by two small windows high in the rocky walls.

The little room was presently unfurnished but for two trestles, the boards laid across them, and the sheeted shape that lay silently upon the boards. Reflexively, Ingrey signed himself, touching forehead, lip, navel, groin, and heart, spreading his hand over his heart: one theological point for each of the five gods. *Daughter-Bastard-Mother-Father-Son. And where were all of You when this happened?*

As Ingrey waited for his eyes to adjust to the shadows, Ulkra swallowed and said, "The hallow king—how did he take the news?"

"It is hard to say," said Ingrey, with politic vagueness. "Sealmaster Lord Hetwar sent me."

"Of course."

Ingrey could read little in the housemaster's reaction, except the obvious, that Ulkra was glad to be handing responsibility for this on to someone else. Uneasily, Ulkra folded back the pale cloth covering his dead master. Ingrey frowned at the body.

Prince Boleso kin Stagthorne had been the youngest of the hallow king's surviving—of the hallow king's sons, Ingrey corrected his thought in flight. Boleso was still a young man, for all he had come to his full growth and strength some years ago. Tall, muscular, he shared the long jaw of his family, masked with a short brown beard. The darker brown hair of his head was tangled now, and matted with blood. His booming energy was stilled; drained of it, his face lost its former fascination, and left Ingrey wondering how he had once been fooled into thinking it handsome. He moved forward, hands cradling the skull, probing the wound. Wounds. The shattered bone beneath the scalp gave beneath his thumbs' pressure on either side of a pair of deep lacerations, blackened with dried gore.

"What weapon did this?"

"The prince's own war hammer. It was on the stand with his armor, in his bedchamber."

"How very . . . unexpected. To him as well." Grimly, Ingrey considered the fates of princes. All his short life, according to Hetwar, Boleso had been alternately petted and neglected by parents and servants both, the natural arrogance of his blood tainted with a precarious hunger for honor, fame, reward. The arrogance—or was it the anxiety?—had bloated of late to something overweening, desperately out of balance. *And that which is out of balance . . . falls.*

The prince wore a short open robe of worked wool, lined with fur, blood-splashed. He must have been wearing it when he'd died. Nothing more. No other recent wounds marked his pale skin. When the housemaster said they had

waited for instructions, Ingrey decided, he had understated
the case. The prince's retainers had evidently been so be-
numbed by the shocking event, they had not even dared
wash or garb the corpse. Grime darkened the folds of
Boleso's body . . . no, not grime. Ingrey ran a finger along a
groove of chill flesh, and stared warily at the smear of color,
dull blue and stamen yellow and where they blended a sickly
green. Dye, paint, some colored powder? The dark fur of the
inner robe, too, showed faint smears.

Ingrey straightened, and his eye fell on what he had at
first taken for a bundle of furs laid along the far wall. He
stepped closer and knelt down.

It was a dead leopard. Leopardess, he amended, turning
the beast partly over. The fur was fine and soft, fascinating
beneath his hands. He traced the cold curving ears, the stiff
white whiskers, the pattern of dark whorls upon golden silk.
He picked up one heavy paw, feeling the leathery pads, the
thick ivory claws. The claws had been clipped. A red silk
cord was bound tightly around the neck, biting deeply into
the fur. Its end was cut off. Ingrey's hairs prickled, a reaction
he quelled.

Ingrey glanced up. Ulkra, watching him, looked even
more bleakly blank than before.

"This is no creature of *our* woods. Where in the world did
it come from?"

Ulkra cleared his throat. "The prince obtained it from
some Darthacan merchants. He proposed to start a
menagerie here at the castle. Or possibly train it for hunting.
He said."

"How long ago was this?"

"A few weeks. Just before his lady sister stopped here."

Ingrey fingered the red cord, letting his brows rise. He
nodded at the dead animal. "And how did this happen?"

"We found it hanging from a beam in the prince's bed-
room. When we, um, went in."

Ingrey sat back on his heels. He was beginning to see
why no Temple divine had yet been called up to take charge

of the funeral rites. The daubing, the red cord, the oak beam, hinted of an animal not merely slain but sacrificed, of someone dabbling in the old heresies, the forbidden forest magics. Had the sealmaster known of this, when he'd sent Ingrey? If so, he'd given no sign. "Who hung it?"

With the relief of a man telling a truth that could not hurt him, Ulkra said, "I did not see. I could not say. It was alive, leashed up in the corner and lying perfectly placidly, when we brought the girl in. We none of us heard or saw any more after that. Until the screams."

"Whose screams?"

"Well . . . the girl's."

"What was she crying? Or were they . . ." Ingrey cut short the, *just cries.* He'd a shrewd suspicion Ulkra would be a little too glad of the suggestion. "What were her words?"

"She cried for help."

Ingrey stood up from the exotic spotted carcass, his riding leathers creaking in the quiet, and let the weight of his stare fall on Ulkra. "And you responded—how?"

Ulkra turned his head away. "We had our orders to guard the prince's repose. My lord."

"Who heard the cries? Yourself, and . . . ?"

"Two of the prince's guards, who had been told to wait his pleasure."

"Three strong men, sworn to the prince's protection. Who stood—where?"

Ulkra's face might have been carved from rock. "In the corridor. Near his door."

"Who stood in the corridor not ten feet from his murder, and did nothing."

"We dared not. My lord. For *he* did not call. And anyway, the screams . . . stopped. We assumed, um, that the girl had yielded herself. She went in willingly enough."

Willingly? Or despairingly? "She was no servant wench. She was a retainer of Prince Boleso's own lady sister, a dowered maiden of her household. Entrusted to her service by kin Badgerbank, no less."

"Princess Fara herself yielded her up to her brother, my lord, when he begged the girl of her."

Pressured, was how Ingrey had heard the gossip. "Which made her a retainer of *this* house. Did it not?"

Ulkra flinched.

"Even a menial deserves better protection of his masters."

"Any lord in his cups might strike a servant, and misjudge the force of the blow," said Ulkra sturdily. The cadences sounded rehearsed, to Ingrey's ear. How often had Ulkra repeated that excuse to himself in the depths of the night, these past six months?

The ugly incident with the murdered manservant was the reason Prince Boleso had suffered his internal exile to this remote crag. His known love of hunting made it a dubious punishment, but it had got the Temple out of the royal seal-master's thinning hair. Too little payment for a crime, too much for an accident; Ingrey, who had observed the shambles next morning for Lord Hetwar before it had all been cleaned away, had judged it neither.

"*Any lord* would not then go on to skin and butcher his kill, Ulkra. There was more than drink behind that wild act. It was madness, and we all knew it." And when the king and his retainers had let their judgment be swayed, after that night's fury, by an appeal to loyalty—not to the prince's own soul's need, but to the appearance, the reputation of his high house—this disaster had been laid in train.

Boleso would have been expected to re-appear at court in another half-year, duly chastened, or at least duly pretending to be. But Fara had broken her journey here from her earl-ordainer husband's holdings to her father's sickbed, and so her—Ingrey presumed, pretty—lady-in-waiting had fallen under the bored prince's eye. One could take one's pick of tales from the princess's retinue, arriving barely before the bad news at the king's hall in Easthome, whether the cursed girl had yielded her virtue in terror to the prince's importunate lusts, or in calculation to her own vaulting ambition.

If it had been calculation, it had gone badly awry. Ingrey sighed. "Take me to the prince's bedchamber."

The late prince's room lay high in the central keep. The corridor outside was short and dim. Ingrey pictured Boleso's retainers huddled at the far end in the wavering candlelight, waiting for the screams to stop, then had to unset his teeth. The room's solid door featured a wooden bar on the inside, as well as an iron lock.

The appointments were few and countrified: a bed with hangings, barely long enough for the prince's height, chests, the stand with his second-best armor in one corner. A scattering of rugs on the wide floorboards. One was soaked with a dark stain. The sparse furnishings left just room enough for a quarry to dodge and run, a gasping chase. To turn at bay and swing . . .

The windows to the right of the armor stand were narrow, with thick wavery circles of glass set in their leads. Ingrey pulled the casements inward, swung wide the shutters, and gazed out upon the green forested folds of countryside falling away from the crag. In the watery light, wisps of mist rose from the ravines like the ghosts of streams. At the bottom of the valley, a small farming village hacked out of the woods pushed back the tide of trees: source, no doubt, of food, servants, firewood for the castle, all crude and simple.

The fall from the sill to the stones below was lethal, the jump to the walls beyond quite impossible even for anyone slim enough to wriggle out the opening. In the dark and the rain. No escape by that route, except to death. A half-turn from the window, the armor stand would be under a panicked prey's groping hands. A battle ax, its handle inlaid with gold and ruddy copper, still rested there.

The matching war hammer lay tossed upon the rumpled bed. Its claw-rimmed iron head—very like an animal's paw—was smeared with dried gore like the blotch on the rug. Ingrey measured it against his palm, noted the congruity with the wounds he had just seen. The hammer had been swung two handed, with all the strength that terror might lend. But only a woman's strength, after all. The prince, half-stunned—half-mad?—had apparently kept coming. The second blow had been harder.

Ingrey strolled the length of the room, looking all around and then up at the beams. Ulkra, hands clutching one another, backed out of his way. Just above the bed dangled a frayed length of red cord. Ingrey stepped up on the bed frame, drew his belt knife, stretched upward, cut it through, and tucked the coil away in his jerkin.

He jumped down and turned to the hovering Ulkra. "Boleso is to be buried at Easthome. Have his wounds and his body washed—more thoroughly—and pack him in salt for transport. Find a cart, a team—better hitch two pairs, with the mud on the roads—and a competent driver. Set the prince's guards as outriders; their ineptitude can do him no more harm now. Clean this room, set the keep to rights, appoint a caretaker, and follow on with the rest of his household and valuables." Ingrey's gaze drifted around the chamber. Nothing else here . . . "Burn the leopard. Scatter its ashes."

Ulkra gulped and nodded. "When do you wish to depart, my lord? Will you stay the night?"

Should he and his captive travel with the slow cortege, or push on ahead? He wanted to be away from this place as swiftly as he could—it made his neck-muscles ache—but the light was shortening with autumn's advent, and the day was half-spent already. "I must speak to the prisoner before I decide. Take me to her."

It was a brief step, down one floor to a windowless, but dry, storeroom. Not dungeon, certainly not guest room, the choice of prisons bespoke a deep uncertainty over the status of its occupant. Ulkra rapped on the door, called, "My lady? You have a visitor," unlocked it, and swung it wide. Ingrey stepped forward.

From the darkness, a pair of glowing eyes flashed up at him like some great cat's from a covert, in a forest that whispered. Ingrey recoiled, hand flying to his hilt. His blade had rasped halfway out when his elbow struck the jamb, pain tingling hotly from shoulder to fingertips; he backed further to gain turning room, to lunge and strike.

Ulkra's startled grip fell on his forearm. The housemaster was staring at him in astonishment.

Ingrey froze, then jerked away so that Ulkra might not feel his trembling. His first concern was to quell the violent impulse blaring through his limbs, cursing his legacy anew—he had not been caught by surprise by it since . . . for a long time. *I deny you, wolf-within. You shall not ascend.* He slid his blade back into its sheath, snicked it firmly home, slowly unwrapped his fingers, and placed his palm flat against his leather-clad thigh.

He stared again into the little room, forcing sense upon his mind. In the shadows, the ghostly shape of a young woman was rising from a straw pallet on the floor. There seemed to be bedding enough, a down-stuffed quilt, tray and pitcher, a covered chamber pot, necessities decently addressed. This prison secured; it did not, yet, punish.

Ingrey licked dry lips. "I cannot see you in that den." *And what I saw, I disavow.* "Step into the light."

The lift of a chin, the toss of a dark mane; she padded forward. She wore a fine linen dress dyed pale yellow, embroidered with flowers along the curving neckline; if not court dress then certainly clothing of a maiden of rank. A dark brown spatter crossed it in a diagonal. In the light, her tumbling black hair grew reddish. Brilliant hazel eyes looked not up, but across, at Ingrey. Ingrey was of middle height for a man, compactly built; the girl was well grown for her sex, to match him so.

Hazel eyes, almost amber in this light, circled in black at the iris rim. Not glowing green. Not . . .

With a wary glance at him, Ulkra began speaking, performing the introduction as formally as if he were playing Boleso's housemaster at some festal feast. "Lady Ijada, this is Lord Ingrey kin Wolfcliff, who is Sealmaster Lord Hetwar's man. He is come to take you in charge. Lord Ingrey,

Lady Ijada dy Castos, by her mother's blood kin Badger-bank."

Ingrey blinked. Hetwar had named her only, *Lady Ijada, some minor heiress in the Badgerbank tangle, five gods help us.* "That is an Ibran patronymic, surely."

"Chalionese," she corrected coolly. "My father was a Lord Dedicat of the Son's Order, and captain of a Temple fort on the western marches of the Weald, when I was a child. He married a Wealding lady of kin Badgerbank."

"And they are . . . dead?" Ingrey hazarded.

She tilted her head in cold irony. "I should have been better protected, else."

She was not distraught, not weeping, or at least, not recently. Not, apparently, deranged. Four days in that closet to sort through her thoughts had left her composed, but for a certain tightness in her voice, a faint vibrato of fear or anger. Ingrey looked around the bare hall, glanced at Ulkra. "Bring us to where we may sit and speak. Some place apart. In the light."